# STACY M. JONES

# Dead Senate

*For Evan*

# Acknowledgement

Thank you to the detectives, special agents, and forensics teams I've had the pleasure of working with through the years and the knowledge and expertise shared with me.  Special thanks to 17 Studio Book Design for bringing my stories to life with amazing covers.  Thank you to Dj Hendrickson for your insightful editing and Liza Wood for proofreading and revisions. Thank you to my early readers for their feedback and my loyal and new readers who have truly made this series a success.

# CHAPTER 1

FBI Special Agent Kate Walsh gripped the cold metal handrail, her body rocking forward then back as the ferry chugged out through the choppy sea on its way to Martha's Vineyard. The harbor became nothing more than three ominous orange lights as the fog descended. A Category 3 hurricane churned up the eastern seaboard with Long Island and then Cape Cod and its outer islands in its path. Rain and fog already blanketed the region.

Kate watched as the lights in the harbor finally disappeared – the last bit of the mainland faded in the distance. A call from their boss, Martin Spade, while they were still at the scene of a previous case had them rushing back to Boston to pack and then to the ferry. Kate barely had time to process the prior case before being thrust into the next. She closed her eyes and let her body sway with the rocking boat. Kate had never minded the ferry to Martha's Vineyard. It had just been a long time since she made the trip.

"You should come inside, Kate. We have a little time to go over the initial case information Spade sent," said Agent Declan James, Kate's partner and best friend. He put a hand on the back of her wet windbreaker. "The captain said we made the last ferry. They didn't run many today because of the weather and this is the final one until the storm passes. He said that once we're on the island, we'll be staying there until the weather clears. It looks like it's going to be a rough one."

Kate turned to look up at him. He had the hood of his FBI-issued windbreaker pulled over his head with the brim of his ballcap sticking out. "I assumed that's why the ferry is nearly empty." There were only a handful of other passengers and three vehicles including Declan's SUV.

"Everyone is headed the other way. There's been no evacuation order yet, but I'm sure people don't want to chance it." Declan nodded his head toward the covered seats. When Kate didn't follow, he put a hand on her arm. "Are you okay? Seasick?"

Kate shook her head. "Anxious about this case." She'd be foolish not to be anxious about it. Seven senators from both sides of the aisle as well as the vice president had gone to Martha's Vineyard together for reasons still unknown. They had with them a few senatorial aides and the Secret Service.

Two senators were dead and the suspect remained at large. All of them had been sequestered in the home where they had been staying on a remote part of the island, awaiting the FBI. The local police refused to let anyone leave – the crime unprecedented.

Declan reached his icy fingers out and tickled the back of her neck, making Kate jump at the touch. She pushed his hands away. "There," he said, laughing, "you aren't thinking about the case."

Kate looked at him wide-eyed. "Our careers are riding on this case."

Declan didn't hide his boyish grin. "That's why we have to keep each other sane. We are about to head into a quagmire and all we have is each other. You know we aren't going to be able to trust any of them." Declan rarely spoke of his total disdain for politics. He couldn't, given the nature of his job. But it is what made him a good choice for the case. He wasn't blinded by politics because he hated them all.

Kate, on the other hand, had grown up in a politically active family. Her father, Joseph Walsh, an American history professor at Harvard, had been an ambassador. He and Kate's mother were killed during an embassy bombing. That single act was what pushed Kate into her career as an FBI agent and drove her to be one of the best profilers in the bureau. She and Declan were members of an elite unit. It's why they were headed to Martha's Vineyard alone. They had been called in instead of another FBI team in Boston.

While she had been mired down in political talk at home when she was younger, Kate didn't like politics any more than Declan. She leaned her head back, trying to warm the spot on the back of her neck where she could still feel his icy fingers. The rain dripped down as she shivered and headed under the cover of the ferry.

Declan followed without saying anything else. They had worked together for so long they knew each other's rhythms – when to push and when to give space. That was something that came in handy since they were living together in Kate's brownstone in Boston's Back Bay. Since Declan's divorce, he needed a place to crash and she had more than enough room.

Kate sat at a four-seater table far away from the three men seated at the front of the ferry. She didn't see anyone else around. When Declan slid into the seat across from her, she said, "Let's go over what we know about the case. Spade only had sparse details when he called me earlier today. I know that he's spoken to you since."

Declan drummed his fingers on the tabletop. "Senator Loraine Abbott from Illinois was shot once in the back of the head in her bedroom. Senator Grady Cutcliffe from Texas was shot once in the chest and then once in the head. From what Spade said, it appeared Abbott was taken by surprise whereas Cutcliffe faced his attacker head on."

Kate asked what she thought was the most logical first question. "Did anyone hear anything?"

"No one heard a thing. The killer must have used a suppressor.

That's the Secret Service's theory anyway. I'd tend to agree given how many people are in the house," Declan explained. "Their bodies were found by their aides early the next morning when they didn't arrive for breakfast. Their respective aides went to their rooms to check on them and found them dead on the floor. Both were wearing pajamas. Evidence suggested it was overnight, but not so late they were sleeping given where their bodies were found. No signs of a struggle. No defensive wounds either."

"When I spoke to Spade, he said they had already dispatched a crime scene unit," Kate said, wanting to close her eyes. The rocking of the boat was easier on her stomach with her eyes closed.

"That's confirmed. A team was sent from the FBI field office in Boston within the hour of when the bodies were found."

Kate raised her head. "Spade didn't say anything to me about the post-mortem. Have any decisions been made about that? I'd assume the bodies were flown out to Boston."

"That's not what happened," Declan explained, surprising Kate. "There was an official request that the Office of the Chief Medical Examiner in Boston send their best to Martha's Vineyard. I assume the pathologist would have arrived already."

Kate rested her head in her hand and her elbow on the table. "I don't understand. Why wouldn't they have sent the bodies to Boston? Martha's Vineyard doesn't have the facilities for that. Their one hospital doesn't even have a morgue. The whole island only has one funeral home. The Dukes County Medical Examiner's Office is in Boston. It would have made more sense after the crime scene techs were done to send the bodies there."

It was clear by Declan's surprised reaction that this was the first he was hearing this. "I had no idea that it was that limited on the island."

"Martha's Vineyard isn't known for its murders, Declan. They aren't equipped like most places. I think the last murder they had was in

2019. The last unsolved homicide was so many years ago I'm not sure. 1940, maybe?"

Declan didn't know either. "If they had asked me, I would have told them to fly the bodies to Boston. Nobody asked us. The airports in Boston and Martha's Vineyard closed earlier today. That may be why the decision was made. I think they are trying to minimize exposure to the press. No official announcement has been made." Declan looked down at his watch. "Assuming they were killed sometime last night, we aren't even twenty-four hours into this thing."

Kate hoped that wouldn't be a problem. "The ferry was running so I'm sure they should have been able to get the bodies to Boston. I hope that doesn't come back to bite us later."

"Kate, I don't think anyone knows what to do," Declan said, resting his arms on the table. "You're dealing with two United States Senators. I'm sure people panicked."

"You're right," Kate said, conceding. She sat back and turned her head to look out at the water, only there wasn't any water to see. It was a thick dense film of white. She didn't want to know how the boat captain was navigating in this. She didn't want to consider how he was getting them there, only that they'd get there safely. Kate pinched the bridge of her nose. The amount of information they didn't have about the case was staggering. "Who took charge of the scene right after the bodies were found?"

"The head of Secret Service on site. I haven't been given much information about him yet. We will meet with him this evening at seven." Declan checked his watch again. "That's assuming we get there on time."

"We won't. It's nearing six already and we have to drive across the island once we pull into the harbor." They were already behind schedule. She raised her eyes to Declan. "Do we know why they were meeting? All Spade said was that it was an off the books meeting. The few people who had been informed of the murders had been surprised they were all together in Martha's Vineyard and not in Washington D.C. Actually, they were surprised that they were all together at all. The senators involved aren't a group known to be friendly with each other."

Declan said, "Spade didn't know."

"What do we know about where they are staying?"

"The Eldridge Estate in Aquinnah, which is the westernmost town on the Vineyard. I heard it's near cliffs. I have some notes from Spade," Declan said, pulling out his phone.

"I know where it is," Kate said, cutting him off. "The estate has fifteen bedrooms and several smaller cottages around the property. The land was bought by a developer twenty years ago and then construction started. It's been used for all kinds of events, weddings, corporate meetings, and such. It offers more privacy than any other place on the island, not only because it's remote but because it's up on a hill behind a gated driveway."

Declan whistled. "Makes sense that's why they chose the location for the meeting place. How do you know all of this?"

"My grandparents' home is in Chilmark, not far from there. I remember people talking about the Eldridge Estate. No one seemed happy about it."

"How close will we be?"

"About five miles. It's a short distance usually. We still won't make it in time for the meeting with the Secret Service." She pointed to his cellphone. "Do you have service?"

Declan checked his cellphone. "A few bars. I'll call and let them know we will be late. Do you have a time you want to give them?"

Kate shook her head. As hard as it was for her to admit, she said, "Nothing is in our control right now."

Declan made the call and ended up leaving a message that they'd be late and would be in touch when they knew more about an estimated time of arrival.

Kate's head swirled with questions about the case. The more she knew going into a scene the better. When Declan ended the call, she asked, "When were the two senators last seen?"

"Last night before bed," Declan explained. "Spade said he was told they had dinner around seven that evening and continued the conversation later in another room. My understanding is that they all separated to their bedrooms around nine."

The boat rocked dramatically to one side and then to the other. Kate took a breath. "Given where they are staying, I can understand how they have been able to keep this a secret." Kate sat back and rested her eyes. It was easier to go with the rocking of the boat with her eyes closed.

"You're looking a little green. Let's talk about this after we are on land," Declan said.

Kate readily agreed and they rode the rest of the way in quiet, except for the rain that pelted the top of the ferry roof.

Nearly forty minutes later, more than a half hour late, the ferry docked. Kate breathed a sigh of relief. Without too much hassle, they settled themselves in the SUV and Declan drove off the ferry and navigated to State Road, which took them across the island.

"When was the last time you were here?" Declan asked.

"It's been at least a year. The caretaker does everything I need at the house for me while I'm away. I called ahead and we should have everything we need." Kate looked out the window but all she saw was fog and the mist from the rain. It was probably better she didn't see the familiar landscape which would only remind her of summers with her parents. That was the last time she had regularly used the house in Martha's Vineyard. Since working for the FBI, she didn't have the time nor the desire to relive those happier times. They were memories

Kate kept locked away.

"Do you want to stop at your house first or go right to the scene?"

Kate turned her head from the window to Declan. "The scene. I'm sure they are getting frustrated without us being there."

Declan nodded. "Spade said as soon as we get there, we are in charge. I'm sure it will be a battle with the Secret Service."

"I hope not," was all Kate said as she stared ahead. She could only see a few feet in front of the car and they were inching along the road going much slower than the speed limit.

Nearly twenty minutes later, as they approached the area of the Eldridge Estate, Kate gave Declan directions, having them turn right and then left and then right again. The road finally dead-ended at the iron fence. Kate guessed it was about ten-feet high and unscalable.

Declan pulled right up to the locked gate, put down his window, and then pushed the intercom button. A man's voice came through the speaker asking them to identify themselves. Declan said both their names and held up his badge so they could verify his credentials on the remote camera.

The intercom crackled and the gate slowly opened. As Declan pulled forward, they heard an ominous message. "We are glad you're here, Agent James. There's been another murder."

# CHAPTER 2

As Kate put her feet on the pavement, the rain intensified. She hadn't bothered with an umbrella and only had the protection of an already drenched windbreaker. She pulled the hood up and made a run for it toward the front door with Declan steps behind her. Surprisingly absent so far were the Secret Service agents Kate had anticipated would be at the gate and the front door.

They reached the door as it was pulled open by a tall, slender man with blond hair wearing khaki pants and a red polo shirt. His badge read Stanton. Kate pulled the chain from her neck and flashed her shield. "FBI Agent Kate Walsh," she said, stepping inside the foyer. She pulled off her hood and extended her hand to the man.

"I'm the house manager." He returned the gesture, providing a firm handshake. "Michael Brooks with the Secret Service is waiting for you." He shook Declan's hand and pointed to where they could hang up their wet windbreakers. Then he led them off to the left of the foyer and down a long narrow hallway.

At the far end of the house, Stanton opened a large wooden door to what he said was the library. "Should I prepare rooms for you both for the night? No one mentioned if you'd be staying or not. We have an extra cottage if you need it."

Kate thanked him. "We have accommodations."

He nodded once. "Let me know if I can get you anything," he said and then disappeared back the way he came.

Declan leaned into Kate and whispered, "The butler did it."

Kate held back her smile as she stepped into the large room. Her senses overwhelmed her for a moment. The smell of a cigar that had recently been burned. The dark wood of the floor-to-ceiling bookshelves. The plushness of a red patterned rug that covered lighter wood floors. The crackle of the fire in the ornate fireplace off to Kate's right. The room was masculine in every sense and so was the man standing in front of the wall of windows in the back of the room.

He stood about six-four and had broad shoulders that cut to well-defined arms. His dark hair stuck up a little in the back, a cowlick that probably annoyed him. He was dressed in pressed pants and a crisp white button-down shirt. He had loafers on his feet that would do little for him in a chase.

"Michael Brooks," Kate said, announcing themselves. The man turned to her, and it was then she noticed the badge on his belt and the holster with his gun at his hip. She was surprised that he'd have his back to the door. That was pretty much police work 101. He didn't seem to be concerned about an attack on his person though. "I'm Agent Kate Walsh and this is Agent Declan James."

Michael had a strong squared jaw and handsome face similar to many Secret Service agents. When Kate was in the FBI Academy, there was a joke going around that the Secret Service shopped for their agents out of a catalog. They often all had the same clean-cut look. Michael rested his gaze on Kate. He had bright blue eyes and a disarming smile.

After he took them in, Michael walked over and extended his hand to her. "I'm sorry we are meeting under such difficult circumstances. It was good of you to come here in the storm. Let me call Stanton and get you some towels so you can dry off and some coffee. It's the least we can do while I catch you up on the case. Then we can proceed from there."

Everything about Kate felt damp – from her hair and the back of her shirt to the front of her pants and shoes. "A few warm towels and coffee would be great. We appreciate the gesture." She said yes because they really could use those things, but she also wanted to seem amenable to Michael's suggestions. The easier they could work together, the easier they could solve the case.

When Michael left the room, Kate squeezed water from her ponytail and Declan shook his head like a dog, letting the water fly. Kate pulled her shirt from her body where it stuck against her. "We could use a change of clothes," she said, running a hand down her face. She was sure every last drop of makeup she had put on before leaving was gone.

"Do you want me to go back out in the rain and get our suitcases?" Declan offered.

"Towels will do for now. There's no point dragging all that in here." Kate glanced around the room. She felt a bit like they had been sequestered there. Michael hadn't told them to stay put, but she didn't think he'd appreciate them wandering off. "I wonder who answered the intercom."

Declan shrugged. "Probably a Secret Service agent. He said there was another murder. Doesn't seem like anyone is in a hurry and there were no crime scene techs out front. I wonder if the medical examiner has removed the body."

"The body is still on the scene," Michael said as he entered the room with towels. He handed one to each of them. "The murder happened not long ago. I knew you were on your way. I wanted to wait to see what you wanted to do. We'll have to get the medical examiner and crime scene techs back, but the storm is getting worse. They just said on the news they are calling for evacuation orders for those on the coast. Luckily, we are on high ground here and won't flood. Not that anyone can get off the island now anyway with the ferry service down and the airports closed."

Kate wasn't worried about flooding. It was wind damage that would impact them the most. That wasn't the most pressing issue. There was still a dead body on the grounds. "Where is the rest of your team? The vice president? Senators?"

Michael pointed toward the door. "The vice president and senators are in the main living room with my partner. They are secure for now."

Kate toweled off her hair and brushed it down her shirt to sop up some water. "Who was most recently killed and where did it happen?" Kate wanted to get there now before doing anything else.

Michael didn't seem to be in a hurry. He sat in one of the high-back leather chairs. "Let's sit and we can talk."

Declan looked over at Kate, concern written all over his face. Neither one of them enjoyed feeling like they weren't in control of the investigation. Michael's tone of voice indicated he wouldn't be giving up control as easily as they had hoped. Declan finished drying off his clothes and sat down on the couch.

Kate didn't want to sit but followed right after him. "Where is the rest of your team?" she asked, her tone stern.

"As I said, Agent Barry Noble is in the living room with everyone else. He's standing guard."

Declan spoke up then. "You have *just one* agent with the vice president? That can't be protocol."

Michael raised his head to Declan and then looked away just as quickly. "I wouldn't say anything about this weekend has gone according to protocol. There will be a lot to answer for after this. It's part of the reason I suggested we don't make a public announcement yet."

"You need to start explaining," Kate demanded and then softened her tone. "We weren't given much information. Please start with why the rest of your team isn't here."

Michael's eyelids fluttered. "It's easier for me to tell you that there were three Secret Service agents here this weekend and now one of them is dead – shot in the same way as the two senators."

Declan lurched forward on the couch. Kate audibly gasped – both that there were only three agents assigned to the vice president and that now one of them had been murdered.

"Do you have any idea what's happening?" she asked, trying to stop her voice from creaking as she spoke.

"Sadly, I don't," Michael said, his head shaking in confusion and disbelief. "One of the reasons I asked to meet with you alone is because there is a lot I don't know and the three of us need to be on the same page if we are going to figure out what's happening."

Kate couldn't agree more with that statement. Although, she couldn't help but acknowledge that as far as she was concerned Michael was a person of interest as was everyone else in the house. For now, she'd feign trust to get the ball rolling. "Let's start with the most basic question. Why were seven senators and the vice president meeting outside of Washington D.C.?"

"I don't know," Michael said with resignation in his voice.

"How can you *not* know?" Declan asked, his anger rising. "That's the most ridiculous thing I've ever heard. The Secret Service doesn't do anything without advanced planning. I assume an advanced team arrived here before the vice president, so you must have had some idea why you were coming here."

"There was an advance team. They secured the house and did the appropriate background check on Stanton." Michael gestured toward the door. "He's the only one here connected to the Eldridge Estate and that's only because the estate refused to allow us occupancy without keeping Stanton around. The cook and the service staff are all from the vice president's residence. We brought them with us to cut down on the number of people who'd be aware that they were meeting."

"But you don't know why they are meeting?" Kate asked, casting a glance over at Declan who was now sitting on the edge of the couch. Her frustration at the situation had already been jacked up. She couldn't imagine what Declan was feeling. He had less patience than she did when information that should be readily available was less than forthcoming.

"No. I don't know. Only that the vice president..."

Declan interrupted, his impatience getting the better of him. "I'm going to get right to the point. Why are you stonewalling us?" He stood and took a step toward Michael. "I assure you we have the security clearances to know what's going on here. If it's territorial issues, we don't have time to play games. Any delay on your part will reflect badly on you in our report and on the outcome of this investigation."

Kate wanted to tug on the back of his shirt and pull him back to the couch. She didn't want to undermine his authority though. He had a point and she was glad Declan was asserting himself. To Michael, she said, "Declan is frustrated by this case as am I. We were ripped away from another scene to be here, in a hurricane no less. We need to work collaboratively, which means you need to share information and keep nothing from us."

Michael remained calm and collected. "Are you two done having a tantrum?"

Kate thought Declan might lunge for the man then, but he turned back to her and raised his eyes in a question. She didn't know quite what he was asking. Cooler heads had to prevail. She got up from the couch and stood next to Declan. "If there is something you know about why they are meeting, this is the time to tell us."

Michael looked up at her and swallowed hard. "I honestly don't know. It pains me to say that because we should have been told. We were only told that the vice president had a meeting in Martha's Vineyard and that we had to secure the scene. Then we were told that we were only bringing a three-person team to keep the meeting quiet. I was assured that with the work of the advanced team we wouldn't need more than three agents, given how remote and secure the location is and how secret the meeting would be."

Kate believed him. "Who decided all of that?"

"The word came from higher up at the Secret Service, possibly from the top." Michael stood and went back to the window where Kate first saw him. He shoved his hands in his pockets and stared out the window. "I've been in the Secret Service for twenty years and nothing like this has ever happened on my watch. Nothing like this has ever gone down this way either. I'm not trying to hold back information. I simply don't know. I'm embarrassed that I don't know given everything that has happened. It's my job to know and I've failed."

There was enough regret and embarrassment in his voice that Kate believed him. "If you don't know why they were meeting, then I assume you don't know why those particular senators were here either."

"That's correct." Michael turned to face them. "This was supposed to be a short trip over the weekend. We'd come up on Friday and be back on Monday. I was given strict orders that while the vice president and senators were meeting, the Secret Service was to be out of the room. I was told no more than that even when I pressed for more information."

Declan asked, "What about the aides the senators brought with them? Were they privy to the information?"

"Not that I'm aware of. I've not questioned anyone. We sequestered everyone in the living room and that's where they have been the majority of the day."

Kate thought that was a smart idea. "Has there been a Secret Service agent with them the whole time?"

Michael shook his head. "That wasn't possible given all we had to do after the bodies were found. But we figured if they were all in one place, they'd be safer. The senators were killed when they were alone." Michael looked toward the door. "Let me take you to the scenes and then we can talk more."

As Michael passed them and went to the door, Declan pulled Kate back to him. "Do you trust him?"

"We don't have a choice right now. I'll give him my trust until he proves otherwise." That answer satisfied Declan and they followed Michael out of the room. They put their wet windbreakers back on and followed Michael to the back of the house. The door led them to a covered walkway that connected eight small cottages. A grassy area with a large fountain in the middle filled the space between the cottages and the main house.

"He was killed in number seven," Michael said and then walked off toward the building with Kate and Declan trailing behind.

# CHAPTER 3

A s they approached the number seven cottage, Declan asked, "Who found the body?"

"I did," Michael said, turning to look at him. "Matt Pike had been a Secret Service agent for the past twelve years. He had an impeccable record. The three of us took turns on rounds to double-check the perimeter and check the cottages. When he didn't return inside after his shift and didn't respond to a radio call, I came in search." He rubbed his forehead and cursed. "It could have been any one of us."

Kate knew Michael was right that it could have been any one of them. They were far too understaffed to handle the situation, especially now one man down. The wind whipped around them as the rain pelted them. "Can we see the scene now?" she asked, hoping to hurry him along.

"Of course." Michael pulled out a set of keys and unlocked the door. The cottages had no porches and the doors were right off the walkway. On either side of the door were two empty window boxes. Kate imagined they probably held pretty flowers in the spring and summer. The cottages were painted beach colors of light blues and tans.

Michael pushed open the door enough that they could see inside. Matt Pike was sprawled on the floor on his back. Kate focused on him and then tore her eyes away to take in the rest of the scene. Matt was killed in a small sitting room closest to the cottage's front door. The room had a television and a couch and recliner. Beyond that, Michael explained there was a bedroom and bathroom. There was no kitchenette and guests were expected to eat in the main house.

"Did you go inside?" Kate asked, standing at the threshold of the door.

Michael nodded. "I found him here just like this. The door was slightly ajar. I pushed it open and saw him. I rushed inside to check for a pulse. I hoped that he was still alive. When I realized that he had already expired, I left and locked up. I didn't touch anything inside other than Matt when checking for a pulse. He had a bullet wound to his chest. Either it killed him instantly or he bled out here before he could radio for help."

"No vest?" Kate asked, knowing that the Secret Service usually wore bulletproof vests under their clothing.

Michael looked away. "We were too relaxed given the situation and those present. We failed on many levels. We only did the security rounds because the senators were sleeping in the cottages."

Kate didn't want to judge him for going off protocol in every way. Still, she couldn't understand well-experienced Secret Service agents being so lax. Kate wanted to go inside, but they had no protective covering for their feet or gloves for their hands. She didn't want to contaminate the crime scene further. All their equipment was still in Declan's SUV. Kate turned to him. "I can run back to the car and get everything," she offered.

"I'll go," Declan said and then took off in a jog back toward the house.

When he was gone, Michael asked, "Is he always so intense?"

It was a strange question from a Secret Service agent, who were all intense. This was also quite the role reversal for Kate. Normally, it was people asking Declan if she was always so intense. She hadn't thought of Declan as intense, only concerned about the crime and the lack of proper security.

She told Michael as much. "Declan is easier to work with than I am. We are both taken a bit by surprise about the situation, especially given the Secret Service doesn't even know why they are here. I'll call my boss, Martin Spade. I'm sure he can call your boss and get some answers for us."

There weren't too many people who hadn't heard of Martin Spade. He ran the specialized unit that Kate and Declan called home and his reach went as far as the White House.

"That would be good. I'd like to know what we are dealing with here." Michael locked his gaze on Kate. "For the record, I expressed my disagreement with this trip and the lack of the vice president's full security detail. I was told by the vice president to know my place and that was the end of that. The estate was secured and that's all that mattered. Even when we initially got here and had our normal security posturing, we were told to stop and relax. It changed the dynamic."

"Except it wasn't secure and no one was safe," Kate countered, raising her eyebrows at him. "There's been three murders in less than twenty-four hours."

"Right," Michael said and put a hand on the back of his neck while looking at Kate with an expression she couldn't read. "I doubt a larger security detail would have done much if the threat is coming from the inside. These are people we all trusted."

"You're sure of that?" Kate knew it was times like this when everyone's guard was down that things like this often happened.

Michael's face reddened and his voice had a tinge of anger. "There's no way in or out without going through that gate. We all had the front gate security video open on an app on our phones. As soon as someone rings from the gate, it alerts us. It alerts us when the gate is opened. The fence you saw out front runs the perimeter of the property except for one side which goes over the cliff down to the sea below. No one could scale that cliff and no one can scale that fence. It's impossible, especially in this weather."

Kate would need to see the area and assess it for herself. The property did sound secure enough, but she still disagreed with the smaller security detail. Arguing with him about the off-protocol lax security wouldn't help anything. She changed her focus. "Do you think Matt was the intended target or killed to shrink the size of the security detail?"

"I assume to decrease the security. I've known Matt for years and have never known anyone to have a problem with him. He's worked through a few administrations and people request him for their detail. He's that good." Michael looked over at Matt's body. "That is, he *was* that good. This killer is unfortunately better."

Kate felt a swell of emotion for him. She had faced losing Declan a few times and she couldn't bear the thought of it. She put a hand on his arm. "We'll get justice for Matt and the others."

Before Michael could respond, Declan was back with their gear. They put gloves on their hands and booties on their feet and then the three of them entered the room. "Were these cottages locked when Matt entered?"

Michael nodded. "We had a set of master keys as does Stanton. Those staying in the cottages have their own keys."

That meant there were multiple keys to the rooms floating around. Kate didn't think that was all that safe. She stood in the middle of the living room, taking in the scene. There were no signs of a struggle and no signs that anything in the room had been disrupted. Matt hadn't even had time to unholster his gun. It was still in its holster on his hip. So was his badge.

Declan must have been thinking the same thing as Kate. He leaned over Matt. "He must have been taken by surprise. The shot could have come from someone standing in the open doorway." He eyed Matt's position on the floor and walked to the door and looked outside. He scanned the middle grassy area and then looked back at the body. "Do you leave the doors open when you're doing your rounds?"

"I don't, but I'm not sure about Matt. We can ask Barry what he does." Michael looked down at Matt and then back up at Declan. "Are you wondering if he answered the door or was just standing in the doorway when it happened?"

Declan paused before he responded. "All I know is that he was definitely taken by surprise. Either Matt had the door open while he did his check or he willingly let in the killer, unconcerned about his safety. He's not close enough to the door to have answered it and then been shot. His body is too far back into the room. If he answered the door, he let them in and then turned to face them and was shot. He didn't even have time to draw his gun. If he was as good as you said, he would have responded quickly to a threat."

"That's true," Michael said, agreeing with Declan's summation. "Then I have to assume what I just said to Kate is true – we are dealing with an inside threat. Anyone outside of the people already here, Matt would have been on guard. Unless, as you said, he simply had the door open."

"Wouldn't he have had his guard up regardless whether he knew them or not, given the two dead senators?" Kate countered. She wanted to drive home the point he should have had his vest on as well. She'd not be lowering her guard at all around any of them. She had a hard time believing that a Secret Service agent would either – at any point while on duty. A lot was amiss.

"Point taken, Kate," Michael said, drawing a deep breath. "I can't account for any of this. What do we do now? We can't just leave him laying here. I can call in the medical examiner and the crime scene techs who were here earlier."

Kate asked, "What medical examiner took the other two bodies?"

"Dr. Shelia Coburn was sent from the Boston office. She arrived and made arrangements with the local funeral home and the hospital. I assume the bodies are at the funeral home right now. She provided me with her contact information." Michael pulled out his phone and gave the doctor's information to Kate who added it to her contacts. "Maybe it's best we call her first."

"We'll do both," Kate said and then glanced around the area. "Where were the two other bodies found?  We might as well look at those crime scenes right now."

"Cottage one and two," Michael said, snapping off his gloves and taking the booties from his feet. "The vice president is staying in the main house in the top suite and each senator has a cottage."

Kate looked down at the body one more time as Michael was speaking. She assumed the shot to the chest had killed him instantly. Matt didn't look like he had rolled around in pain or tried to reach for his phone for help. "Does he have a phone on him and what about his earpiece and microphone?"

Kate knew that Secret Service agents had a small earpiece in their ear and a microphone that rested inside of the agent's sleeves. It's what allowed them to communicate so quickly and effectively. It was the first time Kate wondered if either Michael or Barry had heard anything that had happened.

Michael stumbled for a response. "He should have his earpiece still in and mic in his sleeve. We didn't hear cause for concern when he was shot. We didn't even hear the shot."

Declan glanced over at Kate. There was something off about the situation. Michael seemed far too rattled and unsure of himself – particularly for one with his breadth and depth of experience.

Declan bent to check the dead man's ears for the earpiece and then the microphone. Both were there. He righted himself. "I'd assume given you didn't hear anything that he was shot with a suppressor, which I understand would have been the case with the other two murders."

"I'd assume so," Michael said, his voice still faltering. He closed the door and remained near the body while Kate and Declan first searched the living room and then the attached bathroom and bedroom. Nothing seemed out of place.

Before they left the bathroom, Declan asked, "Where are the local cops? I thought they were the ones who told the Secret Service they couldn't leave. I'd have assumed they'd be on site."

"Maybe they got called away because of the storm."

When they came back into the living room, Declan asked, "How long was Matt radio silent while doing his search?"

"He announced that he was entering cottage seven," Michael said. "That's what we'd do – announce when we arrived at a cottage and then give the all-clear when we were leaving. Matt announced his arrival and then we never heard from him again. That's what made me come here to look for him."

Neither Kate nor Declan had an answer for him. She pulled off her gloves and booties and stepped outside. "Let's see the other crime scenes and we can make a plan from there."

Michael showed them the two other cottages and they did a cursory sweep, given the crime scene techs had already been through. On the walk back to the main house, they lagged behind Michael.

In a voice barely above a whisper, Kate asked, "What is going on here?"

"I don't know," Declan said, shaking his head. "I have a feeling this is big, whatever it is, and it goes far beyond a few murders."

Kate knew Declan was right and that worried her most of all.

# CHAPTER 4

Once back in the house, Kate saw the vice president's head of white hair above the back of his seat before she saw anything else in the room. Mitchell Kramer was a controversial figure, disliked on both sides of the aisle. At seventy-one, he had served most of his life in the Senate and then was chosen as a running mate for reasons most people didn't understand – even his party. He had a confidence that bordered on cocky and an attitude that he was always the smartest person in the room. His views were antiquated about nearly everything. Kate had read somewhere that the loudest person in any conversation was usually the least intelligent on the subject and that fit Vice President Kramer to a T.

The living room was much like the library except larger and more formal. The plush chairs and couches in shades of tan and navy gave this room a brighter feel than the other room. A large television was affixed to the wall and there was a small wet bar on the far wall. A fire crackled in the fireplace that was as grand as the other. Even though the furnishings in this room were brighter than the others, there were fewer windows in this room, which Kate assumed was why it was chosen as a place to sequester them all. From her vantage point, she could see that two windows overlooked the side of the property going toward the cliff. The grass went on and on until it met the horizon.

As Kate glanced around the room, she counted thirteen people in addition to Kramer and Secret Service Agent Barry Noble, who sat perched on a stool near the bar. He had his dark hair slicked back and looked to be the same size and build as Michael. There was a youthfulness to his face that Kate didn't see much with Secret Service agents. The rest of the people were largely unknown to Kate, except for a few senators she recognized. She assumed the rest were senatorial aides.

Michael cleared his throat and announced his presence. "I want to introduce you all to FBI Agent Kate Walsh. Her partner, Agent Declan James, is in the library making calls, and will join us soon."

After assessing the scenes, Declan had walked back to the library to call the medical examiner, crime scene techs, and the local police. He had asked for privacy. Kate figured that was a good time for her to be introduced to everyone sequestered in the main living room, awaiting answers.

After Michael's introduction, Vice President Kramer stood to his five-foot-nine height and turned to Kate. He shook a finger at her and demanded, "When can we leave? I don't appreciate being held against my will. Trust me, your boss is going to hear about this."

Kramer was no match for Spade, who had been in government so long Kate wasn't even sure how many administrations he had worked through.

Kate extended her hand to the man and then retracted it when it was clear that he would not return the gesture. She didn't bother addressing who her boss was. "We were notified earlier today about the murders while we were on another case. Given the storm, the ferry was slower than usual. We are sorry for the delay. My understanding is that it was the local police who asked that you remain here. With the storm that was probably a good idea. We only arrived about an hour ago and had to look at the most recent crime scene."

Kramer screwed his face up. "What recent crime scene? Michael, what is she yammering on about?" he demanded, taking steps toward them both.

Michael looked like he had his hand caught in the cookie jar. It was clear he hadn't told them about Matt. "There's been another murder. Matt Pike was shot during his security checks of the cottages. We've assessed the scene and Agent Declan James is handling calls to the proper authorities. I didn't want to alarm anyone until I knew more and the FBI was here."

There were gasps and one of the female aides stumbled back onto a couch. Her complexion paled and she had fear in her eyes, rightly so. Kate watched everyone's reaction, hoping to catch a guilty party. All she saw were the same shocked and horrified faces.

If the killer was in the room, they were a good actor.

Kramer's whole body began to shake. At first, Kate thought it was fear, but one look in his eyes told her it was rage. He jammed a stubby finger into Michael's chest and cursed a tirade at him. When he settled down, he barked, "Why am I still here? You need to get me out of here right now!"

"There's nowhere to go, sir," Michael said, his voice stern even in the face of abuse. "The local police didn't want us to leave and they had jurisdiction. We had to stay until the FBI arrived and could investigate. With the storm, we are safest right here." He paused and shifted his eyes to Kate, but didn't wait for her approval of what he said next. He turned back to Kramer. "The reality is, Mr. Vice President, all of you are suspects and we couldn't take you back to Washington."

Kramer stumbled back as if he'd been slapped. "How could you say something like that?" He looked over at his colleagues for support but none of them said a word. He spun around back to Michael, gesturing wildly with his hands as he spoke. "How could you accuse us of that? There's not one person in this room capable of such a thing." His face slowly turned the color of a tomato and he breathed out of his nostrils like a bull.

Kate had to get this back under control. She started to speak, but a senator she recognized, Senator Carley Stone from Montana, cursed at Kramer. She stood from her chair and calmly walked over to Kate and Michael. She turned her head to Kramer. "You are such an old fool. Michael only said what we've all been thinking. Of course, one of us is the killer. Who else even knows we are here? There's a traitor among us and I want to know who it is." She turned to face the rest of the senators with her hands on her hips and her head jutted out in defiance.

Kate knew it wouldn't elicit a confession. The stance was strong and bold and shut Kramer up. He went back to his chair and breathed a heavy sigh. Kate said, "I promise my partner and I will get this sorted out as soon as we can."

Senator Stone looked Kate square in the eyes. "What do you need from us to do your job efficiently?"

"Right now, I need some time. It's nearing nine and we aren't going to get much accomplished this evening. We need a plan for the night. Even if I wanted to let all of you go, there is nowhere to go, and won't be for a few days until the storm passes. We took the last ferry in and the airports are closed." Kate watched as the news sunk in that no one was going anywhere and for better or worse, they were stuck with a killer among them.

"What about bringing in more security?" Stone asked.

Kate nodded. "We are looking into that. Agent James is making a call to the local police right now. As I'm sure you know, Martha's Vineyard police aren't large in numbers and they will have several responsibilities given the storm. We might be on our own for now."

Kate wanted to dive in and start asking questions but held off. It was clear from the looks of everyone they were exhausted and irritable. She'd rather start fresh with interviews in the morning. "What would help me best is to get an account of everyone who is here – names and titles and such. That would include all the kitchen and other staff too."

"I can get you that," Michael said. "I have a list in the other room."

"Great," Kate said, wondering what kind of plan they could work out for the night. It's not like they could all camp out in the living room. "Who is staying here in the main house?"

"The senatorial aides have the smaller upstairs bedrooms and Vice President Kramer has the main suite on the third floor," Senator Stone explained. "The senators have the cottages for privacy and comfort. That's where my colleagues were murdered. I don't know that we are safe out there now."

Kate didn't think going back to those cottages was an option either. Five senators remained. "Is there room to bring everyone inside the main house?" Kate asked, turning to Michael.

"I can speak to Stanton." Michael turned and left the room.

Kate looked at all the worried faces. "I think it's wise to have everyone inside the main house so that no one is alone and isolated."

Kramer let out a snort. "Right. So now we'll all be in the main house with the killer." He sat back and folded his arms across his chest. He muttered to himself how he was the vice president and should be able to do whatever he wanted when he wanted.

For Kate, it was akin to watching a toddler throw a tantrum. She was sure he was used to getting his way. Circumstances had changed and it seemed like everyone else was willing to roll with it. She ignored Kramer for now. "I'll need to speak with you individually but that can wait until morning. It would be helpful to understand if anyone has any idea why Senator Loraine Abbott and Senator Grady Cutcliffe were targeted. Does anyone have any ideas?"

The room was silent with each of them looking at the others. When no one spoke up, Kate asked, "It's my understanding there was a meeting taking place this weekend. Would anyone like to tell me the reason for the meeting?"

Senator Stone turned away from Kate, shaking her head.

"It's none of your business and above your pay grade," barked Vice President Kramer.

Kate had assumed after what Michael told her that she was going to be met with that kind of response. Still, the question needed an answer. She scanned the room looking at the aides, mostly young women plus two young men. Kate assumed she'd have to get one of them to flip if they knew anything at all. Given that Michael didn't know why they were meeting – provided he was telling the truth – Kate wondered if the aides had been left out of the loop as well.

She spoke evenly and calmly. "I can appreciate that you don't want to share your reasons for meeting. However, it's possible that the reason is why those senators were targeted. At this point, I have to assume that others of you are potential targets." When Kramer started to bluster, Kate shut him down quickly. "This is the FBI's jurisdiction now and we will get answers one way or another. Michael has been able to keep the story out of the press for now. That won't hold for long. The news will leak and all your reputations are at stake. We have to get to the bottom of what's happened."

Kramer was back on his feet again, this time marching toward Kate. She stood her ground even when Kramer got right up in her face, cursing so violently that spittle hit her face. "I demand the name of your supervisor. You're never going to work another day in the FBI. Do you hear me, young lady?"

Kate wiped the moisture from her face. "Sir, you'll address me as Agent Walsh. Do you understand?" She glared slightly up at him and did not break eye contact. Kramer looked away first. She wasn't going to deal with his disrespect. She didn't care if he was the vice president or the president himself. It wasn't going to happen. She had more than earned her title.

Kramer might have looked away first but he wasn't going to back down, even when the senators told him to cool it and take a seat. "I want the name of your supervisory agent," he demanded again. When Kate didn't offer it, he screamed, "Now!"

Kate had been waiting for this moment and she relished it as she had always done in the past. "I report directly to Martin Spade. You're free to call him."

Kramer blinked rapidly and took a step back. "*The* Martin Spade?" he asked, his voice faltering. "Martin Spade, who runs an elite unit of the FBI?"

"The very one." Kate pulled out her cellphone. "I'd be happy to call him and have you speak with him. We can inform him together of your displeasure over how we are running this investigation." She tried to hide her smirk. "Would you like me to call him?"

Kramer swallowed hard. His mouth opened to speak but no words came out. He simply shook his head and sat back down, all the fire and bluster leaving his body. Out of the corner of her eye, Kate caught Senator Stone smiling. Barry Noble tipped his head to her once, a smile on his face.

"Okay, then that's settled." Kate put her phone back in her pocket.

Before she could address anything else, Michael came back in with Stanton who provided room assignments to each of the senators. There was another wing of the estate that hadn't been in use since the senators wanted more privacy in the cottages.

He assigned them each a room and then Kate and Michael walked each senator separately to gather their belongings from their cottage. They remained with the senators back to the main house and into their rooms. It was a long arduous process and Kate was anxious to reconnect with Declan.

Kate wasn't sure having them all in the same house would prevent another death, but it might make it harder since none of them would be as isolated as they had been. If Kate couldn't prevent another murder, she was counting on making it harder for the killer. Given the storm and the few staff around for security, she didn't think she had many more options.

# CHAPTER 5

After getting the senators settled in their new rooms, the vice president locked in his upstairs suite, and dismissing the aides back to their rooms, Barry, Michael and Kate went to the library to check on Declan and make a plan for the night.

Declan was finishing up a call when they entered. He held up his phone. "Let me give you a quick rundown. There are eight police departments on the island including the sheriff's office, state police, and departments in Aquinnah, Edgartown, Chilmark, Tisbury, West Tisbury, and Oak Bluffs. In total, there are one hundred and ten officers and five state police officers on the island. It was officers from the Aquinnah Police Department who responded to the initial call and requested that everyone remain in place. The state police were never notified. Why is that?" he asked, looking directly at Michael for an explanation.

He shifted his eyes toward Kate. "We were trying to keep things quiet until the FBI arrived. We figured there was no point getting the state police involved when the Aquinnah Police Department had already sent officers. We knew no matter what local or state police arrived it would be the FBI's jurisdiction and so we collectively agreed to keep it quiet for now."

"Well," Declan said dragging out the word. "They know now and they are sending two officers to help us with security for tonight. They can spare them for now."

Kate was glad that the added security would be there and explained to Declan about moving the senators from the outer cottages into the main house. "We have everyone all under one roof now, so it should be easier to keep track of everyone. We need to consider if we want to go back to my house or remain here."

"There are no more rooms inside. You'll have to take the cottages," Michael informed them.

"We'll talk about it later and then decide," Declan said, tabling that for now. "The medical examiner is on her way here with the funeral director. I spoke with Sharon Esposito, with the FBI forensics unit in Boston. She was out here earlier with the crime scene unit. She sent her team back with the evidence on the last ferry out but remained on the island. She said she got the feeling she might be needed again. She's at a local hotel near where the ferry docked. She'll be riding out with the medical examiner. The state police said we could use their lab. It's small and not a full forensic lab, but Sharon assured me it would do the job. I'm expecting them as soon as they can make it with the fog and rain."

Kate was glad Sharon had remained. She had been a vital part of their team on other investigations. "What else do we need to do tonight?"

Declan pointed between Barry and Michael. "Let's do an initial interview separately and then we can figure out where we are staying tonight. We have a little time before the others arrive. If you're both here, who is with the vice president?"

"He's locked in his suite. He wanted to meet alone with his aide," Barry said.

"Is that wise?" Declan asked.

"Nothing about any of this is wise, but the vice president insisted and I'm tired of arguing with him."

Neither Michael nor Declan thought it was a good idea. Declan pointed to the ceiling. "Let's you and I head upstairs and we can find a spot to talk while keeping an eye on the vice president's room. Kate can speak with Barry here. Once the state police arrive, we can figure out a schedule for the night." He didn't leave them any room for argument. Declan left the room with Michael right behind him.

Kate was pleased that Declan had decided to interview Michael. She had been building a rapport with him and Declan would be a more challenging interviewer. Kate gestured to the leather chairs. "Barry, let's sit and chat. This shouldn't take too long."

"I like the way you handled Kramer in there. He's been nothing but contemptuous since we arrived." Barry relaxed back in the chair. "I'll be happy to answer anything you want to know. As far as your earlier question, I have no idea why we are here this weekend. Michael might have already told you, but we were left out of the loop as per the reason for the meeting. It's certainly an odd setup. That's for sure."

Kate sat down across from him, her damp pants sticking to the chair. All she wanted was a change of clothes and to warm up. Even though the fire was still burning, she was chilled to the bone. Stanton had never brought that coffee Michael had requested. Just as well, she might not sleep. She got as comfortable as she could and asked, "Odd, how?"

Barry shrugged. "You know not all of them get along well, different sides of the aisle and all. Even the ones on the same side rarely agree on anything and no one likes the vice president, not even his wife." He laughed and then blushed, embarrassed that he spoke in such a way. "I'm sorry for the informality. I'm just a bit frustrated with this whole thing as you can imagine."

Kate had never seen a Secret Service agent so relaxed, especially given the circumstances. "How long have you been on the vice president's detail?"

"Since he was on the campaign trail. Then I was asked to stay on. I'm sure you know we usually have a few more people. It was scaled down for this weekend."

Kate nodded. "Michael told me that and said it was against what he wanted."

"Yeah, this is an anomaly, for sure," Barry agreed. "It's been bothering Michael since he found out the details of this weekend. I've never seen him so shaken up by something."

"Since you arrived here or before?"

"Before. I think he had an instinct about this weekend."

Kate's curiosity was piqued. "What do you mean by that?"

"I'm not sure I can explain it exactly." Barry considered his words. "Michael is normally calm and cool under any sort of pressure. It's what we train for and what our job requires. Ever since he found out about this weekend and the decreased security, he's been on edge. It didn't help that no one would tell us the reason for the meeting. I've never seen Michael unsure about himself a day in his life. Here, he's second-guessing every decision. The way he's been deferring to you…" Barry shook his head and laughed. "I've never seen him defer to anyone that way. It's like he knows he needs the help. I can't explain it otherwise. He's just not himself."

Kate narrowed her gaze at him. "Has Michael ever told you in the past he didn't have a good feeling about something?"

"Yeah, and he's usually right." Barry leaned forward in the chair. "You have to understand. I don't think there's one person in this whole country who likes the vice president. His favorability is something historically low like twenty-two percent. If you want my opinion, the only reason why the president chose him was to get in good with a small sub-section of his party. The sad part is, I'm not even sure they like him. There have been several threats made against the vice president. We are always on high alert, so when the news came down from above that we were coming here with reduced security, it didn't make a lot of sense. Kramer usually doesn't stonewall us from doing our job like he's been doing this weekend." Barry pointed to the ceiling. "I should be up there right now. I can't do my job effectively when he's behaving like he is."

Kate turned her head slightly to the side, considering if the vice president might be the real target and everything else was just a warm-up. "The advance team approved the trip so there couldn't have been an active threat, correct?"

Even though they were both government employees, it didn't mean Kate knew all the ins and outs of the Secret Service. She probably knew far less than she assumed she did.

"From my understanding, we were cleared to come here with the reduced security. I trust the guys on the advance team. I've worked with them for years." Barry winked an eye closed and tsked. "That doesn't mean I don't think there's something hinky going on from above."

"You're questioning the ultimate decision-making of having a reduced team here?" Kate asked and then added, "I want to make sure I'm understanding you correctly."

Barry nodded. "It's not only that. It's the fact that we have no idea why this meeting is taking place or why it's so secret. The vice president won't even let us near the room when they are meeting. Normally, we have agents standing outside the door. He doesn't want that. We've been rendered fairly obsolete on this trip. We make decisions based on threat assessments and safety. None of this is safe. Yet, none of this is in our control. When the murders happened and Michael called headquarters, we wanted to make arrangements to bring the vice president back to D.C. immediately, no matter what the local cops said. The storm wasn't that bad this morning and we knew we'd be able to get off the island. We weren't given clearance to do that. Can you tell me why that is?" He asked a question that Kate knew was rhetorical. She had no more idea than he had.

"You've raised some valid concerns," Kate said. "I will put a call in to Spade and see what he can find out."

Barry raised his eyebrows. "Is Martin Spade *really* your boss?"

Kate confirmed and was amused by the shock on his face. "That wasn't just something I was saying. I report directly to him."

Barry sighed. "He should know then, and if he doesn't, then we are all in trouble."

Kate had the same thought. "Can you tell me about your arrival here and what happened after?"

Barry described a routine flight on Air Force Two from D.C. to Martha's Vineyard that carried the vice president and the staff from Number One Observatory Circle, the vice president's official residence. They arrived at eleven in the morning, were assigned their rooms, got settled, and then had lunch in the main dining room. The senators and their aides arrived separately.

"What about after they settled in and had lunch? When did the official meeting take place?" Kate asked the question but didn't give him time to respond before she added, "During the meeting, were the aides involved?"

Barry offered her a smile. "You're certainly asking the right questions. Lunch ended at close to one-thirty and then we were all dismissed. Kramer and the senators retired to the living room to meet. We were told not to disturb them. Every room is equipped with a phone that goes to the kitchen, much like in hotels. At three, they called for snacks and coffee. Senator Cutcliffe asked for a scotch. They met in the same closed-door fashion until five when they retired to their rooms to rest and refresh. They had dinner at seven and then met again shortly after. The senators went to the cottages around nine while the aides still milled about the house for a while, some in the library while others in their bedrooms. Most people were anxious, still not understanding why they were here. I overheard a few of the aides asking each other if they knew why the meeting was taking place. No one seemed to know."

"Is there a reason they brought their aides with them?"

"They were handling incoming calls, emails, and that sort of thing." Barry shrugged and leaned back in the chair. "I assume Kramer and the senators wanted them close. A few of the aides had their laptops and they sat in the dining room during the meetings in case they were called on for data or research, but so far, they haven't been needed for anything. They were rendered as obsolete as we were."

None of the information surprised Kate. Still, there were so many gaps in what was happening. She hoped that by morning Spade would be able to fill in the blanks. "I know that we don't have a time of death for the two senators. Could you give me a rundown of the night? Who was where and such?"

Barry shifted in his seat and breathed out a long heavy sigh. "By early evening, all the staff and aides had retired for the night. Michael, Matt, and I discussed the overnight plan. There are no cameras except on the outside fence and that didn't need to be manned because we all had an app on our phones that would alert us. There's no security system in the house. Michael decided it would be best if two of us were awake while the third slept. I took the first sleep shift while Michael was in the main house on guard and Matt patrolled the cottages and the perimeter of the property. Then we switched at one in the morning and again at five. Breakfast was scheduled for eight. By nine, when Senators Cutcliffe and Abbott weren't in the dining room for breakfast, their aides became worried dead went to check on them. The bodies were discovered then and the ball got rolling."

A few key points stood out to Kate. She'd address the easiest first. "How were their aides able to get into their rooms? Did they have the keys or were the doors unlocked?"

Barry seemed surprised by the question. "To tell you the truth, I don't know. Matt was just getting up at that point. I was guarding the house and Michael was the one outside. He responded first. By the time I got outside, he was inside the cottages. I never asked that question. Michael has a set of master keys. Otherwise, the senators had a room key but no one else did and all the rooms have a deadbolt inside that can't be unlocked from the outside."

"It stands to reason then that the senators opened the doors to their killer if there were no signs of forced entry." Kate hadn't seen any signs of forced entry when she viewed the cottages earlier. No doors or windows were broken and she'd assumed no one had windows open with the weather as chilly and rainy as it had been last night.

"That's a good point." Barry shrugged. "You'll have to ask Michael that. I don't know."

Kate didn't know how well Barry knew Matt and she wasn't sure how he'd respond. The question needed to be asked. "You said Matt was the first person patrolling outside and that the shift started at nine. We suspect the senators might have been killed during this time and now Matt is dead. Is it possible that he was killed because the killer thought he might know more?"

Kate's words sunk in as Barry considered it. At first, his expression registered disbelief and then he seemed resigned. "Michael and I thought it was to kill off another layer of security. I hadn't thought that Matt had witnessed something."

"It's possible he hadn't," Kate said, correcting him. "What I wonder is if the killer suspected that he might have last night. After Matt's shift, did he say anything about hearing or seeing anything strange? Did he have any concerns?"

"No concerns," he said. "I took the shift outside right after him. All was quiet. The doors to all the cottages were closed and the lights off.

I thought they were all sleeping. I had no reason to believe otherwise."

Before Kate could ask anything else, Declan and Michael returned. "Kate, the rest of the team is here. We'll need to wrap up these interviews tomorrow. The state police want a game plan."

Kate thanked Barry for the information and they made a plan to speak the next day. She stood and met Declan in the hall. The rest of the night was a swirl of meeting the medical examiner and state police, connecting Sharon to the right cottage to do her work, and then planning for the rest of the night. Kate ran on pure adrenaline.

# CHAPTER 6

At one in the morning, Kate and Declan finally arrived at her house a few miles away from the Eldridge Estate. They were wet, starving, and tired but grateful the state police had made a call to some local police departments and were able to add some extra security for the night. It allowed Kate and Declan to leave and rest. She had worried they'd be pulling double duty with both security and investigation. Thankfully, they'd have a reprieve and could focus on the investigation.

The two-story traditional Cape Cod-style house had gray cedar shake siding, black shutters on all the windows, and a light blue front door. There were four bedrooms, two on the first floor and two upstairs on either side of the house with a shared bathroom in between them. The rooms had dormers that jutted out like eyes. The area had a window seat and a reading nook. One of the bedrooms Kate had used as a young girl. She had modernized the furnishings and used the same room as she had grown older and came to the house on her own. She didn't use the two downstairs bedrooms – one had been her parents' and the other a guest room. On the first floor, there was a large eat-in kitchen, formal dining room, and living room with a wood-burning fireplace. Off the kitchen in the back, there was a screened-in porch that could be used for three seasons of the year. It was one of Kate's favorite places in the house.

As Kate went through the home, flipping on lights, Declan commented, "This is nice, Kate. I'm surprised you don't come up here more."

"If only time allowed," she said, even though that wasn't technically the truth. After the lights were on throughout the house, she went back through the living room to the stairs. "You can take the bedroom across from mine. The caretaker said he stocked the fridge and cabinets for me. I'm sure there is something we can scrounge together for dinner."

Declan was amenable to her suggestions. When they got to the top of the stairs, Kate went off to the left and Declan to the right in the small hallway. She dropped her suitcase on the floor and immediately peeled her wet shirt over her head and unbuttoned her pants and shoved them down her legs. All she wanted was a hot shower. She grabbed her robe from the closet. "I'm taking a hot shower before we do anything," she said and headed for the bathroom.

"Don't use all the hot water," Declan teased as she closed the bathroom door.

All Kate wanted was the hot water to run down her back and loosen the muscles in her shoulders and neck. As the night wore on, her muscles had tightened with stress.

Before they'd left the estate, Dr. Shelia Coburn had removed Matt Pike's body and updated the estimated time of death of the two senators to be close to eleven, which put their murders right in the middle of Matt's shift. He might have witnessed something. Kate saw no other reason to kill the man other than decreasing the amount of security. But even as Kate considered that, it didn't make any sense. Killing off one Secret Service agent with the FBI on the way would only bring more scrutiny and now more security than they had before.

Her interview with Barry was solid and she believed what he had told her. Declan hadn't told her much about his interview with Michael. He had been busy helping Sharon with the forensics in the room where

Matt had been shot. Before they slept for the night, they had promised to trade notes. Kate was glad Sharon had remained on the island and the local police were giving her some workspace. Dr. Coburn was pleasant, professional, and a clear expert in the field. She and Sharon had worked together before, so there was some familiarity between them. Kate was glad that the first thing they had done was put a solid team together, even if not much else had been accomplished. After her shower, Kate towel dried her hair and then went into her bedroom while Declan showered.

Thirty minutes later, they were sitting at the kitchen table eating turkey sandwiches and chips. It wasn't fancy but it was satisfying. They went over the interviews with Michael and Barry and compared notes. At the end of the discussion, Kate was happy that both men had said the same thing. There were no glaring discrepancies that they'd have to address tomorrow.

"What do you think? Do we trust Michael and Barry?" Declan asked, finishing off the last of his sandwich.

"I don't see a reason not to." Kate sighed in frustration. Even though she had said the words there was still something that wasn't sitting right with her. "Barry said that Michael seemed off and that he was concerned about the weekend. I want to speak to him tomorrow to better understand what concerns he had. I understand not having enough security, but it had to be something more than that to throw him off his game. He's a senior-level Secret Service agent. The agents I've met aren't rattled by much. Until the murders happened, there wasn't anything that should have rattled him. Did he mention anything like that to you?"

"He was concerned about the impending storm. They had been watching the hurricane come up the coast and Michael knew Martha's Vineyard was in its path. He kept coming back to not only why was the meeting called but what was the rush for it to happen here this weekend." Declan stood from the table and grabbed his empty plate and Kate's and carried them to the sink. He ran water over them and then turned and leaned against the counter. "I didn't like Michael at first. There was something about him that wasn't sitting right with me. One-on-one though, he was better. I do agree with him – what could have been so important that they all had to risk getting together without security in the path of a hurricane?"

That was what they were missing. "Who do you think is our best bet for the truth? Barry said even the aides didn't know."

"One of them could be lying," Declan countered, leaning back and crossing his legs at the ankle. He had flannel pajama bottoms on and a gray tee-shirt. He was barefoot though, and on the hardwoods, Kate wondered how he wasn't freezing. "We'll need to interview them tomorrow and find out if that's true. If not, maybe Spade can get us some answers."

Kate hadn't called their boss yet. She planned to do it first thing in the morning after Declan and she shared notes. She was hoping by then Dr. Coburn and Sharon might have some additional information to share.

Kate was staring off into space, still wondering how Declan wasn't cold, when he laughed. "I know I look sexy in these flannels but I've never seen you stare so long."

Kate raised her eyes to his, trying to process what he said because she hadn't heard him fully. When she saw his face and his eyebrows bobbing up and down dramatically, she laughed. "I was wondering how you're not cold." She pointed to her fuzzy socks. "These floors are freezing."

Declan held out a hand to her and pulled her up from the chair and wrapped her in a hug. "I'm not cold now," he said giving her an extra squeeze. "We might need to snuggle up tonight to keep warm."

Kate shoved him away playfully, but he reached for her hand again and pulled her close. "You'll be fine in your bed. The house will be warmer soon."

Declan kept his seafoam green eyes focused on her, a hint of a smile teasing his lips. "You're making it hard for me to resist you in those pajamas." He stepped back from her and leaned down, squinting at her thighs, and laughed. "Are those reindeer? It's not even Halloween yet and you're sporting Christmas reindeer." He let out a low gutter growl. "It's so sexy. I can't stand it."

"They were the only warm pajamas I had," she said trying not to laugh.

He spun her around in a twirl. "They are driving me crazy with lust. Come on, let me take you upstairs right now."

Kate rolled her eyes and shoved him away again. She was so tired that she didn't realize until she was laughing that it was exactly what she needed. She couldn't even remember when she last had a full night's sleep.

As the laughing died down and silence fell over the two of them with only the sounds of the rain beating hard against the windows, Declan pulled her into his arms and kissed her forehead. "All kidding aside, I haven't even had a chance to say how glad I am that we made it out of that last case alive. Do we need to talk about that kiss you planted on me before we went into the house and neutralized that lunatic who called himself the Fuse?"

Kate laid her head against Declan's chest. "I think you kissed me."

"Not the way I remember it," he said, his voice husky. "We can leave it at that if you want."

Kate didn't want to leave it at that.

Declan pulled back and looked down into her eyes. "We were stressed, Kate. We didn't know if we'd make it out of that house alive. I'm not complaining about the kiss. If you kissed me or I kissed you, I'm okay that it happened. I only wanted to know if we needed to talk about it now that we finally have a few minutes alone. I don't want to cross boundaries you don't want me to cross. Our friendship and partnership mean everything to me."

Words caught in her throat. They were dancing around dangerous territory and it was starting to seem inevitable that they were going to cross lines they probably shouldn't. Kate's attraction for Declan had hit her the moment they met when they were in the FBI Academy together. How could it not? He had a kind handsome face, dark boyish hair that always looked like he rolled out of bed, and eyes and a smile that made most women swoon. She had relied on his tall muscular frame to hold her when she was sad and shield her from harm. Kate understood why any woman could fall for him. But in the FBI Academy, that's as far as it went.

Declan's running around with women and drinking had put her off and she "friend-zoned" him without ever being aware of the term for it. Then they became partners. Declan married shortly after their partnership started and that was it.

Since then, their friendship had become the single most important relationship in her life. She had no close family and few friends. Then Declan divorced and moved into her brownstone while he navigated the legal proceedings to end his marriage and still be able to afford his alimony. Kate enjoyed having him there and she hated the thought of him leaving now that she had adjusted to his presence.

It was on their two previous cases that their chemistry had bubbled up, both of them finally admitting a mutual attraction. Outside of some ill-timed kissing, they hadn't gone further. Now, here he was looking down at her with a mix of lust and apprehension, waiting for her to make the call.

Kate stared up into his eyes. She slowly drew her teeth across her lower lip. "I'm not sure what we should do. I know what I want to do. I just don't want anything to ruin what we already have. I couldn't bear not having you in my life. As much as I hated having you as a partner in the beginning, if I didn't have you now, I think I'd quit and do something else."

Declan nodded. "I feel the same way. We don't have to do anything or decide anything tonight, Kate. We are both exhausted. I wanted to make sure that you were all right – that we were still good after the last case. It was a whirlwind and now we've walked into another mess. All I care about is that you're happy and comfortable and that I haven't done anything that upset you."

His concern was so genuine that a smile spread across her face. "We're better than good, Declan." His name came out in a whisper and she leaned on tiptoes to kiss his lips. That was all the invitation he needed.

Declan cupped her face with his hands and leaned down to kiss her more passionately. She moved her body into his, enjoying the kiss. He pulled her closer to him until she was practically standing on his bare toes. She dug her fingers into his back as the kissing grew more intense. Her mind swirled with what would happen next. A moment later, she felt a rush of disappointment when he released her and stepped back. He looked at her as if he wasn't sure what to say. Declan held up his hand and she stood there waiting, worried that he was going to change his mind about kissing her.

"Did I do something wrong?" she asked after too many seconds of silence.

Declan reached for her. "Of course not. I want to take you upstairs and do unmentionable things to you but not tonight and not this rushed. We have to be back at the estate at eight and it's nearing two-thirty. What we both need more than anything is sleep."

Kate couldn't disagree with him. She felt her cheeks redden. "You're a good kisser," she said with surprise in her voice that made him smile. "I assumed you were, but…"

"I know what you're trying to say. I feel the same," he said, saving her from the embarrassment of stumbling over her words. He leaned over and flicked off the kitchen light. "Come on, let's go to sleep."

At the top of the stairs, Kate turned to her room and waited to see what he would do. When he turned to the right, she was mixed with disappointment and relief. He was right they needed sleep more than anything.

Before Declan closed the door behind him, he leaned against it. "Promise me one thing, Kate."

"What's that?" she said, standing in her bedroom doorway.

"No matter what happens between us, you'll keep telling me how you feel. You can shut down and go inside your head and it scares me a little. I need to know - good or bad, okay?"

Kate liked that he knew her that well. "I promise." Then they both said goodnight. Kate wasn't sure what was going to happen, but she was going to relish the anticipation.

# CHAPTER 7

The next morning the fog and rain had temporarily let up and been replaced by a growing strong wind. Kate saw on the news that the outer wind bands of the hurricane would be there soon enough. The hurricane was a slow-moving storm that kept stalling out. The weather people were having difficulty predicting what exactly it was going to do and when it would hit Martha's Vineyard. All they knew for sure was that it would and the storm would be unlike any the island had seen in years, probably since Hurricane Bob in 1991.

At the crack of dawn, Declan received a call from Dr. Coburn that put Matt's time of death at four in the afternoon right in the middle of his security shift patrolling the cottages. She also confirmed that it was the same 9mm pulled out of Matt that she had pulled out of the two dead senators. The markings on the bullets indicated the gun was a Sig Sauer. Not that there had been any question if the cases were connected but the ballistics was a good confirmation.

Sharon had also called to explain that the crime scene forensics were as limited as they had been with the two senators. The killer had picked up the shell casings and left no prints or fibers behind. The only one who had touched Matt's body was Michael and he had admitted that. These kinds of gun cases were difficult. The killer didn't need to come close to the victim and so there was little transference of evidence.

The night before, Sharon had wanted to test everyone's hands for gunshot residue. It was something she had wanted to do after the deaths of the senators but many had balked at the idea. The vice president even insisted that they get a warrant to test him.

After Sharon made the request again and everyone declined, Declan explained that it was the fastest way to clear people, find the guilty party, and get them all out of there. He considered that only those who might have something to hide would balk at the idea of testing. It had worked and everyone agreed. Kate assumed that the killer would have been savvy enough to wear gloves and the test wouldn't rule anyone out. Agreeing to the test was a test in and of itself to see who would be willing. Everyone passed and they were no more ahead than they had been.

Before leaving the house that morning for the estate, Kate and Declan sat at the kitchen table and placed a call to Spade. He had been anticipating their call but hadn't liked that they had made so little progress.

"What can I do to help you?" he asked with frustration evident in his voice after they explained the current state of the investigation.

"We need to know why they are meeting," Kate said and Declan agreed. "There is something big we are missing, and I'm assuming it might go right to motive. If we can figure out why they have all come together and the reason for the lax security, we might start to understand the motive and narrow down a suspect. We have interviews with everyone planned for today. I'm going to try to get one of the aides to tell me. If Barry is correct, then they don't know anything either."

Spade agreed with the plan. "What about the two Secret Service agents? Do they seem credible?"

Kate caught Declan's look and she knew what he was thinking.

"There is something off about Michael Brooks. Even Barry said that he hasn't been acting himself. One of the things we need to do today is figure out who had access."

Spade clarified what he meant. "I was thinking of the gun, Kate. Both of those agents are armed with the same kind of weapon and bullets used in these murders. They know how to use a suppressor. They'd be your easiest persons of interest on the case."

Kate knew everything Spade was saying was true. She was hard-pressed to think that a Secret Service agent could kill two senators and one of their own. "Can you get us official background on the three agents assigned to the vice president? I want to know more about their backgrounds, their financials, and any risk assessment on them that might lead them to commit an act such as this before we start accusing them or getting too rough with them in an interview. We are working collaboratively and I don't want anything to get in the way of that."

"We aren't working too collaboratively," Declan clarified and looked over at Kate to see if she agreed. When she nodded, he added, "We are only sharing information with Sharon. I'm worried that we don't have a full picture of what's happening, so Sharon is the only person we trust to know the full scope of what we know. Kate is right that we need more information. I'm particularly curious who authorized the lax security."

Spade agreed with Declan's assessment. Before they ended the call, he reassured them. "I'll get to the bottom of the reason for the meeting and the security issue. For right now, do you have everything you need?"

"We do," Kate said. "With the added local security, we can focus on investigating the case. We've also moved everyone inside the main house. I don't think the senators were too happy about it, but it was better than keeping them isolated as they had been. The vice president is on the third floor alone and we have one officer who remains up there for his protection."

"It sounds like you're doing everything you can given the circumstances you've been dealt." That was the last Spade said before hanging up.

Kate and Declan arrived at Eldridge Estate a little after eight that morning. Stanton could be heard guiding the two servers who had come with the vice president from his residence. The smell coming from the kitchen wafted into the dining room where most of the senators, except for one, and the aides were assembled. Kate introduced Declan, who hadn't met all of them the night before in the flurry of activity. After introductions, they went in search of Michael who was in the library.

Kate found him sitting in the leather chair reading from a tablet. "Good morning, Michael. Was everything okay over night?"

Michael briefed them that all had gone fine the night before. "It was nice to have the extra security and be able to sleep in longer shifts. Both Barry and I are a little more rested than we were yesterday. Did you find out anything from your boss?"

Kate shook her head, not letting him know they had only spoken to Spade that morning. "He'll get back to us soon and I'll share what I can." She sat down on the chair and Declan took the one next to Michael. "I had a follow-up question from last night. Barry said that he wasn't sure if the doors were locked when the bodies of the senators were found that morning. Do you know?"

Michael kept his eyes focused on Kate as he explained what happened. "Both doors were unlocked. Their aides went out at the same time to let them know breakfast was ready. Allison Manning was Senator Loraine Abbott's aide and Chase Sims was working with Senator Grady Cutcliffe. They are the ones who found their bodies. If you noticed the young woman visibly upset yesterday after finding out about Matt Pike, that was Allison. I've been concerned about her well-being. Finding a dead body certainly can take its toll on a person. She seemed unusually distressed, in my opinion."

"The average person doesn't expect to find a murdered victim's body, Michael," Declan said evenly. "You and I are trained to see that kind of horror. It probably never crossed the young woman's mind that she'd find herself in that position. Not to mention, finding her boss that way. Are you saying her reaction was beyond what you'd expect from any young, untrained person in that situation?"

Michael adjusted in his seat and reached for a cup of coffee he had on the table next to him. He took a sip, seeming to delay his response to Declan. When he was ready, he answered, "Yes."

It was a curious response for a man who had been verbose in earlier meetings. Kate didn't understand the one-word response. "We need you to elaborate on that, please."

"I don't want to say that I think Allison might know more than she's told us because I don't know that for sure. But her response was over the top to me, far more than Chase's response. He was visibly shaken and upset. Allison kept muttering that she knew something like this might happen. She was saying it in a way that I don't believe she intended anyone else to hear. When I asked her about it, she denied that she had said it." Michael gestured toward the door. "You saw her yesterday when you told her about Matt Pike. She paled and was shaking. To my understanding, she didn't even know Matt."

"Okay," Kate said, agreeing that what Allison had muttered might be significant. "I'll start with interviewing her this morning. Back to the doors. They were unlocked?"

"Yes. Both of them." Michael fixed his gaze on her. "That's partly why I know this is an inside job. Those senators let their killer in. Dr. Coburn confirmed that when she told us the time of death. I don't know if the senators were still awake or in bed when they let their killer in. I can't imagine that either of them had left their doors unlocked."

That was a good point. Kate didn't believe either senator would be so careless as to leave their doors unlocked, even in a remote area such as this. They knew how risky that could be.

Declan looked over at Kate, but she gestured for him to ask his questions. He focused on Michael. "You have said a few times you think this is an inside job. Do you have a potential suspect?"

Michael appeared uncertain if he should respond. Kate encouraged, "Even if you don't have any evidence, what's your instinct on this? You've been around these people probably more than anyone. Do you have a feeling one way or another?"

"I couldn't even venture a guess who'd be responsible," Michael said calmly and evenly. He paused as if he wanted to add something. Kate pressed him more and he finally shrugged. "I'd start with Allison who seems to know more than the rest of us. Her response about worrying something like this would happen sparked my interest. I wouldn't say she's a person of interest, but she is someone who might have a clue as to what's happening."

Kate agreed with that assessment. "What about the other keys? You said yesterday you have a master set as does Stanton. Anyone else?"

Michael pulled a set of keys out of his pocket. "The doors use keys, not keycards like a regular hotel. I have the master set of keys for the main doors, cottage doors, and upstairs bedroom doors. That said, each of the bedrooms and cottages has an extra deadbolt inside that I can't access with these keys. The doors can be double locked and the master keys only provide access to one lock. If the senators had deadbolted the doors and had been killed by someone who escaped through the window, we would have had to go in the same window or break down the door. I believe the killer walked in and out the front door, and I believe they were let in."

"I'd tend to agree with that assessment." Kate turned her eyes to Declan who was nodding his head in agreement. She refocused on Michael. "Let's keep this room as a command room for all of us. We need to establish a timeline of events and know where every person was minute by minute. Do we know where everyone was when the senators were killed?"

"That's not going to be possible," Michael said and furrowed his brow. "All the senators and vice president had gone to bed at that point. Matt Pike was outside patrolling the cottages and the grounds, Barry had gone off to bed, and I was patrolling the inside of the main house. As you can imagine, there is a lot of room to cover on three floors. Some of the aides were still up and watching television, others had gone to bed. I don't have an accounting of where everyone was during those murders."

That's what Kate had been afraid of after her interview with Barry yesterday. It would make alibiing anyone near impossible. "What about during Matt Pike's murder? You said that you had sequestered everyone in the dining room so you could better keep an eye on them."

"That's partially true, yes. The senators still broke off to continue their meeting in the main living room and the aides were all in the dining room. We weren't holding them there though. They were free to move about the main house. If a senator wanted to go out to the cottages, either Barry or I would walk with them and the other would stay in the main house."

Declan stood at that point, growing frustrated. "That living room has two doors, one into the hallway that connects to the dining room but it also has a back door that goes out onto the yard with a direct path to the cottages. Isn't it possible that a senator left out that door and you and Barry would be none the wiser?"

"Yes," Michael admitted. "I told you yesterday we were doing the best we could with the circumstances at hand. I couldn't hold all those people hostage in the dining room all day. The senators and vice president wanted to continue meeting. It seemed more important than ever."

With resignation in her voice, Kate said, "Give Declan and me a moment alone, and then we can get started."

Michael rose from his chair. "I know a lot of blame falls on me for what happened."

"No one is blaming you, Michael." Kate stood and took a step toward him. "We have to ask these questions to fully understand the scope of the situation. I'd love to be able to start ruling people out today and to do that I need to alibi everyone. The circumstances make that nearly impossible so we have to corroborate through interviews where everyone was. Do you have photos of each person?" Kate assumed he had files on all of them.

Michael nodded. "I'll bring those in here. I can also speak to Stanton about a dry-erase board or something similar."

Kate thanked him and he left. When they were alone, they decided that Declan would start with Stanton, the cook, and two service staff people. Kate would start with Allison and then Chase.

# CHAPTER 8

Down the hall from the library, Kate found what Michael had referred to as the sunroom. It was styled in the same tans and blues as the main living room but did not have a fireplace. There were two oversized chairs with ottomans and a couch. The windows overlooked the front lawn and driveway down to the gate. Kate would use this as her interview space with Allison.

She led Allison to the room and closed the door behind them. The young woman's hands shook as she eased herself down on the couch. Allison hadn't said a word to Kate as they walked the long narrow hallways, even when Kate tried to make light conversation.

"I'm not sure what I can tell you," Allison said before Kate even asked a question.

Kate sat across from the young woman. "It's just a conversation, Allison. No reason to be concerned. This is routine. My partner and I will be speaking with everyone. He is interviewing the cook and service staff right now."

Allison nodded her head once. "All of this has me quite upset. I've never experienced anything like this before. I'm sure you know I found Senator Abbott." She sniffed back tears and lowered her head to look at her hands folded in her lap. Allison did not relax back. She remained rigidly perched on the end of the couch cushion with her knees together at an angle from her body. It was the primmest way of sitting and Kate wondered about her background.

Kate would start with something easy. "How long have you worked for Senator Abbott?"

"Four years. I was a junior aide when I started and moved up the ranks quickly. I'm her most senior aide now."

"What about your background – where you grew up, schooling, and such?"

Allison explained that she was born and raised in Connecticut and had gone first to Dartmouth and then to Georgetown University for her master's degree in political science. She started working with Senator Abbott right out of grad school. It was not the first political appointment she'd had though. "I worked for a state senator in New Hampshire while in undergrad. My father was a state senator in Connecticut when I was younger. He runs a corporate law firm in New York City now."

Kate asked several routine questions about her working environment with Senator Abbott. Allison said that it was fairly easy and that everyone loved their jobs.

When Kate realized she wasn't getting anywhere with that line of questions, she shifted gears. "I'm sure you get threats from constituents and others who do not like Senator Abbott and her positions. She was quite outspoken and had made a name for herself during her tenure in the Senate. Some had even speculated that she might make a run at the White House. Were there any specific threats made against her that concerned you?"

Allison lowered her eyes and wouldn't meet Kate's. "There are always threats."

Kate knew by the energy shift in the room that Allison knew more than she was saying. "Yes, I'd assume there are always threats. I'm asking about specific threats that raised a level of concern. I can tell there's something you're holding back. It's important that you share it with me. It might relate to what's happened."

Allison didn't seem to understand. "Both Senator Abbott and Senator Cutcliffe were murdered the same way. How would a threat against Senator Abbott impact Senator Cutcliffe? They are different political parties and didn't vote the same way on any legislation. They are opposed in every way imaginable." Allison shifted and now faced Kate more squarely. She leaned forward and lowered her voice. "If I'm being honest with you, Agent Walsh, Senator Abbott hated Senator Cutcliffe. If she wasn't dead, I might have suspected her of killing him."

Allison's expression suggested she couldn't believe she had said that aloud. Kate assumed it was for show and she knew exactly what she was saying. Kate crossed her legs. "If I can rule out anyone, it's Senator Abbott and Senator Cutcliffe. That does bring up the question though about who'd want both of them dead. Who stands to benefit with both of them gone?"

"I don't know because they had nothing in common other than being United States Senators. They weren't even on the same committees. Senator Abbott was on the judiciary committee while Cutcliffe was on the foreign relations committee. I can't think of one similar cause they had between them."

"Yet, here they are this weekend with a select few senators." Kate zeroed in on her now. "Allison, do you know why they were meeting this weekend or who arranged it?"

She shrugged and averted her eyes again. "I couldn't say."

That phrasing struck Kate as significant. "You can't say because you aren't allowed to say or you can't say because you don't know? There is a marked difference."

Allison remained tight-lipped and didn't respond.

Kate worried if she pushed her more right then, she'd shut down. "Tell me about finding Senator Abbott's body. My understanding is you were worried when she didn't show up for breakfast."

"That's correct," she said, looking at Kate again. "Senator Abbott keeps a fairly strict schedule. Nine is late for breakfast but she's never one to be late for a meeting or make anyone else wait for her. She prides herself on her punctuality. When she was late, I became concerned. Senator Cutcliffe was late too, but Chase said that happens frequently so he wasn't worried. But he walked outside with me to check. That's when we both found the senators dead." Allison wiped her wet tear-filled eyes. "It was a horrible thing to see – she was lying there on the floor facedown. I didn't go into the room very far. I could tell from close to the doorway that she was dead. How could she not be, shot like that?"

"How did you find the door when you arrived?"

"It was closed but unlocked," she responded with confidence. "I knocked twice and when no one answered, I tried the handle. I pushed the door open, took a step in, and called her name. That's when I realized she was lying there on the floor. Chase said I screamed but I don't remember it."

That all sounded plausible to Kate. "Did you have a key to the senator's room?"

Allison shook her head. "She didn't share that with me and there would be no reason to. When she turned in for the night, if she needed anything, she'd have texted me."

"How safety conscious was Senator Abbott?" When Allison asked what Kate meant, she added, "Did she lock her door? Make sure the windows were closed and locked? Did she take risks with her safety?"

"Oh, no," Allison said, shaking her head firmly. "Senator Abbott always made sure doors were locked. She wouldn't even jog alone. She either went to the gym or had one of her staffers go with her. She wasn't one to take risks like that."

That was what Kate had suspected. She asked a few more routine questions about Senator Abbott and when she was satisfied, Kate pressed again on the tougher questions. "When you found Senator Abbott, you were overheard saying you thought something like this might happen. What did you mean?"

Allison looked away again, which was becoming a tell that the young woman didn't want to answer the question. Kate knew there was more right under the surface. "I don't remember saying that," she lied too obviously for Kate to let it go.

"Even if you don't remember saying it, do you know why you might have?" When Allison wouldn't respond, Kate pushed harder. "I want to remind you that lying to a federal agent is a crime and so is obstruction of justice. We have two murdered United States Senators and a murdered Secret Service agent. No one is leaving here until I figure out what's going on. So, if you have pertinent information, I need you to share it now."

Allison sat primly with her hands folded in her lap.

Kate's growing frustration bubbled over. "Allison, you have made a name for yourself with Senator Abbott. You could easily get a job with another senator. That's not going to happen if you create a reputation for yourself as being noncompliant with the FBI." In truth, Kate figured stonewalling the FBI would make her a hero with some senators, but not anyone Allison would consider for employment. "You know more than you're saying. I can help you."

"I was told never to speak about it to anyone no matter what happened."

Kate's instinct was right. "Then you do know why Senator Abbott was murdered?"

"I'm not sure that it all relates. I would assume it does." Allison wrung her hands and it was clear the young woman was conflicted about whatever she was about to say.

Kate knew she had her right on the edge. "Allison, whatever you know could be relevant. If it's not, I'll never disclose what you told me. Senator Abbott is dead. If you promised her something, it doesn't matter now. You could help find the person responsible for her death and prevent another." Kate let that sit and didn't push further.

Allison remained quiet for several moments and just as she opened her mouth to speak, a scream pierced the quiet and both of them turned their heads to the door. Kate stood and drew her gun, holding her hand out for Allison to wait there. She went to the door and opened it a crack and looked out down the hall left and then right. There was no one there.

Kate stood there for a moment, waiting to see if there was another scream. She was ready to close the door and brush it off, thinking Michael or Barry would take care of it. The scream happened again. This time someone screamed the name Chase louder and more piercing than the previous scream. It was followed by a rush of terrified voices.

"Wait here, Allison," Kate commanded as she stepped out into the hallway and closed the door behind her. She was halfway down the hall when she considered that it wasn't a good idea to leave the young woman alone. Kate ran back and opened the door. "I don't want to leave you alone. Come with me but follow behind me."

They made it down the long narrow hallway to the foyer where they saw the crowd of people huddled in a circle. Kate couldn't tell what they were looking at until she was standing nearly on top of them. Then she saw the brown shoes of a man and his right pant leg pushed up showing his sock. Kate shoved through everyone until she got to the body.

Chase was sprawled out on his back with one arm thrown over his head and the other at his side. His legs were twisted in an unnatural way that certainly wasn't bothering him now. His eyes were still open and the bullet wound in his forehead dripped blood. She didn't need to check for a pulse. It was clear to all of them that he was dead.

Kate raised her eyes from the body and met Declan's who stood on the other side of Chase. She knew the panic she was seeing on his face was reflected in her own. They had to take control of the scene. "Everyone back to the main living room now." She wasn't going to give them time to do anything other than get into the same room. As she passed by Declan, she whispered, "We need to search for the gun. No one is getting out of my sight until I search them all."

He nodded once. "I'll stay here and secure the scene and call Sharon and Dr. Coburn."

As Kate ushered people down the hall, Michael came from the dining room. "What's happened?" he said with confusion on his face. He looked to the side around Kate as all the senators and aides walked back toward the living room.

"There's been another murder. Where are Barry and Vice President Kramer?"

Michael pointed to the end of the hallway. "They were headed to the back staircase up to the vice president's suite. He said he needed to do a few things before speaking with anyone."

"Has he been out of Barry's sight?"

"I don't know, Kate. I was outside patrolling the grounds." Michael ran a hand down his face. "The extra security we had last night left this morning. They said they'd be back tonight. They can't spare the staff during the day with the storm."

Kate pushed everyone to the living room until she could figure out the best course of action.

# CHAPTER 9

Once Kate had everyone in the living room, she stared at the group of frightened senators and aides. They looked at one another in both confusion and fear. There was a killer among them, possibly. Kate hadn't ruled out the noticeably absent vice president. She hadn't asked Michael to go upstairs and get him, but she had asked him to radio Barry and have Vice President Kramer remain in his suite.

Kate cast glances around the room. "I need you to empty your bags and pockets and purses." She thought the senators might balk at the idea but they got up and started emptying the few belongings they had with them. The aides followed. Kate walked around the group, checking their bags, purses, briefcases, and persons. There was no gun in anyone's possession.

Michael stood at the edge of the room watching her. She knew he had the same make and model gun that was used in the other murders. Kate wouldn't outright accuse him in front of the others or do anything to bring his character into question. She needed them to trust Michael even if she didn't. She looked over at him and he nodded his head toward the door.

When Kate stepped into the hallway, Michael handed her his weapon. "Check it if you like – full magazine. This weapon hasn't been fired in the last few weeks. I haven't even gone to the range."

Kate didn't touch the gun but she raised her eyes at him. "Where were you coming from when I saw you in the hallway?"

He holstered his weapon. "As I said, I was out in the rain patrolling the grounds. My windbreaker and umbrella are drying off in the library. I dropped my wet things there and then headed toward the dining room. Chase passed me in the hallway. He said that he had an interview with you. When I didn't see anyone in the dining room, I went to the living room. Most of the people were in there, except for Barry and the vice president. I was told by one of his aides they were upstairs in the suite. I made it to the second floor when I heard the scream. I rushed back down and through the hall and then bumped into you as you were coming from the foyer."

Kate glanced down at his wet shoes. It was a sign he had been telling the truth, or at least, it fit the story he told. For all she knew, he had run outside and stashed another gun. Kate wasn't sure why she suddenly had mistrust for him. It's not like he had done anything to garner that. "You said you looked in the living room, was everyone in there?"

"I don't know, Kate. I don't remember. Chase was the only person who passed me in the hall. It was a blur of people who I saw. I can make you a list of who I remember. But not remembering someone doesn't mean they weren't in there."

"Understood," Kate said. "I have to search the house and the bedrooms. Someone might have stashed the gun in their room."

"I was headed up the staircase when the scream happened. Don't you think I would have seen someone pass me?"

"There are two staircases. The one in the main area of the house and one off the back kitchen. Someone could have slipped into the dining room and then into the kitchen and up the back stairs without you noticing. It's a long way around but certainly possible." Kate assumed it was possible. She'd need to check with Stanton, the cook, and the two servers to see where they were.

"Okay," Michael said not agreeing or disagreeing. "Do you want me to stay with everyone while you go search the rest of the house?"

"I need to ask permission to search their rooms. We don't have a warrant." Kate moved past Michael and back into the living room. She didn't want to dance around it. "I'd like to search your bedrooms during my search of the rest of the house. I need your permission to do that. Does everyone consent?"

None of the aides made a move to agree or not. All of them turned to look at the senators.

"Go right ahead," Senator Nancy Yates of Vermont said, standing. She had a key in her hand and offered it to Kate. She turned back to her colleagues. "No one else should have a problem consenting to this either unless they have something to hide."

Kate had hoped someone would take the lead. She waved off Senator Yates. "I appreciate the key but Michael has the master key I can use. I appreciate you taking the lead on this."

"Someone has to." She stood about five-foot-two but was a powerhouse in the Senate. She had her hair cut in a blunt dark bob. She folded her arms across her chest and looked over at the aides. "I assume all of you consent to a search of your rooms." It wasn't a question.

There was a volley of slow responses all confirming. Kate hated to do it but she needed each one of them to say yes and provide their name and room number. She took notes on her phone as she went through them one by one. She didn't need anyone coming back saying the search wasn't legal or that she had violated their rights. She also needed Declan to help the search go faster.

When she was done with the aides, Kate raised her eyes to the other senators. One by one they complied even though two of them looked like they were ready to give Kate an issue with it. The conjecture of having something to hide forced their hands. "I appreciate all of you making this so easy for me. I'll have Stanton bring in some snacks and coffee while you wait. We will need you all to remain in this room as a group for now."

"We're being held here?" one of the aides asked.

"For now," Kate said, turning to leave. At the doorway, she stopped long enough to ask Michael to remain with them all and not to leave the room or allow any of them to leave the room. He didn't fight her on that and Kate was grateful. He handed her the master key as she left.

She closed the door behind her and took a moment in the hall to collect herself. She took a few deep breaths in and out to calm her mind and settle the racing thoughts. Things were happening so fast that they barely had time to get a handle on one thing before another started. The rain that had let up this morning was again coming down hard enough to sound like small pellets hitting the windows and roof. The wind was picking up too. It would only be a short time before they lost power. She had a generator at her house and assumed the estate would as well. It might make it impossible for the local cops to make it back for their added night security. Kate couldn't worry about that now.

She headed down the hall toward the foyer. Declan was in a squat position over the body. His gloved hands were fishing around in the man's pockets. He pulled out a phone and held it up for Kate. "I thought I'd take a look and see what kind of messages he's been exchanging."

That reminded Kate about the phones from the dead senators and Matt Pike. "Has anyone gone through the other victims' phones?"

Declan shook his head. "They have a passcode and we can't get in. The FBI field office tech person is working on it." He held the phone up for Kate to see it. "We got lucky here. It's a fingerprint scan entry." Declan held Chase's index finger against the scanner. It accepted the scan and unlocked the phone.

While Declan skimmed through the phone, Kate said, "I have them all sequestered in the living room and the vice president and Barry are upstairs. I need your help to search their rooms."

Declan's eyes snapped up. "Everyone gave you permission to search?"

"Senator Nancy Yates guilt-tripped them into it. She said if someone said no, they'd look guilty. No one said no." Kate looked down at Chase lying there. She didn't want to leave the body exposed like this but didn't have a choice. "Are Sharon and Dr. Coburn on their way?"

"Yeah, they were as horrified as we were. Dr. Coburn said it's only a matter of time before this is leaked to the media. She's doing her best but she's sharing space and there are people at the hospital who know. They are watching her work on body after body. Two senators, a Secret Service agent, and, now, a senatorial aide." Declan pointed down to the phone. "Since Chase was Senator Cutcliffe's aide and he found the senator's body maybe he knew something or maybe he saw something he shouldn't have like Matt Pike."

"It's possible," Kate said. It's what she had been thinking. "Allison knows more. She was on the brink of telling me when we heard the scream. Who was it that found the body?"

"Senator Yates. She was headed to find Stanton to ask for more coffee. She couldn't find him because he was sitting with me being interviewed. She came out here to the foyer looking for him and found Chase instead."

That meant neither Allison nor Stanton had killed Chase. "At least we can rule out a couple of people."

"Rule out all the service people too," Declan said and then explained. "Stanton was finishing up with me, but from where I was sitting in the staff kitchen, I could see the cook and the two servers. I had my eyes on them the whole time and none of them would have had time to sneak out to shoot Chase."

"We can rule them out of that murder then."

"What does that mean, Kate?"

"Just what I said. We can rule those people out of Chase's murder. We don't know if any of these people are working together." Kate tightened her ponytail and tucked the errant strands behind her ears. "We don't know any more than we did yesterday. I agree with Michael that we need to know why they are meeting. It's an odd bunch to bring together."

Declan nodded his head toward the hall where the stairs to the second floor were. "Why don't you go start the search and as soon as Sharon and Dr. Coburn are here, I'll be up. I don't want to leave Chase's body here alone."

Kate explained that he could because Michael had everyone sequestered. "Okay," he said relenting, "let's get this search over with and back to interviewing people."

They headed for the stairs and once on the second landing, Kate went to the far end of the hall and unlocked the first door. Before they got started, Declan handed Kate the extra pair of gloves he had in his back pocket and they got down to work.

They split the rooms in half. Kate worked on the right while Declan took the left. Kate took the bathrooms while Declan took the closet and desk drawers. They moved swiftly but methodically through each room – all of them including each of the senators. At some point, Sharon texted that she and Dr. Coburn were there. Kate continued the search alone while Declan went to speak to them and then joined her again. They continued through the rooms until they reached the final one. The search had been futile and nothing had been found.

As she closed the last door, Kate raised her eyes to the ceiling. "You know where we have to go next, don't you?"

"Vice President Kramer," Declan said. He didn't appear to be any more excited by the prospect than Kate. "He's not going to give us an easy time of this. He might even flat-out refuse to let us search."

"Which he has every right to do." Kate knew that unless she had solid evidence there was no way she was getting a warrant to search the vice president's room and belongings. She hoped that he'd be at least willing to speak to them. "Only one way we are going to find out."

# CHAPTER 10

The third floor of the house was nothing but one large suite. It had a large living room area and a small dining room along with a bedroom and a full bathroom including a clawfoot tub that was made to look like an antique but was quite new and fitted with modern jets. Kate had read all of that on the estate's website. Seeing it in person, Kate realized the photos on the website didn't quite do it justice. It was a retreat of the senses capped by the sweet smell in the air of something Kate couldn't quite distinguish. Lavender, maybe. Jasmine. Kate wasn't sure but it was lovely and soothing. She almost didn't want to disturb the vibe of the space.

Kate had assumed Barry would be in the hallway, but he wasn't there or outside of the suite's door. She knocked once and then stepped back with Declan to wait. Barry answered the door a moment later. "We need to speak with you and Vice President Kramer."

Barry opened the door wider and let them in. "The vice president is in the living room watching the news about the storm. He also just had a call with the president. They have both accepted that the vice president is stuck here for now. Kramer was trying everything in his power to get off the island, regardless of what the FBI wanted. He's not in the best mood."

"Is he ever?" Declan asked with a chuckle.

Barry cracked a smile. "Fair point." He led them into the living room area to the left. "Vice President Kramer, Agents Walsh and James are here to speak with you."

Kramer waved them in without turning in their direction. He was kind enough to turn down the volume of the television. "What do you people want now?"

"There's been another murder," Kate said, stepping toward him. "Chase, Senator Cutcliffe's aide, was shot in the foyer."

Kramer cast his eyes up to Kate's. "Shouldn't you people have stopped that? Isn't that why you're here? It doesn't seem like you're doing much good at all. I just spoke to the president about you both. I'd be prepared for a demotion after this case."

Neither Kate nor Declan was going to take the bait. Kate started to speak but stopped when Declan reached for her arm, willing to throw himself on the sword. He stood his ground. "Vice President Kramer, we need to search your room and your belongings."

Kramer shot up from the couch and cursed at them. "You're treating me like a common criminal. I'm not letting you search my room. Get out now!" Red crept up from his neck to his cheeks and Kate caught the faint smell of alcohol. She wondered how much he'd had to drink so early in the morning.

"Sir, we searched the aides' rooms as well as the senators. We are just looking for the murder weapon. All we are trying to do is rule people out," Kate assured him. "It won't take us long."

"The senators allowed you to search?" Kramer asked, sounding as if he doubted it.

"Yes, we just finished doing that now." Kate pointed toward the door. "Sharon, with the FBI forensics team, and Dr. Coburn are downstairs processing the crime scene. We are doing the best we can under the circumstances. I had just started to interview the aides when we were interrupted by a scream. Where were you when the murder happened?"

"I was in the dining room." Kramer looked over at Barry and gave a slight head nod.

"That's right," Barry said, agreeing. "Vice President Kramer was finishing up his coffee and reading some news when we heard the scream. I didn't know what happened so I quickly rushed him up the stairs. We haven't left the suite since."

That wasn't what Michael had told her. "Are you sure you were in the dining room when you heard the scream and not already up here?"

Barry held his stare on Kate and barely even blinked. "I believe we were in the dining room."

Kramer stepped around Kate. "Maybe we were up here already. What does it matter? I certainly didn't kill an aide." He waved his hand as if he were swatting away a fly. "Go search the room. I don't care. I don't have anything to hide."

"I'll get started," Declan said, giving Kate a look that it was okay if she took Barry aside and questioned him.

Kramer sat back down on the couch and Kate asked Barry to step out into the hall with her. When the door closed behind them, she said, "I thought you and I had a good rapport yesterday."

"We did," he said nodding.

"Why are you lying to me? I can tell by your expression that you were lying about where the vice president was when the scream happened. You weren't in the dining room." That was a guess on Kate's part.

Barry stared off down the hall and then raked a hand over his head. He kept his eyes focused on Kate's. After a few moments of silence, he capitulated. "You're right, Agent Walsh. We weren't in the dining room. Vice President Kramer asked me to lie. To be honest with you, I don't know where he was at the time of the murder. I was in the dining room with him initially and he said he was walking to the bathroom. When I tried to follow, he told me to stay put. We were all downstairs so I didn't think anything of it. The bathroom is right in the hall near the library. That's about the time Chase left saying he was meeting with you. A few minutes later, Kramer came rushing into the room and told me he needed to go upstairs and so we headed that way. We were back here in the room when we heard the scream."

Kate sucked in a sharp breath. "Do you understand the implications of what you're telling me? Vice President Kramer was unaccounted for during the time of the murder and asked you to lie about it."

"I understand." Barry leaned into Kate to get closer. "I was going to tell you I swear. I just didn't want to say anything in front of him. If he's the one who is doing this, I didn't want to tip him off that we knew."

Kate wasn't sure she believed that. "Did Kramer have anything on him when he came up here? Any bags with him or a place to stash a gun?"

"He's been wearing the same heavy brown cardigan since we arrived. I thought he was cold. It has deep pockets, and it looked like it was weighed down by something. I didn't ask though. When we got back upstairs, he went directly into the bedroom and returned without the cardigan."

"Did it occur to you that the vice president might have killed Chase?"

Barry shook his head. "I didn't even know that anything happened until we were up here and heard a scream. I tried to radio down to Michael, but he didn't respond. Then after a few minutes, he said that Chase was dead. Then yes, it occurred to me that the vice president was unaccounted for during that time. But I don't believe, even now, that he could have done something like that."

"I assume people can account for you being there?"

"Yes. I was speaking to Senator Yates about the plan for the day. They were eager to get back to the meeting. She said they still had a lot to discuss and hoped that the investigation wouldn't take away from the reason they were there. The vice president said something along those lines as well. Even with the murders, they felt they had much to accomplish. She left the room to look for Stanton for more coffee. The others can account for me being there the rest of the time."

Kate locked her gaze on him. "You still have no idea what they were discussing?"

"No."

"What about the other murders? Where was Kramer then?"

Barry looked a bit taken aback by the question. "I assume when the senators were killed, he was up here either asleep or getting ready for bed. I wasn't with him then. When Matt Pike was killed, I believe he was in the living room with the senators."

Kate clicked her tongue. "That sounds like a lot of assuming to me."

Barry leaned in as if he couldn't believe what he was hearing. "You can't seriously think that the vice president killed senators and his own Secret Service agent, can you?" Before Kate could respond, Barry said *no* several times. "You won't convince me."

"I'm not laying blame, but it's not out of the question. Stranger things have happened."

"What would be his motive?"

"We don't have a motive for any of it. That's something still left to be explored." Kate knew that just by asking the question she was risking Barry going back to tell the vice president. She had to take the risk and assumed Spade would back her up if there were any repercussions. "I want to be clear that I'm not outright accusing the vice president of anything. I'm saying that he lied and asked you to lie during the time of a murder. He's making himself look guilty and it's something we have to explore. As far as I'm concerned, everyone is a potential suspect until they are cleared."

Barry touched his chest. "I'm a suspect, too?"

"Everyone is until I can clear them," Kate said but then threw him a bone. "Coming out here and telling me the truth helps you. It matches other information we have. I'm sure others in the room can account for you there. If you weren't responsible for the murders, you'll be cleared quickly."

"I'll do whatever I can to help you. I had nothing to do with any of this."

"Good. That will help us." Kate excused herself and went back into the room, Kramer was parked in front of the television watching the Weather Channel.

Kate made her way past the living room and into the bedroom. "Did you find anything?" she asked Declan as she entered. He was on his knees looking under the bed.

"Nothing so far."

"What about a brown cardigan? Did you search the closet yet?"

"I haven't searched the closet. I started in the living room and worked my way back." Declan stood and scanned around the room. "I don't think there's anything here, Kate."

Kate opened the closet door and turned her head over her shoulder to look at him. She explained that Kramer had lied about where he was during the murder. "He's unaccounted for, Declan. Barry admitted that to me outside."

"But he's the vice president, Kate." Declan was making the same face that Barry had.

"Everyone here is someone, Declan. Would this investigation go smoother if we found out one of the aides was involved? That would make the arrest less high-profile. We don't know what we don't know, so everyone is suspect, including the vice president."

Declan could tell she was getting heated by the tone of her voice. He reached out and squeezed her shoulder. "I'm on your side, Kate. If we find it's the vice president, I'll arrest him myself and perp walk him through a sea of reporters."

"*Perp walk*. It's been a long time since I heard the phrase," Kate said, allowing herself to smile. It was a common law enforcement phrase for making sure that the arrest or court proceeding where they brought the suspect out in handcuffs was on full display for the media.

Kate turned her attention back to the closet. She found the brown cardigan but its pockets were empty. She felt down the pants and shirts and found no gun. There were three pairs of shoes on the floor that were empty as well. Even though Kate was frustrated by not finding the gun, she was glad it hadn't been in the closet.

"If we are done, we can head back downstairs," she said.

Declan was finishing up the search of the dresser. "Yeah, I'm done here. Nothing at all."

They made their way back to Vice President Kramer. "I appreciate you letting us search, sir," Kate said as she entered the living room. "You are free to go back downstairs. Everyone is sequestered in the living room, but if you'd like to get back to your meeting, we can move the aides to the dining room. I suggest Barry remains with you in the living room."

"Absolutely not," Kramer said, glancing over at her. "As I'm sure you've heard, this is a private meeting."

"Can you tell me what the meeting is regarding?"

Kramer shook his head and turned his attention back to the television. It was his signal he was done with the conversation. He made no move to get up and head downstairs either. Kate wasn't sure what he was going to do other than sit there and continue to watch the Weather Channel.

Kate thanked Barry as they headed out the door. She looked down the hallway past Kramer's suite and asked Declan, "What are those two doors at the end of the hallway?"

"I have no idea," he said. "Stanton mentioned there was laundry service up on this floor, but I thought he meant the suite had laundry inside, which I didn't see." He walked down the hall ahead of Kate and tried one door and found it locked.  He tried the next door and it opened to a small laundry room.  There wasn't much in the room beside a commercial washer and dryer and a shelf above it with detergent and a stack of plastic hangers. He bent and pulled open the washer door and then closed it.

When he opened the dryer, Declan stepped back and cursed.

"What?" Kate asked, rushing toward him. He pointed to the inside of the dryer and Kate bent to get a better look.  Sitting right in the middle of the tumbler was a handgun.

Declan reached in and pulled it out with his gloved hand. He slipped it into an evidence bag he'd had in his pocket.

"Anyone could have put that there, Declan," Kate said, now sounding like him earlier. With the evidence right in front of her, she didn't want to believe the vice president could be a killer.

Declan held the bag up and pointed with his other hand toward the locked door. "What do you want to bet that door is the one at the end of the hall between the bedroom and the bathroom?"

Kate didn't even want to consider. All she wanted to do was check the door herself and see how quickly Kramer could go from the bedroom to the laundry without being seen.

# CHAPTER 11

While Declan waited in the hallway with the gun, Kate knocked on the door to the vice president's suite. Barry answered. "I thought you were done?" he asked with confusion on his face.

"We were done but we've…" Kate didn't want to give away what they had found just yet. She pointed down the hall. "There are two doors down there. One goes to a laundry room and I'm assuming from what Declan said the other door goes into the hallway with the bedroom and bathroom. I need to see it."

Barry stepped out of the way and let her in. It didn't look like Kramer had moved from the couch. He didn't even turn to acknowledge her. Kate made her way back to the bedroom and stopped just outside the door in the short hallway. The bathroom door had been left wide open blocking the wall at the end of the hall. Kate hadn't even noticed it before. She closed the bathroom door to reveal the other door that Declan had mentioned.

Kate unlocked the bolt and pulled the door open, stepping right back into the main hallway. The laundry room wasn't more than a few steps away. Kramer could have said he was going to his bedroom, stepped out the door, stashed the gun, and returned without Barry noticing. It would have taken him less than twenty seconds from start to finish. They had a problem on their hands and would need to speak to Spade before going further.

Kate walked back into the main living room area and pointed at Barry and then to the door. She left first without saying anything to Kramer with Barry right behind her. Once they were in the hall and down from the door, Kate called to Declan who was waiting by the stairs.

Declan turned and held up the evidence bag with the gun. "I'll give you three guesses where we found this."

Barry paled and remained fixated on the gun. "The laundry room?"

"The laundry room," Declan confirmed, lowering the bag to his side. "You have any idea how it got in there?"

Barry's mouth remained in a firm line and he slowly shook his head. He seemed to be in a state of shock and couldn't take his eyes off the gun.

Kate said his name to get his attention. When he turned to her, she asked, "Is it possible when you came back into the suite earlier that Vice President Kramer slipped out that door and stashed the gun before going into the bedroom?"

Barry took a deep breath and paused. His answer was clear by the look on his face. Kate didn't need to hear him say it. She was glad when he finally nodded his head. "It's possible. I didn't follow him down the hall to the bedroom. I walked into the living room. When we were coming into the suite, Kramer said he wanted an update about the storm. When he went to his bedroom, I went directly to the television and flipped through the channels to find the weather. He had plenty of time to go out that door and stash the gun. He was gone probably fifteen minutes before he came back out. As you can imagine, I'm not in a position to question what Vice President Kramer is doing in his bedroom."

Kramer had the perfect cover. "I appreciate you telling us the truth," Kate said.

"What are you going to do now?"

"Run it through forensics and see if there are prints and the ballistics match." Kate looked to Declan to see if he had anything to add. When he didn't, she focused on Barry. "I agree with what you said earlier about not wildly accusing the vice president of murder. That's not something I'm prepared to do. Other than telling you, I'll tell Michael and our team that *a gun* was found. I see no need to disclose that to anyone else downstairs. We don't even know for sure that this is the murder weapon. I'd ask you not to tell the vice president either. It would be just as easy for someone to come up to the third floor and stash the gun. While it doesn't look good for Kramer, this doesn't definitively tell us anything."

"Understood." Barry turned back to the closed suite door. "What about the vice president's safety?"

"That's up to you. My recommendation would be to keep him up here sequestered alone. I don't see him agreeing to that though. If you want a fight on your hands, go for it."

"That's not going to work."

Declan said, "Take him downstairs to the living room and clear the space except for the senators. I would search the room and then allow them to continue their meeting. You can stay right outside the door. If anyone needs to leave, Michael can escort them. You remain as close to the vice president as possible for the rest of the day and night."

"What about patrolling the grounds as we had been doing?"

"No need," Declan said and a roll of thunder overhead reinforced that decision. "The storm is getting worse and I think it's safe to say the threat is coming from the inside. That's where you and Michael should remain while Kate and I continue interviewing people. The killer is striking when people are alone. We have to make sure that no one is ever alone even inside the house."

Barry confirmed that it was a good plan. His expression didn't indicate that it would be successful.  He turned and left Kate and Declan standing there and went back to the suite.

"Do we trust him?" Declan asked as they descended the stairs.

It was a question he had been asking Kate since the start of the case. She tossed it back to him because she wasn't sure. "Do you trust him?"

"I don't know," Declan said wryly.  "I'm not sure that we should. What choice do we have?"

Kate furrowed her brow. "Then stop asking me." She realized as soon as the words left her mouth how sharp and angry she sounded. She looked back at his wounded expression. "I'm sorry. I'm not angry with you. I don't know any more than you do and we may be about to accuse the Vice President of the United States of murder."

"It's big, Kate. We knew going in this was either going to make or break our careers." At the bottom of the stairs, he reached out to stop her from walking. "No matter what happens, we'll both be fine. You can write a book and go on the lecture circuit or teach and I can be your housekeeper. I'll have dinner ready for you when you get home every night. I'll even do all the laundry and fold the towels in that weird little square that you like."

That made her smile. If they went down in disgrace, they had had a good run. "Why don't you check on Sharon and Dr. Coburn and I'll update Michael before Kramer comes downstairs." Kate stopped briefly in the living room and updated the senators that the vice president would be down and they could resume their meeting. Kate requested the aides head to the dining room and remain together. They all wanted an update but Kate didn't have one to give them. Noticeably absent from the group were Allison and Michael, who she had asked to watch them all. When she asked Senator Yates where they were, she said that Allison had been upset and Michael took her to the library to calm down.

Kate made her way back to the front of the house into the foyer where Sharon was still working. Dr. Coburn had already left with the body. Sharon was standing near the front door talking to Declan. She waved hello to Kate as she entered.

"This is some case, huh? It's got to be like some kind of record. This isn't the kind of house party I'd want to be invited to."

Kate agreed with Sharon and then asked, "Senator Yates said Michael and Allison headed this way. Have you seen them?"

Sharon pointed to the hallway that led to the library. "They went that way. That young woman was hysterical. She tried to leave out the front door and that tall good-looking agent stopped her. He had to chase after her out of the room." Sharon gestured her hand down toward the floor still covered in blood. "Obviously, she didn't get far."

Kate took a deep breath through her nose. "I'm heading there now and will speak to her. I was interviewing her when Chase was found. Was it the same caliber weapon as the other murders?"

"We won't know until Dr. Coburn does the autopsy. She didn't say much and wouldn't even venture a guess. The rest of the evidence looks about the same to me. I'm going to take this gun into my possession and run some tests. I'll let you know as soon as I know."

Kate thanked her and then made her way down the other hall toward the library. She got a few feet from the door when she heard Allison's sobs. Michael was doing his best to try to calm her down and ask her why she was crying. He was also gently urging her to tell him what she knew. Kate waited just outside the door to see if either would say anything incriminating or something they might not say to her. She heard nothing but Michael trying to calm her down.

Kate knocked on the door and then pushed it open without being asked to enter. Allison was sitting on the couch and Michael was standing near her holding a box of tissues. There were several wadded-up tissues on the couch next to Allison and her face was puffy and red.

She looked up at Kate. "I want to go home right now."

"That's not possible, Allison. Not only because we can't let anyone leave but there's nowhere for you to go. Besides, if you're out there on your own you wouldn't be safe. If this killer can murder senators in this proximity to other people, then he can get to you wherever you are." That was the first time Kate considered why the killer had chosen this weekend. Sure, they were all congregated in one place. It made it easier, but it was also riskier than getting to them one by one back in D.C. Just like the senators and aides had nowhere to run, neither did the killer.

*Why murder them and why now?* Those were the most pressing questions.

"I'm not safe here," Allison whined, reaching for another tissue and blowing her nose. "I didn't sign up for this. I'm a researcher and handle Senator Abbott's schedule and communicate with her constituents. The hardest thing I do is write talking points on subjects that aren't always clear to me. I told her this was too much for us to handle on our own. I told her that we needed to go to the police. She said, no, that she would handle it. How is she handling it if she's dead?"

Allison had tears streaming down her face and her words were coming out like hot jabbing knives as her anger grew and finally bubbled over. She stared straight ahead cursing Senator Abbott and the poor decisions she had made in a situation that still wasn't clear to Kate or Michael. Neither one of them was going to ask a question or stop her. Kate didn't even want to breathe too loudly for fear that something might shake Allison out of her rant and quiet her down. She wasn't being clear but she was talking. Kate took in every word.

Allison blew her nose and kept going. "I told her when she got the first letter, do not give in. Do not negotiate. I told her she had to go to the cops. It didn't matter what I said or did, she thought she could solve it all on her own and now she's dead. I don't even know if it's all related, but what else am I supposed to think? I'm probably going to die and I haven't even had a real relationship yet. I'm going to die never having had a real boyfriend all for something I didn't do." Allison bent forward at the waist and held her face in her hands. She sobbed uncontrollably.

Kate's eyes locked on Michael's and he raised his shoulders in a shrug as if he wasn't sure how to handle such an outburst of emotion. She hitched her head to the side toward the door. "You head out. We found something in our search and Declan can update you."

"Thank you," he said as he passed by Kate, handing her the tissue box and looking relieved. He moved as quickly as he could to get out of the room and closed the door behind him.

Kate pulled a tissue out of the box and sat down next to Allison. She rubbed the girl's back and tried to offer soothing words. Kate felt as ill-equipped to handle the outburst as Michael did. She wasn't one for strong emotions and had even been accused of being emotionless and cold in a few relationships. It wasn't that she was cold. Kate's brain worked far more on logic than emotion.

"Allison." Kate said the young woman's name and the sobbing started to quiet. "I know this is difficult for you and you're obviously keeping a secret for Senator Abbott. It can't hurt her anymore. If you think this might have led to her murder, that's all the more reason to tell me. I want to stop this killer, but the only way for me to do that is to understand what's going on." Kate let her words settle between them as Allison cried the last little bit.

She raised her head and sniffed and then blew her nose again. She wiped off her face and then turned to Kate. "Senator Abbott was being blackmailed. The letters started about six months ago. They said if she didn't pay her secret would be exposed. She paid close to two-hundred-thousand dollars so far but the blackmailer wanted more and more. The threats went from exposing her secret to killing her.

Last month, Senator Abbott didn't make a payment and now she's dead."

If Allison had punched Kate in the face the impact might have landed softer than the secret Allison disclosed. Someone had been blackmailing a United States Senator and now she's dead. Kate wondered if the same thing was happening to the rest of those who had been killed. The implications were far-reaching and staggering. It was hard to even fathom let alone process.

# CHAPTER 12

When Kate found it in her to speak again, she asked, "Do you know if Senator Cutcliffe or Chase was being blackmailed?"

"It wasn't Chase. It was Senator Cutcliffe. He was getting the same letters as Senator Abbott. They started around the same time," Allison said, wiping the tears from her face. She paused for a moment to further collect herself. When she was ready, she explained. "Chase and I went to graduate school together at Georgetown so we knew each other well. Even though we were on different sides of the political spectrum, we got along and shared information sometimes. Nothing that we shouldn't have, except this," she made sure to clarify.

"Did you tell Chase about the blackmail or did he go to you?" Kate wasn't sure that it mattered.

"He came to me and wanted to know what he should do," Allison looked up at her with big eyes. "How would I know what to do? We compared notes and had been trying to figure out who was sending them." Allison looked up at the ceiling and blew out a sharp breath. "We didn't know how to investigate anything. We were trying to keep it quiet. I hadn't told Senator Abbott that Senator Cutcliffe received the same letters until a month ago. I figured she'd be angry with me and she was when I told her. Then she calmed down and said she'd speak to him. That was the last I heard about it – she wasn't going to pay and she was going to talk to Senator Cutcliffe. After that meeting, she told me not to worry about it and that it was handled. Senator Cutcliffe told Chase the same thing."

"Did you believe that it had been handled?"

"Right after she told me, yes. But a week later, we received another letter. Senator Abbott had it in her office and didn't think I saw it but I did. I never read it fully but the demand for payment was clear. The threat to her life was clear too. I wanted to say something to her, but I didn't want her to know that I had briefly snooped on her desk." Allison held her hands up in defeat. "I should have said something. I should have gone to the FBI even though she told me not to. If I had, maybe this wouldn't have happened. I feel responsible."

"You aren't responsible for this. Whoever was blackmailing her is responsible." Kate wasn't going to pile on Allison's grief. She should have gone to the FBI immediately. Not only would it have been the safer thing to do, but technically, she had been hiding that a crime was being committed. There was no point to address all of that.

Kate asked the question she had already assumed. "Do you know if any of the other senators here this weekend are being blackmailed?"

"I haven't spoken to the other aides. It would bring suspicion back on Senator Abbott and me. I don't know why we are here this weekend and that's the truth. About two weeks ago, she told me to clear the schedule from Thursday to Monday, that we were going to Martha's Vineyard for a meeting. I asked her for details like I normally did, but she wouldn't share anything. I didn't even know until I arrived that Vice President Kramer was going to be here."

Allison was an intelligent woman, and Kate got the feeling she was underplaying her hand. Her body posturing with her eyes cast down and hands together would give anyone the impression that Allison was a soft-spoken young woman who might not get herself involved in such matters. Kate knew by Allison's title and the way she had worked her way up to Senator Abbott's right-hand woman, she was holding back. The meek don't make it in D.C. They get eaten up and spit out early on. Aides like Allison are tough and commanding and highly intelligent. They are fighters.

"Given the circumstances, you and Chase must have speculated about the meeting." When Allison didn't respond, Kate pushed harder. "Allison, you and Chase were both harboring a secret so when this meeting was called, I'm sure you spoke to each other. You had to wonder if this was what it was about. I need to know if Chase told you anything about the meeting. He might have had a different relationship with Senator Cutcliffe than you had with Senator Abbott."

Allison pulled back, affronted by Kate's comment. "If you're suggesting that Senator Abbott didn't trust me like Senator Cutcliffe trusted Chase, you're wrong. Chase never pushed as hard as I did for Senator Abbott to call the FBI. I'm sure she didn't tell me the details of the meeting because she'd have known I might have refused to come along with her on this."

In her lack of answering the question directly, she still told Kate what she wanted to know. She just didn't realize it. "When Chase told you what the meeting was about, did you tell anyone?"

Allison realized then and she turned her face up to Kate to deny knowing. Kate remained firm and the young woman backed down. She turned away from Kate while she corrected herself. "I didn't know the vice president was going to be here. That was a surprise to even Chase. He told me we were coming here to talk about the blackmail, but he didn't know how many people were involved until we arrived. When we first got here, we thought maybe they were all meeting about something else and thought Senator Abbott and Senator Cutcliffe might meet on their own time to discuss it. The meeting itself was so hush-hush that we figured out quickly this must be impacting all of them."

"Do you have any idea what Senator Abbott was being blackmailed over?"

"I shouldn't say."

Kate wasn't having it. "You must. Someone is killing the senators and it's possible they killed Matt Pike and Chase to cover their trail. I need to know what Senator Abbott and Senator Cutcliffe were being blackmailed over. Don't tell me you don't know because you do." Kate rose from the couch and stared down at the young woman. The time for being sympathetic and babying her was done. Kate had had enough of whatever game she was playing. "Allison, we don't have time for this little meek and mild game you're playing. We both know that you're a strong capable woman. I need your help and you're going to help me."

Allison straightened her back. "I don't want to speak about Senator Cutcliffe. It's not my place to say."

Kate stared down at Allison. "What about Senator Abbott?"

Allison closed her eyes, clearly conflicted about spilling the senator's secret. When she opened them, she explained, "If I tell you this, it's not just going to impact Senator Abbott. I mean would have impacted her. It would impact her whole family. If this gets out, it will change a lot for a lot of people."

Kate had a feeling where this was going. She had heard it before with women Senator Abbott's age. She had just turned sixty-one a month ago. "Did she have a child out of wedlock?"

"How did you know?" Allison asked with suspicion in her voice. She smiled nervously. "I'm surprised you know. I didn't think anyone knew. Senator Abbott said she didn't tell anyone other than her parents. They sent her away to a home for pregnant girls. They told her school, neighbors, and family that she had to go to another state to help take care of a sick aunt. She had the baby and then came home as if nothing had ever happened. It was a closed adoption and

Senator Abbott never spoke of it again – well, until she told me." She blinked rapidly a few times and asked her question again. "How did you know?"

"It was a guess," Kate admitted. "It happened to a lot of young women of that era. It must have been hard for her to keep the secret."

Kate couldn't imagine having to carry a secret like that for her whole life and then facing the threat of exposure. She wasn't sure she would have taken Senator Abbott's path of paying the blackmailer. As hard as it would have been, the secret might have drawn sympathy for Senator Abbott rather than ruin her reputation. Kate was sure there was more than that factoring into her decision-making.

"Senator Abbott said that as strange as it sounded, she didn't think about it much. She was sure the child she placed for adoption would have a good home and she had made her decision and didn't look back."

Kate wanted to ask if it had been Senator Abbott's decision or her parents' but figured Allison wouldn't know that. "You said the letters started about six months back. Did you know right away that it was blackmail?"

"Within a couple of weeks," Allison said and crossed her legs, sitting back on the couch a little. Her face was more animated as she spoke, some of the tears drying and her normal personality coming through. "Senator Abbott took me out to lunch one day, which wasn't usual. We often had working lunches, but she took me outside of D.C. to Alexandria to a little hole in the wall. We had a back table, very private. That's where she told me all about getting pregnant at fifteen and her trip away to give birth. She told me that before she told me about the blackmail. After she told me about the baby, Senator Abbott sat back and slipped the letter across the table for me to read. I was shocked and horrified. Not at the secret but that someone would try to blackmail her to keep it quiet."

Kate could believe it. People would do anything for money and a secret like that was a juicy one. "Can you recall what the letter said?"

"The letter asked Senator Abbott to pay them fifty thousand dollars to keep quiet."

"How did she know the blackmailer was serious – that they had evidence to expose her?"

Allison pulled her phone from her pants pocket and scrolled through to a photo. She handed it over to Kate as she said, "There's a record of her living at the girls' home. Her name is right there in black and white and it lists her as four months pregnant when she arrived. I have no idea how someone got the record. Senator Abbott had assumed they were sealed or destroyed at this late stage. The place she was staying – St. Catherine's – had closed years before. But the blackmailer sent her a photocopy of the record and then said they had other evidence. A second letter claimed they had found Senator Abbott's child but they didn't provide additional details, so she didn't know if that was true or not."

Kate assessed the photo but it wasn't easy. She had to squint down at the writing to be able to read it. The document had faded over time and the script of the handwriting wasn't all that clear. Kate stared at it until she could start to make out the senator's name and birthday. Across from that was the notation that she was pregnant. Her parents' names were also listed as well as the city where she had been born. If someone got their hands on this, and it was clear they did, it would be ripe for blackmail.

Kate handed the phone back to Allison and asked her to text the photo. "I need it as evidence or I wouldn't ask," she said when the young woman hesitated. "Did the letters come by regular mail? Anything electric like email?"

"Regular mail with the 20515 Washington D.C. postmark. It's like whoever was doing this was looking at Senator Abbott's office as they mailed it."

"How many letters in all?"

"Five that I'm aware of, but I'm not sure she showed me all of them." Kate asked her about how the senator paid. Allison explained, "Senator Abbott hoped after the first payment it would end. Of course, it didn't. I told her before the first payment that if she paid, they'd ask for more. And they did. They kept demanding more and more money. She kept paying for a while. Each letter would specify a specific drop place. I was the one who dropped the money for her. We tried to do some surveillance on the location but we never caught the person."

Kate assumed they wouldn't have. Whoever was doing this was probably smart enough to send someone else to pick up the money. "How many payments in all?"

"Four, that I delivered. Senator Abbott grew frustrated and just didn't have more money to give. She said she needed to stop and let the secret come out if that's what they were going to do. That's when the threats of physical violence started if she didn't keep paying. We should have gone to the FBI with the first letter. That was a mistake, but it was even more of a mistake not to address the physical threats."

It was too late for that. The blackmailer was already making good. They talked for a little while longer about what Chase knew and any details they might have gathered about the blackmailer. The result was little more than Kate already knew. She was going to have to address this with each senator. Someone among them knew everyone's secrets and now Kate needed to know theirs.

# CHAPTER 13

Declan cursed softly and then louder, his words and tone grew angrier with each outburst. They were standing in the library after Kate had escorted Allison back to the dining room with the other aides. Michael was keeping watch. The vice president had finally left his room and came down to the first floor to continue the meeting with the remaining senators. Barry was standing guard outside and Kate wanted to be in the room finally getting to the bottom of everything. She was still debating what would be the right approach – to confront them all at once with the information she had learned or take it one by one.

Declan had finished with Sharon. Now the two of them were going through everything Kate had learned. As it had been for her, Declan was having trouble understanding the extent of what was happening. While the situation frustrated Kate, it enraged Declan.

He jabbed his finger toward the door. "You're telling me we are up here in the middle of a hurricane with lax security because each one of them is being blackmailed and they don't want anyone to find out?"

"That's exactly why we are here." Kate reached for him, hoping a comforting gesture would calm him down. He stepped out of her reach oblivious to anything but his anger. "Declan, that's not all. I assume the blackmailer is also here with us. Who else would be killing them? Senator Abbott refused to pay anymore and received a threat before this weekend."

"Even then she refused to call the FBI," Declan said, his words coming out sharp like daggers. If Senator Abbott hadn't already been dead, Kate was sure Declan would have torn out of the room and given her a piece of his mind. "How are we supposed to solve this if no one is going to be honest with us?"

"I don't think they want it solved. I assume they know why they are being targeted and whatever secrets they hold are more important than their lives." The impact and implications of what Kate said knocked both of them back. They'd be hard-pressed to get any senator on the record for why they were being blackmailed. It was going to be one of the only ways to find a common denominator.

"We need to call Spade before we proceed," Declan said, saying aloud what Kate was thinking. He walked to the window. "This is going to be a mess."

Kate's biggest concern at the moment was who to trust. She knew she couldn't trust any of the aides, the senators, or the vice president. She didn't know if she could trust Michael or Barry and she desperately needed to trust one of them. Kate approached him and put a hand on his back. "Declan, is there anyone in the house we can trust? We need another ally in this."

"I don't know. Both Michael and Barry seem squirrelly to me."

Kate explained, "Barry already lied to me to protect the vice president. Who knows what else he's lying about?"

Declan folded his arms across his chest. "There's also something off about Michael."

"Barry said that too, but now I question if he was telling me the truth or redirecting the focus away from himself." Kate left Declan's side and went to the table near the couch and picked up her phone. "I'm going to call Spade and see how he'd like us to proceed. I hope he's received an answer by now about the lax security. You'd think with a threat, there'd be more." Then again, Kate reminded herself, no one knew about it.

Declan turned his head to look at her over his shoulder. "Unless the vice president is the blackmailer and asked for less security so he'd have more freedom of movement around the house."

That had occurred to Kate but she hadn't dared to speak it. Now that Declan had, it couldn't be ignored. "We need to tell Spade all our suspicions. When I call him, don't hold anything back. If we are going to proceed with anything, we need to know he has our backs."

Declan left his post at the window and came over to Kate while she made the call. Before Spade picked up, Declan pointed to the door, asking if she was sure that it was closed tight. Kate nodded and then said hello as Spade answered.

"I'm getting the runaround about the security issue, Kate," Spade said as he answered. "I've gone right to the top with it and still don't have an answer that satisfies me."

That surprised Kate as she'd never known a time when Spade couldn't get what he wanted. "What answer are you being given?"

"That the vice president called off his full security detail and the Secret Service went along with it. That isn't how it works. The vice president doesn't get to decide his detail. It sounds to me like Kramer went over the head of his security detail supervisor and straight to the top of the Secret Service. The decision came down from above."

"That's what Michael said, Spade. He didn't understand why at the time." Kate was glad Michael had told her the truth. "We found out information that's delicate and we need to know how you want us to handle it."

Spade laughed. "It must be incredibly delicate if you're asking the question. I've never known the pair of you to ask permission for anything." He grew quiet for a moment, probably waiting for Kate to say it. When she didn't because she was still trying to figure out how best to explain what she had heard, Spade urged her to go on. "Even if it's speculation at this point, that's better than what we have now, which is nothing."

Kate realized then she had been so desperate for information that she had taken Allison at her word. There was the small photo of the report from St. Catherine's but that didn't prove the blackmail. Kate took a breath. "I've not been able to corroborate this yet, but Senator Abbott's aide, Allison, just told me that the senator was being blackmailed for a teen pregnancy. She placed the child for adoption and never spoke of it again. Allison also told me that Senator Cutcliffe was being blackmailed but didn't tell me the reason. If Allison is to be believed, and I do think she was credible, then someone has dug up the secrets of all the people here and is blackmailing them. Allison said that once Senator Abbott decided not to pay any more, threats were made against her life."

"That certainly is delicate," Spade said in a clipped no-nonsense tone. "We have to corroborate this first. Have you gone through any of the belongings of the deceased senators? Have you spoken to Chase?"

"Chase is dead, Spade," Declan answered before Kate could say anything else. "He was shot in the hallway while Kate was speaking to Allison. He would have been the only one that could have corroborated what Allison had to say. According to Allison, they compared notes early on. His death confirms that not only is the killer someone in this house but they are brazen and daring. Chase was shot with people on the same floor and only feet away." Declan cast his eyes up to Kate.

She took it from there as if what they had just disclosed wasn't already enough. "We found what we believe is the murder weapon outside of Vice President Kramer's suite. He is unaccounted for during the time of the murder. Then right after the murder, before the body was found, he headed up to his suite and had enough time to ditch the gun." When Spade didn't say anything, Kate added, "It's possible someone else stashed the gun there. The area is accessible to anyone in the house. He and Barry Noble, the Secret Service agent who was protecting him, lied at first. When confronted, Barry said that Kramer could have had enough time out of his sight to place the gun in the dryer where it was found."

"Is Barry Noble the only person who knows about the gun?"

Kate looked to Declan but he indicated he hadn't had time to tell Michael yet. "Yes, only Barry knows."

"You need to tell Michael Brooks what's going on and see if he's heard anything or has suspicions about Kramer."

Declan asked, "Can we trust him, Spade?"

"I'd say if there is anyone there you can trust it's him. He's been a decorated Secret Service agent for the past twenty years. There is no reason to suspect him of any wrongdoing."

Kate recounted what Barry said about his concerns about Michael and she added her interactions with him. "I get an odd feeling about him that I can't quite place. It's not mistrust, but I don't feel like he's been leveling with us. It may be that he knows more and has been trying not to disclose information he shouldn't."

Spade considered that. "Kate, if Kramer isn't the killer and is a victim of this blackmailer then I'd assume Michael is aware. That may be what he's holding back from you. He might feel the pull to be loyal to the vice president even at the cost of not being straight with an FBI agent. Not a smart move on his part, but I can see how he'd be conflicted."

Kate hadn't even had time to consider that. Spade brought up a good point. "If you're comfortable with us disclosing all this information to Michael, then I'll talk to him again. We will also search the deceased senators' belongings as well as whatever Chase brought with him in the hopes of confirming the blackmail. I'd like to confirm that the blackmailer is getting accurate information."

Spade reassured them they had free rein within the law to do whatever they needed to do to solve the case. "Will you have backup security tonight too?"

"We should," Declan said. "Do you think since we found the gun that the murders are over? Is it possible the rest made contact with the blackmailer to let them know they'd continue paying?"

"I'd hope it's over, but I doubt it," Spade said and then wished them both luck. He promised he'd be in touch when he knew more.

When the call ended, Kate sat down on the couch and put her hands on her knees. "I think we should split up. You can tackle searching Chase's room while I speak to Michael."

"Who is going to keep an eye on the aides?"

Kate had forgotten about that. "You said you trusted Stanton. Can he watch over them?"

Declan looked skeptical. "He's not security, Kate. He doesn't have any authority or training."

"He's better than no one. I need Barry to remain standing guard outside the room with Kramer and the senators. That seems more important right now than the aides." They were in a tough situation and Kate didn't mind having to improvise to make the best of it. Mostly all they needed were eyes they trusted on the people they didn't trust. She explained that to Declan.

He held his hands up in defeat. "I'll make sure that happens before I go upstairs and search Chase's room." Declan reached his hand out to pull Kate from the couch. "You sure you're going to be okay with Michael?"

Kate nodded. "I have a fairly good rapport with him and think he'd be more open if we are one on one."

Declan smiled. "I don't think he likes me much."

"He said the same about you." Kate didn't have time to worry about their egos. There was too much that had to be done. As they were leaving the library, the lights flickered as a gust of wind rattled the windows. "It's getting worse out there."

"Stanton has the generator prepared should the power go out. He went over the storm preparedness with me."

At the foyer, where Chase's blood streaked the floor in the blocked-off area, they went their separate ways. Declan toward the kitchen to get Stanton and Kate to the dining room to get Michael.

Kate stood outside the door for a moment, listening to the conversation. There was nothing other than chatter about the storm and worry about what would happen to them all. She opened the door and found Michael sitting perched on a high stool. "Declan went to get Stanton, who will sit here with the aides. I need you out at the cottages." She turned to the aides who all looked at her wide-eyed. "Please remain in this room. Stanton, the house manager, will be in here with you momentarily."

As they stepped out into the hall, Kate said, "We need to search Senator Abbott's and Senator Cutcliffe's rooms. I received information that I need to corroborate and I'm hoping there is evidence in their belongings. You said that no one searched it yet, correct?"

Michael nodded. "I didn't feel right going through their things before the FBI arrived. I figured you'd handle that." He stepped back from Kate and squinted down at her. "Can you tell me what information you uncovered?"

"Yes, but not here in the house. Once we get to the cottages, I'll tell you what I know." Kate maintained steady eye contact with him. "You have to tell me everything you know. I know that you know something you're not sharing and it's causing me not to trust you. I can't have that."

Michael released a heavy sigh. "I'll tell you what I know."

# CHAPTER 14

Kate had no choice but to put her windbreaker back on with the hood up to cross the short courtyard to the cottages. They had to fight the wind and sideways rain as they ran from the main house to the first cottage door. Michael had offered an umbrella, but Kate was sure it would have been turned inside out at the first step outside.

Michael unlocked the door to Senator Abbott's cottage and they stepped inside, trying not to drip water all over the floor. Kate peeled the wet windbreaker over her head and hung it on a nearby chair. They were in the living room and the crime scene techs had already done their job going through the room looking for evidence. The senator's belongings had been left untouched, which wasn't the purview of the crime scene investigators anyway.

Kate gestured toward the back of the cottage away from where the murder had occurred. There was a small two-seater table in the back where they could talk before they started their search. As they sat, Kate said, "Michael, I know you might feel like you're breaking your oath by disclosing information to us, but I can't stress enough how important it is for us to know what you know."

With a pained expression, Michael sat. "It wasn't that I was trying to hide information. I just didn't know of its relevance to what was happening."

"What's changed?"

It took Michael a moment to consider Kate's question. "I guess nothing has changed other than more deaths. I don't know why I thought it might stop with the two senators. I figured that Matt had seen something on his rounds. With Chase..." Michael shook his head as if he couldn't make sense of it. "They are targeting certain people."

Kate folded her hands on the tabletop. "Do you know why that is?"

"I can't say for sure. I can assume the information I have might be a factor, but if that was the case, I'm sure they would have gone after the vice president already."

Kate had an inkling he knew about the blackmail. She wasn't going to show her hand too early. "Why is that, Michael? Why do you believe the killer would have gone after Kramer?"

He looked right at her. "Should I assume you know about the blackmail?"

"I only heard about it recently," Kate said not disclosing the vice president hadn't been named. "How much has Kramer paid so far?"

"Three hundred thousand dollars but they keep asking for more." Michael sat back and folded his thick arms over his chest. "No one else knows about this. Kramer's secretary knows because she opened all the letters, but she has no idea that he paid the money. He told me and swore me to secrecy. Kramer told me that he didn't tell anyone else."

"What does the blackmailer know?" Kate wondered if it was related to the alcohol. He had all the signs of being an alcoholic from the red face to the irritability and the fact that he smelled like alcohol whenever she got close to him. What Michael said next was not something she would have ever guessed.

"The blackmailer is alleging multiple affairs. I don't know if it's true. Kramer adamantly denies it, but of course, he would. He's the candidate of choice for the Christian Coalition. Even the hint of a rumor would rock all his political ambitions."

Kate wasn't sure what more political ambitions he would have. "Is Kramer considering running for president?"

"There are only a handful of people who know this, Kate," Michael said and then waited for a few beats. "Kramer is planning to primary the current president in the next term."

"But she'll be running again," Kate said shocked. "I don't know that I can remember when a current vice president has primaried a current sitting president."

Michael sighed and shrugged. "It's what the plan is, but that's all going away if his secret gets out. True or not."

Kate wasn't sure about that. Other presidents had been able to weather affairs. "You've never seen any proof?"

Michael shook his head. "I asked his secretary, Margaret, but she wouldn't tell me anything that was in the letters. Kramer only showed me the first letter. It referenced a photo as evidence, but he wouldn't show me the photo. I don't even know the names of the women. I'm operating on very little information."

"Why wasn't the FBI called immediately?"

Michael cocked his head to the side and looked over at her as if it was a stupid question. "Come on, Kate. I was sworn to secrecy. The rest of Kramer's Secret Service detail didn't even know. He made his secretary sign a non-disclosure agreement for even seeing the letter and he denied it over and over again. Margaret is as loyal as you can find. She's been with him since his time in the Senate. She wasn't going to tell anyone."

Kate had known his answer for why no one called the FBI before he gave it. She still had to ask. "Who dropped the money off for him?"

"I did." Michael sat back in the chair and then leaned forward as if he couldn't get comfortable. "I know I shouldn't have, but what else was I supposed to do? I left the money at the drop locations and waited. I was never able to catch the person."

Spade had been right. Not only was Michael hiding the secret about Kramer, but he was also hiding how incredibly dumb he'd been to make the decisions he had. "You told me that it was Kramer's request to have lax security this trip. Did you suspect that it was because of the blackmail?"

Michael offered a half-hearted shrug. "We had sent the advance team well before I knew I'd have a limited team with me. I learned about that the night before we left. As I told you, I questioned Kramer and then called my boss. All I was told was that it was approved as it stood and to do my job. I tried to argue about the reasonableness of the plan but was shot down." Michael leaned forward on the table. "I don't know all the ins and outs about how the FBI works, but I have one job and one job only and that's to make sure the vice president is protected at all costs – even if it costs me my life. When you put that much on the line and you are denied the very protection needed to do your job effectively, you start to question what's really at play."

Kate didn't want to explain she had Spade look into it. "Who told you the security detail would be smaller?"

"My direct supervisor, but he said the order came down from above. When I pressed him on that he just said it went all the way to the top. No explanation was ever given. I can tell you that my direct supervisor wasn't happy with the decision either. It was setting us up for disaster. No one could have predicted this though."

Maybe that was the goal. Kate expressed that to Michael who didn't even flinch. She was sure he had considered the same. "Do you believe that Kramer is the only person being blackmailed?"

Michael jolted forward. "There's more?" he asked with genuine shock and confusion in his voice.

Kate nodded slowly. "At least two others that I'm aware of right now."

"Are they here this weekend?"

Kate locked her gaze on him. "They're dead, Michael. It was Senator Abbott and Senator Cutcliffe. Allison told me the details she knew about Abbott. Either she didn't know about Senator Cutcliffe or she wouldn't tell me. Chase knew but he's dead too."

Michael's mouth fell open and he snapped his jaw shut. "I can't believe this."

"Believe it because there are two things I know for a fact." Kate held up each finger as she made her point. "First, they are here discussing the blackmail, and second, the blackmailer or their hired gun is here inside this house. I need to see one of those letters because I might be able to form a profile from that. Tell me everything you know about this person."

Michael recounted basically what Allison had said. The letters came to the office from a local postmark in D.C. The money drop locations were around the nation's capital. Unmarked cash payments were made from Kramer's accounts and Michael never saw who picked up the money no matter how hard he tried to locate the person. He threw his hands up in disgust. "It's very little information as I said. Kramer kept paying and paying even when I advised him to stop. He never missed a payment."

There was something Kate didn't understand. "You don't take your orders from the vice president. You take them from your command. Why would you keep Kramer's secret when you should have reported it?"

Michael didn't move a muscle. His mouth was set in a firm line and he stared at Kate while she assumed he contemplated either telling her the truth or coming up with a lie. His actions had been careless, reckless, illegal, and he could lose his job and pension if Kate wanted to pursue action against him. Lying to a federal officer wouldn't do him any favors.

Finally, Michael's shoulders relaxed and he let his arms drop loose at his sides. "Kramer threatened to ruin my career if I said anything. He told me he'd say I was negligent in my duties and report me. He meant what he said, Kate. He could make real trouble for any of us if he wanted to. You don't know how powerful he is."

"Instead, you do that all on your own." Kate read down the list of offenses he had committed by not coming forward with the information. Michael nodded his head in agreement at each point. He wasn't unaware of what he had done. "Then why do it? You'd ruin your career either way. Does Kramer have something over you? Is there proof of something?"

Michael shook his head. "I thought it was a prank at first since Kramer denied it. I didn't think he'd pay the blackmailer. After I made that first drop, I knew I was in deep then. I should have gone to my supervisor. I can't explain why I didn't. I acted in poor judgment and deserve to lose my job and pension."

Kate could see that he had a real sense of guilt. That's why he had been acting so strangely – not only holding in this secret that could destroy his career but he had immense guilt for not coming forward sooner. "Don't get ahead of yourself. I have no plans to arrest you or go to your supervisor. The Secret Service put you in a perilous situation and I imagine they might already know what's going on in some capacity." Kate began to wonder if it wasn't someone high up in the Secret Service who might be responsible for all of this. There's no way they should have approved less security no matter what Kramer requested.

Michael gave her a sad smile and nodded. "What can I do to help?"

Kate stood and tucked errant wet strands of hair behind her ears. "You can continue to tell me the truth and help me search for anything that looks like it might have come from the blackmailer. The letters, additional correspondence, proof of the blackmailer's claims –

anything could be helpful. You start in the front and I'll start in the back and we'll work our way to the middle." As Michael turned to leave, Kate needed to confirm one last thing. "Are you sure no one has gone through Senator Abbott's things? Not even Allison?"

"No," Michael said, standing. His voice was calm and even, now. His typical staunch agent demeanor had returned. "I didn't allow anyone in here after Senator Abbott's body was found. Not even Allison, and she had asked to collect some papers from the senator after her death. I didn't allow her to do that. Your crime scene investigator was here and the medical examiner and that was it. I closed and locked the door after them. You and Declan were the first in the room after that when you looked after your arrival. It's been closed and locked since that time. I assumed you'd want to go through everything."

The only part of what he said that mattered to Kate was that Allison wanted *papers*. "Do you know what Allison wanted specifically?"

"She said it was legislative information. She said what she wanted should be in a desk drawer and she'd only take a second to grab it. I never looked in the desk to confirm. There was just no way I was letting her in here to take anything."

Kate put her hand on his arm. "That was the right decision. When I interviewed Allison, I believed what she said, but I didn't necessarily trust her." Kate headed right for the desk in the far corner of the bedroom. It was a simple white desk with three drawers on the right-hand side and a thin rectangle drawer that pulled out from under the desktop. Kate went for the side drawers first, but they were empty except for a few basic office supplies the estate provided for guests.

It was in the thin drawer Kate found what Allison had been after. She slipped the green two-pocket folder out of the drawer and opened it. The first letter was dated nearly six months ago. Kate pulled that one forward to see what was behind it – another letter and then another and eight more. That was ten letters in all, far more than Allison had known about or admitted to. The other side of the folder contained old documents and information on adoption. It appeared as if Senator Abbott might have been searching for the child she had placed for adoption or it was the evidence the blackmailer had sent her. Kate couldn't be sure, but it looked at first glance that she was close to finding the child – a son.

Kate turned and yelled for Michael. "I found it but keep searching and see what else we might come across." They continued the search but found nothing else. Kate only hoped the evidence for Senator Cutcliffe would be as easy to find.

# CHAPTER 15

Senator Cutcliffe's cottage wasn't as neat as Senator Abbott's had been. Kate searched the desk first but found nothing. The desktop was a mess of newspapers and other official documents. There was nothing marked classified and Kate was thankful for that. She didn't want to deal with securing classified records in the middle of a crime scene. The papers looked like committee meeting minutes and other documents.

Kate slid open the closet door and found the senator had made a half-hearted attempt at hanging his clothes in the closet. The shirts were half on the hangers with the shoulders nearly dropping off. Some shirts had completely fallen and lay in a rumbled heap on the floor on top of his shoes. Just outside of the closet, two shirts hung off the back of a chair.

Kate closed the closet door and assessed the rest of the room. She scanned around at the pile of clothes on the bed and the floor. The man had more clothes than Kate, and it appeared he changed them so frequently he left messy piles all over the place.

"Did he have a briefcase or a laptop bag or anything with him where he kept documents?" The mess was distracting her. It didn't appear like someone had ransacked the suite but rather he wasn't good at picking up after himself. Kate stuck her head in the bathroom and grimaced, shaking her head in disgust. There were toiletries all over the place and hair lining the sink. A line of toothpaste dripped across the bathroom counter leading to an open tube.

Michael yelled from the suite's front room. "He had a messenger bag that first day. It was an Army green color. Did you find anything like that?"

"No," Kate said absently as she went through more of the mess in the room and then turned her attention back to the closet. She picked up the shirt that had fallen in a heap. She felt it down for any pockets and then put it on the bed behind her. She did the same with more shirts and then a pair of pants. On the other side of the closet, a crumpled towel sat where it had been discarded. She searched the shoes and patted down the other clothes.

As Kate stood on tiptoe to reach something hiding on the top shelf, a gunshot rang out, startling her and leaving her scrambling back and reaching for her Glock on her hip.

"Michael!" Kate screamed his name as she ducked low and pulled her service weapon from her side. "Michael!"

The second gunshot rang out shattering the front window and then a third and a fourth made contact with what sounded like the living room furniture. Kate took a breath and belly-crawled along the floor to the front to check on Michael. She wanted to stand and look to see who was shooting but she didn't dare risk it. "Michael!" she called again. "Are you hit?"

"I'm fine, Kate. Pinned down in the corner. I have a clear shot of the door if he tries to enter."

Kate reached her hand out along the wall and stood slowly, trying to look out the front broken window. Another shot came again as soon as she got her head above the window line. She threw herself back on the floor wondering where Declan was and hoping he'd come to their rescue. The shots were loud enough that surely they were heard in the house.

"Do we have anywhere we can get a line of sight outside?" Kate asked as she continued her belly-crawl through the living room, dodging broken glass, toward the front shattered window. One of them needed to be able to get a shot off.

Kate got to the window and raised her head slowly as she positioned her gun on the window ledge. The shooter was faster and a volley of more shots ripped through the front window and into the living room tearing through the furniture and hitting the back wall. Kate cursed and shrank back hoping she'd still have a chance to take a shot at him. She didn't see how though. She couldn't see out and as soon as she raised herself even slightly the firing continued.

Suddenly, Declan's voice rose above the gunshots. Kate was flooded with a sense of relief. She heard one shot and then another and Declan yelled commands for the shooter to stop. Then there was nothing except for the rain pelting off the roof and the wind howling through the open window.

"We should be clear now," Kate said after longer than probably needed. She looked over at Michael and noticed the blood staining the sleeve of his shirt. "You've been hit in the arm. We need to get you medical attention."

He turned his head to look to where Kate had pointed. "I didn't notice," he said absently as he assessed the wound. "I need to get this shirt off so I can see the damage. I think it's just a graze. Probably didn't feel it with my adrenaline running."

Kate got up slowly again, being cautious just in case. As she stood to her full height, she took a few steps toward the middle of the window to try to look out. Glass crunched at her feet and her movement kicked up the white cotton stuffing from the furniture. She pulled back the curtain and had anticipated seeing Declan on top of the shooter in the wet grass in front of the cottage but the area was clear.

Panic set in then. She reached for her windbreaker and, as quickly as she could, tugged it on over her head. "Michael, you wait here. Declan didn't apprehend the shooter. No one is out here."

As Kate reached the door to brace herself against the wind, her phone rang. She looked quickly and saw that it was Declan. Relief and fear blended together as she answered. "Where are you?"

"I'm okay, Kate, but the shooter got away. I chased them and they disappeared in the tree line going toward the back fence. I followed but they disappeared among the trees. There has got to be a break in the fence. I've searched up here but don't see anyone."

"You're sure they got away?" Kate asked, looking back at Michael who had his shirt off and was tending to his gunshot wound. He was right that it was just a graze. Kate was so focused on Michael that she hadn't heard Declan's response. "I'm sorry, what did you say? Michael was shot in the arm."

"Is he okay?"

"Looks like it was just a graze." Kate stepped back from the doorway where the rain was hitting her legs. "Should I head your way?"

"Yes, if you can. We need to find the hole in the fence. We can't have a breach like this. We have enough to deal with inside."

Kate had no idea how they'd fix the fence. They certainly couldn't get anyone out there to fix it in the storm. She confirmed with Declan that she'd be there and he promised he'd walk back to the tree line so she could find him. He also assured her that Barry was in the house protecting everyone. She turned to Michael before she left. "Declan thinks the shooter must have gotten through the fence. He said he was at the tree line at the back of the property. Your team did an advanced assessment. Where do the woods go?"

He made a triangle shape with his fingers. "We are right here at the point of the cliff. One direction goes directly off the side of the cliff. No one could survive that fall or jump. The other way doubles back toward the property next door and the main road leading up here, but my team said that fence was impenetrable. There's a little land in the back beyond the woods. Past the fence, there's enough to walk about and then a straight drop down to the water below. No one could survive jumping off the cliff."

"You said the side doubles back to the property next door and the beach. Is there a path?"

Michael nodded. "It's steep but it's doable. There's a dirt path."

"The fence line covers that area?"

"Yeah, but no one is getting through that fence," Michael said his voice filled with confidence. "The fence covers two areas – the back and the side with beach access. The property drops off on the other side and there is no fence."

That sounded dangerous to Kate. "Someone could walk right up to the ledge and fall off?"

"That's correct. I have no idea why it was designed that way but that's how it is. Be careful out there, especially in the rain. There is a gradual slope up on the lawn and then the drop-off."

Kate pointed to his phone. "Has the front gate been opened?"

Michael reached for his phone, pressed his finger on the biometrics, and unlocked it. He checked the app. "No alerts."

Kate didn't know how much she trusted the technology. There always seemed to be ways around it. "You head into the house with Barry and figure out if you're going to need stitches. I'm going to meet up with Declan and check the fence." Kate nearly forgot about the folder sitting on Senator Cutcliffe's bed with the evidence they had found in Senator Abbott's room. She turned and walked through the suite, grabbed the file, and returned, handing it to Michael. "Keep that safe."

"What about evidence that could still be here in the room?"

"Can you finish searching with your arm like that?" Above all, Kate wanted to make sure that he was okay. He'd be no good to them injured. "If you need to tend to your arm, do that. We can always come back here later. I hate to call Sharon out here for this scene, but we need to. I'm sure there are shell casings out there being washed away by the rain."

Michael told her not to worry about that now. "Let me finish looking for that bag and then I'll head into the main house and tend to my arm." He glanced down at it. "The bleeding has almost stopped. I'll be fine."

Kate trusted his judgment. "Let's meet back in the library. Please don't tell Barry about what we found. I assume he doesn't know about Kramer's blackmail letters."

"No one knows."

"Let's keep it that way for now." With that, Kate pulled the hood of the windbreaker over her head and stepped out into the rain with the gun still in her hand. She had no idea if the threat was over or if there was someone still lurking on the property. Kate assumed the person who had escaped into the tree line wasn't someone from inside the house. Their absence would be apparent. It would be easy enough to confirm when they went back in.

The rain stung her face as she fought against the wind to meet Declan. He was standing with his windbreaker flapping in the wind as he steadied himself keeping watch. When she reached him, Kate pointed into the trees. "Show me where they went and let's get out of this rain." Kate felt like she was shouting to be heard above the pounding rain and wind.

Declan led her into a wooded area with thick trees so dense it was hard to walk through. She could see why the Secret Service might not be concerned. The rocky terrain wasn't the easiest to navigate especially wet. The trees and roots created a mazelike obstacle course. It wasn't that the distance was far. It was just uneven and difficult terrain to cover in the present conditions.

They made it to the back fence. Declan said, "They headed this way and then they were gone." He turned back to look at the house the way they had come and pointed. "As you can see, it's dense so you can't see much. They were headed in this direction, and by the time I made it up here, they were gone. They got a shot off at me when I exited the house and then I took a shot at them. I don't think I hit them. I wouldn't be surprised if I missed them completely."

Kate couldn't blame him under the circumstances. She stepped right up to the wrought iron fence. It had to be about ten feet high with large spikes at the top of each post that were spaced so closely together that no one, not even a small child, could slip through. Kate wasn't sure a dog could get through the space. Maybe a small one.

Beyond the fence was a few feet of grass and then nothing. It dropped off as Michael said it would. "Let's walk along the fence line and see if there are any breaks. Michael said there is beach access on the side of the property, but he didn't mention if there was a gate and I didn't ask."

Together they walked the fence line. The terrain wasn't any easier there than among the trees. Kate could understand why the Secret Service thought they were safe. Kate reached out and held onto the fence, one post after another, as they walked. The fence line curved to the side as Michael said it would and probably fifty feet down the side Kate couldn't believe what she saw.

Someone had cut through the fencing. "How is it possible someone cut through it?" Kate asked, bending with Declan to take a look. Six of the posts were cut at mid-height. Enough for a person to crouch down and crawl through.

Declan examined the damage left behind and then turned to look over at her. "They didn't cut it, Kate. Someone used a blowtorch on this." He met her eyes. "Let's follow the path they took."

Kate didn't want to but there wasn't another option. She slipped through the hole in the fence first, her belly and legs bearing the brunt of the muddy earth. When she reached the other side and stood, she brushed the mud from her clothing. Before she took a step toward the dirt trail, she saw the footprints.

"There, Declan," she said pointing, knowing they had to do something before the evidence was washed away.

# CHAPTER 16

More than an hour later, Kate peeled her wet windbreaker over her head and discarded muddy boots at the side staff entrance of the estate. Declan followed right behind her. Every inch of their clothing was wet and caked in muddy dirt and sand.

Upon seeing them, Stanton led them down a narrow hallway to a staff bathroom that had three shower stalls, towels, freshly washed robes, and toiletries. "Let me see if I can get you a change of clothes," he said before he disappeared.

Kate stepped into the shower and pulled the curtain closed behind her. Declan was in the stall next to her. She considered waiting for Stanton's return but ached to feel the hot water against her skin. She turned on the water, holding her hand under it until she got just the right temperature, and then stepped under the spray, letting it warm her.

She and Declan had followed the trail down to the small secluded beach. They weren't sure if the area was frequented by locals or tourists, but it seemed fairly isolated. A short walk down the beach led to a parking lot that would have fit three or four cars. It was empty by the time they arrived.

Declan snapped a few photos of the area and then suggested that they time themselves from the parking lot back up to the fence and see not only how long it took to climb but how difficult it was in the current conditions. It took them twenty-three minutes and sixteen seconds to reach the top. Kate was sure the shooter was someone with a good deal of strength and agility not only to be using the dirt trail in the current conditions but sneaking into and out of the house without getting caught. Declan had even suggested that the shooter might be a professional, which would be a game-changer for sure.

In the middle of her shower, Stanton yelled from outside the privacy curtain that he was setting clothes for them on the sink counter. Kate and Declan thanked him and then he left them alone to finish.

The clothes included gray sweatpants that tied at the waist, warm socks, a blue tee shirt, and a cardigan. Declan had the same but a crew neck rather than a cardigan. "I wonder if he just keeps these on hand," Declan asked, tugging the sweater over his head. "It fits great too."

Kate finished dressing and then wiped her hand across the fogged mirror. She towel dried her wet hair enough to twist it on top of her head. Without makeup, she looked even younger than her mid-thirties. "What's the plan, Declan? We aren't going to get someone out there to fix the fence in this weather. The island doesn't have more security for us until tonight and everyone here is hiding a secret."

Declan had been relatively quiet and it wasn't sitting well with Kate. She needed to feel like he wasn't just along for the ride. When he hesitated, she asked, "Is there something wrong?"

Declan didn't respond but rather reached for his phone and handed it to her. "Pull up the first few photos. I found that searching Chase's room. I didn't get a chance to tell you before."

Kate lowered her head to the photos. She had to enlarge each one to read it more clearly. They were non-disclosure agreements – nine in all signed by women and Senator Cutcliffe. Other documents showed that he had paid them each twenty-five thousand dollars to keep their claims of sexual harassment quiet.

When Kate got to the last of the signed agreements, she sucked in a breath. There were non-disclosure agreements signed by Allison Manning and by Maven Vale, who was there that weekend as an aide to the vice president. Kate hadn't spoken to her yet but knew who she was. Kate swiped to another photo, which contained a ledger, and enlarged that.

"You've got to be kidding me," she said to no one in particular. She raised her eyes to Declan. "He paid this out of campaign finance money."

"That's what Chase indicates." Declan pointed toward the right-hand bottom corner of the photo. "There's a handwritten note at the bottom there. Read what it says."

"Senator Cutcliffe has to pay. They are all liars and frauds." Kate read the words and recognized immediately that they could be taken several ways. "Does he mean all these women are liars and frauds?"

"It could mean that or it could mean he's indicating that Senator Cutcliffe has to pay for his crimes and that all the senators are liars and frauds. Chase might have been complicit in the blackmail."

Kate handed Declan back the phone. "We don't even know if Chase wrote that."

"Let's ask Allison. You're going to need to question her about the senator's payoff, which I assume she didn't mention. If she's that close to Chase, she can probably recognize his handwriting."

Kate didn't know about that. With all the texting and emailing and social media, handwriting wasn't as common as it used to be. She wasn't even sure she could pick Declan's handwriting out from a few samples. "Was there anything else I missed when Michael and I were searching the cottages?"

Declan shook his head. "All the staff are cleared in my opinion. The Secret Service ran a background check on Stanton and he checks out. The rest of the staff here are connected to the vice president and have been vetted. No red flags when I interviewed them."

Kate realized then she hadn't told Declan about Vice President Kramer's secret. "Michael told me that Kramer was being blackmailed for several affairs."

Declan raised his eyebrows. "The loudest condemning voice in the room when it comes to others' affairs? That doesn't surprise me. Is it true though?"

"Michael doesn't have other details," Kate admitted. "Kramer wouldn't share the content of the blackmail letters with him. No one else on his security detail knows."

"I don't see what the big deal is. I'm not saying having an affair is right, but other politicians have survived it." Declan shrugged for emphasis.

"He's backed by the Christian Coalition, Declan. He's spoken out against marital infidelity. He called a female senator a whore on national television when she was caught having an affair. He practically wanted to brand her with an A like it was the 1600s in Puritan times. He's railed on about the destruction of the family. It's his number one talking point. Of course, it matters for him." Kate also considered the man's family. "He has a wife and children, Declan. This could be a devastating blow for all of them."

"I didn't realize all that." Declan leaned back against the counter and folded his arms across his chest. "What do we do? Figure out who didn't have any secrets among them and consider them the blackmailer?"

"I was suspicious of Kramer when we found the gun, but now, I'm not sure. I highly doubt he'd fake his blackmail, not with a secret like that," Kate said with her tone thoughtful and even. She had grown frustrated with the process and needed to shake it up in a way that might not work. She was willing to take the risk. "We need to start being more direct. I want to put them all into the same room and let them know we know about the blackmail. I want to see their reactions and go from there. I could bring them in one by one and interview them but you know they are going to lie to us."

"Allison didn't lie to you. Don't you think being direct like that might offend them or make them uncooperative?" Declan asked.

"Since when are you worried about being direct?" Kate searched his face to see his response. When he remained firm, she tsked. "Shake out of the choir boy routine, Declan. I know there are some heavy hitters here but we have a job to do. You said it yourself. What's the worst that's going to happen? We destroy our careers? Okay, then we do something else. We set up a consulting firm. Spade has our backs."

Declan remained tight-lipped, watching her.

"Is that why you've been so hesitant on this case? You've been walking on eggshells."

Declan stood there with a thoughtful expression on his face. Then he laughed it off. "I don't want to say I'm intimidated, but I'm off my game." He reached out and squeezed her shoulder. "I'm trying to be respectful and realize now that they are all suspects no matter their title and power in D.C."

"You said the same to me on the way."

"Yeah, but then I got here and met them." He ran a hand down his face and laughed again. "You forget they are real people, Kate. I can't explain it any better than that. The seat of power in the United States is in their hands. They can make or break my career. It's easy to brush off in the abstract. When it's right in front of your face, it's something else entirely."

Kate understood what he was saying. She hadn't felt that way. Maybe it was because of her father, she had been used to being around powerful people for most of her life. She also wasn't easily impressed. "Under their titles and power, they are just people and one of them is our suspect."

"Okay, so let's go get them." He turned and reached for the knob on the bathroom door.

Kate asked him to wait. "I want to speak to Michael first before we go into the room. I just want to make sure he's okay and ask if he found anything in Senator Cutcliffe's room."

"I'll go get him and bring him into the hall." Declan left Kate standing in the bathroom. She took one last look at herself in the mirror and then down at the heap of dirty clothing. She gathered up her and then Declan's and carried them out to the kitchen. "Is there somewhere I can throw these into the wash?" she asked the young woman standing at the counter.

"I'll take them for you," she said, walking to Kate with her arms outstretched. Kate was hesitant to have this young woman do her laundry, but she wasn't sure what choice she had. "Do you work for Vice President Kramer?" Kate asked.

The young woman smiled shyly and nodded once. "I've worked with him for the last couple of years. First when he was a senator and now as vice president."

"Do you enjoy it?" Kate asked and then felt foolish for the question. It was just that there was something in the young woman's expression that struck Kate's curiosity. Her demeanor and the way she spoke portrayed someone young and unsure of themselves, much the way Allison first presented. The fine lines around the young woman's eyes and the stiff gait of her walk indicated that she might be older.

"Vice President Kramer is a good boss," she said without any hint of affect in her voice and then turned her back to Kate and walked the dirty clothes to the laundry room across the kitchen. It was an odd interaction that left Kate unsure of what more to say. She brushed it off and headed back toward the hallway with the dining and living rooms.

She met Michael in the hallway. He had a bandage around his bicep that had already soaked through with blood. "I thought it was just a graze," she asked, jutting her chin toward the wound.

"It is," Michael said, running his hand over it. "It started bleeding again after I bandaged it. It will stop soon."

"Michael, if you need medical attention, you should go get it."

"I'm fine, really," he said stiffly and then changed the subject. "I found the evidence we were looking for in Senator Cutcliffe's room. There were letters from the blackmailer hinting that Cutcliffe had sexually harassed a few young women. No one was named in the letters I found, but the threat to go public was there. It seemed similar to what you told me about Senator Abbott. Senator Cutcliffe paid the blackmailer for a while but when the demands kept coming, he decided to cut them off. The letters turned threatening. There was nothing in any of his papers indicating he had found out who the blackmailer was though."

Kate nodded along as he spoke. "This confirms what Declan found in Chase's room. Senator Cutcliffe had them sign non-disclosure agreements. It looked like some of the dates pre-date the blackmail while others were after the blackmail had started. Two of the young women are here."

"Here?" Michael said, his voice and expression registering shock. "You mean he went after senatorial aides?"

"Allison and Maven. I don't know if Allison disclosed anything to Senator Abbott. It certainly puts a spin on what Allison told me. Chase knew what had happened between Senator Cutcliffe and Allison. I wonder if he brought her the non-disclosure agreement and the pay-off money." Kate held back that the hush money was paid with campaign finance money. She wondered now if the money paid to the blackmailer came out of the same fund. "We can address all of that later. Right now, I want to go in and shake things up a little."

"Shake them up?" Michael said with hesitancy in his voice. "You don't think they are shaken up enough already? They were all freaked out with the gunman outside. Barry said they all dropped to the floor and were scrambling to safety."

"All of them were accounted for then?" Kate hadn't asked that question yet. It was one she was going to wait to ask until they were all in the room. Going in with more information couldn't hurt.

"Barry said that all were accounted for. Stanton confirmed that no aides were out of the room at that time either. I assume that means we're looking at someone from the outside?" There was hope in Michael's voice.

Kate hadn't wanted to dash them so soon. "It's probably best if we don't assume anything. For all we know, someone from the inside is working with them. They seem to be able to slip in and out of here with ease."

"What about the fence? What did you find?"

Kate explained what she and Declan had found out there along with the boot print in the mud. "I can understand why you didn't think anyone could get through. Who thinks someone's going to take a blowtorch to the fence."

"How are we going to get it fixed? We can't just leave a breach open like that."

Kate shook her head. "Not now and definitely not in this weather." Michael's face fell and Kate pointed down the hall. "Only so much we can do. Let's go shake them up a little and see what we get." Michael's expression indicated he wasn't convinced, but when Kate headed down the hall, he was right behind her.

# CHAPTER 17

Barry stood on the other side of the door in the living room as Kate and Michael entered. He raised his eyebrows in a way that showed he knew something was up. Kate assumed Declan hadn't told him anything, which had been the plan. Since finding out he lied to her and her finding the gun upstairs, he had fallen down the short list of people Kate trusted.

She walked farther into the room and spotted Declan perched on a stool across the room. There were a few windows to his left that looked out over the area of the property with the drop-off, but after being shot at once, Kate was wary of any rooms with windows. If she could tuck them all away in some underground bunker, that's what she'd do. For now, she had to accept the status quo of what was in front of them.

Before Kate could get started, Declan explained that everyone wanted to gather in the living room rather than the dining room for comfort and warmth. Kate appreciated that too. The roaring fire felt good. Not even the hot shower had warmed her enough from being outside in the rain and wind.

As soon as Kate turned her attention to the senators, aides, and Vice President Kramer, there was a flood of voices shouting questions at her. She held her hand up like a teacher in a classroom of noisy students. "I have a few things to say before I answer your questions."

She waited for an argument but none came.

Kate took the time to update them about the shooting outside and the breach in the fence. She explained how she and Declan walked the fence perimeter, found the cutout and then followed a dirt trail to the parking lot below. Someone asked about a gate in the fence and Kate confirmed that there hadn't been one. While the dirt path did go to the beach, it had never been intended as access from the estate, the path was simply too steep to be safe. As Kate finished her explanation, Kramer interrupted her.

"What are you going to do about it?" he shouted from his high-back chair right near the fireplace. He was sitting slightly off from the senators and had his arms crossed over his chest and his legs crossed at his ankles.

Something had riled him up since she saw him earlier in the day. Kate wasn't going to assume that it was the fact that someone had shot at Michael and her. She didn't think Kramer cared that much. "Sir, we are doing the best we can with limited resources. Right now, you're looking at all the security we have available. The locals said they could send a few officers in the evening. No one can come out in this storm and fix the fence."

Kramer slammed his fist down on the arm of the chair. "I demand that it's fixed now!"

Kate held firm despite his outburst and face reddening. He'd get worse before this was all over. "That's simply not possible. We don't have the materials or the tools needed to fix the fence and there is no repair shop on the island that is coming out to do that in this storm." Kate pinned her gaze right on him. "If you were that concerned about safety, then maybe you should have allowed your entire security team to accompany you on this trip. You'd be a lot better off had you done that."

Kramer raised his eyes to her and he looked like he was sitting on the precipice of scolding her, but he held his tongue. "What's the plan then?" he asked, letting his arms hang loose and sinking back into the chair.

"We need to address the elephant in the room. The reason for the meeting."

There was a rush of voices all saying no at once. From a chair off to Kate's left, not far from Declan, Senator Nancy Yates said, "That isn't possible. There are matters of national security at play here and you don't have the security clearance. We've told the Secret Service team the same. If they aren't privy to the information then you certainly aren't either." The other senators and the vice president agreed, shouting similar things at Kate.

She had assumed they would try that angle. Kate smiled and waited for them to settle down. "Vice President Kramer. Senators," she said and then made eye contact with each of them to drive home her point. "You misunderstand me. I wasn't asking why you're all here this weekend. I said that we need to discuss it." They started their chatter once again.

Above the din, Kate raised her voice nearly to a shout. "I already know why you're here. I know each of you is being blackmailed. I also know why some of you are being blackmailed and that Senator Abbott and Senator Cutcliffe refused to pay the blackmailer any longer."

Each of them turned to the others, their faces paling. The murmurs from the aides grew louder. No one was surprised by what Kate said. The surprise was that she knew about it.

Senator Nancy Yates started to speak but was cut off by Senator Scott Bailey from California, who hadn't said much until now. He was the youngest among the senators, only serving his second term. If Kate remembered correctly, he had just turned forty-three. During his first campaign, his opponent, the incumbent senator who had been in the position for more than twenty years, joked that Bailey might win only because he was so good-looking that women would have to vote for him.

At the time, Kate knew Bailey's opponent had just made a fatal mistake, suggesting women can't see past a pretty face and vote on real issues.  He had enraged women in the state and drove record voter turn-out. Whatever the incumbent senator had thought he was trying to do had backfired spectacularly. Senator Bailey had won by a landslide. Now he was here with a terrible secret so bad that he was being blackmailed.

Bailey stood to his full six-foot-two height and shoved his hands in his pockets. He didn't deny what Kate said. He asked, "How did you find out?"

"I was informed by a witness and we found concrete evidence including the blackmail letters in the rooms of Senator Cutcliffe and Senator Abbott. We also found evidence in Chase's room." Kate paused to see if Senator Bailey would say anything else. When he didn't, she looked over at the aides. "I also know that two of the aides here were sexually harassed by Senator Cutcliffe. They signed non-disclosure agreements and were paid twenty-five thousand dollars each to keep quiet. We suspect they were paid off with campaign finance money."

The vice president was on his feet then. He took a few steps and jabbed a finger toward Kate. "You can't make wild accusations like this. You're tarnishing the names of good people. Who'd want to blackmail us? I don't have any secrets to hide," he said and then looked to his colleagues who wouldn't meet his eyes. Kramer wasn't going to back down. He'd stand by his statement. "Well, I have nothing to hide. I'm like an open book."

Kate wasn't going to tell the man's secrets in front of his colleagues. She had only shared the information about Senator Cutcliffe because he was deceased and she had more than enough evidence to prove that the allegations were true.  Kate started to respond to the vice president when Maven, his aide, stood up from the couch. She was holding Allison's hand as she did, but let go as she stood to her full height.

She tucked her bob-length dark hair behind her ears and then pulled her ribbed purple shirt down father over the top of her black skirt. Maven stood with her shoulders back, head held high, and her hands folded in front of her. She spoke loudly and clearly. "Agent Walsh is telling the truth, Vice President Kramer. Before I came to work with you, I worked for Senator Cutcliffe. I was just out of graduate school and it was my first job as a senatorial aide. His behavior was inappropriate from the first day. I was told to keep my head down and ignore it and eventually he'd stop when he got the hint that I wasn't going to sleep with him. It never stopped."

"Who gave you that stupid advice?" Senator Yates asked with condescension in her tone.

"His secretary who had been with him for years," Maven said, glancing in her direction. The two shared a look that Kate felt deep. That was the advice that many older women in government who had worked through the years had told their young female colleagues. Kate had received the same advice when she first joined the FBI. There were only a handful of women among the ranks, and some men didn't like that Kate was there or getting the prime assignments. That had been in the days before she was recruited to join Spade's team.

As if on cue, Kramer said what Kate had grown to expect the man to say. "Maven, you must have done something to lead Senator Cutcliffe on. Something you wore or said must have given him the wrong idea. Maybe you flirted with him unintentionally. You had to have dropped some hint that he had a chance with you."

"A chance for what?" Senator Yates asked, standing now too. "A chance for some sixty-year-old fat grubby man to put his paws all over her? You've missed the boat, Kramer. That behavior is no longer tolerated and we are not blaming women for the abuse leveled against them."

"I'm just saying that Senator Cut…"

"I know exactly what you're saying," Maven said, shoving up the sleeves of her shirt and releasing a laugh with an edge to it. "You think the only way a man behaves like that towards a woman is if we invite it or if we do something that sparks their lust. You think we are somehow responsible for a man's lust and he's just so overcome that he no longer has control of himself so he must act on it. That it's my responsibility to not elicit that lust at the start and to fend it off when it's directed my way. Let me ask you, Vice President Kramer, when are men responsible for their actions? When do they accept responsibility for the things they think, say, and do?"

Kramer turned on her then. His nostrils flared. "Don't you dare speak to me that way, young lady!"

Maven let out another laugh then, followed by a snort. "Young lady? Are you kidding me? No, sir, don't you dare speak to *me* that way." She was on a roll now. It was like she had held in the secret for so long that Maven was finally exploding and nothing was going to stop her. "After it was clear that Senator Cutcliffe wasn't going to stop, I applied to be your aide, Vice President Kramer, because I thought, if anything, you had some morals. Do you know why I signed the non-disclosure agreement when Chase brought it to me? I'll tell you why. Because the message to me was that if I didn't sign it Senator Cutcliffe would tell you that I had stolen money from him for an abortion."

"Is that what happened?" Kramer asked. That was met with a collective groan.

Kate thought Senator Yates was going to knock the man on his backside. "Of course that didn't happen, you old fool," Yates shouted at him. Then she turned to Maven, "I'm sorry on behalf of my colleagues that you had to deal with that. When did you sign the non-disclosure agreement?"

"About nine months ago. It was odd timing because I had long since quit. I didn't understand why it was coming up then. Then Chase explained that Senator Cutcliffe was being blackmailed over it and by signing it we were admitting that we weren't the blackmailer and that we'd also remain quiet should the blackmailer go public. If none of the victims report, there is no story."

"I assume you didn't want to sign it," Kate said.

"I didn't want to sign it," Maven admitted. "I was more than willing to come forward if I had support from others. Otherwise, I was a lone voice without much proof."

Senator Carley Stone stood up then too. "How many women have come forward?"

Maven shrugged but Kate responded, "There were nine signed non-disclosure agreements."

"You said initially that there were two women in this room." Senator Stone looked over at the aides, most of whom were women. "Does anyone else want to admit this?"

"I don't think that's necessary," Kate said, trying to protect Allison who didn't seem to want to out herself in the way that Maven had. That was fine by Kate. "I brought it up because we can prove what Senator Cutcliffe did. We know that there is a blackmailer. I need to know what all your experiences are."

"You're not going to address what Senator Cutcliffe did?" Stone asked with eyebrows raised as if daring Kate to not condemn the man.

Kate shook her head. "That's not what I'm saying at all. There will be time to judge him on his actions and get support for the victims if they choose to access it. What's important right now is that the rest of you start talking. The more I can learn about this blackmailer, the faster I can create a profile of them. All of you are at risk. I'm trying to stop another murder." Kate noted that none of them except for Vice

President Kramer had denied they were being blackmailed.

Senator Stone blinked rapidly several times. "What is it you want to know?"

"I need to know everything from start to finish about the blackmail each of you has experienced," Kate said calmly and let the words settle in the room. "That's the only way we are going to catch the killer."

Still standing near Senator Yates, Maven asked, "Do you think the killer is in this room or someone from the outside?"

Kate could have easily let them all off the hook. She needed to keep the pressure on. "I'm convinced we are focused on someone on the inside and that the blackmailer may have hired a professional killer. Either way, someone in this room is complicit in these crimes."

A hush fell over the room as each one looked to the others, wondering who among them was the guilty party.

# CHAPTER 18

"The aides need to leave," Senator Yates said. Senators Stone and Bailey echoed the same along with the two other remaining Senators Kip Harrison from Florida and Stan Taft from New York.

Maven had disgust written all over her face. "Don't you think we already know what's going on? You rely on us for everything. Even when you don't think we are listening, we are." She turned her body to face the other aides. "We've also shared everything we know." There was no hesitation in her admission.

Kate was sure Maven had been waiting for the opportunity to tell them all exactly what she had been thinking. She wasn't sure whether to be impressed or concerned. There was a current of anger bubbling just below the surface.

Senator Yates stepped toward the group of them. "Is this true? All of you knew that we were being blackmailed?"

Most of the aides looked down at their hands. It was Allison who finally had a shot of courage and responded. "I didn't know all the ins and outs until you brought us all here this weekend. I knew about Senator Cutcliffe from Chase who I told about what was happening with Senator Abbott. When we arrived, we all met while you were meeting and exchanged information."

The senators started to yell at their aides. It was Declan who finally pushed himself off the stool and came to stand by Kate. "That's enough. I know that you're in an uncomfortable situation and you don't want your private business exposed. But you need to look at the bigger picture." Kate didn't think it mattered what Declan said. His loud, deep voice was enough to get them to quiet down.

Once everyone had stopped talking, Declan asked, "Who called for the meeting this weekend? We aren't sure of a lot of things, but what I'd like to know is how all of you figured out the others were being blackmailed."

"It was Senator Abbott who initiated all of this," Yates said, stepping back from the aides. She looked past Kate and didn't fix her eyes on anything other than the wall. There was defeat in her voice. "Senator Abbott found out from Allison that Senator Cutcliffe was also being blackmailed. A few days later, she and I were at lunch when she disclosed to me that she was being blackmailed and was being threatened. She wasn't sure what she should do. It was then I told her the same thing was happening to me. We quietly started asking our colleagues, and over a couple of weeks, had identified all of us." She raised her shoulder to shrug but she sighed deeply instead. "I should say, we identified all those who were willing to admit it. For all I know, there are more who wouldn't admit it."

Senator Bailey added, "We came together this weekend to compare notes and figure out what we are going to do. We thought a coordinated and united front might put an end to all of this. The blackmailer could attack each of us individually, but if we were united, we thought they might back down. They are going after United States senators and the vice president." It was the first time that anyone had acknowledged that the vice president was also being blackmailed. Kate wanted to address that but Declan spoke first.

With frustration in his voice, he said to Senator Bailey, "I assume none of the options included calling the FBI?"

Bailey shook his head. "Honestly, it should have been the first call we all made even before going to each other. You have to understand that the things we are being accused of are embarrassing and could destroy our careers."

"Accused of or what you actually did because there is a difference," Declan responded.

"I didn't do what that sicko said I did," Vice President Kramer said, pushing himself up from the chair. "None of the information in my letters was accurate."

Kate had to walk a fine line because she didn't want to betray Michael. "Do you want to explain further, sir? What did the blackmailer accuse you of doing?"

He narrowed his eyes at Kate and furrowed his brow. He seethed in anger. "Of having several affairs over the years I've been in politics. That never happened. That would never happen. It's disgusting to even think about." Kramer went on for several more moments ranting about how he'd never do that and that anyone who would think that was sick in the head. Everyone in the room remained quiet as the vice president wound himself up and then settled his tirade.

Kate remained calm even though inside she was cringing at how he spoke. "Senators Abbott and Cutcliffe had evidence sent with their blackmail letters. Was that provided in yours?"

"I just said it didn't happen. How is there going to be evidence of something that didn't happen?" he barked and scowled at her.

"I assume you paid the ransom money. Why pay for something that can't be proved?"

That question seemed to stump him. He took a step back from Kate and raised a hand to his heart and rubbed his chest. After far too long waiting as the silence hung around them, Kramer said, "The blackmailer sent photos of me with women I know. They weren't compromising photos but the blackmailer indicated that he had some and that he'd release them. I know for a fact no such photos exist, but we all know how people can doctor photos today. I had no idea what he was going to do and I wasn't going to have my career destroyed over it. It would hurt my family too."

Kramer was so convincing Kate believed him. She turned to each of the senators. "What about all of you? Did you do what you were accused of in the blackmail letters?"

Slowly, they all nodded. Senator Yates stepped forward. "I had a drug problem early in my career. I went to a treatment center and got help. I've been clean for nearly thirty years."

Senator Bailey raised his hand. "I had a gambling problem a couple of years ago. I got into debt to the mob and my father-in-law paid them off. No one knew about it."

"That didn't come up in your security clearance background check?" Declan asked and then shot Kate a look. It was the FBI who performed those security checks.

Senator Bailey tucked his chin down to his chest and let out a loud breathy sigh. "I admit that I lied during that process and my father-in-law and family lied as well. Everyone knew that it would be a major complication and they wanted me to succeed in the Senate."

Something like gambling addiction could impact federal security clearances, and without them, he'd be barred from confidential and top-level security documents. It would render him unable to do his job in Congress. One of the factors they considered when doing the security clearance background checks is what kind of information in the person's past could set them up for blackmail. Senator Yates's substance abuse could be a factor as well, but probably less so because it was so long ago.

Kate looked over at Senators Stone, Harrison, and Taft. "Would you like to disclose what you're being blackmailed for so we can get all of this out into the open?"

Senator Harrison, who was in his early fifties and still looked like he had just stepped off a football field, raked a hand through his thinning dark hair. He hitched up his pants and said, "I was accused of hazing when I was a senior in college. The allegation is true. My fraternity brothers and I hazed a sophomore and put him in the hospital. He had alcohol poisoning and physical injuries and nearly died. My parents paid his medical bills and we settled on compensation before a civil suit could be brought against me. My father also talked the prosecutor's office out of filing criminal charges against all of us. I learned valuable lessons and put it behind me."

"None of that was public information at the time?" Kate asked, wondering how something that should have been public knowledge was being used to blackmail him now.

Senator Harrison shook his head. "No, Agent Walsh. I'm not proud of it but my father bought off everyone involved. He wanted me to have a life in politics and did what he thought he had to do to make that happen. There were a few newspaper reports but I was never mentioned."

Declan cleared his throat. "Who was blamed for what happened?"

Senator Harrison wouldn't meet Declan's eyes. "After the family was paid off, they made a statement to the press that no one hazed the young man and that he was responsible for his actions."

Declan grunted in disgust. "So, you all blamed the victim? Is that correct?"

"That's correct," Harrison said without any trace of guilt in his voice. Kate assumed he had trained himself over time to the right expressions to make and the way to show his body language to indicate he felt remorse or guilt for what he had done but there wasn't a trace of it in his voice.

Kate asked, "Is there any chance that the victim would be seeking revenge?"

"No, that's not possible. He died a few years back unmarried and without children. His parents had preceded him in death." Harrison focused on Kate instead of Declan. "Unless one of my old fraternity brothers ratted me out, I don't know how the blackmailer got the information. He had too many details about what happened the night of the hazing and afterward."

Kate turned away from him and focused on Senator Stone.

"Real estate fraud," she said finally, admitting her humiliation. "I'd blame my husband on his bad business dealings, but that doesn't seem like the responsible thing to do even though he's the one who got me involved in it in the first place. I knew what was going on and then I covered it up. Apparently, I didn't do a good enough job because I've been exposed."

All eyes turned to Senator Stan Taft, who seemed like the cleanest cut of the bunch. He had pressed khaki pants and a button-down shirt under his sweater vest. He was the quietest of the bunch when Kate and Declan were around. Kate knew he was in his early forties and had a wife and two teenage daughters. He had already served two terms in the senate and was fairly popular on both sides of the aisle. Most considered him an independent on the political spectrum.

Taft stood even though he didn't have to and walked toward Kate. "You have to understand that I never meant to deceive anyone. It all just got so out of hand." He closed his eyes as if wishing it all away. When he opened them, they were moist. "I never graduated from Yale or Wharton. I had started at Yale as an undergraduate, but then my father died. I had to drop out to take care of my mother and sisters. I went to work and supported my family. Later, when I ran into people from high school the assumption was that I had graduated. I don't know why but I said yes and then talked about going on to graduate school. I spent a lot of time reading and probably could have easily passed Wharton's MBA program. I never graduated from undergrad and never attended graduate school."

His lie might not have been so bad had it not been that his degree made him a prime member of the Senate Committee on Finance. "Who would know this information other than you?"

"I don't know," Taft said. "My wife doesn't even know. I've been telling the lie for so long that I even convinced my siblings of it. It's been on my resume since my first job. When no one verified my education and I got the job, that was all the backing I needed for later employment. No one ever questioned me."

Kate could understand how if he had stayed in the private sector that would have been true, but he had run a campaign. The opposition research would have easily caught something like that not to mention the federal security background check. There was more to the story than he was saying. "Senator Taft, while I appreciate you telling me, I know that's not the full story. There's no way you could have kept that hidden during your campaign. I know for a fact the FBI would have caught it during your background check. One of the first things we do is confirm education."

Taft held his hand up to stop her. "You're right," he said three times in a row. "Before I ran for my Senate seat, I hired someone, a hacker, who went into the college databases and added me in. That way when someone checked the record, they'd find my information and my graduation date and GPA."

Confused by what he said, Kate asked, "You mean they created an entire fake transcript for you at both universities?"

"Yes. That's what he did. I looked at the websites and determined what courses I would have taken and what professors taught then and created transcripts for myself. The hacker I used then manipulated the databases. For Yale, he added to the transcript they already had for me, but with Wharton, he had to create a new student profile. I don't know how anyone didn't catch it. The man I paid to do it said he was the best and it seems he was. It was seamless. I even get alumni information for Yale and Wharton." Taft looked surprised that anyone believed his lie. "I've attended alumni events and no one ever caught it."

Declan appeared as dumbfounded as Kate felt. She wasn't sure she had ever heard anyone take such drastic steps to fake an education. The lie certainly had made Taft's career. "Do you think the hacker could have outed you?"

Taft shook his head. "I doubt it. I was small potatoes for the work that he was doing. I was probably nothing more than an easy paycheck to him. He had some serious skills and was going after much bigger fish."

Declan rubbed his fingers across his brow line the way he did when he was stressed. "Do you remember the hacker's name?"

"Not his real name. No. I paid in cash." Senator Taft pursed his lips in thought. "He had a weird name. I think it was Ditch or something like that."

Kate looked up at the ceiling and let out a string of curses that made even the vice president embarrassed for her.

# CHAPTER 19

The revelation made by Senator Taft had Declan and Kate scrambling for more information and trying to make sense of the news that had been delivered. At the first opportune moment, she excused them both to the library to process what had been said. She had given the aides, senators, and vice president a break. It worked out because Stanton was in the process of bringing them snacks and drinks.

Kate held everything in until they were secured in the library alone and the door closed and locked behind them. She had even kept Michael out of the conversation. She leaned against a shelf for support. "Declan, it can't be the same person, can it?"

Declan didn't look surprised or as shaken by the revelation as Kate. "We knew what he was before Spade hired him. I don't doubt that it's him. This whole thing might be him. Who else could get all that kind of information on senators and the vice president? A hacker surely could."

"Declan, don't say such things. You're accusing an FBI consultant, one of our teammates, of one of the worst crimes imaginable." Kate heard herself say the words and even she didn't believe it. She slumped down to the floor and leaned back against the bookcase. She wasn't sure why this had shaken her so badly when she was used to dealing with horrific crimes all the time. But thinking that one of her teammates could be involved in something of this magnitude was a little much for her to take.

Declan wasn't going to give Ditch any slack or wiggle room. "He's done worse, Kate."

Kate didn't want to consider it, but Declan was right. He had never liked Ditch and hadn't liked that the man could go from being a criminal to working with the FBI without the usual hoops that everyone had to jump through including passing the background check – something Ditch would never pass. His employment with the FBI had come about differently than theirs.

Ditch – Kevin Detrick at birth – was a hacker who had been arrested by the FBI. In addition to being wanted by the U.S. government, he was wanted by Saudi Arabia, the Chinese, and the Russians for a swath of international espionage, money laundering, and insider trading. He had made fools out of some of the most powerful leaders around the globe. They wanted him dead, and Kate was sure they had planned some unimaginable torture before taking him out completely.

Spade had sprung him, and as they say, made him an offer he couldn't refuse. For the past two years, Ditch had been the computer forensics expert on Spade's team and his secret weapon. Kate wasn't sure what else he did for Spade, but if there was a computer forensics job to be done, Spade didn't need to send in a whole team – he sent in Ditch.

Much to Declan's chagrin, Kate had a soft spot for the genius hacker. She wasn't sure why because he was moodier than anyone she'd ever met and he acted like he was a gift to women. He had blue eyes, a chiseled jaw, a swoop of dirty blond hair, and abs that looked like they had been carved on him with a knife. He was a California boy at heart and a surfer to his core. Declan thought it cliché except even he couldn't rule out Ditch's intelligence.

Kate pointed to the door. "What do we do? We can't go out there and admit that Ditch works for the FBI and is on our team. That's going to put a serious kink in our credibility."

"That's why I don't like him, Kate. Where Ditch goes, trouble follows." Declan sat down on the arm of the chair, thinking. After a moment, he exhaled through his nose loud enough for Kate to hear. "We have to call Spade and let him know. I also want to know where Ditch is right now. I want eyes on him during the rest of this case."

Kate pushed herself up from the floor and pulled out her cellphone. The phone rang a few times before Spade answered, which wasn't his norm. Most times, Kate wondered if he was sitting on top of his phone perched and ready to answer all the time. "Spade, we have a complication," she said as he answered.

"Hit me with it."

Kate explained what Senator Taft had done and that it was why he was being blackmailed. She saved the most important for last. "Taft said the name of the guy who changed the records was Ditch. Unless you know other hackers named Ditch, we might have a problem."

Spade's silence said it all.

"Where is he right now?" Declan asked.

The question was met with more silence. Then Spade said he'd call them back and hung up, leaving them both confused and unsure of what had happened.

"What was that about?" Kate asked, looking over at him with a curious expression on her face.

Declan shook his head. "Maybe Spade is questioning his choice of bringing Ditch onto the team."

"He's rarely wrong," Kate countered. She couldn't explain Spade's reaction because it wasn't what she had been anticipating. She expected to hear concern and that he'd address it. If not that, then maybe a denial that there is no way Ditch could have done something like that.

"He's wrong sometimes, Kate. I respect Spade and what he's done for the United States and all the good he's done for the FBI and the intelligence community. Even Spade can make a mistake."

"You're a bit jaded. Don't you think? I know you've had issues with Ditch from the start. I just thought…" Kate trailed off because she didn't want to say what she was thinking.

Declan had no problem addressing the elephant in the room. "You think I don't like him because he flirts with you. That I'm acting like a jealous boyfriend."

"Aren't you?" If he was going to go there, Kate wouldn't shy away.

Declan didn't answer her right away. He stared at her, their eyes meeting for several seconds before she looked away. "It's not the only reason. Even if I didn't feel the way I do, I wouldn't want you with him. He's a criminal, Kate, and once a criminal always a criminal."

"That's not fair. People can change."

"Not people like Ditch." Declan had the final say in the matter because Spade called back. "What's going on, Spade? You left us sitting here in suspense and we need to get back in the room and continue our interviews."

Spade wasn't one to apologize for anything. "I asked Ditch directly if he was involved. There's no point beating around the bush about it. I find being direct works best with him. He confirmed he was the one who falsified Taft's college record. He said Taft isn't the only one he did that for but wouldn't elaborate."

Ditch's admission brought it home for Kate. The way Spade explained it made it seem like Ditch had no problem with what he had done and didn't see the further-reaching implications of it. "Spade, do you have any concern that Ditch might be involved in all of this?"

Declan interrupted, his anger getting the better of him. "What Kate is nicely trying to say is where is he and is he involved in blackmailing these senators? It would take a hacker with Ditch's skillset and his criminal background to pull off something like this and not get caught."

That again was met with a deafening silence and no denial from Spade. It took him a moment. "Is there something about what's been happening that would indicate Ditch is involved?"

Kate noted that Spade hadn't told them where Ditch was located right now. Last they knew he had been in Manhattan. Kate didn't answer Spade's question, but rather, asked Declan's again. "Is there a reason you can't tell us where Ditch is right now?"

"I don't want to raise your level of concern unless I feel like I have reason to."

Kate raised her eyes to Declan's and they shared a concerned look. "Are you trying to tell us that Ditch is here in Martha's Vineyard?"

"Yes," Spade said and then waited. When neither of them said anything, Spade filled the silence. "As soon as I heard about this case, I figured you might need some computer support. Call it a hunch on my part but I sent Ditch there. He arrived before the two of you did, that's why you didn't see him on the ferry. He's at a local hotel." The sounds of rustling paper came through the phone line while heat flushed Declan's face. She laid a hand on his arm for him to remain calm and not jump to conclusions. Spade provided them with the name of the hotel, Ditch's room number, and the hotel's phone number.

Declan made a note in his phone while Kate tried to find the right words to ask her question again. "Spade, we have some concerns that Ditch might be involved. When exactly did you send him here? You said you sent him after the first murders happened?"

"Yes, that's correct. The two senators had already been murdered. I was notified and called Ditch and then called both of you." Spade remained quiet for a moment. Then thoughtfully, he said, "Kate. Declan. I know neither of you approves of Ditch being on the team given his criminal past. Yes, him doing what he's done for Senator Taft is not ideal in this case. We've known that Ditch's past might come back on a case or two. Granted one involving such high-value stakes is cumbersome, but it's not the end of the world. I highly doubt that Ditch is blackmailing and murdering senators."

Declan wasn't convinced. He pressed harder. "We know the last time we saw Ditch in Manhattan, but do we have any proof when he made it here to Martha's Vineyard? When you spoke to him, did you call his cellphone?"

"Yes," Spade said with hesitation not normally heard. "I can't imagine that…" His voice trailed off as he seemed to reconsider. "I thought you said this threat was coming from the inside."

"That was before someone shot at Michael and Kate while they were searching for documents in one of the cottages. I gave chase and they took off into the trees. We found that someone had used a blowtorch on the wrought iron fence and got in that way." Declan looked over at Kate. "We believe there might be someone here involved too. We know for sure that we are also dealing with an outside threat. I feel comfortable saying that we are sure now that there are multiple people involved."

Kate was comfortable with Declan's admission. She would have liked more solid information before taking it to her boss. Under the circumstances, Declan made the right call. "Spade, we need to interview Ditch and at least rule him out." Kate thought that was the fairest thing she could say. If it had been up to Declan, he would have gone after Ditch with full force. She understood that a more delicate touch was needed. She had also learned something about her boss – not only was he rarely wrong but convincing him he might be wrong would take an act of God.

Spade relented. "Go talk to him, Kate. Go easy because you know how Ditch is when he's set off. If you go in there making wild accusations, he'll shut down. When I asked about Taft, he readily admitted it to me. I hardly think he'd do that if he was blackmailing him."

Kate agreed to go easy with him. When the call ended, she saw Declan's expression. "Don't give me that look. Just because I told Spade I'd go easy doesn't mean that's what I'm going to do. Given that we know he's here, that changes things for me. I like evidence, Declan, and you used to as well. Spade is right that we can't make wild accusations."

"What do we tell everyone else?"

"Nothing. We let it lie until we know more. There's no point admitting that Ditch works for the FBI unless we have to. I don't know what kind of arrangement Spade made with the FBI director about Ditch's employment. I don't want to ruffle political feathers unnecessarily."

"Then let's hope he hasn't blackmailed or killed anyone or else we are all going to be testifying before Congress." Declan raked a hand through his messy dark hair that hadn't been brushed since his shower. It dried in wavy curls that Kate knew he tamed with gel. She liked his hair wild and wavy more than she should.

Kate brought herself to the present and took a moment to gather her thoughts. "We need to start running some background information on all the aides and Michael and Barry. Also, anything we can find on the vice president. We need to tap into that data first. I don't think that will be in our database."

Declan shook his head. "We won't be able to readily access it. You go back in the room with them and continue finding out all you can while I make a few calls." As Kate started to head out of the room, he called her back. "We need to consider if this is just a domestic threat."

"Right," Kate said slowly, hoping that this wasn't an international terror threat or a bad actor blackmailing them for something much worse than money. "I'll assess that when I go back in. I still need to read over the letters we found in Senator Cutcliffe's room."

Declan held up his phone. "I'll be in as soon as I finish up here."

# CHAPTER 20

Kate steadied herself against the wall as she watched the aides and senators mingle with each other and eat the snacks that had been provided. The only person removed from the scene was Vice President Kramer, who sat sipping coffee in the same chair he was in earlier.

Right when she walked into the room, Michael approached to ask if everything was okay. She assured him that all was fine. She inquired about his arm and he said the bleeding stopped. There was at least that if there wasn't any other good news.

Kate hated to say it but the news that Ditch was nearby and had been the hacker Senator Taft had employed didn't sit well with her. She wasn't as angry as Declan had been or as dismissive about the whole thing as Spade. She was shaken by the news in a way she was having trouble identifying. An FBI agent betraying the oath they took to their country was something that Kate knew happened. She wasn't living under a rock. It was just to have met and worked with that person felt like something different. Then again, Ditch wasn't one of their own. He was a criminal who Spade turned to the good side.

"Are you all right, Agent Walsh?" Senator Carley Stone asked, approaching Kate with a cup of coffee in her hand and a few cookies on a napkin. She offered them to Kate. "You need to eat something. You look pale."

Kate accepted the kind gesture as her stomach growled in response to the smell of food. "I appreciate that. There's so much to be done neither Declan nor I have taken a moment to stop."

"We asked Stanton for a late lunch since we've been delayed this morning. He's preparing it now. You'll join us whether it's protocol or not." Senator Stone's tone left little room for argument. "Have you any idea who is doing all of this?"

Kate hated to admit it. "No. Not so far. We know that there is someone from the outside who shot at Michael and me. We also suspect someone from the inside might be involved, but we have no clear suspect yet." Kate wasn't sure that was exactly true. There had been the gun found outside of Vice President Kramer's room. While she assumed he put it there, Kate couldn't be sure. She wasn't even sure that it was the murder weapon. She wouldn't know that until Sharon got back to them with an update after processing the gun and Chase's crime scene.

Senator Stone put her hand on Kate's back. "I'm willing to help in any way I can to make sure the rest of us get out of here alive. We should have gone to the FBI immediately. I don't know what we were thinking."

Kate offered her a smile. "You were thinking about protecting your reputation. People never realize that it's nearly impossible to outwit a blackmailer. They are usually five or ten steps ahead."

Senator Stone gave a solemn nod. "I'm glad you're here now. Eat up and then we can get started."

Kate took a sip of the coffee, which was warm and too sweet for her liking. She wouldn't complain though. She drank it down and ate a couple of cookies. The chocolate chips were warmer and better than the last batch she had made at home. Not that she had a lot of time for baking. It was something she had enjoyed with her mother when she was a child and reminded Kate of her still. It wasn't long before the dull headache that had started to form over the last hour eased off. Kate finished the last of the coffee and then set the cup on the sideboard.

Stanton approached and retrieved her empty cup. "Senator Taft said to make sure that you and Agent James have lunch. I can have it ready in the dining room with everyone else or in the library, whichever you prefer."

Kate didn't want to get too social with everyone. "In the library will be fine, Stanton. Thank you for the clothing as well. I appreciate your help today."

He offered her a smile and then headed into the hallway. Once he was gone, Kate eased the door closed and asked for everyone's attention. "While Declan and I spoke in the other room during your break, something came to our attention that we should have considered earlier. We are barely into the details of your blackmail and I need to know more. First and foremost, help me to understand what the blackmailer wanted in exchange. Was it always money?" Kate didn't want to suggest it was anything else and hoped to elicit the information naturally if more had occurred.

Each of the senators started responding at once, throwing out a range of financial payoffs that had been made. "I know what you're getting at," Senator Harrison said, hitching up his pant legs as he sat down on the couch not far from the vice president. "You're wondering if the blackmailer asked us for anything that only we could provide like secrets or classified information."

"That's the concern with any blackmail case, particularly given your stature and access to information." Kate scanned their faces to see if anyone might have a worried expression or might be hiding something. She didn't see that reflected in any of them. There was an undercurrent of conversation that rose from them like a constant humming sound. They were looking at one another as if this was the first time the question had been asked.

Senator Stone looked back at Kate. "I wasn't asked for anything like that and it doesn't appear my colleagues were either. If we had been, that might have changed how we approached this. I know I would have been much more willing to call the FBI had that been the case."

Kate thanked her for the information and looked to the rest of them for confirmation. All of them, including the vice president, echoed that it was just financial compensation the blackmailer requested. "That's good to hear. Given that, I'd say we are dealing with a domestic blackmailer rather than an international one. You've met a few times since arriving this weekend. What conclusions have you drawn?"

"Not many," Senator Stone said, speaking first. She raised her eyes to the rest of them who either didn't respond or shrugged. She turned back to Kate. "It's been an exercise in futility. We started by going through all the people we might have had in common to see if we had any connections. You can imagine how many people that would be. We set that aside and then considered our pasts, where we went to school and such, but that didn't turn out to be productive either. We explored that maybe it was someone connected to the Democratic National Committee or the Republican National Committee but that didn't get us very far. The reality is Washington D.C. is a small place and most of us are connected. There are about two degrees of separation so the list was miles and miles long."

Kate assumed it would be. "Is there anything all of you have in common that your other colleagues do not? Did you use the same person to run your campaigns or share a staffer at some point?"

"We didn't use the same staffers or campaign managers," Senator Harrison said, looking up at his colleagues. "We aren't even all on the same side of the aisle or the same state."

"What about public relations or marketing firms? Is there any commonality there?" Kate knew she was starting to stretch for commonality, but she couldn't think of one either unless the blackmailer was one of their own and close to all of them in Congress. The one thing she knew for sure was that it was someone who had figured out that they all had a secret to hide and would be willing to pay to keep it quiet.

Each of the senators turned to each other and went over their public relations and marketing people and there were no commonalities. Senator Harrison threw his hands up. "This seems like a useless exercise."

Kate agreed with him on that. "This might seem like a basic question, but when this first started who did each of you suspect? Is there someone in your life that knew your secret?"

Senator Bailey raised his hand slightly. "I thought it might be my father-in-law. He paid off my debts and hates me. I figured he was just messing with me when I got the first letter. I didn't even pay anything until the third letter when the threats on my life started. That spooked me and I figured I better scrape the money together." Bailey let out a nervous laugh. "Turns out, I had to go to my father-in-law to get the money because I didn't have it. That's really when I knew it wasn't him."

"Did you tell him what it was for?" Senator Harrison asked.

"I had no choice," Bailey said with sadness in his voice. "That's when I asked him if he told anyone about my gambling debts. He said he didn't tell a soul, not even his wife or mine. He said it was just between the two of us and the bookie I used. I don't think he's telling anyone or blackmailing me. There'd be no point. He knows I'm broke." Senator Bailey looked up at Kate and winced.

That was interesting to Kate. She wondered if others were the same. "Did all of you pay when you got the first letter or did you wait?" She knew from Allison that Senators Abbott and Cutcliffe had paid after the first letter. It made Kate wonder if the blackmailer had other victims who simply refused to pay and didn't even respond with threats.

"I paid right away.  I wasn't going to chance this information becoming public," Senator Stone said about her real estate fraud. It made sense to Kate because it sounded like she had committed several federal crimes.

Harrison responded next. "I didn't pay right away. What happened in college was a done deal for me. I had let it go. I didn't think there was much that could be proven from that time anyway. Besides, I was never charged or arrested. Then the proof came and I paid up."

Kate didn't want to remind him that he should have had legal or civil recourse for what he had done, but his father had swept it all under the rug. "Who could have known about that?"

"As I said before, I have no idea. My other fraternity brothers would be implicating themselves with any release of information about the incident, and the guy and his family are all deceased.  Beats me." Harrison had a nonchalance about him that Kate didn't like. He was far too blasé about hurting another student even if he was young and in college. Harrison had the same reputation in the Senate for being unperturbed about everything and often showing a lack of emotion and empathy. He frequently voted no on disaster relief for other states that were impacted by hurricanes, earthquakes, and the like. He didn't have a problem accepting federal funding for his home state though.

"What about you, Senator Taft?"

"I paid right away.  I wasn't going to chance a big secret like that coming out."

"Was there anyone you suspected?"

"Ditch is the only one who knew." Taft raised his eyes to Kate. "Not only would this secret devastate my career, but it would also implode my family. My wife would never recover her trust in me with this kind of lie. My entire career is built on a lie."

Kate didn't want to encourage him but that wasn't necessarily true. "All the hard work that you've done and accomplishments you've had throughout your career are yours. I can't speak for your wife, but I'd assume she might factor that in when deciding how she feels. You've earned experience even if you faked your education. That doesn't make what you did right. I'm just saying don't discount everything you've accomplished."

"Thank you for saying that," Taft said and then looked at Senator Yates, who was the only one besides Vice President Kramer who hadn't answered yet.

Senator Yates pursed her lips. "I didn't pay right away and I only paid once. Unlike my colleagues here who made multiple payments, there was a part of me that didn't care if my secret came out. It might hurt my career but it was so long ago. I've remained clean and sober since then. It was a great accomplishment that, once the blackmailer threatened to expose me, I had to consider how bad it would be to be exposed."

"Yet, there was something that made you pay for them to keep the secret," Senator Stone said, calling her on what she was saying.

Senator Yates nodded. "My children. I had never told them and I was ashamed of my past. I didn't want them to know."

Kate assumed some people in her past had to know. "Does your husband and other family know?"

"Not my husband but my sisters and my brother. It was a family secret at the time. Of course, others saw me around that time and suspected I might have had a problem. I don't know that they ever really knew for sure. I got clean and sober and never went back. If there was any talk it died down a long time ago." Senator Yates stepped back as if she was struck by something important. She opened her mouth to speak but it took several seconds before she said anything. "There was only one other time it came up. During opposition research from my opponent early on. It was the second campaign I ran and my opponent threatened to use the information. I don't know why they didn't. I had prepared for it to come out."

"Do you know who found the information then?" Kate asked, feeling like they might have cracked a sliver of light into the case.

"John Huntly.  He was one of the most ruthless for opposition research at the time. Everyone wanted him because there was nothing that could be hidden from him," Senator Yates said and then saw Kate's face. "He's dead, Agent Walsh. He died about a year ago."

Kate wasn't deterred. "Then we need to know who had access to all the secrets he uncovered over the years."

# CHAPTER 21

Kate stood still for a moment fighting against her instinct, which was to leave them in the room and chase down the lead on John Huntly. Her training taught her she should break them apart now and interview them all one by one. Only that would take far too long and she didn't think it would illicit any more information than she had now. A few of the aides hadn't said much at all, but Allison and Maven and even the information found in Chase's room had helped her have a clear picture of their role in all of this.

Kate said, "I want to follow up on some leads. I'm going to the library to make a few phone calls."

"What do you want us to do?" Senator Yates asked. "Let us be productive while we are all stuck here."

"Continuing to talk through the people all of you might have in common is important. You never know what you might hit on. Do any of you have your blackmail letters with you?"

"All of us," Senator Bailey said. "Do you want to see them?"

"I need to. I need to ensure the letters are all coming from the same person, and the only way to do that is to compare them. Have you done that already?"

Everyone said no at the same time. Senator Yates said, "Maybe Michael can walk us to our rooms one by one, and we can gather the materials that were sent to us. We can then share that with you. I don't have any extra copies, so I'd need mine back."

Kate wasn't sure what would be kept as evidence. She could always ask Stanton about making copies for their files. "We'll figure it out," she said without committing to anything. She glanced over at Michael who was already on his feet. "When you have the materials, just drop them off to me in the library."

"We'll be quick about it," Michael said, gesturing toward Senator Yates and then the door with his good arm.

Kate walked out first and was halfway down the hall in the opposite direction when she turned and called to them. It occurred to Kate to track down the information she needed that credible sources were right in front of her. "As each person gathers their information, I'd like to speak to them alone for a few moments."

Senator Yates raised her eyebrows and an expression of concern fell over her face. "Would this be a formal FBI interview? Maybe I should speak to my lawyer first."

"Nothing like that," Kate assured her and took a few steps to close the distance between them. She wasn't sure where the feeling was coming from because there was no reason behind it, but Kate trusted Senator Yates. "I want to track down your opponents and see who they used for opposition research. If it all comes back to John Huntly then we might have hit on something that needs to be explored more."

Yates shook her head confused. "He's dead though. A dead man can't blackmail us."

Kate realized then this would take some convincing. "Senator Yates, Huntly had people working with him. I'm sure he didn't do that work all alone, not with how popular he was. Countless politicians sought out his help. It was too much for one person There is also the question of what happened to his confidential files once he passed." Kate wasn't even sure the lead would go anywhere, but it was about the most solid lead they had so far. Huntly would have inevitably found the kinds of information they were all being blackmailed for now.

Kate recalled the few sparse details she knew about the man. She hadn't even known he had died, but his name was one to be feared around Washington D.C. He had been a retired homicide detective turned private investigator, who focused only on opposition research. His entire business was based on exposing the secrets of those in politics. Kate knew more rumors about him than she knew facts. He was an interesting character and a middle-of-the-road independent, so he didn't favor one side of the aisle over the other. He was in it for the money and the challenge. At least, that's what he had told a reporter who dared ask why he did what he did. The last Kate had heard about him he was celebrating his seventy-fifth birthday but that was a few years ago.

When Kate snapped herself back to the present, she asked, "Was Huntly still working up to his death?"

Senator Yates chuckled. "He was, right up until the moment he died. I don't know if it's true or not, but I heard he had a heart attack while doing surveillance. Metro D.C. police found him parked in his truck outside a known D.C. brothel. No one knows who he was spying on that night. It's been a swirling mystery since he passed."

Kate wondered if that guy was being blackmailed too. "He must have had someone working with him."

"If he did, it's one of the best-kept secrets in D.C." Senator Yates chuckled to herself. "It's probably the only secret being kept in D.C. But you're right that Huntly's associates could be a lead. He was known for being ruthless but fair. He uncovered things that should have remained hidden forever. I know the things he dug up on my opponents I'd have never known otherwise."

Kate hadn't realized Senator Yates had used him. "Did you seek his services recently?"

Yates shook her head. "This was early on in my political career. If

I'm remembering correctly, it was my second senate race. I was up against a tough opponent and needed a competitive edge. I never ended up using the information that was found because it was so damning. I couldn't play dirty like that."

Kate didn't have the stomach for politics. "If Huntly worked for one senator, does that mean he'd never work for their opponent down the road?"

"Huntly didn't have loyalty like that. He never played favorites," Senator Yates explained evenly. There was no animosity in her voice. She spoke it simply and plainly as the truth. "I don't even know if Huntly saw us as people other than little figureheads with pasts he could dig around in and make a mess. His loyalty remained to his paying client for as long as the money flowed. That's who he answered to – the person with the most money."

That could get a person in trouble. Seeing that he was already dead, Kate wasn't going to worry about the trouble Huntly could cause for himself. "How did you reach him?"

"The telephone but that was years ago, Agent Walsh. I know that Senator Bailey used him recently for his campaign. While I'm upstairs, getting the docs you need, ask him. I'm sure he could help you out." Senator Yates turned and walked toward the staircase with Michael.

Kate headed back into the living room and gestured for Senator Bailey. Once in the hallway, she asked about how to contact John Huntly. "Did you ever speak to anyone else in his office?"

"There was a secretary but I can't remember her name." Senator Bailey provided Kate with the information she needed to contact John Huntly. "Mostly, I called his cellphone directly. Well…" he paused as if to walk back what he said. "I didn't call him. It was my campaign manager who was the main point of contact. I was kept up to date with the information that was found."

"Did you use the information that was found?"

Senator Bailey shook his head. "There wasn't much on my opponent. A couple of unpaid parking tickets and he cheated on an English test in high school and got suspended."

Kate had a bemused smile on her face. "Huntly went back that far?"

"He'd interview your kindergarten teacher if he thought it would find some dirt on you."

Kate raised her eyes to him. "Given you worked with him recently, do you think there could be anything to this lead?"

Senator Bailey stood there for a moment, just looking at Kate. She couldn't read the expression on his face. He looked off down the hall and then stepped closer to her. "I had only one conversation with John Huntly and that was before he'd take me on as a client. He interviews all his prospective clients before he takes the first retainer payment. I asked him why he does what he does. Do you have any idea of his answer?"

Kate shook her head. "I couldn't even venture a guess."

"Huntly hated politics and politicians. He said we were all dirty, so he might as well make a living exposing us for the frauds and hypocrites that we are. He said even the ones who came to Washington D.C. starry-eyed and eager to make change were nothing but egomaniacal narcissistic frauds. I got the sense he hated all of us."

"Are you sure he died?" Kate asked because he sounded like he'd be the prime suspect. Even his last name reinforced his work. He could have easily hunted down all the secrets and then used it all as blackmail at the end of his life. Cash in a big payment and then ride off into the sunset.

Senator Bailey crashed Kate's fantasy. "I went to his wake. He has grown children who didn't seem too pleased with their father's life work. They looked downright embarrassed when I met them."

"How many children did he have?"

"Four and he has ten or twelve grandchildren. I really can't see anyone in his family involved."

Kate wasn't going to rule out anyone that easily. "What about mentors or other investigators who worked for him?"

"I wouldn't know anything about that."

Kate thanked him for the information and then waited as he walked back into the living room. Her mind reeled with the possibilities. If Huntly meant what he told Senator Bailey about politicians and that they should all be exposed, it stood to reason that if he had been a mentor to another investigator that he might have passed on his bias against politicians or his other investigator just saw a cash grab after the boss died.

Kate walked through the foyer that still needed to be cleaned and down the hall that dead-ended at the library. She found Declan in one of the leather chairs speaking to someone on the phone. He gestured her in and pointed to a notepad he had sitting on the arm of the chair.

Kate picked up the notes and scanned them. Declan had been busy tracking Ditch's movements from the hotel to Martha's Vineyard. He had taken the train up from the city to Boston and then the ferry over to the island. The most pertinent information – the time – was missing from his notes. Kate waited while he wrapped up his call.

"I think I might have a viable suspect," Kate said when he hung up.

"Me too," Declan said with a sly smile. "Do you know that Ditch arrived in Martha's Vineyard by lunch on the day we arrived?"

"How is that possible? We left him in New York City. Spade said he called him right before he called us."

Declan put a hand on her shoulder and leaned in. "That's right, Kate. That means Ditch left New York City and headed here to Martha's Vineyard before there was official word about the murders."

"Right," Kate said still not understanding. "Ditch wasn't here in enough time to commit the murders. He got here after they had occurred, so he can't be our suspect. That would clear him."

Declan still had the same sly smile spread across his face that made Kate feel like she was missing out on the punchline. "Ditch got here after the murders but he met with someone as soon as he arrived at the hotel. The clerk at the front desk heard them talking in the front lobby. The man asked Ditch if anyone knew he was there on the island. He said no one knew and that he had timed it to arrive at just the right time. Ditch asked the man if it was done. The man confirmed."

Kate stepped back from Declan. "That doesn't mean anything. The *it* they were talking about could be anything, Declan. I highly doubt Ditch is going to stand in the lobby of a hotel talking so casually about the murder of two senators."

"Either way, Kate. He was here well before he was informed about the murders." He stood back from her and planted his hands on his hips. "We don't believe in coincidences like that."

Kate held her hand up in defeat. They'd get nowhere continuing to argue about it. Kate wasn't going to convince Declan that Ditch was innocent. The only thing that would prove it was actual evidence. "Ditch needs to be interviewed. I'm not arguing that. It's just not a slam dunk for me."

Kate told Declan about the lead she had uncovered and highlighted each of their blackmail cases. "We need to run down leads and find out who took over for John Huntly or if his business went belly up. Someone had access to those records. We should call Spade."

"We don't need to call Spade. I know who took over for Huntly."

Kate's mouth fell open. "How do you know?"

"I'm not sure how I know to be honest with you. Maybe it was Spade who told me."

"Well, who is it?"

"Conner Fitzgerald." Declan saw Kate's confused face. "He's the homicide detective who solved that rash of stabbings in D.C. about ten years ago. His face was splashed all over the news then. Turns out

Huntly was looking for a partner and Fitz was more than happy to oblige."

# CHAPTER 22

Kate didn't remember much, only that the Metro D.C. cops handling the case hadn't wanted to call in the FBI. They had resisted all offers of help and the lead detective, who was a young detective in his mid-thirties, wasn't going to let anyone get in the way of solving it himself. He was determined to solve it even if it meant tanking his career in the process.

Kate went through her memories trying to recall the television footage around the time of the case. "Is Fitz the tall, good-looking detective who the reporters fell all over themselves trying to interview?"

Declan nodded. "After that case, I heard he even got a modeling offer. Good Morning America interviewed him. Then he made the late-night television show circuit. Fitz ended up with more fame than he bargained for and had a hard time working back at Metro. My understanding is he went private and that's when he sought out Huntly. The two made quite the pair before Huntly wanted to retire."

"Wait, he retired?" Kate asked, confused because Senator Yates had said he died while on surveillance and Senator Bailey had said he'd recently used him. Kate explained that to Declan.

Declan shrugged. "I'm not sure, Kate. All I know is that Fitz took over for Huntly after working for him. He runs the firm now. I'm sure of that."

"Then we need to get in touch with Conner Fitzgerald immediately because I want to know where all of Huntly's case files went." Kate reached for her cellphone and went to the search engine but didn't get far. A knock on the door interrupted her. It was Senator Yates with Michael.

She walked in with a file folder in her hand. "This is everything you asked for."

Kate took the file and set it down at a nearby table. "Declan believes a former Metro detective by the name of Conner Fitzgerald took over for John Huntly. Is that a name familiar to you?"

Senator Yates thought for a moment. "He solved that D.C. stabbing case, right?"

"That's him," Declan said and waited.

Senator Yates didn't know. "I haven't needed such services recently so I wouldn't know." She pointed to the file folder. "I'll be in the other room if you have questions. It's all fairly straightforward."

Kate wanted to speak to Yates as she went through the file. She turned to Declan. "Can you run down the leads about Conner Fitzgerald while I go through the information?"

Michael offered him another quiet place to work and then the two of them left the room. When Kate was alone with Senator Yates, she said, "Before I go through the evidence that was sent to you, is there anything you want to tell me now that we are alone?"

Senator Yates glanced around the room and then spotted what she was seeking. She made her way to a small mini bar at the far end of the library and dug a can of soda out of the fridge. She poured it into a glass and took a sip. "I can't even tell you how much I'd like to add whiskey to this. That's the thing about addiction. Some days it's a breeze and other days, even these many years on, the temptation is there, even if it's just for a shot for courage."

Kate wasn't sure what to make of the woman. "Is there something you need courage about, Senator Yates?"

She rolled the soda around the glass but didn't take another sip. "I don't have any reason to say what I'm going to say. If you wanted to use it to tank my career, you could very well do that."

"What you tell me doesn't have to leave this room," Kate said, trying to reassure her.

Yates sat down on the chair across from Kate and crossed her legs. She wasn't looking at Kate but rather at the liquid she swished around in the glass. "It's possible I want this information to leave the room. It might be why I'm telling you."

Kate leaned forward confused by that. "It sounds like you're telling me two different things. If I tell someone it could ruin your career, but also you might want the information to be public. I don't understand both at once. Maybe you just tell me whatever it is and then we can decide the best course of action."

Senator Yates smiled over at Kate and then rested the glass on a nearby table. "I like you, Agent Walsh. You seem highly intelligent and logical, two things missing in D.C. these days. I trust you and I can't remember the last time I felt that way about anyone."

"What about your senatorial aide?" Kate asked, realizing then she wasn't sure which aide was hers.

Yates didn't answer the question. She took a deep breath and exhaled slowly. "I don't trust Vice President Kramer. I don't just mean that I don't trust him because he's on the other side of the aisle and we disagree on nearly everything. I don't trust him because I don't believe his blackmail story. I don't think he's being blackmailed. I think he's making it up and might be behind all of this."

Kate chose her words carefully, knowing that if Kramer was lying then Michael was too. Unless Kramer was bluffing his own Secret Service agent. "Why do you think that?"

"He's never shown us proof. We all showed each other the letters we received. Kramer has never done that even when we asked him to." Senator Yates paused to collect her thoughts and then answered Kate's question before she had a chance to ask it. "It was Senator Cutcliffe who told Kramer about the blackmail. Those two were thick as thieves. Cutcliffe told us that when he mentioned it to the vice president, he paused kind of funny like, but then admitted he too had been blackmailed. When Cutcliffe asked about his letters, he didn't seem to have any details."

"Could it be that the nature of the details was something Kramer didn't want to share," Kate suggested, knowing how adamantly the vice president had denied the affairs. "His was rather life-altering and seems to fly in the face of everything he stands for."

"I had considered that, but when we asked him if he contacted the other women to warn them, he said no. We were all willing to show each other the proof that this is occurring. I don't believe Kramer will be that forthcoming with you."

Kate was sure that he wouldn't be. "I'll cross that bridge when I come to it. Is there any other reason you don't trust him?"

Senator Yates stared at her long and hard before she said, "He's armed, Agent Walsh. Vice President Kramer came to this meeting with a gun stashed in his luggage. What does he need that for when he has the Secret Service? Of course, we were surprised that he came with less than half his Secret Service detail. No one can seem to explain why that's happened and now we are paying a price for it. But he's armed himself instead of using the security that's been provided for him. I find that curious."

"Did you see the gun?"

"No," she said in a clipped tone. "But I heard about it and that was enough for me."

Kate tucked that info away for later. "What are you saying? Do you think Vice President Kramer might be responsible for some of this?"

"Some of it?" she said with a laugh. "I think he's responsible for all of it."

"How would that serve him?" Kate asked, still not understanding what the motive could be if it was the vice president. He was already in power and had everything he needed.

"Oh, you don't know," Senator Yates said and Kate shook her head. "His wife has bankrupted him. They are lucky they are living in the vice president's mansion otherwise they might be living on the street. He's got nothing left. They are broke."

Kate hadn't heard that before. "How do you know that?"

Senator Yates picked up the glass and sipped. Over the rim, she watched Kate's reaction to the news. "Agent Walsh, everyone in Washington D.C. knows that. Vice President Kramer has consistently made bad investments and his wife has a serious shopping addiction. It's common knowledge."

"You think he's blackmailing all of you for the money then?"

"Partly, but I think it's something more sinister than that."

Kate raised her eyebrows in a question.

"He wants influence over all of us. Consider who is out there in that room. You reach just about every sector of the vote – both sides of the aisle and senatorial leaders on major issues. Not to mention, leaders on several committees. If he has those senators in his pocket, Kramer wields far more power than most vice presidents."

Kate sat back, surprised by the admission. She hadn't considered that before. If she were being honest with herself, even though she had her suspicions about the vice president, Kate hadn't seriously considered the implications or motive of Vice President Kramer being the blackmailer. It didn't seem feasible to her. Someone else would have to be involved. She sat there tight-lipped considering all the angles.

"You don't believe me?" Senator Yates asked after a moment of quiet.

Kate raised her head and looked over her. "It's not that I don't believe you. I have suspicions about Kramer. I was just trying to figure out how he'd pull off something like that. It seems to me that someone would have to be helping him. It's not like Kramer can sneak away from the Secret Service and pick up the blackmail payments or even mail the letters. Someone is always with him. Either he's sending someone to do that for him or it's not him."

"I'd speak to his aide, Nathan Channing. He's always at the vice president's side. If there is anyone that I think would be helping him, it's Nathan. He's been with him since his days in the Senate."

Kate knew Nathan was older than some of the other aides. She'd bump Nathan up on the list of those whose background she needed to investigate. Kate flipped through the evidence Senator Yates had given her from the blackmailer and asked a few questions that didn't provide more than she already knew. At the end, Kate asked, "Is there anything else you want me to know? Anyone else you don't trust?"

Senator Yates stood and took one long sip of the soda until the glass was empty. "I don't trust any of them, Agent Walsh, and you shouldn't either. Each one of those people is out for their own gain and to cover their backsides. They'd hand over the lot of us if it meant protecting themselves. They'd do anything to remain in power." She started to walk toward the door and then turned back to Kate. "Anything," she said again, stressing the word. She left her empty glass on the bookcase closest to the door and then stepped out into the hallway.

"Wait," Kate said, yelling her name. "Let me walk you back to the living room."

Senator Yates allowed Kate to walk her back to the living room with the others. She asked Senator Bailey to come with her. Kate spent the next half hour going over all his evidence and didn't learn much more. After that, it was a revolving door of senators until it was the vice president's turn. She asked Michael to bring him to her when the last senator left.

Michael returned empty-handed. "He won't meet with you, Kate," he said evenly and closed the library door behind him. "He also refuses to show you any of the evidence. Kramer said you had the rest and didn't need what he had."

"Senator Yates told me Kramer would do that. She doesn't trust him." Kate knew she was divulging something she shouldn't but it was just to Michael. She gestured for him to sit. After checking on his arm and being assured he was fine, Kate asked, "Michael, do you think there is any way that Vice President Kramer is behind the blackmail?" Michael expressed the appropriate amount of shock Kate would have expected. There was more he wasn't saying. She pressed him. "There is either something more you know or something you're not sure of that you don't want to say. I need you to say it now."

"I don't know what more to say." Michael folded his hands in his lap and gave Kate a sympathetic smile. "I'd tell you if I knew. If I suspected Kramer was involved, I'd tell you. You said you found that gun. Do we know if it ties back to anyone?"

"I assume the vice president. Senator Yates said she heard he had a gun with him," Kate said with more force than she had intended. She waited for Michael to respond.

"That's not true, Kate. She's lying to you or she's misinformed. I've never known Kramer to have or to handle a gun. I'm not even sure he'd know how."

"What if one of you is involved?" Kate knew leveling that kind of accusation without any facts to substantiate it against the Secret Service crossed a line. She couldn't help it, she wanted Michael's reaction to it. She was disappointed though because he remained stone-faced.

"They'd have to be very good at lying to me," Michael said and then considered. What struck Kate the most was that he didn't seem surprised by the idea. "That would mean Kramer lied to me and sent me to drop off blackmail money to keep the ruse going while enlisting one of the agents who I supervise to help him pull it off."

"Maybe we got it wrong and that's why Matt was killed. Maybe Kramer is cleaning house and getting rid of those who helped him." It was such a stretch that Kate felt silly even saying the words aloud.

It was no laughing matter when Michael looked her dead in the face and said, "It's hard for me to believe that could be true, but at this point, anything is possible."

# CHAPTER 23

Kate didn't have time to react to Michael because both of them were on their feet as Declan burst through the library door. His face was flushed and his eyes wild. "You are not going to believe what I just found out." He crossed the room holding his phone out so Kate could see the photo. "Look at this. I don't know what this means but we are getting closer, Kate. I can feel it."

She wanted to tell him to calm down, worried about how Michael might react to Declan's outburst. When she looked down at his phone though she had no idea what he was going on about. "Who is this, Declan?" She knew it was Ditch but she had no idea who the man was that he was meeting with in the photo.

Declan jabbed his finger down on the screen. "That is Conner Fitzgerald and this is taken from the surveillance video at the hotel right after Ditch arrived, before Spade requested that he come here. The conversation that the clerk overheard was between them, Kate. This is proof that not only was Ditch here before Spade ever sent him, it's proof that he knows and is working with Conner Fitzgerald."

Kate brought the photo closer to her face. It was the kind of grainy photo that had been taken from a video. It wasn't a closeup shot but rather from a ceiling in the corner of the room. She could easily make out Ditch because she knew him, but the man he was with was harder to pinpoint. If Declan thought it was Conner Fitzgerald, she couldn't argue with it. She handed the phone to Michael, explaining their connection to Ditch. "I didn't want to explain in the room with everyone that Ditch works for the FBI."

"Probably smart to keep that to yourself for now," Michael said as he glanced down at the photo. "That's Conner Fitzgerald."

Kate looked at Declan. "Does Conner Fitzgerald make it more or less likely that Ditch is involved in this?"

"More," Declan said, stressing the point. "What more evidence do you need that Ditch is up to no good?" he asked Kate who didn't have an answer for him. "I know that you don't want to admit that he could be involved in this, Kate. We need to go interview him."

"I should do that alone," she said nearly holding her breath while she waited for Declan's reaction. She expected him to blow up or tell her she wasn't being objective. He surprised her.

"That's fine by me, but I'm going to the hotel with you. I'm not leaving you alone with him."

Kate knew they'd need to leave the house. "What about security here while we are gone?"

"Barry and I can handle it," Michael said, and then added, "Stanton is here in case we need anything." When he saw the worry on Kate's face, he reassured her. "It will be fine. Everyone is staying in the living room. If anyone needs to leave, either Barry or I can escort them. You'll be back as soon as you can."

Kate didn't feel like she had any choice but to agree. She collected all the files that the senators had provided her. "I'm going to take these with me and create a profile as soon as I can."

Before they left, Stanton returned their clothes that were washed and dried. They changed and put their rain gear back on. Kate checked the weather before leaving and to see the road conditions. They had to drive along State Road back to Oak Bluffs to the hotel where Ditch was staying.

"He's in a carriage house behind the main building," Declan explained once they were in his SUV.

"That should give us some privacy. When was he seen inside with Conner?"

"When he checked in apparently." Declan took his eyes off the road to look over at her. "I know you don't want to believe that Ditch could be involved. Please keep an open mind when you interview him."

"I always do," Kate said with an edge in her voice. "Please don't second guess my objectivity."

Declan didn't respond but turned his head to keep his eyes on the road. Stiffness was creeping into Kate's shoulders and neck. That's where she held all her tension and she was starting to feel like they were spinning their wheels with this case. They were no closer to finding a killer than when they had arrived. The blackmail gave them a better understanding of it all, but it didn't narrow down the possibilities.

Kate flipped open the first file that Senator Yates had provided and read through the letters. They were the same style of writing that had been sent to Senators Abbott and Cutcliffe. The series of letters were the same too, starting with basic blackmail and then growing with threats later on. Kate went through each file and read the first of the letters for each senator. They all started the same way. *Dear Senator – you have been keeping secrets and it's time you're exposed for the fraud that you are. No one can hide in the shadows forever. I am your judge and jury.*

The blackmailer called themselves the judge and jury in each letter but did not close the letter with any salutation. They did not call themselves anything, which surprised Kate. The requests for money came in twenty-five thousand and fifty-thousand increments. Each letter had a request. All the drop-off places were around Washington D.C. – all in the northwest quadrant, which was the seat of power of government. It was where everything was located including the National Mall and major landmarks, Smithsonian museums and the

White House.

Kate wasn't sure if the blackmailer was making it easy for the senators to drop off the money or if they were mocking them by operating right under their noses. It might have been both. Each letter also demanded that they do not go to the FBI or local law enforcement and that any hint that they had would result in exposure and deadly consequences.

Kate rested the pages on her lap and turned her head to look at Declan. "Does it strike you as odd that the blackmailer never exposed Senators Cutcliffe and Abbott? They went straight to murder. It says here the blackmailer was willing to do both. With most blackmail cases we see, exposure is the first step and they rarely resort to violence, even if they aren't paid. Usually, exposure is enough to satisfy them."

Declan shifted his eyes to her. "Maybe it wasn't about blackmail all along. It's possible murder was the ultimate plan and the blackmail was a way to get money from them first – kill two birds with one stone, so to speak."

It didn't make much sense to Kate. "They could have easily killed off each senator in D.C. It would have been much easier to get them on a morning jog or even in their home. How would the blackmailer even know that he'd be able to get them all alone out here with lax security during a hurricane?"

"It's got to be an inside job, Kate. Someone arranged all of this and was pulling the strings from the inside."

"Then how do Ditch or Conner Fitzgerald factor in? They couldn't have set this up, so what you just said doesn't match them as suspects." Declan didn't respond to that, not that Kate needed him to. They were going round and round about Ditch's involvement because they didn't have any other viable suspects. It was easy to focus on the low-hanging fruit and Ditch tended to make himself look suspicious.

What Declan said about murder being the ultimate motive rang true for Kate. There was something this killer wanted and Kate wasn't sure what that was. The killer used a gun in each murder. It was done without a level of passion. They were cold and remote. It could be a hired contract killer as they had suspected. They had gotten away from Declan after all and dared to shoot at the FBI and Secret Service Agents.

"Ditch wouldn't try to kill me," Kate said absently almost to herself.

"What?" Declan asked absently as he slowed down at a traffic light. There were few cars out in the storm and the light changed quickly to green. "What does that mean?" he asked again when Kate didn't respond.

"If Ditch is involved in this, then he must have been okay with someone trying to kill me and I don't think he'd be involved in that."

Declan took a breath and let it out slowly, not arguing with her. "We are almost there. Do you know what you're going to ask him? I know we aren't walking in with much evidence but don't let him off the hook easily."

"I won't," Kate promised as she thought about the letters. The blackmailer seemed well-educated and it took a lot of time and planning, even possibly some money. While Kate thought the blackmailer was toying with the senators by operating right under their noses, she didn't get the sense that like some killers they wanted any notoriety or credit for their crimes. The act of getting away with it seemed enough for them.

Declan parked the car in a space on the road in front of the small boutique hotel. The street was nearly empty and most of the shops were closed and dark. Kate got out of the car, her foot landing in a sizeable puddle. She shook the water free, pulled her hood up on the windbreaker, and ran towards the front porch of the hotel, trying to get out of the rain as quickly as possible. Kate waited for Declan who seemed to be taking his time scoping out the area.

He pointed down the driveway toward the back of the property. "Back there, Kate. It's the small carriage house in the back." He joined her up on the porch. "What do you want me to do while you're meeting with Ditch?"

"Can you go inside and see if Conner is staying here? I'd like to interview him as well. It's suspicious that he's here but cuts down on our work. I thought it might be difficult to track him down."

"Do you want me to interview him or just hold him until you can interview him?"

"Interview him," Kate said. They had no reason to hold anyone right now and they might as well take any chance they got even if it wasn't ideal. She told Declan a few of the questions she'd want to be answered and then dashed off the porch toward the back of the property.

The small carriage house's blue front door was covered by a small overhang. Two windows sat adjacent to the left of the door. A light was burning bright inside. She rapped her knuckles against the door and contemplated calling Ditch's name. She remained quiet hoping he'd just answer. She knocked again and waited.

Ditch pulled the door open a moment later. He was wearing a white long-sleeved shirt, gray sweatpants, and thick orange socks, which were a striking contrast to the rest of his attire. He towel dried his hair as a smile spread across his face. "Come on in out of the rain, Katie," Ditch said, calling her the nickname that normally only Declan used and stepping back and letting her in. As Kate entered, he moved quickly through the living room and disappeared down a hallway.

He came back a moment later, carrying a thick white towel. "Dry off. It's miserable out there." Ditch left her by the doorway and went into the small living room area and plopped down on the couch. He patted the seat next to him. "I have a nice little fire going. Come on over and let me warm you up."

Kate peeled the wet windbreaker off and used the towel to dry the rest of her. She was forced to kick off her sneakers otherwise she'd track water and dirt onto the floors. She joined Ditch in the living room but didn't sit down. "I'm not here for a social call, Ditch. I'm not even here to go over case information. I'm only here for one reason."

"What's that? Did Declan leave you and you need a new partner?" Ditch asked with a laugh.

Kate stood with her hands on her hips. She wasn't in the mood for his flirting. "I want to know why you arrived on the island hours before Spade asked you to come here. We know you checked out of your hotel in New York City and then took the train to Boston and the ferry over. Why were you here before you were requested to be here?"

Ditch slumped back in the seat, watching her. "You know about that." It was stated as fact not an admission of guilt. He didn't seem particularly bothered by the fact that she knew.

"We know that and a lot more, Ditch. Declan thinks you're the blackmailer."

"I'm not the blackmailer, Kate. I haven't had anything to do with what's happening," Ditch said evenly, seeming nonplussed by the mention of a blackmailer. The thing that stuck out to Kate was that he hadn't asked *what blackmail*. "I know Senator Taft mentioned me. Spade already asked me about that. It was a long time ago, Kate. Long before I started working with the FBI."

"Did Spade tell you about the blackmail? We only found out about it after we arrived."

Ditch raised his eyes at her. "Do you want the truth or the lie, Katie?"

Kate cursed in an exhaled breath. "I always want the truth, Ditch."

"Then you better get comfortable."

# CHAPTER 24

"What have you gotten yourself involved with, Ditch?" Kate asked wearily as she sat down in the chair across from him. "Don't you dare lie to me. If you're in trouble, I need to know that right now."

"I'm not in trouble. I promise you that." Ditch locked his blue eyes on her, staring intently. "You may not like what I've done but I assure you it's nothing illegal. It does relate to your case though."

"Senator Taft?" she asked with eyebrows raised.

Ditch shook his head. "Conner Fitzgerald. He goes by Fitz, which is how most people know him. Do you know the name?"

"He was a Metro homicide detective who took over from John Huntly."

"That's correct. Fitz came to me because someone hacked into his system, which he thought was so secure it couldn't be hacked. That was his first mistake. His second was keeping all that data he had on a server."

"Data? You mean opposition research he was doing for his clients?"

"Unfortunately, yes. He digitized all of Huntly's old records, so there was information going back forty to fifty years on there and the hacker got everything." Ditch opened his arms wide as if to say, it happens. "Fitz was too cocky. He had good security but this hacker was better. Not long after the hack, he heard through the D.C. grapevine that

Senator Cutcliffe was being blackmailed. He had just done some research on him for a client."

Kate shook her head not understanding. "He wasn't up for reelection. Why would a client be asking for research on him?"

"It wasn't that kind of client, Kate," Ditch said, leveling a look at her that Kate didn't understand. When she pressed him, he said, "Fitz doesn't just do opposition research like John Huntly did. Fitz expanded the business and is a bit of a D.C. fixer."

"What does that mean? Does he do illegal things?"

Ditch wouldn't meet her eyes then. He shrugged off the question. "He does what he has to do."

Kate was trying to put two and two together but it still wasn't adding up. "I don't have time to play games. Yes or no. Do you know who hired Fitz to research Senator Cutcliffe?"

"I know," Ditch said.

"Then tell me," she demanded with anger in her voice. Kate could feel the heat rise against the back of her neck. He was being purposefully evasive and it was testing her last ounce of patience.

"I can't, Kate. Fitz has confidentiality agreements with all his clients. This isn't my information to share."

"Ditch," Kate said sternly. "If you know the client, then I can know the client. We are on the same team."

Ditch still shook his head. "Kate, the only reason I know is that I was doing some work for him and it was among some of the data that was lost."

"You're not allowed to be doing work for anyone outside the scope of your work at the FBI."

He gave her an impish smile. "That's why I'm hoping you don't say anything to Spade. Fitz didn't know who else to turn to. He got my name and knew I'm the best around. He had no idea I was working for the FBI. We struck up a little deal and I'll get a big payout when I find the hacker. I put in better safeguards and was trying to retrace the hacker's steps in the hopes of identifying him. I haven't so far if you're curious. That's why I was here. I got a lead on the hacker and met Fitz. Then Spade called and said there were two high-profile murders and you might need my support. I didn't know how to tell him I was already here since he thought I was in New York City."

"Are you telling me it's all a coincidence that you were here?" Kate asked, not believing what she was hearing.

"I don't think it's a coincidence. I think the hacker is the one who stole the information and is using it to blackmail the senators," Ditch said as if he couldn't believe Kate hadn't thought of that sooner. "When Spade mentioned Senator Cutcliffe had been murdered, I thought about the blackmail the client mentioned. I assumed it was happening to the rest of them given the data breach."

Kate didn't think he was lying. She wasn't happy that he was doing side work and Spade would come down on him hard if she told him. "You don't know who the blackmailer is though?"

"If I knew that I wouldn't be here. I don't know for sure that the hacker and the blackmailer are the same person, but it's a high likelihood that they are working together."

"Who is better than you?" Kate asked and she watched his face fall.

"I wouldn't say better. I'm the best there is, but Fitz's hacker did a good job of covering their tracks. It's taken me a while to even get an IP address for them and I traced them here to Martha's Vineyard, which didn't make a lot of sense to me."

"Do you have a specific address here on the island?"

"Coffee shop down the road. Before you ask, no they don't have cameras. I already called. I thought it was kind of pointless to come here but Fitz wanted to check it out." Ditch got quiet for a moment. "I don't know, Kate. I told Fitz that just because we found this address, it didn't mean the hacker was ever here. There are a lot of ways to block your real IP address or reroute the information. Fitz still wanted to be here."

"Do you trust him?"

Ditch shrugged. "I don't have any reason why not to." He squinted over at Kate and rubbed his jawline. "You don't think Fitz is the blackmailer, do you? He cares too much about his business. Besides, if he did something like that and anyone found out, he'd be ruined."

"Is he having financial difficulties?"

Ditch laughed and shook his head. "Are you kidding me? That guy is loaded. He just bought a house in Chevy Chase, some crazy five-thousand-square-foot monstrosity. It set him back millions and he paid cash. If he's involved, it's not for the money. Fitz has a good thing going. I don't think he'd risk it."

Kate believed Ditch was telling her the truth. "Someone tried to kill me and a Secret Service agent. We have four murders now – the two dead senators, a Secret Service agent, and one of the aides. We don't even have a viable suspect."

"Where's your sidekick?" Ditch asked, looking toward the door. "Do I need to be worried about him charging in here and knocking me out?"

"Probably," Kate said and finally cracked a smile. "He thinks you're involved in this and he wasn't wrong. You're just not involved in the way he thought you were."

"You going to rat me out?"

"Declan and I don't keep secrets from one another, especially on cases. That isn't the way partnership works."

Ditch cursed softly. "I might as well tell Spade myself then. I don't need Declan holding this over my head. He's such a hypocrite..." Ditch didn't finish his thought. He stood and went to the back of the cottage. Kate assumed toward the bedroom. He came out carrying his cellphone.

"Why don't you wait on calling Spade," she said softly. "I'll make sure Declan doesn't tell Spade and gives you a chance to do that." Kate locked her gaze on him. "You have to tell Spade though. I can buy you some time but that's about all you're getting if you agree to help us."

"What do you need?" Ditch asked, slipping his phone into his pocket.

"I need to know everything Fitz told you, even if he said it was confidential. For all we know, one of his clients is the blackmailer. They might have seen the kind of information that Fitz can find and then sought the help of a hacker to get the rest." Ditch didn't seem convinced but Kate continued. "Ditch, think about this. The client comes to Fitz and gathers as much information as they can by going through his process. They ask questions about what kind of information he can gather and how he goes about it. Maybe they ask how far back he can get information or if he interviews friends and family of the subject of the investigation. All the while, this client is playing him and hiring him basically as a ruse. Maybe they are even meeting in his office and learning the lay of the land."

Ditch considered it for a few moments. He admitted, "I didn't think of that. Fitz is a smart guy and has good instincts, but if someone is coming to him as a client, he might not suspect."

"Where is he now?"

Ditch hitched his thumb over his shoulder. "Back in the main part of the hotel. He has a suite up on the top floor. They had openings given the hurricane. That was the other reason I thought Fitz was crazy for wanting to come here now. We should have waited until the storm passed. He wants to find this hacker, Kate. It's his livelihood and driving him crazy."

"What have you been doing since you arrived?"

Ditch held his arms wide. "You're looking at it. There's not much to do. We spoke to the owner of the coffee shop but it's closed like everything else. I've been working on another case that Spade asked for my help on and trying to review more of Fitz's breach to track down the hacker. Haven't made much progress with anything. The Wi-Fi also keeps going out and the signal is weak."

Kate relaxed back into the chair. She had known in her gut that Ditch wasn't going to double-cross them no matter what Declan might have suspected. He was right not to fully trust Ditch given his extracurricular activities. She chose at that moment to share information with Ditch. "Each of the senators has been blackmailed as well as the vice president but he won't show us any of the blackmailer's correspondence with him." Kate wanted to share that they had found a gun outside of the vice president's room, but she didn't want to give away the whole farm.

"Are you close to creating a profile on the blackmailer?" Ditch asked, looking at Kate with hope in his eyes. She was sure that if she had a profile of the blackmailer, it might also help him find the hacker. When Kate confessed that she wasn't even close, he asked, "What senators are being blackmailed? I've seen all the info that was stolen from Fitz. I can confirm if there is information about them that was stolen."

Kate didn't want to tell Ditch the senators' secrets. She held that back while answering his question. "There are seven in all. Senators Abbott and Cutcliffe are dead. The remaining five are Senators Yates, Stone, Harrison, Bailey, and Taft. They are each being blackmailed for something specific in their backgrounds."

"Senator Bailey's blackmail isn't in his past. He still has a wicked gambling addiction."

"How do you know that?" Kate asked.

"It's part of the files that Fitz has. We discussed it because he was concerned about the data that was stolen. He was probably most concerned about Senator Bailey because it's active information. As you said, the rest of them it's the past." Ditch got up then and walked to the back of the cottage, leaving Kate to sit there alone. While he was gone, Kate checked her phone and sent a quick text to Declan to bring Fitz back to Ditch's cottage because she thought they should all meet. He responded almost immediately that he'd be there soon.

Ditch came back carrying one of his laptops and a mug of something with steam rising above it. He handed Kate the cup. "I had some coffee brewing and you look like you could use some. Sit on the couch with me and I'll show you what I've uncovered from Fitz's hack."

Kate sipped the coffee, grateful that he had thought of it. She stood and followed him to the couch. "I asked Declan and Fitz to join us. I figured we'd all better get on the same page right now." Kate wasn't sure she should say what was on her mind but thought if she was going to say it, now would be the time. "Try not to antagonize Declan when he's here. Remember you're on the same team. Also, I know that you've been working with Fitz and he's former law enforcement, but I don't trust him, so don't expect me to. Understand?"

"You'll get no arguments from me." Ditch turned his head to her slightly and smiled. "But you know I don't do anything to antagonize Declan. My mere presence does that."

That was partially true. "Don't call me Katie. It sets him off."

Ditch laughed. "Okay, okay. I won't call you his cute little nickname for you. You two do it yet? You've got all this bubbling sexual tension. I'm sure that's half the reason Declan is so miserable. Just bang one out and put the poor man out of his misery already."

Kate felt her cheeks warm. "It's not like that, Ditch." That's all she'd say about that. She barely knew what was between her and Declan. She certainly didn't want to discuss it with anyone else. The one thing she knew for sure though was it wasn't crass like Ditch had described. It never would be between them. They'd be all in or not at all. Kate couldn't imagine a middle ground if they crossed that line.

A knock and then the door creaking open interrupted her thoughts.

Declan stepped in first followed by Fitz who took up most of the doorway. Kate had only ever seen him on television. He had dark hair cut close to his head, a scruff of a beard, and intense dark eyes. He also stood a few inches taller than Declan's six-foot and had probably thirty pounds more muscle. He was a beast of a man and not at all what Kate had been expecting.

"Agent Walsh," he said, stepping toward them. He locked his gaze on Kate and for the first time in a long time, she felt small and wholly feminine under his gaze. "Agent James filled me in about what's happening. I'm sorry that my work has caused such a thing. You have to know it wasn't intended. I thought my server was secure."

"Of course," Kate said, feeling uncomfortably disarmed by him. "We don't know for sure that your hack is the cause, but it's certainly a possibility. Ditch has filled me in some but we have more questions."

Fitz sat in the chair taking up the whole thing. "I'm at your disposal."

# CHAPTER 25

The cottage suddenly felt too small for the four of them. Kate was also aware that Declan watched her closely as she interacted with Fitz. He remained near the door and didn't sit down with the rest of them.

"Fitz admitted to me that his server was hacked and that he employed Ditch to find the hacker," Declan said, keeping his line of sight on Kate.

Kate nodded. "Ditch told me the same and that it was Fitz who requested Ditch meet him here." She turned her attention to Fitz. "Ditch explained to me that you cannot share much because of the confidentiality you have with your clients. I'm concerned that one of your clients might have come to you only to learn your process and the kind of information you can uncover to see if hacking your system would be worth the effort."

Fitz cleared his throat and gave a curt nod. "I considered the same. What do you need to know from me? As I told Agent James, I'm willing to forgo the confidentiality of my clients without forcing the FBI to get a search warrant. I know people will look down on the work that I do, especially stepping away from law enforcement to take on this work. I feel passionate that we have a right to know the background, even the secrets, of those we are putting in charge of the country. I just never expected that my work would get people killed."

Kate went over the last question she had asked Ditch about the information on the specific senators involved. As Kate mentioned each name, Fitz gave a nod of his head. When she was done, she said, "Vice President Kramer is also involved. He did not share with me what the blackmailer sent but did mention that they had accused him of being romantically involved with several women. Is that information you uncovered?"

Fitz seemed surprised by the information. "I've never investigated the vice president. No one ever asked me to do that. Kramer was one of my clients from the last election. He asked me to uncover dirt on his opponent, which he used during the election."

"Kramer denies that it's true but he did pay the blackmailer, so I'm not sure what to believe."

Fitz asked, "You have proof that he paid?"

"According to Michael, the head of his Secret Service detail. I trust him." Kate looked up at Declan and he echoed the same. "One of the Secret Service agents was shot and killed and the other…" Kate trailed off because she still wasn't sure how she felt about Barry. She had lost trust in him over the small lies he had told. Kate explained that to Fitz and Ditch. "I'm just trying to get a handle on what's happening. The reason for their meeting this weekend was to strategize how to handle the blackmailer and figure out who it could be, but they haven't made much progress. We haven't made much progress either," she said with an edge of frustration in her voice.

Declan added, "Part of the issue is that they weren't forthcoming from the start. It was one of the aides who told us about the blackmail. Kate had to confront them about it."

"After I didn't give them a choice, they started talking," Kate said softening her voice. "They didn't try to hide it, not that I gave them much choice. My goal was to find out how the blackmailer was getting the information. One of the senators mentioned John Huntly." Kate needed to challenge Fitz. She fixed her eyes on him. "I'll be honest with you. I had some doubts about your work and assumed it would have been easy for you to blackmail them. I don't know if you're someone I can trust."

Fitz seemed unfazed by Kate's admission. "You can trust me, Agent Walsh. I'd lose my business if I blackmailed the subjects of my investigations or my clients. As it is, I might lose my business if this breach comes to light. I've not made it public."

"The murders haven't been made public either," Kate echoed, trying hard not to believe Fitz. She wanted him to be guilty because it made the most sense. She could arrest him right now and call it a day. "I need to ask where both of you were today."

"We were here," Ditch said. "We met early for breakfast and then we worked in my cottage for the majority of the day. We only took a break about twenty minutes before you arrived."

Kate looked to Fitz who said the same thing. "Are you armed?"

"Always," Fitz said. "I haven't fired my weapon since I was at the range two weeks ago. I'd be happy to have you check. Is there a reason you're asking?"

"I didn't share with him what happened today, Kate," Declan said and then focused his attention on Fitz. He explained about the earlier shooting and following the trail down to the beach and the remote parking lot. "It's not just the senators and aides who have been targeted. It's been all of us. The vice president's security detail was cut for reasons we still can't understand and it's been a challenge to add local cops given the weather. We are working with our hands tied behind our backs."

Fitz pointed to Ditch's computer. "What were you doing when we came in?"

"I was about to go over your information with Kate," Ditch said and then paused as if waiting for an argument. When Fitz gave none, he continued, "I was hoping to compare the information you had on the senators with what we know about the blackmail. If we can confirm reasonably that the blackmail information came from your hack, we might be one step closer to solving both of our issues."

Fitz agreed with that. "We don't have anything on Vice President Kramer. As I said, he was a client but not the subject of an investigation."

Kate suggested, "The blackmailer could have come by it by other means. Ditch said you recently investigated Senators Bailey and Cutcliffe. I'd like to know who hired you to do that."

Fitz shifted in his chair uncomfortably. It was the first time Kate saw him look uncertain about how to proceed. He had projected confidence up until this moment. There was something in his eyes that told Kate he felt conflicted about sharing that information.

Declan saw it too. "We understand, Fitz, that you're breaking confidentiality, which is a death sentence in your line of work. If your clients can't trust you, then you're out of business. You said you wanted to help without us needing a search warrant. It's important to know who asked you to dig into these two senators."

"No, you're right. Nature of the business." Fitz sat back in the chair. "Senator Bailey's father-in-law requested that I look into his gambling debts. He had paid off one debt that was substantial and was concerned, and rightly so, that Bailey was continuing to gamble. Not only was his father-in-law concerned about his daughter's well-being but the gambling made Bailey a blackmail risk. I found that he was in deep for more than one-hundred-thousand dollars."

Declan whistled. "Is that before or after the debt the father-in-law paid?"

"After. Bailey never stopped betting on games and horse racing even after his father-in-law paid the debt. Bailey promised the family that he had stopped. He even went for counseling and joined a twelve-step program." Fitz frowned and shrugged. "The addiction was just too strong and the debts kept increasing."

"Senator Bailey admitted that he was using a bookie," Kate said and Fitz confirmed. "Could that be the source of the blackmail?"

"I wouldn't think so. The bookie is a low-level player in the mob. He'd be more about breaking kneecaps and taking a pound of flesh rather than an elaborate blackmail scheme."

Kate said she understood and then gave him a moment to tell her about Senator Cutcliffe. When Fitz didn't say anything, she asked, "Is there a reason you're hesitant to tell us about who wanted Senator Cutcliffe investigated?"

Fitz folded his meaty hands in his lap. "I feel a sense of loyalty to this client, probably greater than any client that has come to me given the nature of their concerns. It's a delicate situation and has far-reaching implications."

Kate realized then that neither she nor Declan had told him what they already knew about Cutcliffe. "We know that he was sexually harassing some staffers and that he had them sign non-disclosure agreements and paid them off. That happened around the time of the blackmail letters."

Fitz waited for a beat and then admitted, "My clients were one of the victims and someone close to Senator Cutcliffe. They had concerns that there were more victims and wanted to know the full scope of his abuse. They were trying to determine the best course of action but they were faced with an uphill battle."

"What were they going to do with the information?" Declan asked, sitting down in the chair opposite Fitz.

"Lawsuit. That's what they told me anyway. They had given me the contact of their attorney but I never called. The allegations were serious enough that I was willing to work with them even if it wasn't going to court. The victim was compelling."

"Allison Manning?" Kate asked.

Fitz shook his head. "Maven Vale and Chase Sims, who said he was Cutcliffe's top aide. They were credible, Agent Walsh. The information I found confirmed it too. There were at least twenty other victims who went on the record with me."

Kate shouldn't have been surprised but she was. "We were only aware of nine victims. When did they hire you?"

"Roughly seven or eight months ago."

Kate was surprised. "That was after Senator Cutcliffe had Maven sign a non-disclosure agreement."

Fitz smiled and had a hint of mischief in his eyes. "That's what angered her the most. She used his payment to her to fund my work."

For some reason that didn't surprise Kate. "What did you find during your investigation?"

"I found more than twenty victims," Fitz said his voice steady. "It wasn't hard actually. It seemed to be something people were already talking about. Even those who hadn't been victims had heard the rumors."

"Do you still have the attorney's name? I'd like to follow up with him. Maven is here this weekend and Chase is one of the victims."

"Chase is dead?" Fitz asked, his voice dropping an octave in surprise. When Kate confirmed, he ran a hand across his stubbled cheek. "He was a nice guy and seemed genuinely concerned that Senator Cutcliffe was doing this. Chase said that Cutcliffe needed to be stopped but he wasn't sure how to go about it other than finding all the victims and giving the evidence to an attorney."

"What about criminal charges?" Declan asked, looking between Fitz and Kate.

Kate knew that in sexual harassment cases, criminal charges were difficult. "Did it ever go beyond harassment?"

"Not that anyone would admit but I had my suspicions," Fitz said with frustration in his voice. "I wanted to be able to help them, Agent

Walsh. They had a compelling reason for wanting the information. Knowing the full scope of the senator's harassment also gave them the information they needed if they were going to pursue anything legally. You know these cases don't happen in a vacuum. Victims are not always believed. If one victim comes forward, it's generally swept under the rug. But when they come out in mass, it's harder to ignore. They were arming themselves with as much information as possible before going after the senator."

Kate had seen many cases go just that way. There was one caveat to all this that Fitz didn't seem to know. Kate explained, "We found the non-disclosure agreements with Chase's belongings. Is there any way he was playing both sides of the fence?"

Declan spoke up before Fitz could. "He might not have had a choice. Since the rash of cases that have come forward in Hollywood, the media, and beyond, those kinds of non-disclosure agreements aren't holding up in court. Legislation last year changed how they could be utilized. Chase was probably pressured to get the women to sign them. He could have just been doing his job."

Fitz shifted in his seat to fully face Kate. "Chase thought Senator Cutcliffe was suspicious of him and did it to test his loyalty. Chase was angry about what was happening to these young women. He said he had spoken up a few times to Senator Cutcliffe and told him that it wasn't okay what he was doing. Of course, he was shut down and his job was threatened. He worked hard and I know was looking for other jobs. In the meantime, he was going to do what he had to do to help these young women."

Ditch turned his attention to Kate. "If Chase was working to expose the senator and so was the blackmailer, it seems they'd be on the same side. It makes me wonder what got him killed."

That was exactly what Kate had been wondering.

# CHAPTER 26

On the drive back to the estate, Declan pulled over to the side of the road and parked. He kept the car running for heat but turned the wipers off and let the rain beat down on the windshield. It was coming in torrents, nearly sideways, and made visibility nearly impossible. Kate assumed he was stopping to wait for it to let up.

Declan took off his seatbelt and turned to her. "I want to talk before we go back into the estate. We need a plan of action." When she started to remind him of the plan they had just set in motion, he shook his head. "More than what we told Ditch. Yes, he can handle some of the background information on the aides and senators, but we need to decide what we are doing when we go back."

Before they left the meeting with Ditch, Fitz confirmed that all the information being used in the blackmail, except for the information on Vice President Kramer, was information that could have been pulled from his server. Ditch confirmed it was all part of the hack. He and Fitz asked what they could do to help. Kate didn't want Fitz anywhere near the investigation.

Kate had provided Ditch with a list of names and the little information she had already gathered about them. If Ditch could focus on that, she could focus on interviewing each of the senators again as well as the aides, and pressing them in a way she hadn't earlier. She had gone in trying to be friendly and garner information that way and she had succeeded to an extent. Now, it was time to get serious and make a few enemies if it meant getting to the truth.

Kate turned slightly to face Declan. "We have no way to confirm where they all were during the murders. I asked those questions already and tried to cross-reference and at night they were all in their rooms alone and during the day when Matt Pike and Chase were killed, they were all in the house. Everyone can tell me where they were but their memories aren't great about identifying the others with them or who left what room and when. I've tried being nice. I'm going to have to treat them all like suspects and interrogate them."

Declan agreed with that. "Where are we in understanding this crime? I think Fitz's breach started this whole thing or possibly what Senator Cutcliffe did. Do you think the two are connected?"

Kate understood what Declan was trying to do. He was trying to understand her thinking about the crime. He wanted to be a united front when they went back. Kate was in her head so much that she relied on Declan to initiate these conversations and she was grateful when he did.

Kate squinted her eyes and went through the possibilities before she spoke aloud. Finally, she admitted the truth. "I'm not sure which came first. It's kind of the chicken or the egg for me. Given we don't know who hacked the system, the blackmailer could have figured out what Senator Cutcliffe was doing and discovered that Chase and Maven went to Fitz. The idea could have sparked from there or the blackmailer could be one of the victims, so incensed by what happened to her that she wanted to expose everyone's secrets. I don't think Chase and Maven went to Fitz as a guise to learn more about his process to help the blackmailer though. That was a good theory but I don't put much stock in it now."

"I'd assume if it's one of the victims she would have had help."

Kate teased a smile. "Are you being sexist and assuming that a woman couldn't hack Fitz's server?"

Declan rolled his eyes and groaned. "Not at all what I meant. The shooter, Kate, was male. Yes, this mystery woman could have hacked the system, but she had help in pulling off the blackmail and the murders."

"I knew what you meant," Kate said, letting him off the hook. "It's certainly possible but there are only two other female aides besides Allison and Maven. I don't think it was Maven who did this and Allison seems too emotionally fragile. The other two didn't admit they were victims of Senator Cutcliffe when given the opportunity. They also weren't on the non-disclosure list in Chase's room. We should have asked Fitz for a list of the twenty names."

Declan sat back against the driver's seat and rubbed his brow with his eyes closed.

Kate could tell there was something more on his mind. "If you have a theory, tell me."

Declan opened his eyes and turned his head slightly to look at her. "It's not so much a theory. We are missing something. We know Senator Cutcliffe went after the aides. He was almost sixty-six years old, Kate. This behavior didn't start recently. We know that men who sexually harass have a long history of victims. Given how long he's been in the Senate, how many other victims do you think there are that we don't know about?"

Kate had considered that earlier. It was behavior he had probably been engaged in for a long time. "Countless. More than we'll ever know about. I'm also fairly certain it wasn't just the senatorial aides."

"What do you mean?"

Kate thought back on her earlier time at Harvard. She had her own experiences of sexual harassment as she was sure most women had. "Men who do this tend to prey on anyone they think will be weaker than them and it's not just people in lower positions than themselves. I'm sure Senator Cutcliffe had several aides and administrative staff, but we have to consider the possibility it went beyond that to his peers. There could be female senators who have experienced this." There was a catch of emotion in Kate's voice she had tried to hide.

Declan didn't miss it. He reached over and took her hand in his. "Are you speaking from experience?"

Kate had never told Declan anything about this. It was something she was equally ashamed of and embarrassed by, especially her reaction to it. "It was a professor when I was a senior and my parents were out of the country. Nothing ever happened, not for his lack of trying. He'd corner me in buildings and he even showed up at the house a couple of times. I never told anyone and I regret that."

"How did you respond to it?" Declan asked.

"I didn't." Kate glanced over at him and met his gaze. "I said I wasn't interested and made that clear. I started dressing as conservatively as possible, wore little makeup, and kept my hair up. I thought if I made myself as unappealing as possible, he'd stop. He didn't. It finally ended one night he showed up at the house, knowing my father wasn't there because he was an ambassador at that point." Kate smiled now thinking about it a little. "I flipped out, started screaming and yelling on the porch, and made such a scene the neighbors came out to check on me. He left immediately and told me in class the next day he was going to fail me and tell the dean I was mentally unbalanced. I made it clear to him that if he did, I would tell everyone. He said that no one would believe me. I don't know what came over me but I lied and said I had it documented and had a witness."

Declan pushed himself upright in the seat. "How did he respond?"

"He backed down and I graduated without him bothering me again." Kate didn't like thinking about her reaction to it because the guilt was still present to this day. "I didn't handle it correctly. I should have gone to someone the first time it happened or at least told someone later to keep him from doing it to other women."

"Kate," Declan said her name softly and with tender emotion. "You were twenty-two years old. It wasn't your responsibility to stop him from doing that to other women. You need to let it go."

Kate understood his sentiment and his efforts to be kind. It still fell flat for her given her experiences. She looked straight ahead at the rain hitting off the window. "You don't understand, Declan. Whenever a woman is assaulted either physically or verbally, it ends up being her responsibility. Why didn't she tell sooner? Why was she drinking or flirting? What was she wearing? Why didn't she tell him to stop making sexual comments? What did she do in the first place to encourage those comments? She must have liked it if he did it, right? Why didn't she put a stop to it immediately? She would have quit her job, dropped out of school, and totally rearranged her life if she didn't like it, right? Since the dawn of time, women have been made to be responsible for men's actions. Even when they do everything right, they are still responsible or at least made to feel that way by some. You heard Vice President Kramer in there. He said the very same things."

Kate grew quiet for a few moments and they sat there with the rain beating down. Finally, she turned to him and softly said, "Women are tired, Declan."

"Tired enough to fight back?"

Kate released a sardonic laugh. "Tired enough to kill." She said the words sarcastically at first and then as she sat with them, it started to make a certain kind of sense. She started considering all the players involved in the case and adding pieces together she hadn't considered before.

She sat upright sure of her conviction. "The senators that were chosen were targeted, Declan, and not because of their secrets."

"What do you mean?"

Kate wasn't sure how everything fit together, but she explained as she sorted it out in her mind. "Vice President Kramer and Senators Cutcliffe and Harrison were best buddies. The three of them served in the Senate together for years." Kate pulled her phone from her pocket and began furiously searching for the information she knew was there. It took her a few minutes while Declan remained quiet watching her. He knew that once Kate got something in her head nothing would deter her until she found what she was seeking.

"Right here, Declan," she said, handing him the phone. Kate jabbed her finger down on the screen. "Last year, two bills were introduced, one ending forced arbitration in sexual harassment and sexual assault cases and another targeting non-disclosure agreements that force workers to remain silent about sexual harassment and assault in the workplace. You alluded to one of these bills when we were with Ditch. Both were bi-partisan bills with support on both sides of the aisle that passed with ease. There were a handful of no votes though – some surprising. Can you guess who they were?"

Declan opened his eyes wide and pointed out the window toward the direction of the estate. "Everyone meeting this weekend?"

"Yes, every single one of them," Kate said punctuating her words. "There are a few others in the House, but they aren't here this weekend. It's just the senators."

It took Declan a moment to catch up with Kate's thinking. "I assume then the blackmail wasn't to get them to vote a certain way?"

"No. The senators are being targeted for voting no. The vice president was also a vocal opponent of the bill. I assume that's why he's being targeted too."

"The president was for the bill though, right?"

"Yes, she was and Kramer's vocal dissent of it created division. I don't know how he got the senators to vote no, but I'm sure of it now. He's the ringleader for the no votes."

Declan tapped the steering wheel with his hand. "When was the vote, Kate?"

She took the phone back and scanned through the article until she found the information. "The vote was a year ago, so a few months before the hack. The blackmail started six months ago," Kate explained, doing the mental math. It was a tight window but certainly possible for it to add up. "Understanding this doesn't get us any closer to the blackmailer and killer."

"No," Declan agreed. "It doesn't identify the killer but it's certainly the first plausible thing that makes sense. There's something I don't understand. Why would Vice President Kramer go to the trouble if the no votes were never going to swing the vote their way? There were far too many people in favor of this legislation. A handful of votes wasn't going to change the outcome."

"That I don't have an answer to," Kate admitted, knowing that was the main unanswered question in her theory. "It doesn't make a lot of sense on the surface unless it was some kind of power play or loyalty test. Everyone believes that Kramer is going to primary the president and that he was going to choose Senator Cutcliffe as a running mate. It's possible they tried to sway the vote to see who was on their side."

"It's underhanded politics at its finest," Declan said with an edge of disgust in his voice.

"Exactly and our blackmailer is trying to settle the score. It might be why they are being killed and no blackmail info is released. They are being targeted one by one."

"What about Chase and Matt Pike? They don't seem to fit the pattern. No one else has been killed."

Kate didn't have all the answers. "We limited the time people are alone. It might be that the killer can't strike without being caught right now. Chase got those young women to sign the non-disclosure agreements. Maybe the blackmailer doesn't realize what he was doing behind the scenes with Maven. Did you speak to him at any point while we were here?"

Declan nodded. "Briefly. He seemed genuinely concerned about what was happening and what we were going to do to protect them. I don't think either he or Maven had anything to do with the blackmail. I believed Fitz when he said they were trying to go a legal route to stop the harassment. It doesn't mean that the other victims were willing to be that patient."

Kate agreed with him. She recapped what they knew so far, laying out the evidence – the senators voting no on the legislation, Fitz's hack, Maven and Chase going to Fitz, and the blackmail and murder. "There is a connection point among them," she said sure of herself.

Declan took a deep breath and looked toward the estate. "Then that's what we need to find."

# CHAPTER 27

Kate breathed a sigh of relief when she made it back to the estate and found everyone where they had been earlier in the day. The senators and vice president were in the living room talking while the aides were in the dining room in front of laptops. It seemed they had not taken Kate's advice and all worked together as a team. The division was still there and probably always would be no matter what might work in their favor.

As Kate stood at the threshold of the living room, Michael tapped her on the shoulder. "Did everything go as planned?"

Kate turned and smiled up at him. "We figured out a few things. I need to speak to Senators Stone and Yates in the library together. Declan is going to try to interview Vice President Kramer. I'd like to but we decided he might respond better to a man. If it's possible, could you escort Kramer upstairs with Declan and leave Barry down here with the rest of them? I don't want Barry involved in the interview."

Michael stepped back from her. "Are there concerns about him?"

"Not anything more than before, but I trust you and don't trust him."

"Understood," Michael said and then assured her he could make that happen. "I'll take Vice President Kramer upstairs while you use the library."

Kate thanked him and then went back into the living room and asked Senators Stone and Yates to follow her. They both got up from their seats and left the room with Kate without asking any questions. They followed her back to the library and it was only once they were inside that the questions started.

"Did something happen?" Senator Yates asked with concern in her voice.

Senator Stone added, "Did you find the blackmailer?"

Kate didn't answer their questions. She took a seat and gestured for them to do the same. "I've uncovered some information that I feel relates to the case. I need both of you to help me understand the connection."

"Certainly," Senator Yates said, sitting. "Anything we can do to help."

Kate shifted her eyes between them. "I'm confident that there is more than one person involved in the blackmail and murder. It would be impossible for it to be just one person. I still believe there is someone here on the inside. I need to understand what Vice President Kramer used to get you both to vote no on the sexual assault and harassment legislation that passed last year." It was as if Kate had struck them both in the face. A look of shock and horror came over each of them.

"I didn't..." Senator Yates started to say. Kate reminded her that her voting record was a matter of public record. "There were things in the bill I didn't agree with."

"Same," Senator Stone echoed.

Kate shook her head. "I don't believe either of you. I can almost understand Senator Stone's vote. Your track record on voting for anything related to women is terrible, but this bill was co-sponsored by a colleague of yours who votes the same way you do every time. Most of your colleagues voted yes and it's something your constituents wanted. Senator Yates, you champion women's causes. This is the kind of bill that not only would you vote yes on, but I'm surprised you didn't co-sponsor it. I'm only going to ask one more time – why did you vote no?"

Senator Stone turned to Senator Yates and they shared a look.

Kate pressed again. "Help me to understand because it will help me solve the case. I need your honesty."

Senator Stone appeared resigned. "I was promised a cabinet position when the vice president became president. Kramer was going to primary the current president. They claimed she wasn't an effective leader. I know that I'm supposed to agree with them because I'm in the same party. However, I think the president is doing a great job. I wanted that cabinet position more."

Kate turned her eyes to Senator Yates. "I was promised the same." She held her hand up to stop Kate from speaking. "I know I'm not in the same party, but Kramer promised that he'd make the cabinet bi-partisan if he were elected."

If Kramer promised that for her vote, Kate didn't believe him for a second. "Kramer and Cutcliffe didn't threaten or blackmail either of you?"

Senators Yates and Stone shared a second look and both shook their heads.

Senator Stone said, "I wasn't blackmailed by them, I assure you. I was promised a cabinet position and I readily agreed to vote no."

"Agent Walsh, I did the same," Senator Yates said, crossing her legs. "You have to understand how much good I could do in the cabinet. I knew the bills would pass even without my vote. It was a win-win situation for me. Is that who you think is blackmailing us? They were both blackmailed too."

"No, I don't think it's them," Kate said evenly. "It's possible you're being blackmailed because of your no vote. Only the senators who voted no in the Senate are being blackmailed."

Senator Yates sucked in a sharp breath. She put a hand on her chest. "You think because I voted no, I was targeted for blackmail? Who would do such a thing? It was one vote and didn't mean anything. The legislation still passed."

Kate lost respect for Senator Yates justifying voting against her conscience for a cabinet position that probably wouldn't be given to her anyway. "The only senators who were targeted for blackmail voted no and, as you know, the vice president was out front of the bills talking about how they should be defeated. In light of Senator Cutcliffe's sexual harassment allegations, we need to consider that this might be the driving cause. I was informed that an investigation showed more than twenty recent victims. We also have no idea how far this kind of abuse goes back. You had to have known what Senator Cutcliffe was doing."

Senator Yates lowered her head.

"I knew," Senator Stone admitted, keeping her eyes averted. "It had been common knowledge among a handful of us for years. He'd been spoken to many times. I thought he had changed his ways."

"They don't change unless forced to," Kate said sharply, trying to stop her anger from bubbling to the surface. "Even then, I wouldn't trust them to change. You enabled Senator Cutcliffe and others like him. Then you supported his efforts to stop legislation that would help his victims."

Senator Yates gasped again and sank back on the couch. "I'm so ashamed."

"You were trying to get ahead and do what's right on a global stage," Senator Stone chastised her. "Don't listen to Agent Walsh, she doesn't understand how hard it is to make the decisions we have to make. You did what was right at the time."

Senator Stone might have been right that Kate didn't know what it was like to have their kind of power. If in a political office, Kate might have had to make similar hard decisions. The one thing she knew was she wouldn't have compromised her values and sold herself out for more power. "Senator Stone, you said that there were rumblings for years about Senator Cutcliffe. Do you know any of his victims?"

Senator Stone pursed her lips and lifted her nose higher to look down at Kate. "Why are you looking to dig up all this old dirt, Agent Walsh? The poor man is dead, murdered by someone you still haven't caught. Do we have to trash his reputation in death? Let it go already."

"Don't be so stupid!" Senator Yates shouted, turning her whole body to face Senator Stone. "Carley, what is wrong with you? You cannot protect him anymore – any of them. This has been going on for far too long." She held her hands out wide. "Don't you see where this has gotten us? People are dying because of this secret we've all been holding. It's time we come clean."

Kate sat on the edge of her seat, hoping they were finally getting to the heart of all of this. She nearly held her breath waiting for them to go on like she wasn't even in the room. Kate didn't dare speak now. She simply waited and wasn't disappointed.

Senator Stone pushed herself from the couch. She turned to Senator Yates and shook her finger at her like she was scolding a child. "There's no point to any of this. You need to keep what you know to yourself and this will all blow over. We've all done things in the past that we aren't proud of, but you pull yourself up and move on. Look at me. I made some bad business dealings. I admit it and can move on with my life. The statute of limitations has run out. I won't even be in legal jeopardy. What did you do that was that bad? Had a substance abuse issue? So do countless people across the globe. You could be a spokesperson for recovery at this point. You're going to throw your career away for nothing. We paid the blackmailer. We came up here for this stupid meeting. Now, let's leave and put it all behind us."

Senator Yates sat there for a moment. She closed her eyes and breathed deeply. Kate watched as the woman's chest rose and fell. After a few moments, her eyes suddenly opened. "No," she said, standing. "I'm not going to sit by anymore and keep this secret, Carley. We aren't getting out of this alive and all we've done is enable them, just as Agent Walsh said. Don't you understand that by now? There are four people dead. We can't just go back to D.C. and carry on with our lives. If the blackmailer wanted to expose our secrets, they would have done so already. I have no more money to give and neither did Senator Abbott, which is why she's dead. The blackmailer didn't expose her, he killed her!"

"It might not be the case for us," Senator Stone countered.

Senator Yates took two steps forward. She had frustration and fear on her face and she balled her fists tight. "Do you want to risk that? I'm not risking my life for this any longer. What Agent Walsh said about the vote proves what I've been saying all along. This is what the blackmailer wants – he wants us to atone for what we've done wrong. It's got nothing to do with our secrets but what we've been holding for someone else. We are protecting someone who shouldn't be protected and it's destroying all of us."

Senator Stone shook her head furiously back and forth. "You'd be throwing it all away. You have to know that. I've done too much good in my career to go out like this. No. No, Nancy. I'm not willing to go out like this because of the sins of another. We don't even know for sure what happened!"

"We know enough," Senator Yates said with resignation in her voice.

Kate was simply a witness to their argument but it was clear they were talking about more than sexual harassment. "What am I missing?" she asked.

Senator Yates turned to Kate and said a name. "Alexandria Bell. She went by Lexie and she was killed after a birthday party for Vice President Kramer three years ago during the presidential campaign."

"We don't know that she was killed. It was ruled a suicide," Senator Stone corrected and then sat down again. "If you're going to tell her, at least get your facts right."

"That's the problem. No one got the facts right. The official story is just that – a story. And everything was covered up." Senator Yates turned back to Kate. "This party was at a house in Bethesda. It was rented out for the party, which included a whole host of people including D.C. powerbrokers. You had the top echelon of Congress, lobbyists, lawyers, and everyone who wanted to make a name for themselves. There were also a few aides that were invited, mostly attractive young women who were trying to make it in that city. I went for a little while but the drugs and alcohol were overwhelming for me. If I wanted to maintain sobriety, I needed to leave. On my way out, I saw Lexie and tried to get her to leave with me or allow me to call a cab to get her home. She seemed drunk and unstable. That's when Senator Harrison said he'd make sure she got back safe. He led her back into the house before I could do anything. I should have gone after her but I didn't know."

Kate didn't know where the story was going but she had enough of a sense of it as her heart thumped in her chest. She pointed to the door. "Senator Harrison, who is out there?"

Senator Stone confirmed. "I saw Lexie that night. She was Senator Bailey's top aide. He tried to get her to leave after Senator Yates did. Harrison had a good grip on her hand and assured us she'd be fine. That's when she went into a separate room with Senator Cutcliffe and Kramer, a senator at the time who was running for vice president. That was the last we saw of her."

Senator Yates took a deep breath and let it out slowly. She locked her gaze on Kate. "By morning, Lexie was dead."

Kate wasn't sure what they were trying to say. "You think Kramer and Cutcliffe did something to her?"

"I'm sure of it," Senator Yates said. "Word had gotten around that Lexie was talking to a Washington Post reporter and was about to name names in one of the biggest sexual harassment scandals to ever hit D.C. Kramer, Cutcliffe, Harrison – they were all on the list, among others. The rumor was that Lexie had found victims going back years willing to come forward if she broke the dam and went first. I'm sure that's what got her killed."

"It was a suicide," Senator Stone said with anger in her voice.

"No." Senator Yates stood her ground. "We both know that it wasn't. One of those men killed her and all of us covered it up. We're paying for it now."

# CHAPTER 28

Kate steadied herself on the couch, unsure if she was hearing correctly. *Did a United States Senator just accuse the vice president and other senators of murder and a cover-up?* Kate composed herself quickly and stood. "I'm going to need more information because I don't understand anything you're telling me."

"Have you heard about Lexie Bell's murder?" Senator Yates asked sternly and then repeated the question when Senator Stone said again that it was a suicide. Regardless, Kate said she hadn't heard about any of it. Senator Yates went on. "You probably haven't heard about any of it because we all worked to cover it up. Each of us played a part. I denied knowing that Lexie had been sexually harassed by Senator Cutcliffe even though I saw it firsthand in the hallway one afternoon. That's what started it all."

"What did you see?" Kate asked, trying to process it.

Senator Yates nodded. "Senator Cutcliffe never hid the harassment from any of us. He didn't see anything wrong with it. I was walking down the hall and I saw them standing in his office doorway right in view of his secretary. He put his hand on Lexie's backside and squeezed hard while he pulled her close to him. He whispered something in her ear that made her blush and try to pull away. When the cops asked me about Lexie, I said that she was drunk that night and that she'd been known to cause trouble, which was true. It was trouble that needed to be caused. She was starting to fight back against them all and it terrified us. We had all encouraged Senator Bailey to fire her but he refused. Some of us assumed he was having a relationship with her but he denied that."

"I don't think they were having a relationship," Senator Stone said and chuckled. "He's too much of a wimp to cheat on his wife. I think he felt bad for Lexie and kept her on, putting us all at risk. Those freshmen senators don't know how to play the game yet. Too green to know the system."

Senator Yates ignored her colleague and focused her attention on Kate. "Shortly after what I saw with Senator Cutcliffe, the rumors started that Lexie was talking to a reporter with the Washington Post. There were also rumors that she had spoken to other women about the sexual harassment and was making a plan to break the story with the media. We were in the middle of a presidential election year. I was up for reelection too. I had seen what happened and didn't report it. I didn't know what she'd say about me. I was in as much jeopardy as the men who did this. Honestly, none of us could take the scandal."

Kate's rage burned hot as she turned to Senator Stone. "What was your role in this?"

"We're *really* doing this?" Senator Stone asked no one in particular. She threw her hands in the air. "Okay, fine. I pressured Lexie to keep her mouth shut. She was volatile but she was also incredibly bright and had a good future in politics if she just played the game a little more. I told her to ride out the election, but she didn't seem to care what was at stake for all of us. You would have thought she'd be happy with the first real female presidential candidate."

"The current president wasn't the first female candidate," Kate countered.

Senator Stone laughed. "She was the only one who had a shot at winning."

Kate thought that was debatable but she wasn't going to get into an ideological political fight. "Where were you the night of the party?"

"I was there and saw Lexie. I had pulled her aside and told her that she better keep her mouth shut or she'd have some trouble to face. Playing nice wasn't working, so I figured I'd turn up the heat. She had to know what she was going to face if she went public. You know what they do to women, Agent Walsh. They would have torn apart her past and every little thing she said and did. I was trying to protect her."

"How did Lexie respond to that?"

"Lexie said there was nothing I could say or do that was going to stop her and she was going to take us all down – those who harassed the young women and those who protected the harassers. As Senator Yates said, we were all at risk. It would have destroyed our careers."

"Your response to that?" Kate asked, knowing that Senator Stone wouldn't have accepted that answer with any kind of grace or goodwill.

Senator Stone looked Kate right in the eyes. "I deployed other measures."

"Which were?" Kate asked with an edge in her voice.

"I called the reporter and told him Lexie was unreliable and that nothing she said was true. I was willing to go on the record." Senator Stone stood firmly in the middle of the room staring Kate down.

Bile rose in Kate's throat. It was bad enough that men did this to women, but when faced with a woman who was willing to cut down another, Kate was filled with a different emotion – rage. "You were willing to go on the record and lie about Lexie?"

Senator Stone dared to smirk at Kate. "You might be younger than us, but you're a strong woman, Agent Walsh. You know how the game is played. You know this as well as we do. We've all been subjected to the odd flirty comment. We've all had to flirt a little to get ahead. I'm sorry these young women today don't understand how the game is played and want to tear down the whole system. These men don't mean anything by it. So what if you need to laugh and they get a little handsy? It's how it's been for women since the beginning of time. They think they are too good for it, so they whine and complain and go running to the media."

"Systemic, persistent sexual harassment isn't a game," Kate said coldly, wanting to snap at the woman and say what was really on her mind. Kate held her tongue, which was the hardest thing she had to do in an investigation. "I need to know about Lexie's death. Did it happen at her home? The party? Who was involved?"

Senator Stone sighed. "Look, the girl was troubled. Kramer, Cutcliffe, and Harrison spoke with her that night. Maybe she was scared and went home and realized how much trouble she was causing and killed herself. Maybe she realized this was a fight she was never going to win and all she did in the process was destroy her reputation. She was throwing away her entire career."

"Where and how did she die?" Kate asked again, her jaw clenched.

"An overdose of fentanyl in her apartment in Georgetown," Senator Yates explained, holding back emotion. "Lexie was not prescribed the medication nor was she known to take it. No one including her doctor, mother, or roommate had any idea that she had fentanyl in her possession. While the cops ruled it a suicide, her roommate believes Lexie was murdered. She said that when she came home that night, she was certain that someone else was in the home with them. She heard the back door open then close and she went in to check on Lexie. That's when she found her friend unconscious but not dead. Lexie died on the way to the hospital. There was a syringe lying next to her."

That didn't tell Kate much. It could easily be a murder. "Did the cops determine how Lexie got home that night?"

"Senator Bailey drove her home," Senator Stone said with a grunt. "He denied going inside with her, but everyone left at the party said they were all over each other before they left. He admitted to dropping her off, but he held firm that's all he did."

Senator Yates scoffed at that. "Who was left at the party to witness that? Kramer, Harrison, and Cutcliffe? I don't trust anything they have to say."

Kate would need to sort that out later. "What happened after Lexie made it back home?"

Senator Yates focused her attention on Kate and explained, "The neighbor told the cops they heard someone come home around one in the morning, which matches the time Senator Bailey said he dropped her off. The neighbors reported that they heard yelling from a man and a woman. They couldn't hear what was being said though. Then everything was quiet and the next thing they heard was a scream at quarter to two. It was when Lexie's roommate found her."

There was a forty-five-minute gap where anything could have happened. "What about the investigation after Lexie died?" Kate asked.

Senator Yates shrugged. "There wasn't one. None of the other victims of sexual harassment were willing to come forward after Lexie's death, especially given the suspicion around it. The story was effectively shut down. The cops didn't do much of an investigation of her death. The medical examiner ruled it a suicide fairly quickly – case closed."

Kate would need to follow up with all those details. There were things she still didn't understand. "Senator Yates, you said that you covered up a murder. You weren't even there when any of this happened."

She shook her head and wiped a tear from her eye. "As I said, I never told the cops about the sexual harassment. We closed ranks and never disclosed that Lexie was about to go public with the allegations. No one from the Washington Post came forward to the cops either.

Maybe the reporter got spooked because the official report was that Lexie killed herself.  Either way, I covered that up and as a result, the cops never dug deeper." She cast her eyes toward Senator Stone. "She had already told the reporter Lexie was unstable. Once the cops learned about Lexie's supposed instability from my colleagues, it was an open-and-shut case. We all covered up the truth."

Kate knew if the reporter hadn't come forward, it meant that they probably didn't have any suspicion about her death or they hadn't been working on the story for too long. Kate assumed the reporter didn't want to unduly insert themselves into a case. Kate also understood the men's role in this as well as theirs. "What about Senator Abbott? How was she involved in all of this?"

Senator Yates looked like there was something she wanted to say but remained tight lipped. Kate encouraged her to go on. Senator Yates licked her lips nervously. "There was a rumor going around that Lexie confronted Senator Abbott about rumors she had been sexually harassed by then Senator Kramer when she was first in the Senate. Lexie had asked her to go on record. Senator Abbott refused. She said she had a family and that it was all a long time ago.  She wouldn't confirm what had happened to her. Even after Lexie's death, she remained quiet.  I know accepting Kramer's offer to vote no in exchange for a cabinet seat was difficult but he promised her Secretary of Education. If you knew Senator Abbott, that was her life's work."

"That's the part that I don't understand," Kate said, raising her eyes to them, one and then the other. "Knowing all of this. Knowing about the sexual harassment and knowing about Lexie's death, you were still willing to dance with the devil. You were still willing to vote no on legislation that could have helped women just like Lexie. How could you do that?"

"You do what has to be done for the greater good," Senator Stone said, clearly feeling no shame in her decision-making.

Senator Yates slumped down on the couch and held her face in her hands. "I'd say I wasn't thinking clearly, but I was. I was thinking of myself and didn't consider how it would impact those young women." She raised her moist eyes to Kate. "Is that why we are being targeted?"

Kate had thought it was for their vote but now she wasn't so sure. "Do you know if any of those aides knew or worked with Lexie?"

"I'm sure a few of them had to," Senator Stone said but didn't offer more. She went back and sat down on the couch near Senator Yates.

"Maven might have known her. I'm sure Chase did but I can't say for certain. The rest out there are all fairly new except for Nathan Channing. He's been with Kramer since he was a senator. At the time of Lexie's death, there had also been rumors that the two of them were dating but Nathan said that wasn't true. No one else could confirm or deny it so it wasn't followed up."

"What about Lexie's roommate?  I assume if Lexie was dating someone that the roommate might have known."

"My understanding is that the roommate didn't give much of a statement and left town shortly after," Senator Stone said.

"Which was suspicious to me," Senator Yates added. "The roommate is kind of a mystery. I'm sure you can find her name in the police files but the bulk of her statement was that she arrived home, found Lexie, and called 911. She barely knew Lexie's family from what she said. I don't think they were friends, just roommates who probably didn't know each other that well."

Kate only had one question left for them and it was the most important. "You said by the night of the party, Kramer had already received the vice presidential nomination. As a senator, he wouldn't have had Secret Service protection, but when he was campaigning, he would have. Were there Secret Service agents at the party?"

Senator Stone remained quiet and it took a moment of recollection for Senator Yates to answer. "Michael wasn't on his detail yet, but

Matt Pike was there. He knew the rumors about Lexie."

Kate didn't show any emotion on her face when she heard that. She couldn't help but wonder if the murder of Matt Pike wasn't connected to the other murder three years ago. She stood and brushed her hands down her pants. "I'll walk you back to the living room."

"What's the plan now?" Senator Stone said but was met with only Kate's silence.

"Let's head back," Kate reiterated as she walked behind them out the door.

# CHAPTER 29

Kate waited until she was back in the library with Declan with the door not just shut tight but locked. She wasn't going to chance anyone barging in while she explained to him what she had just learned. They sat side by side on the couch.

"Did you find out anything from Kramer?" she asked.

Declan explained that the vice president at first refused to be interviewed. Michael had finally convinced him to go with Declan up to his suite and have a conversation. Kramer insisted Michael be there, which was fine with them both. "He didn't say much, Kate. He adamantly denies the affairs. I hate to say this, but I believed him. When I pressed and asked why someone would say such a thing, Kramer said that it was the single most damaging thing someone could say against him. It was the one factor that would tarnish his reputation among his base the most."

"That makes a certain kind of sense," Kate said evenly, even though with the allegations of sexual harassment she still didn't believe him. She wasn't going to fight Kramer's denials. There'd be no point when she had bigger fish to fry. "Was he willing to show you any of the blackmailer's letters?"

"He was," Declan said and pushed back on the couch. "The blackmailer didn't include any proof like he did with the others. It was all just speculation and the women named in the letters Kramer insists were friends and colleagues, nothing more."

"Did Kramer have any idea who was doing this to him?"

"He blamed everyone from the senators here this weekend to the president and her supporters." Declan breathed out all his frustration in one breath. "Kramer has no idea and said he doesn't have any more money to pay the blackmailer, but that the rumors cannot come up when he makes a play for the presidency. He'd do anything to stop it."

Kate couldn't think of any other time in history where a current vice president primaried a sitting president of the same party. "I don't know how all that is going to play out but we are dealing with a lot more than the blackmail."

Declan raised his eyebrows in concern. "Did Senators Stone and Yates come clean about something?"

"It's the sexual harassment, Declan. We were on the right track, but it goes further back. Have you heard the name Alexandria Bell? She went by Lexie."

Declan shook his head. "Is that a name I should know?"

"I didn't know it either." Kate spent the next few minutes detailing the entire Lexie Bell case from what the senators had told her. There were many gaps in the story and pieces she still needed to confirm. Declan's emotions were easily read on his face and reflected Kate's feelings when she heard the information. He went from surprised to concerned and then angry quickly.

When he calmed down, Kate continued. "It doesn't sound like suicide to me. There was enough motive to want to silence Lexie. Senator Stone even admitted that she had threatened her and told the reporter Lexie was unstable. It looks like all of them either knowingly or unwittingly set her up for murder."

Declan agreed with that. "Do you think Senator Bailey is involved since he was the last to see her conscious?"

Kate had no idea. "We are going to need to interview him. I want to speak to Nathan Channing first or possibly Maven and Allison. I don't know, Declan, this case is getting more complicated by the second."

Declan kneaded the tense muscles of her shoulders. "You've done some great work. If the case was in Georgetown that would be Metro police. Why don't you give Fitz a call and see if he knows anything about it."

Kate wasn't sure why she hadn't thought of that. She chalked it up to a lack of sleep. Instead of calling, Kate wanted to lean into Declan and let him continue to rub her shoulders. His touch was making her sleepy. She shooed his hand away with a good-natured laugh. "You're going to put me to sleep right here on the couch."

"I'll continue later tonight then," he said with a smile.

Kate returned the smile but was having trouble finding the right words to say. Her mind was a cloud of confusing thoughts. She pulled her cellphone from her pocket and called Fitz. He answered after a few rings and Kate asked him about Lexie Bell. "I don't know if you were on the case or were involved. I need more information before I interview everyone else. I have a feeling her case might have started a chain reaction that has led us to where we are now."

"I'm aware of the case," Fitz said much to Kate's relief. "It was ruled a suicide. The medical examiner was sure of that and the detective involved in the case was as well. I was never sure that was the correct ruling, but I had no information to counter it. She came from a party with several senators and was brought home by one. There were rumors she was drunk or possibly unstable in some way if I'm remembering correctly. If not suicide, it might have been an accidental overdose, but there was speculation that Lexie might have been causing trouble."

"Sexual harassment allegations?" Kate asked if that's what he meant.

"That was the rumor," Fitz confirmed. "The detective at the time had heard the rumors about the harassment but everyone he spoke to denied it was happening. They said Lexie was making up stories for attention."

Kate explained about the reporter with the Washington Post. "It sounds like she had several women willing to come forward with her. If the story broke it would have rivaled what happened with the media and Hollywood."

"None of the other women came forward at the time," Fitz explained his voice filled with regret. "Of course, if they believed Lexie had been silenced none of them would have. The rumors were there though."

"What about her relationship with her boss, Senator Bailey? There was some speculation that she was involved with him. Do we know if that's true or not?"

"I heard that as well," Fitz confirmed. He put Kate on hold for a moment and explained the reason for the call to Ditch and then got back on the line. "There was never anything substantiated that they were involved. Senator Bailey dropped Lexie off at home and went right to his house. His wife confirmed it. Based on the distance he drove, it would have only left him about five minutes to go into Lexie's apartment, drug her, and then leave. It didn't make any sense. I wouldn't consider Senator Bailey a suspect in this."

"You said suspect," Kate said with some surprise in her voice. "Does that mean you don't think it was suicide?"

"I believed those sexual harassment rumors could have been true and that Lexie was murdered to keep her quiet," Fitz said with a level of frustration in his voice Kate hadn't heard before. "No one could convince the detective who had the case. Given the high-profile players involved, you can imagine the pressure to close the case as a suicide. That was especially true after the medical examiner's ruling. Lexie's death was swept under the rug. It's why I was so willing and eager to work with Chase and Maven. I thought maybe I could get to the truth."

It was good confirmation that she was on the right track given Fitz thought it might be murder. "Did you ever hear about any viable suspects?"

"No," Fitz said to Kate's disappointment. "I'll tell you though that something happened at that party that night. Senator Bailey alluded to it. He said Lexie was in a back room of the house with Senators Cutcliffe and Harrison and Kramer. She came out of there angry. She told Senator Bailey she needed a ride home and that was it. Lexie never told Senator Bailey what had happened, at least that he was willing to admit."

Kate's mind went in several different directions. "Do you think she could have been sexually assaulted at the party?"

Fitz spoke quickly and with conviction. "No, it wasn't that kind of thing. If anything, now that I know about the Washington Post story, I'd think Kramer and the senators were afraid of her and trying to do damage control. Lexie did text a friend on the ride home and said she was determined to tell her story. No one at the time admitted to knowing what that meant. Her friend wouldn't admit to it either. It ended up being another dead end. But that's another reason I don't think she killed herself."

"It also doesn't sound like a woman who is so drunk or unstable she isn't in control of herself."

"I didn't consider that," Fitz admitted. "Either way, you can speak to Senator Bailey, but I've never had the sense he was involved. He might be a degenerate gambler, but there have never been other accusations leveled against him."

Kate was glad there might be one of them there who wasn't guilty of all of it. "What about Nathan Channing? Was that name ever connected to the case?"

"That's Kramer's aide, right?" When Kate confirmed, Fitz explained he didn't know much about him personally. Nathan had handled a few email exchanges between him and Kramer. "I couldn't say one way or the other."

"What about the Secret Service or Lexie's roommate?"

Fitz seemed shocked by the idea the Secret Service could be involved. "As for Lexie's roommate, she left town and went back to the west coast where she was from, soon after Lexie's death. I got the sense they weren't friends and that she was shaken up by the death. I don't think I'd want to stay in an apartment where my roommate killed herself or was murdered. The roommate was sure she heard someone leaving from the back entrance when she arrived that night. When the cops didn't take her seriously, she didn't feel all that safe."

Kate couldn't blame her for that. She probably would have felt the same. Kate thanked Fitz for the information and asked to speak to Ditch. She asked how the background research was coming along and he promised he'd be in touch soon. Kate ended the call feeling a little more emboldened that she was finally on the right track.

While she had been on the phone, Declan had been listening to Kate's side of the conversation and had picked up most of the details. Kate filled him in on the rest. When she was done, she said, "I'll start with Senator Bailey. Could you interview Nathan for me? You might want to seem sympathetic to Kramer's cause. It might get you further."

Declan started toward the door and then hesitated. He turned around. "Do you think we are wasting time with Lexie's murder? We are pressed for time as it is and I don't want to get too sidetracked. There's still a killer on the loose and we don't even know for certain Lexie was murdered. It might have been a suicide, Kate."

Kate understood Declan's reasoning but she didn't agree. "There are a lot of things about this case that don't make any sense to me. We have Ditch working on the hack as well as running some background for us. Right now, we need to get to the root of this connection between them. I'm convinced it's the ongoing sexual harassment. Lexie seems to be the first break in the dam. All the same people were involved then as now. Let me speak to Senator Bailey and see if I can learn more. Then I'll speak to Allison and Maven again and see if they knew her."

Declan didn't look convinced. "Is there any chance you're going down this path because you didn't go after the professor who sexually harassed you?"

If he had slapped her, Kate wouldn't have felt more stung. "You think I'm doing this because I can't sort out what happened to me all those years ago from the evidence right in front of me? You should know me better than that."

"I didn't mean it like that," Declan said, reaching for her but she stepped out of his grasp. They rarely argued, but when they did, it was serious.

Her eyes grew narrow as her anger rose. "Then how did you mean it?"

Declan stumbled over his words. He pointed toward the door. "They aren't the good guys, Kate. Normally, when we are brought into a case, we are trying to save the innocent. Those people out there aren't innocent – not what they did in the past by covering up what happened to Lexie and what happened to all those other young women and what they are being blackmailed for now. We are stuck here with a hurricane barreling toward us with a murderer who has already tried to kill you still on the loose. Lexie was innocent, so it's easy to focus on what happened to her. That's all I'm saying."

Declan stepped toward her and put his hands on her arms and this time Kate let him. He lowered his head until his forehead was resting against hers. "I'm a horrible person to say this, but I don't care what happened to them. The world is probably a better place without Senator Cutcliffe but we don't know what Chase and Matt Pike or even Senator Abbott have done. You've always fought for the underdog and now you have to fight for the criminals and that's a big shift in perspective."

Kate searched his face and only found sincerity. She nodded once to let him know she understood now and then stepped back. "Please let me do this my way. I'll be mindful of what you said, but I truly believe this is the heart of it."

"I'll trust your process, as always." He kissed her forehead and left the room, leaving Kate still feeling stung by how accurate Declan was more than any unkind word he might have said.

# CHAPTER 30

"Senator Bailey, come in and have a seat," Kate said and gestured toward the couch. "This shouldn't take too long. I have questions that only you can answer."

Senator Bailey had fear in his eyes as he sat down on the couch. He remained perched on the edge with his hands on his knees. "I've told you everything I know about the blackmail."

"You did," Kate said, agreeing with him. "What you didn't tell me is that you still have a gambling problem."

"I don't," he said, starting to argue.

"You do," Kate said, interrupting him and not allowing him to continue the lie. She needed to assert her control early on with him. She had a sense that Senator Bailey would be someone who'd quickly back down when confronted. "Let's not start with lies, Senator Bailey. I'll remind you that lying to a federal agent is a crime. I know for a fact that you have continued gambling and that you've gotten yourself back into debt. That puts you right at the top of my suspect list."

Surprised, Senator Bailey sat back a little on the couch. "I don't have anything to do with this. You're right that I'm still gambling and back in debt, which has made paying the blackmailer all but impossible for me. My father-in-law won't give me any more money and my wife has cut me off too. I'll be surprised if this doesn't lead to a divorce." He raised his head and made steady eye contact with Kate. "I may be a lot of things, Agent Walsh, but I'm not a killer. I don't have the time nor the resources to plan and execute a blackmail scheme like this."

Kate believed him but she wanted him rattled. "Do you have any idea who the blackmailer might be?"

Senator Bailey shifted his eyes to the side and remained quiet. "I've had my suspicions. I considered for a while that it might be Vice President Kramer but the logistics of that seemed unlikely. The Secret Service would have had to be in on it and I can't see that happening. I also considered Senator Stone and even Senator Harrison. They have both had it out for a number of us. I don't have evidence to suspect either but I've questioned it."

Kate tucked that information away for later. "Earlier today, I came to realize that everyone here voted no on two sexual harassment bills, one to stop non-disclosure agreements in the workplace and the other to stop forced arbitration. Funny enough it was only the people here this weekend who voted no. These were two highly successful bipartisan bills. Ones your party favored and nearly everyone voted yes. Is there a reason you voted no on both?"

Senator Bailey sat stone-faced, blinking rapidly. He seemed both surprised and caught off guard by the question. "I didn't like how the bills were worded," he said softly after not responding for far too long.

"We both know that's another lie," Kate said evenly without judgment or anger. "What did Vice President Kramer promise you? I know he's made promises to other senators if he's elected and they voted no on those bills."

Senator Bailey averted his eyes and didn't respond.

"Your silence isn't going to help you, Senator Bailey. I already know that the vice president plans to primary the president and that in the lead up he's been promising certain senators cabinet positions if they voted no. We both know the bills were going to be passed. What Kramer is doing is testing your loyalty and your ability to be controlled." Kate waited to see if Senator Bailey commented or contested her summation but he said nothing. "Is there a reason why Vice President Kramer would want to test your loyalty? You're from different parties so I don't understand why he'd need to have you under his control. That doesn't make a lot of sense to me."

Senator Bailey finally broke his silence with a weak denial. "It's nothing like that. I don't think you're on the right track, Agent Walsh. I didn't like the wording in the bills and I voted my conscience."

Kate stood then and shoved her hands in her pockets. "I see," she said calmly and then counted to ten and turned on him. "I was under the impression that the loyalty test had something to do with your relationship with Alexandria Bell. You know, Lexie Bell, who served as your senatorial aide. She was sexually harassed by Senator Cutcliffe and planned to go to the Washington Post with her story. Then she was murdered after you drove her home from a party, making you a prime suspect in her murder."

Senator Bailey swallowed so hard that Kate saw his throat constrict. His eyelids fluttered again. "I didn't kill Lexie. I know how this all looks, but you have to believe me. It looks suspicious, but I cared about Lexie. Her death..." His voice cracked and he didn't go on.

Kate was taken aback that he didn't give the standard line that she had committed suicide. "Do you believe Lexie was murdered? I know the official record is that she killed herself."

"I don't believe she killed herself. I never did." Senator Bailey took a deep breath causing his chest to rise and fall. "Lexie also wasn't as drunk or unstable as everyone made her out to be. She had been drinking but was coherent on the ride home. She was upset and angry and more determined than ever to right the wrong. That's why I know she didn't kill herself. Everyone left at the party made it seem like she was drunk and out of her mind. I drove her home so I should know. It wasn't like that at all."

"Did you go into her apartment with her?"

"No. The cops checked my alibi. I drove Lexie home, dropped her off, and immediately went home. I was standing in my kitchen talking to my wife about ten minutes after leaving Lexie. I waited there in front of her house only long enough to make sure she made it inside. I drove right home."

Kate believed him, not because she thought he was telling the truth, which he seemed to be allergic to, but because Fitz said the cops had checked his alibi. Kate wanted to know about the party, but more importantly, she wanted to know about the harassment. "When did you first become aware that Lexie was being harassed?"

"Shortly after she started working for me," Senator Bailey said, taking his upper teeth against his lower lip. "I found her in the office crying and she wouldn't tell me what was going on. My secretary did and I went immediately to Senator Cutcliffe and tried to address it. He said Lexie misunderstood his gesture and that she was being sensitive. I was a freshman senator, Agent Walsh. I was learning the ropes myself. This was Lexie's first senatorial aide position and we were both out of our depths. I went back to her to see if there was a chance she misunderstood what was said or see if she was being overly sensitive. I didn't know the full details of what had happened. Lexie was clear that he had groped and propositioned her and that she had pulled away and said no. He threatened that he'd get her fired."

"Did you go back to Senator Cutcliffe to address it?"

"I tried but he shut me down."

"Did you try anything else to address it?" Kate asked.

He nodded. "I went all the way to the Senate Majority Leader, but it was no use. I came to understand this was common behavior for Senator Cutcliffe. He had done similar things with other aides and staffers. His behavior wasn't hidden. It was something that was known. At that point, I told Lexie to avoid him as best she could. I wasn't sure what other action I could take. She shouldn't have needed to have contact with him anyway. My understanding is that Senator Cutcliffe initially sought her out."

"That's what offenders usually do. What about Kramer? I heard that he might have been sexually harassing others as well. Senator Harrison too."

Senator Bailey shook his head. "I'm not sure if Kramer or Harrison was sexually harassing Lexie. I heard the rumors too. My understanding from Lexie is that they were harassing her to keep quiet, which only fueled her need for retribution."

"Retribution?" Kate asked not sure that's the word he meant.

He waved her off. "You have to understand, Agent Walsh. Lexie wasn't like most young senatorial aides. She was strong and confident even from the start. She came back to the office and told my secretary right after it happened. Lexie wasn't going to stay silent. While it upset her and she was crying, the tears were out of anger and frustration rather than fear or sadness. When I came back and told her that I didn't get anywhere by going up the chain of command, Lexie was incensed, as she should have been. I knew she wasn't going to drop it, and I knew that was going to lead to trouble."

Kate assumed that was why so many had told him to fire her. "When I spoke to Senators Yates and Stone, they mentioned that many people told you to fire her. Is that true?"

"It is," Senator Bailey said, nodding. "I wasn't going to do that. Lexie had done nothing wrong. Even though she tried to avoid Senator Cutcliffe, it was like he kept seeking her out, toying with her. He'd stare at her and make snide remarks. He was able to grope her a few more times. One time she hit him but he just laughed. It only made her angry and as that anger bubbled up, she started talking to other women in the Senate office buildings trying to see how many women there were like her. After spending a few months doing that, she felt she had enough to go to the press. I was aware of all of this and cautioned her along the way. I wasn't going to stop her."

Kate wasn't sure if she was impressed he let Lexie go forward with the story or angry that he hadn't been the one leading the charge. He'd left it up to a young woman who didn't share the same power he had. "What happened the night of the party? It doesn't seem like that's something she'd willingly attend."

"At that point, Lexie was already talking to the Washington Post reporter. He wanted something on record, more than just her word. He wanted corroboration of the story. I didn't know what Lexie planned but she went to that party with an agenda." Senator Bailey rubbed his brow. "In hindsight, I should have stopped her. It was too dangerous. I didn't know it until after the fact but she went in there acting crazy and drunk, trying to taunt them into confessing what they had done and trying to get Senator Cutcliffe to harass her while being recorded. She taunted them that she was already speaking to the press and that they were no longer going to be able to sexually harass any young woman again. All it did was enrage them. Toward the end of the evening, Kramer and Cutcliffe agreed to speak to her alone. Lexie thought that was her chance. I don't know what happened but Lexie came out angry and amped up and asked me to take her home. In the car, she kept saying that she got it. I asked her what she meant and she told me she had recorded them on her phone. That it was the proof she needed for the Washington Post."

Kate didn't contain her surprise. "What happened to her phone after her death?"

"That's the thing, Agent Walsh. No one ever found it. That's another reason I think Lexie was murdered. Someone stole her phone that night."

"Are you sure her family doesn't have it? Maybe it was just lost among the evidence." She recalled Fitz talking about the text message to her friend.

"I'm sure.  The police were able to pull her phone records from the provider but never found her phone," Senator Bailey said with as much conviction as Kate had seen from him. "Her mother called and asked me for her phone, thinking she might have left it in the office. I followed up with the cops to see if it had been taken during the search of her room. There was never a phone found. Whoever killed her did so because she had a recording. That's why I know she was murdered. The detective wouldn't listen to me. He was sure it was a suicide."

Kate knew then without question it had been a huge miscarriage of justice that was the tipping point in this whole thing.  "Tell me, knowing all of this, why would you show any loyalty to Kramer?"

"I was the last person to see Lexie conscious. Everyone knew that and Kramer said most people would suspect that I was involved with Lexie.  I was doing everything to subvert those rumors.  Kramer threatened that if I didn't show him loyalty that there'd be trouble for me."

"He didn't promise you a cabinet position?"

Senator Bailey said, "No. Even if he had, I wouldn't have taken it. I'd never work directly for a man like that. I was doing it to protect my marriage and my reputation. As I said earlier, I may have a gambling addiction, but I'd never cheat on my wife or disrespect her like that. I did what I thought I had to do and certainly not out of loyalty to Kramer. I hope he loses his primary and is forced out of politics for good. I'm not sad that Senator Cutcliffe is dead either, but I didn't kill him."

It didn't seem like anyone was sad that Senator Cutcliffe was dead. Kate could be counted among them. "How did Senator Taft factor in? Was he there that night?"

"There are no allegations against Senator Taft that I'm aware of, but he too tried to talk Lexie out of rocking the boat.  He was there at the party that night and could corroborate all the harassment. He's another one who told me to fire her."

The most important question remained unanswered. "Who do you think killed Lexie?"

"I don't know but they put the plan in motion before we ever left that party," Senator Bailey said and waited for Kate's reaction. She encouraged him to continue. "There was no way anyone at that party beat us back to Lexie's apartment. I think they put the plan in motion when she was in the room with them, possibly even before that. Whoever did it was in her apartment waiting for her. I don't know who ordered the hit – Senator Cutcliffe or Kramer – but they were all in on it. They are all guilty of murder."

# CHAPTER 31

After speaking to Senator Bailey, Kate went to find Declan who was sitting in the living room with the rest of them. Night had fallen and dinner was about to be served. Stanton asked if they'd like to join the group and Kate declined. They had never eaten the lunch he made for them.

She gestured for Declan and Michael to follow her back to the library as the others went to their rooms to freshen up for dinner. Barry escorted Vice President Kramer up to his suite while Stanton followed everyone else to their respective rooms. He promised to stand guard in the hall until they were all ready to come back to the dining room.

Once back in the library, Kate explained everything she had learned from Senator Bailey. Michael slumped down in the chair, still favoring his arm. "I can't believe this," he said, a mix of disgust and shock on his face. "I wasn't on Kramer's detail until later in the election. I wasn't brought in until they had surged in the polls and were a favorite to win. I didn't know any of this."

"What about Barry or Matt?" Kate asked. "They were both with Kramer at that time. My understanding is Matt was at the party that night."

"You can ask Barry but neither of them ever told me anything. I've never even heard Lexie's name mentioned."

"You never heard about her suicide?" Declan asked, squinting down at him.

"I heard that one of Senator Bailey's aides had killed herself. I never knew the story surrounding that. Politics is high stakes and the pressure is immense. Suicide wasn't necessarily surprising."

Declan pressed on. "What about the allegations of sexual harassment?"

"There were allegations about a few people, but it was nothing that I had witnessed. Vice President Kramer certainly never did anything like that in front of me. I would have done my best to address and curtail that kind of behavior. Is it possible he stopped once he was the vice president?"

Kate had never known someone who stopped that kind of behavior when they gained more power. She told them as much. "I don't have any current allegations to confront him with. I'm not even sure that it would do us any good to confront him about Lexie. I believe we have found our motive now. Someone is looking for retribution for Lexie and trying to put a stop to the sexual harassment once and for all."

"Does that mean you've identified a suspect?" Michael asked hopefully.

Kate wished she could say yes. "I can say with certainty that there is a professional involved. The shooter was not someone unskilled and they were brazen and bold to attack the way they did. I can't help but feel like someone inside this house also knows more."

Michael frowned. "We haven't made any progress then."

"We've made progress," Declan assured him. "It takes time for cases like this to come together. Look how much we've uncovered in just two days. We understand the motive and that can help us find the killer. Not to mention, Kate has enough to work on a profile. We have other team members doing background work. We are getting there. It just takes time."

Michael looked back and forth between Kate and Declan. "What's the plan for the rest of the night?"

Kate could see that even though he hadn't said it, he was in considerable pain. "You need to get some rest. You should consider getting your arm checked at the hospital." When he assured her he was fine, Kate said, "Then at the very least, you need to get some rest. The extra security should be here soon and you and Barry can rest for the night. Declan and I are going to head back to my house where we can continue to work. I need to clear my head and get some food."

"Why don't you eat here?" Michael offered, standing. "The cook does an amazing job. He said something about making steak for tonight. I don't know that you'll find anything open during the storm. I heard even some of the grocery stores were closing up early."

Kate declined as she had to Stanton. "I want to get out of here and shower and change my clothes. It's been a long day and I need a change of scenery to process my thoughts for the day."

"You also need to rest," Declan reminded her. He turned to Michael. "We appreciate the offer, but we don't want to socialize with the senators and the vice president. After everything we learned today, we need to step back and reassess our plan for tomorrow."

"Understood," Michael said with a curt nod. "If you need anything from me tonight, don't hesitate to call."

Kate gestured toward his arm. "The only thing I want is for you to get some rest and get better." After saying goodbye, Declan and Kate pulled their jackets on and braced themselves again for the wind and the rain. They ran to the car and were safely inside before Kate felt like she could exhale. She had never minded a rainy day or two but this was getting on her last nerve. She also felt her whole body decompress after leaving the house.

"Is it wrong that I don't care what happens to them tonight?" Declan asked as he turned the engine on and put the car in drive.

Kate brushed water down her pants and side-eyed him. "There are a few people in that house I care about. Stanton and the staff didn't do anything wrong and neither did Michael."

"What about the rest?"

Kate remained tight-lipped about that one. She didn't want to lie but the truth wasn't something she wanted to say aloud. Instead, she told Declan she was grateful for him. "I'm glad you were okay with declining dinner. I wanted to get home for the night and clear my head."

Declan yawned and didn't try to stifle it. "I'm exhausted, Kate. I feel like I've been awake for several days straight. All I wanted to do was get out of that house."

Kate didn't even have enough energy to respond. Her clothes were soaked down to her undergarments. All she wanted was a hot shower and her pajamas. They had work to do tonight but at least it would be in the comfort of her home. "If I cook dinner, will you get a fire going in the fireplace?"

Declan agreed and once they made it back, he went directly to the back enclosed porch where Kate's caretaker had stacked enough wood to last them a month if they needed it. Kate headed upstairs to take a shower.

Once she was in her room, she peeled off her wet clothes and left them in a heap on the floor. She stood naked in front of the mirror and appraised her face. She pinched back the skin on her eyes and patted the growing dark circles under them. She probably didn't look any different, but Kate thought she looked like she had aged a few years overnight. She turned on the hot water until steam billowed out and stepped inside and let the hot water beat down her shoulders and back. She tried to shut out thoughts about the case but it was impossible.

There was simply too much riding on her solving it to even take a few minutes break.

Later, Kate and Declan sat in the living room with the lights dim and the fire roaring. Kate sat in the chair with her feet up on the ottoman and a blanket over her legs. She steadied the tray with the turkey sweet potato chili she had made alongside grilled cheese sandwiches. It wasn't fancy but it was good and filling. Kate would have been satisfied with the chili. It was Declan who had asked for the grilled cheese. He said when he was a kid on rainy days, his mom would make him and his brothers gooey grilled cheese sandwiches and it always made him feel better.

They ate in near silence with Declan mumbling how good everything tasted every few bites. Kate laughed every time he did it. She wasn't known for her cooking skills, and at home, he was usually the one making them dinner. When they finished eating, Declan got up from the couch with his tray, took hers from her lap, and carried them into the kitchen. When he returned, he laid back on the couch with his feet up and reached for the other throw blanket, pulling it up to his waist.

"We both know your mind has been on the case since we left," he said after he got comfortable. "What's your assessment?"

Kate stretched her arms overhead. "It's not so much my assessment, but I was trying to make sense of the timing in the hopes that something would shake loose. First, across all of this, we have ongoing sexual harassment by a few members of the Senate. We don't know how widespread this might be, but we know that soon after Lexie Bell started working for Senator Bailey, she experienced it at the hands of Senator Cutcliffe. That set her off and she told Senator Bailey and his secretary what happened. Bailey confronts Cutcliffe and is shut down."

"What does that mean specifically?" Declan asked.

"Bailey said that Cutcliffe wouldn't address it. He said this is just how it was and that these young women like it and had no self-awareness at all. He wasn't willing to be dressed down by Senator Bailey, who was a freshman senator. Bailey then told Lexie to stay away from him. Even though she did that, it kept happening. It wasn't said specifically, so this is me speculating. But I'm sure Lexie was talking to some of the other female aides because, at some point, she decided she was going to break the story in the Washington Post."

"Did the reporter come to her or did she go to him?"

Kate wasn't sure of that answer. "I assume she went to him. The story ended when Lexie died. If the reporter had gone to her, I'd think he'd have other sources and the story would have continued."

"Do you think we need to track down the reporter?"

"Possibly," Kate said with uncertainty in her tone. "As you pointed out earlier, we don't want to get too far down the rabbit hole on Lexie's case. It started all of this, but it's not why we are here."

"What came next?"

"Lexie was murdered before she could take the story public. A few months after that, the new president and vice president were elected. A couple of years pass and Kramer and Cutcliffe convince the others connected to Lexie's case to vote no on those two sexual harassment bills in exchange for cabinet positions when Kramer primaries the president. I assume that was a loyalty test. That vote happened shortly before Chase and Maven connected with Fitz asking for background information on Senator Cutcliffe. They wanted to explore if there were other allegations. I still don't know if this is because they knew Lexie or had heard the stories and it was happening to Maven. Either way, they were going to file a civil lawsuit."

Declan opened his eyes wide. "Fitz's hack followed that and a few months later the blackmail."

Kate nodded. "That about sums it up."

"What about the female senators who were there? Have any of them been victims of harassment?"

Kate had wondered the same thing. "Senator Yates said that Senator Abbott was. Yates didn't say that she was and Senator Stone didn't admit to anything either but brushed off any harassment as something women just needed to deal with. It wouldn't surprise me if both had experienced incidences they brushed off as normal."

Declan shook his head as if he couldn't understand that. "Did they say that Senator Abbott was harassed by Senator Cutcliffe?"

Kate shook her head. "Kramer when he was a senator."

"That's a big disclosure right there," Declan said. "Do you have any feelings after looking at the blackmail letters?"

"The language in the letters is the same except for some slight differences. It's like someone wrote a form letter and then filled in the blanks based on each person. Whoever this is, they are educated and highly intelligent. Gender is hard to pick up but I wouldn't rule out a woman. I didn't want to suspect her before, but I wouldn't be surprised if it was Maven." Kate had been thinking about that all day. She had seen how strong and angry the young woman had become when confronted about the harassment. She had gone with Chase to get background info on Cutcliffe. Kate didn't know if she had hacking skills but that could easily be hired out. She hadn't said anything to anyone about her suspicions but they had grown throughout the day.

"You're sure, Kate?" Declan asked watching her closely.

"I'm sure Maven is on my suspect list. I can't prove it right now based on the evidence we have."

"What about the gun found upstairs in the laundry?"

"We need to get the report from Sharon to see whose prints were found."

Declan said he'd call her first thing in the morning. "Why would Maven shoot Chase if he was on her side?"

Kate wasn't sure about that. "It's possible they were in on it together.

Maven could have killed him to keep him quiet or she double-crossed him and is keeping the money for herself." The thunder clapped loudly making them both jump.

"It's all too diabolical. We should relax and think about more pleasant things. Let's head up to bed." He stood and folded the blanket before walking over to Kate and extending his hand.

Kate hesitated in her chair, wondering what exactly he meant. "Declan, I don't know that tonight…"

He laughed. "I didn't mean anything by that. We are both exhausted. I'm dragging you out of that chair and making sure that you're going straight to sleep in your bed."

"Oh, good," she said laughing with him. "What about the kitchen?"

"I'll clean it in the morning." Declan took her hand in his and pulled her up and then kissed her sweetly on the forehead. Kate leaned into him and felt his warmth and strength and breathed him in. He smelled like the woods and a spice she didn't recognize. She waited there while he shut off all the lights and checked the locks on the doors.

At the top of the stairs, he kissed her lips gently and sent her off to her room. Kate was all too happy to shut her brain off and climb into bed. She shut her eyes and was asleep in a matter of minutes.

# CHAPTER 32

The sound of glass shattering woke Kate with a start. She stared off into the darkness, wondering if it was a vivid dream that woke her.

"Kate," Declan said, his voice a loud whisper. "There's someone downstairs."

"Are you sure?" she said, working to adjust her eyes to the darkness. She swung her feet to the floor and grabbed her Glock from the bedside table. As if answering for them, something scraped along the wood floor downstairs.

Declan was no more dressed than Kate was in her pajamas. He had shorts and a tee shirt and was barefoot. As she looked around the room for something more to put on, a floorboard in the living room creaked.

"They are getting closer, Kate," Declan said with his voice far calmer than Kate felt inside. They had the advantage though. The person didn't know that they were awake and they had to climb the stairs, giving Kate and Declan ample opportunity to aim.

Kate felt glued to the floor in terror. "We have to go on the offense," she said, summoning bravery.

Declan moved toward the door. "We know you're down there. Identify yourself!"

A small silver canister sailed up the stairs and hit the wall on the landing. It exploded – a loud, blinding flash. Kate didn't turn her head in time and was blinded by the flash of light. She rubbed at her eyes but it was no use. A steady hum filled her ears as she tried to get her bearings.

As she wobbled on her feet, all at once Declan shoved her backward off the other side of the bed. She hit the floor hard, banging her right knee and elbow on the floor. The first bullets went over their heads, hitting the wall behind her. The window above her shattered, throwing glass down on top of her.

"Stay down, Kate," Declan shouted to her. "Don't come any closer!" he shouted at the intruder.

A sinister laugh was the response. "There's nothing you can do. I'm going to kill you both and end this for good. I should have killed you both earlier."

The humming in Kate's ears blocked out most of his voice. She didn't dare speak because she was so disoriented that she didn't know if she could form words. Kate reached for Declan but found an empty space. A volley of shots whizzed by her again, slamming into the wall inches above her head.

"Give up!" the man shouted. "You're not going to get out of this alive!"

"If you kill us, there will only be more sent to stop you," Declan shouted. "Put down your gun and we can talk about it."

"We are done talking!"

"Come on, man. We are sympathetic to the cause. We understand what the victims have gone through and we don't mean the senators. We are on your side. I can't condone your approach but let's talk it out. We might be able to get you some leniency with the court."

The floorboard creaked under his feet as he stepped into the bedroom. Kate knew every creak in the house and the last one meant he had entered her bedroom. "You're right on the other side of the bed. I can see you. Stand up with your hands up. One shot and it will be over. I don't want to make you suffer."

Kate knew he had to be talking to her because Declan was nowhere near her. Even in the darkness, she couldn't feel him beside her and her gun was somewhere on the bed, released from her hand when Declan shoved her over the bed. She crouched down lower trying to hide.

From the other side of the room, Declan gave one last warning.

Three shots rang out in rapid succession followed by a low guttural groan as a body hit the floor with a thud. It all felt like it was going in slow motion for Kate. She screamed Declan's name.

"I'm fine, Kate," he assured her. Moments later, the sound of a gun kicked across the hardwood and Declan telling the man not to move let Kate know it was safe to come out from behind the bed. Her vision still had bright spots but it didn't matter. The room was bathed in darkness. Kate felt around on the bed for her gun that had been lost in the shuffle.

"Is he still alive?" she asked as she wrapped her hand around it.

"I thought he was but he's dead. He took a shot to the neck, head, and one to the chest. I don't think anyone could survive that. He's got a vest on so the chest shot didn't do any damage." Declan stood from his crouched position over the body and looked at her with concern. "Are you okay? You took the full force of that flashbang. I'm sorry if I hurt you by throwing you off the bed like that. I knew you couldn't see to shoot."

Kate rubbed her right elbow at the mention of it. "Only sore knees and elbows. Worth it. I'd be dead right now if it wasn't for you." She raised her hand to her head dead rubbed her temples. The ringing in her ears hadn't subsided yet, but her vision was slowly coming back to normal. "What time is it?"

"Just after three," Declan said, looking over at the bedside table. "I'm going to turn on the lights. It might hurt your eyes for a moment." He waited until Kate said she was ready and then flicked on the overhead light.

Both of them turned to look at the man on the floor. He was dressed in black from head to toe. He had a utility knife attached to his hip and another gun strapped to his ankle visible under his raised pant leg. A black ski mask covered his face except for his eyes and mouth.

"Guess it's a good thing I got the shots off when I did."

Kate wasn't sure where Declan was when he took the shots. "I thought you were right next to me on the floor. Where were you in the room?"

Declan pointed behind him. "I crawled over beside the dresser. I figured I could get a better shot off that way. With the lights off, he wasn't going to be able to see me. I had a clean line of sight on him, especially because he kept running his mouth. That's what helped me. It's why I kept him talking. It was too dark to see him. I could only make out his shadow."

Declan pulled up the mask to reveal an unfamiliar face. Kate didn't know him either. He checked the hoodie pockets first and then his pants pockets. As he was searching, he said absently, "I assume he's not carrying identification but you never know."

"He had to get here somehow," Kate said just as Declan found the man's car keys in his back jeans pocket.

He held up the keys and jingled them. "We'll search for that right after we call the local cops. We need to make a report about this and get the medical examiner out here."

"I hate to call them out so early in the morning."

Declan stood and looked over at her. "I don't think we are going to get much sleep now. If you want to try, you can take my bed and I'll stay here with the stiff."

"I'm awake. I'll go down and make some coffee while I make the calls." Kate had to step over the body and sidestep the blood as she went to the hall and then descended the stairs. Her thoughts weren't on how close they had come to death. Her mind shifted to how difficult the blood would be to get out of the hardwoods and how they'd need to quickly replace whatever window he smashed to get into the house.

It was the first time in a long time that Kate acknowledged just how emotionally checked out she had to be to do this job. She'd often thought that maybe therapy was in order, but given her background, she knew what a therapist would say before they said it. She also knew her issues but had never taken steps to resolve them. Kate worried more than anything that a therapist messing around in her brain might change her ability to do her job.

Standing in the middle of the kitchen, Kate placed the call and woke all those that needed to be on the scene. She apologized for waking them, explained the situation, assured each caller that she and Declan were fine, and then gave them directions to her house. Sharon was the most shocked of all. She asked several times what they needed but Kate remained steadfast that they were okay.

When the calls were done, Kate made coffee and then went to the pantry to find the broom and dustpan. The interior kitchen door had been left ajar by the intruder. Kate couldn't remember now if he had on gloves or not but she pulled the door open not from the doorknob but by pulling on the side of it and then stepped out onto the enclosed back porch. She couldn't clean anything now. She had to wait until Sharon was there to take photos and assess the scene. Kate mostly wanted to make sure the rain wasn't coming in and drenching everything in the process. Luckily the exterior porch steps sat under an overhang which was now protecting the door from the onslaught of rain that was still pouring down.

The intruder had broken two panes out of the bottom of the window, reached in, and unlatched the bolt lock. Many people on the island never worried about their safety. Kate could remember times when she was a kid when this door was never locked. She'd run in and out of the house until her mother would yell at her to either stay inside or out. The only time Kate could remember the door being locked was one late summer afternoon after she had come in and out of the door at least twenty times and then went out to play again. When she returned, she found the door locked – her mother had grown frustrated and locked her out. Kate ran to the front and her father let her in. Kate would like to say she had learned her lesson that day, but she was hard-headed. She smiled now at the memory.

"You can't clean that up," Declan said from behind her. He put his hand on her back and then pulled her a little closer to him. "We'll get it cleaned up as soon as we can. I know this house has a lot of meaning for you and this happening here probably…" He trailed off unsure of what he was going to say.

Pulled out of the memory, Kate turned to him. "I know and it's okay. I wanted to make sure there was no rain coming in. Is everything okay upstairs?"

"He's still dead if that's what you're asking." Declan stepped around the glass and peered out the back window next to the door. "Did you see that there's a car in your driveway?"

Kate hadn't even bothered to look. "You don't think he pulled in the driveway to kill us, do you? Who does that?"

"There are no other houses near here, Kate. In your driveway, it doesn't look suspicious. If anyone was going by, they wouldn't even notice the car. If he parked on the road leading up to your house, people would question it. It's genius in its simplicity. Plus, if he died, it's not like he cares if he got caught. He went in knowing it was him or us."

Kate hadn't wanted to think about that. "Are you going to check it out?"

"I'll go out the front way," Declan said and then walked back toward the kitchen. He turned when he got to the interior door. "Katie," he said softly and she turned to look at him. "Are you sure you're okay? You seem a bit off as if you're in shock."

Kate wasn't sure what had settled over her. It could just be a lack of sleep or stress from the case. "I'm overwhelmed with it all."

Declan stepped back onto the porch and wrapped her in a hug. She rested her head against his chest. "I promise you, it's all going to be okay. As we said at the start, if we royally mess up our careers with this case, you can teach or consult and I'll tend to the house since I have zero transferable skills."

Kate didn't want to laugh but she couldn't help herself. She took a deep breath and let it out. "Go check out the car for identification. I'd like some information before everyone gets here."

Declan dropped a kiss on the top of her head and then left to do what Kate asked. She remained on the porch looking at the mess.

# CHAPTER 33

"Nagy Barna," Declan said as he tossed the man's wallet on the kitchen counter. Dr. Shelia Coburn was upstairs working with her team to remove the body while Kate, Declan, and Sharon waited in the kitchen. Sharon had already fingerprinted him and would run his prints in the system when she got back. Dr. Coburn assured them that she'd provide Sharon with a DNA sample so she could run that in the system, too. For now, all they had was the name Declan found in the man's car, which he confirmed was a rental. Declan said the man's name again, this time slower.

Sharon squinted over at him. "Is that a nickname?"

Kate wasn't even sure they were pronouncing it correctly.

Declan threw another document down on the counter. "It's a Hungarian passport. There are other documents in his car with the same name as well as a few others. I don't know what's real or not but that passport sure looks legit. The four driver's licenses from different states look like fakes, so for now, until we know otherwise, he's Nagy Barna."

Kate raised her eyes to meet Declan's. "Professional hitman?"

He shrugged. "That or mercenary for hire. Who knows at this point."

Kate assumed that either was true. That meant someone was paying for his services. "Last night I said that I thought this was Maven. I highly doubt that a young woman her age is going to be coming across the likes of Nagy Barna. How old is he?"

"Forty-eight, if that passport is legit. Otherwise, we have no idea." Declan leaned back against the counter and crossed his legs at his ankles. "I agree with you, Kate. It's unlikely that Maven would come across this guy. Unless we find something in her past that tells us otherwise, I think we need to look in a new direction. That's probably true for all the aides. Most of them are only a few years out of college, in their late twenties." Declan pointed to the ceiling. "This wasn't that guy's first hit. Twice now he's taken risks most professionals wouldn't. I don't think that's because he wasn't skilled. I think he was probably cocky and overconfident and that's what got him killed."

Sharon put her hand on his arm and looked up at him. "How are you handling it, Declan? You've killed two men in a matter of days. Your last case and now this one. That's got to be hard on even the most seasoned agent."

As soon as the words were out of Sharon's mouth, crushing guilt washed over Kate. She had been so focused on herself that she hadn't even considered Declan had not only pulled his gun in two different cases but that he had killed two men in a matter of days.

Declan looked down at Sharon and then over at Kate. "You know the job. You do what you have to do."

"It doesn't mean it's easy, big guy. You better take care of your mental health or your physical health is going to suffer and you're already not fully recovered from a few cases ago," Sharon said, wrapping her arms around his middle and hugging. Sharon and Declan had formed a tight bond during his time working in the FBI Boston field office while Kate was sent alone on an international case with the CIA.

Declan leaned down and hugged her back. Sharon stood several inches shorter than Kate, but she was a powerhouse. She ran marathons for fun. "I promise you, I'm fine. It's just going to take a little time for us to figure this one out."

Sharon stepped back from the hug and looked over at Kate. "Do you need a hug, too?"

Kate accepted one and assured Sharon that she was fine too or would be soon enough. Every once in a while, Kate found moments of humanity and friendship even in the worst circumstances. She couldn't remember who said it, the actor Tom Hanks maybe, but it was all about the hang. Meaning no matter what the job was, it was the people you were doing it with that made the experience either good or bad. Kate couldn't have asked for a better team.

After the hugging was over, Declan asked, "Did you get any prints off that gun we found?"

Sharon shook her head. "It had been wiped clean. If it was Kramer's gun, he did a good job of wiping it down. You think he would have had the time for that?"

Kate wasn't sure. "It doesn't make a lot of sense to me. Anything is possible though." The gun was another dead end for now. It was in a place where anyone could have put it. Kramer was still the most likely suspect.

They stood there chatting until Dr. Coburn and her team brought the body down the front steps and out the front door. The local cops had yet to arrive. Kate wasn't sure Dr. Coburn should technically remove the body, but given this was all part of a federal investigation, there probably wasn't any harm.

Still, Kate walked to the front door and told Dr. Coburn they had called the local cops. "We assumed they would have been here by now. I know it's coming down out there and I'm sure they have other things to do. Can you update them for us when you know more?"

Dr. Coburn let her team bring the body to the van while she went back to talk to Kate. "I wouldn't worry about it. I called them too and they assured me I was free to do what I needed to do. They are hands-off as long as the two of you have handled this. They aren't equipped for this kind of carnage. I think the locals might even be a little intimidated by it all."

Kate could understand that. "If the state police or whoever wants an update, we are happy to provide it."

"I'll let them know. I'll call you when I know more." Dr. Coburn left and Kate waited until she was in the van before she closed the door and went back to the kitchen. "Sharon, you might as well do what you need to do. It doesn't sound like the local cops are coming out for this." To Declan, she said, "We should call Spade and update him. See what he wants us to do."

"Probably more paperwork," Declan said with a groan and then sat down at the table with Kate. They called Spade and he answered as if he'd been sitting at his desk awaiting their call.

"The shooter came after us, Spade," Kate said after she apologized for calling so early. "This time he broke into my house, threw a flash grenade up the stairs, and then tried to attack. I couldn't tell you how many rounds are in my wall. Declan shot and killed him."

Spade remained silent for a moment. Then he clicked his tongue. "The threat is neutralized then. That's about all we could have asked for. Do you know his identity?"

Declan explained about the car and finding the man's identification and passport. "I can't say for certain that any of it is accurate because he had several IDs in his car. The passport looks fairly authentic. Can you run his name and ask around?"

Spade asked Declan to spell the man's name and then promised he'd be back with some information. "If he's professional, then someone has hired him."

"We considered that," Declan said and then looked to Kate to see if she wanted to say anything. When she didn't, he added, "We are doing our best here, but we don't have a viable suspect yet." Declan then gave Spade the overview of the case including how the Lexie Bell murder might be tied in.

"What name did you say?" Spade asked, interrupting.

Kate leaned toward the phone. "Alexandria Bell. She went by Lexie. Do you know the name?" Kate took a moment to give Spade more background and how she might be connected to the case.

"I know the name and remember when the story hit the news. There were rumors around Washington that it hadn't been a suicide, but the local Metro detective shut down the case fairly quickly. The medical examiner ruled it a suicide."

"That's what we keep hearing," Kate said dryly. They talked for a few more minutes about the case and then Spade said he'd try to find more information. Kate appreciated that. She was going to need a flow chart soon of all the people running down information for them. They ended the call without much resolution.

Kate checked the clock on the wall. It was close to five-thirty and they'd need to be back at the estate by eight. "I need to find something to board up that window until we can get it replaced," she said, standing. "I'm also going to need to get a cleaner in here to take care of that bedroom."

"It will all get done, Kate," Declan reassured.

At close to eight, Kate and Declan arrived at the estate already overwhelmed and exhausted from the morning. This time they brought a change of clothes and other personal items in case they got stuck there for the night. Kate had heard on the morning news that a few of the roads were starting to wash away and there was some flooding on the island. She wanted to be prepared for anything.

They had decided on the way there that they would not tell anyone what had happened in the wee hours of the morning. Kate and Declan would show up alive and unharmed and watch carefully to see everyone's reaction.

Michael was the first to greet them at the front entrance. He seemed bright and alert and had nearly full range of motion of his arm. "It doesn't even hurt today," he assured Kate when she inquired. "You don't look like you've slept much."

"I look old and haggard is what you're trying to say," Kate said, trying to make light of it.

Michael blushed and shook his head. "I'm sorry. I didn't mean to say it like that. You both look a little tired is all. Was it a late night?"

"We stayed up strategizing," Declan said before Kate could answer. "How'd everything go here?"

"No issues. It was a quiet night and the local cops who are here said they could stay for the remainder of the time. Barry and I are letting them sleep during the day and they will take the night shift. Barry is sleeping in Vice President Kramer's room at night on the couch to give him extra protection."

"Is there a reason for that other than the added security?" Declan asked what Kate had wondered.

"With everything going on, Barry told me last night it seemed Kate suggested Kramer might be in some kind of trouble. Barry was thinking that keeping an eye on him night and day might offer everyone else protection if he's up to something."

Kate said, "Here's something I don't understand, Michael. The vice president is heavily guarded at all times. If Kramer was involved in the blackmail, wouldn't someone on your team know that?"

"If anyone should know, it's me," Michael said, his tone tinged with frustration. "I assume if Kramer was going to do something like this that he wouldn't tell me because he knows I'd put a stop to it. I paid his ransom but didn't want to. As I said, I was conflicted about it and wanted to call the FBI. I asked him several times if we could. He shut that down. I should have done it on my own. I'd never help him commit a crime."

Declan leaned against the wall. "What about everyone else on the team? Some of the members aren't here this weekend. Could they be involved?"

"They are all accounted for this weekend. None of them could be the killer."

Kate knew that because the killer was dead and he certainly wasn't a Secret Service agent. She had a tightrope to walk. "Let's set aside the killer for a moment. We suspect he might be a professional anyway. Is it possible that someone on your team was helping Kramer blackmail the others and might have hired a hitter to take them out this weekend?"

Michael considered the question but soon shook his head. "I can't imagine it. Everyone on my team is loyal to the core. I know the Secret Service has had its issues over the years. I'd stake my life that we aren't involved in this. What I did was bad enough. I was simply trying to do my job and protect the vice president from a scandal that he adamantly denied. Even the hint of the rumor could destroy his political career as well as his family."

Michael was still trying to justify his actions, which Kate didn't need him to do. "Do me a favor and give it a little more thought. Maybe someone wasn't where they were supposed to be or were unaccounted for during periods they shouldn't have been. Just consider it. That's all I'm asking."

"I'll continue to do whatever I can to help."

Kate thanked him. "I'm going back in the library and will start some interviews right after I say good morning to everyone."

# CHAPTER 34

Kate entered the dining room where they were all seated around the table having breakfast. Kate cleared her throat and then loudly said good morning.  She scanned their reactions but didn't see any surprise or shock among them, except for Senator Harrison. His head snapped up from his plate at the sound of Kate's voice and he fixed his gaze on her.

"You're back," he said, surprising himself as the words left his mouth. He darted his eyes back and forth. His cheeks reddened and he lowered his eyes back to his plate. "I just meant with the weather and all."

Kate assumed he hadn't meant to say it aloud. "There's still lots of work to be done."

"How was your night?" Senator Yates asked, standing with a cup of coffee in hand. She pointed across the room to a coffee cart. "There's hot coffee and pastries if you'd like anything. I'm sure Stanton could whip you up something if you asked."

Kate waved her off. "We are fine, thanks. We need to get back to interviewing people. I'd like to speak to Maven." Kate looked over at the young woman who sat at the end of the table right beside Allison. She didn't even look surprised that Kate wanted to speak to her.

"Watch what you say, Maven," Vice President Kramer cautioned her. "The FBI can twist your words."

Kate zeroed in on him. "You know trying to intimidate or threaten a witness is a felony."

Kramer smirked as he looked over his iPad at her. "No one is arresting the Vice President of the United States, certainly not a lowly FBI agent like yourself."

Kate hoped he was guilty of something because she wanted the satisfaction of cuffing him and throwing him in a cell. Kate returned the smirk. "The FBI doesn't discriminate who we arrest." She didn't even give him a chance to respond. Kate turned to Maven. "Let's go."

"Let me grab some more coffee and I'll be there," Maven said evenly, seeming unphased by what Kramer had told her. She rose from the table, grabbed a messenger bag from the back of the chair, and refilled her coffee. Then she followed Kate out of the room.

While Kate was doing that, Declan would interview the handful of other senatorial aides they hadn't spoken to yet. Kate wished she could speak to all of them one-on-one. The timing just wasn't going to make that possible.

Once they reached the library, Kate pushed open the door and was glad to see that someone had started a fire in the fireplace for them. "Someone was thinking ahead," Kate said and then took a seat in the chair facing the couch. "Please, sit down. I'm sure Allison told you this shouldn't be too painful. I'm just trying to understand what's going on."

Maven sat back on the couch and set her bag on the floor next to her feet. She sipped from her coffee and smiled over at Kate. "I'm not nervous to speak to you, Agent Walsh. I know that you're here to help us. I'm willing to tell you everything I know." Her tone was confident, unbothered, and even.

Where that might have indicated she was confident, Kate was concerned that Maven was far too unaffected by what was going on around them. It might indicate she knew more than she was saying. Kate wanted to start building rapport first. "I appreciate that you admitted in front of everyone that Senator Cutcliffe had been sexually harassing you. Is that the first time you told anyone?"

"Allison knew and so did Chase. I also had conversations with some of the other aides who aren't here." Maven rested the cup in her lap and gestured with one hand as she spoke. "It wasn't any secret that Senator Cutcliffe sexually harassed women. It might have been for a long time, but a few years ago one brave young woman stepped forward and then paid for it with her life."

"Lexie Bell," Kate said and watched as Maven frowned.

"That's right. I'm glad you know her name. Senator Yates mentioned that you talked about her yesterday. She tried to talk to everyone last night, but she was shut down quickly by some of the men, particularly Vice President Kramer and Senator Harrison. They didn't want to rehash it."

"Did you know Lexie?"

"Around the office, but I didn't know her well. I was one of the women willing to come forward for her story with the Washington Post. As I said before, it happened to me and I was ready to tell someone. I had already been talking to people about my experiences but not openly. Talking to my peers was one thing, but doing something Lexie was willing to do was entirely different. There is safety in numbers, at least that's what we thought. That is until Lexie…" Maven didn't finish as she turned away from Kate. Tears formed in the corners of her eyes.

"Do you believe Lexie was murdered?"

Maven still didn't turn back to Kate. "I think everyone *knows* she was murdered."

"What about you, Maven? What were you willing to do to make the harassment stop?"

She took a sip of her coffee and looked over at Kate. "For a few years, other than changing who I worked for, there wasn't much I was willing to do. I wasn't brave like Lexie. I was a coward, but then I came to realize how pervasive the harassment had become." She paused then and reframed. "It probably had always been bad, but I was noticing more with younger senatorial aides. They had started to become more vocal about it. Not many of them knew about Lexie and I was worried about what would happen to them. I felt protective in a way."

"What did you do?"

Maven took a deep breath, puffing up her chest. "I decided that I needed to do something about it and Chase offered to help me. He was getting tired of having a front-row seat to Senator Cutcliffe's behavior and the fact that no one was stopping him. We teamed up."

Maven then went on to explain how they had spoken to a civil attorney who suggested they go to Fitz to help them build a case. She explained that she had used some of the money from Senator Cutcliffe's non-disclosure agreement but that Chase covered some of the other bills. "He said that someone was willing to help us but they wanted to remain anonymous."

"Do you have any idea who that might have been?"

Maven shook her head. "Chase was tightlipped about it and I didn't want to pressure him. He was helping and I wanted to respect the fact that he had gotten us added help. There was no point being disrespectful and pushing him to tell me something he didn't want to disclose."

Kate believed her as she felt another potential lead slipping away. "I'm sure you were curious. Did you ever suspect anyone?"

Maven shrugged. "I assumed it was one of the other senators." She pinned her gaze on Kate, holding steady eye contact. "You and I both know that these men didn't just target the senatorial aides. I'm sure there are at least a handful of freshmen senators who experienced sexual harassment. All we want is to come to work and be left alone to do our jobs."

Kate wanted badly to sympathize with her, but for all she knew Maven was a blackmailer. "Did you have any particular senator in mind?"

"I considered both Senators Yates and Abbott. They always seemed most sympathetic to our cause. I knew Senator Abbott had even spoken to Lexie when she was trying to gather support for the article." She saw the look on Kate's face and added, "I don't know what they talked about. Lexie was great at keeping things private unless she was given express permission to share what she learned."

"What had you learned from the information Fitz provided?"

"He continued Lexie's work for us. That reporter she was working with flaked after her death. He had more than enough for a story with the rest of us who might have come forward had he pushed us as Lexie did. Once he started asking us questions about Lexie's mental health, we knew we couldn't trust him. Someone had poisoned the well if you know what I mean." Maven sat quietly for a moment and then smiled. "Fitz is one of the good ones. He rallied things for us. If not for him the civil lawsuit wouldn't have been able to go forward."

"Now that Senator Cutcliffe and Chase are dead, what will happen?"

"I don't know," Maven said sadly. "Senator Cutcliffe might have been the primary person we were targeting but there are many other men in the senate who have been guilty of sexual harassment. We don't have the bandwidth to go after them all."

"What about Vice President Kramer? Has he ever harassed you?"

Maven shook her head. "No. I wouldn't have asked to join his staff if he had."

"But you've heard the rumors about the other women?"

"I have," Maven said with an edge to her voice. She paused and collected herself, took another sip of coffee, and leaned forward. "Do you think I'm smart, Agent Walsh?"

"Very," Kate said, and then more pointed, she added, "and calculating. That's why I'd like to know the real reason you chose to work as one of the vice president's aides. I suspect that it had nothing to do with your career prospects."

Maven sat back and laughed. "No one should underestimate you. Taking a job as an aide to Vice President Kramer had nothing at all to do with my career prospects or working my way into a better position for later in my career. I wanted proof that he killed Lexie. That's what I've been doing for the last two years. Doing everything I could to get close enough to him to prove that he had murdered her or had her murdered. I sat in on every meeting I could, went through every document of his I could get my hands on, and talked to everyone close to him. You would not believe the lengths I've gone to get proof he was responsible. He doesn't scare me, Agent Walsh. Letting this continue unchecked terrifies me."

The venom in her voice unnerved Kate. She was going to take down the Vice President of the United States if it was the last thing she did. Kate returned the same calm icy demeanor. "What are those lengths, Maven? Did they include blackmail?"

"No," she said with disappointment on her face. "I wish I could take credit for something that ingenious. I was simply working from the inside as if I were undercover to find the information I needed. It was also why Chase didn't quit working for Senator Cutcliffe. Lexie's death galvanized us all. No one wanted to take the allegations of sexual harassment seriously, not even the media who is usually an ally. We had no choice but to take it upon ourselves *from the inside*," she stressed again. "Whoever is blackmailing them is a genius."

"What about the deaths? People have been killed including Chase and Matt Pike."

Maven kept her focus on Kate with the same air of confidence. "I've been thinking about that and the deaths don't make any sense.

We all know Senator Cutcliffe was a bad guy but Chase, Matt Pike, and Senator Abbott were on our side. They cared about what was happening to young women in the Senate. I was starting to wonder if Senator Cutcliffe's death was different than the other three. Maybe you have two killers and they aren't connected."

Kate had thought about that but hadn't given it too much consideration. "Are you suggesting this isn't about the blackmail then?"

"I'm not sure I'm suggesting anything," Maven said and breathed out sharply. "They might all be connected considering they were all shot. I'm just saying that the three of them have something in common that doesn't match up with Senator Cutcliffe who was the reason all of this started. I know he wasn't the only one being blackmailed, but if you think about it, the blackmail for the men was worse than the women."

Kate could debate that. Secrets were secrets and each individual had a reason why they didn't want to come out. Still, she was curious how Maven saw it. "How are they that different?"

Maven looked over as if she couldn't believe Kate had missed it. "All of the men committed career-ending crimes but the women didn't."

"That's not necessarily true," Kate countered. "Senator Stone committed real estate fraud and what Vice President Kramer was accused of isn't criminal."

"It was a death sentence for him. It might as well have been a murder and Senator Stone's crimes were in the past." She held her hand up to stop Kate. "I know you'll say Senator Harrison's crime was in the past too, but that's a far more serious allegation than real estate fraud."

Kate didn't get much of a chance to consider what Maven said because her cellphone rang. She pulled the phone from her pocket. It was Ditch. "I need to take this," Kate said, standing and walking toward the door. She opened it and stepped into the hallway as she said hello.

"I found the hacker," Ditch said with excitement in his voice. "You were right to look into their backgrounds. I dug further and looked at their families."

"Is it Maven Vale?" Kate asked, looking back at the closed library door.

"Her background was clean. Allison Manning's brother, Eric, is a hacker. I did a little digging and found that one of his addresses tracks back to one of the IP addresses related to the hack. That can't be a coincidence."

Kate was sure it wasn't. "Where is he?"

Ditch remained quiet, forcing Kate to wait out the dramatic pause. She was ready to shout at him to stop playing games when he said, "Washington D.C. He has the same address as his sister. I pulled the property records and it's a two-bedroom apartment with a heavy price tag. I'm sure Eric pays the rent. Kate, he has a cushy government job. I know you guys think I'm bad but this guy is a national security threat."

Kate thanked him and hung up unsure of her next move. If it was Eric, then surely Allison was involved.

# CHAPTER 35

Kate went back into the room with Maven with added determination to get to the bottom of what was happening. She didn't want to show her hand too early. "Sorry for the interruption," Kate said as she sat down. She didn't give Maven a chance to ask any questions. Kate went right into it. "I want to back up a little bit. Could you tell me how you first connected with Chase and decided to move forward with the lawsuit and hire Fitz to help you?"

Maven watched Kate carefully. It was clear by her expression she had questions about the phone call but she didn't ask them. "Chase and I worked together for Senator Cutcliffe. He had been a witness to the harassment and he said he knew of other women it had happened to. After Lexie, we both wanted to put a stop to it. It took us a while to come up with a plan."

"Who suggested the lawsuit?"

"Chase," Maven said without missing a beat. "I was focused on connecting Vice President Kramer to Lexie's murder."

Kate held her hand up to stop her. "Why would you think it was Kramer? Lexie was harassed by Senator Cutcliffe. Wouldn't you have thought he'd be responsible?"

Maven cracked a smile and crossed her legs. "You searched his room earlier. You had to have seen that he's a total slob. That went for every area of his life. I don't think a day went by he didn't have a stain on his shirt or that his desk was such a mess he couldn't find anything. There was nothing covert about his harassment. He'd grab your backside in the middle of the hall in front of people. Do you think he could have pulled off a murder as clean as Lexie's? That was cold and calculated and precise. The killer got away making it look like a suicide. Senator Cutcliffe couldn't have pulled that off."

"He could have hired someone to do it," Kate argued.

Maven shook her head, adamant about her feeling. "They don't go to outside help. Maybe they'd get some opposition research from someone, but that's handled through a campaign manager. Men like Senator Cutcliffe and Vice President Kramer handle things in-house. When they need something done, they do it themselves or use someone close to them. They aren't going to risk the exposure of an outside person unless there is extreme trust. Senator Cutcliffe's harassment took place in the Senate office building. He wasn't doing that at parties or where there were outsiders around. They both felt safe in the confines of their environment. It's why they got away with it for so long. It was insular and both were arrogant enough to think no one close would betray them."

Kate would have to take her word for it. "Who do you think is behind the blackmail?"

"That I don't know. It seems to have come out of the blue. In a lot of ways, it's a distraction from what Chase and I were trying to do."

"Who else was involved with you and Chase?"

Maven squinted as if she wasn't sure of the question. "No one," she said slowly after a moment. "It was just Chase and me and the person who funded us. We didn't tell anyone else what we were doing. We left it all up to Fitz. He kept us anonymous even to the people he interviewed."

"What about Allison? How was she involved?"

Maven shook her head. "She wasn't. Chase knew she had been sexually harassed by Senator Cutcliffe, but we didn't ask her to be involved in what we were doing. We didn't want anything to get out there too quickly and be shut down as Lexie had been. We were concerned for our safety." She gestured toward the door. "Given Chase is dead, I'd say we were right to be afraid."

"Are you afraid?" Kate asked even though it didn't seem like Maven was afraid of anything.

"I wouldn't say afraid, no. I'm concerned about what will happen now."

"There's still a killer on the loose," Kate said evenly. "I think if I were you, I'd be afraid."

Maven didn't offer up anything at that.

Kate pressed on. "Do you socialize with Allison outside of work? Do you know her family?"

"We meet for drinks sometimes but that's about it. It's rarely Allison and me alone. It's a big group of us. I don't know her family."

"What about her brother, Eric?"

"I didn't even know she had a brother," Maven said with the same air of confidence.

Kate believed her. She didn't seem to be hiding anything. Kate asked a few more questions that didn't help her get any closer to the killer. She asked one final question. "If you had to guess who the blackmailer was, who would you say?"

"The person to gain the most from getting those senators out of the way," Maven said without missing a beat. "I'd also consider that one of them may be lying and not being blackmailed. Saying they are makes them look less guilty."

Kate stood and thanked her for the information. "You don't seem afraid of Vice President Kramer. He warned you about speaking with me before you came in and you didn't even flinch."

"I don't much care what he thinks. As I said, I'm only working with him to get to the truth. If he fires me, I'll just find another way."

Before they headed toward the door, Kate asked, "Do you work much with Nathan Channing?"

"I do but I don't trust him. I don't think there's anything he wouldn't do for Vice President Kramer."

Kate cocked her head to the side slightly. "Do you have suspicions about Nathan related to Lexie?"

Maven nodded. "Suspicions but no proof. There were rumors at the time that they were dating. I'm not sure if that's true or not. If it were true, I'd suspect Nathan was only dating her to keep her quiet or to find out what she was up to. Nathan is a lot like his boss and neither one of them can be trusted."

"I'll take that under advisement." Kate walked Maven back to the living room where everyone had moved from the dining room. She wasn't sure who she wanted to speak to next. Kate watched as Maven sat down next to Allison. The two huddled their heads together to talk and then Maven looked over at Kate and lowered her head again.

Kate couldn't be sure what they were discussing but wondered if Maven was telling Allison that she had mentioned her brother. The way the two women sat together, Kate had a hard time believing they barely knew each other. It seemed like a strong bond between them.

Kate gestured toward Michael who was standing on the far side of the room. When he got up and walked over, she asked, "Do you know where Declan is?"

"He is in the office interviewing the rest of the aides as you requested. I spoke to him a few minutes ago and he seemed to indicate that he was hitting dead ends."

"I'll speak to Senator Harrison next."

"Good luck with him. He's a hard egg to crack."

Kate smiled up at Michael then turned to the rest of the room and called to Senator Harrison. "I'd like to speak to you next."

Senator Harrison hesitated for only a moment and then got to his feet. He came over to the doorway, flashed a big smile, and said, "Is this necessary, sweetie? We talked once yesterday."

"Don't call me sweetie," Kate said her voice low and confident. "You'll address me as Agent Walsh as I address you as Senator Harrison."

"Don't make such a big deal about it. You're a beautiful woman. You'd think you'd enjoy some attention like that. It's a sign of endearment. I'm sure if you let your hair down and relaxed a little more, you might have a ring on that finger. I've been watching you and the way you move. You need to release some of that tension."

Kate looked up at him and it took everything she had not to hit him. "Are you so bold that you're attempting to sexually harass me right in front of everyone?" She knew exactly what he was doing. He wanted to shake her confidence and throw her off her game before going into the interview. He wasn't smart enough to realize that it wasn't going to work on her.

He tsked. "Why do you have to take it there? I was being nice to you. Women today take everything to such an extreme. A man can't even flirt with a pretty woman and express how beautiful she is without being called a predator."

Kate narrowed her eyes and pushed a breath out of her nose like a raging bull. She stepped out of the door and made a sweeping gesture with her hand. "Let's go, Senator Harrison."

He brushed past her with a smirk on his face. "Is Agent James going to be sitting in on this interview with us? I'm not sure if you can handle this on your own or if it might be good to have a male perspective."

Kate ignored his question and marched down the hall through the foyer and into the library. She pointed to the chair and told him to sit. It wasn't the most respectful way to speak to a United States Senator, but Kate wasn't going to take his disrespect lightly.

"There are a few more things I need to know," she said as she sat down on the couch. "First, start with why you were so surprised to see me this morning."

"I told you it was the weather," he said dismissively. "I had heard the roads were closed."

Kate didn't believe him but she had more pressing concerns at the moment. She watched him carefully, waiting to see if he'd fill the silence.

Senator Harrison folded his hands in his lap. "I've told you everything I know about the blackmail. There's not much more I know. I don't know anything about the murders either."

"Where were you when Matt Pike was killed?"

Senator Harrison shook his head. "I don't know for sure. My understanding is that at the time he was killed we were all in the living room and the aides were in the dining room. People were moving around freely at that point. Michael and Barry hadn't been restricting our movements. I could have been in the living room or could have run up to the bedroom to get something or even been in the bathroom."

Kate believed that was probably the most honest thing someone had told her. An inexperienced interviewer might assume he was creating a false alibi or being evasive or even trying to explain his absence in the room at the time of the murder. His tone and the uncertainty in his voice said more to Kate than his actual words. He wasn't sure given she didn't know the exact moment Matt Pike had been murdered. None of them knew it. It was an estimated time of death.

"Do you leave the room frequently when you're meeting?" Kate asked in response, trying to pin him down.

"I get too antsy sitting there going over the same thing over and over again. We have no idea who the blackmailer is and sitting in that room among the group of us was never going to solve it." He looked over at Kate. "I was opposed to this meeting from the start. It's a total waste of time."

Kate realized that line of questioning was a total waste of time. She needed to get him angry and uncomfortable. She gave him no warning of the topic shift when she asked, "You were at the party that night when Lexie Bell was murdered, right?"

"I, well…" Senator Harrison started to speak and then pulled back in surprise. "What does *she* have to do with what's happening now?"

"I'm asking the questions, Senator Harrison," Kate reminded him. "Were you there that night?"

"I was there but so were a lot of us. We were celebrating Vice President Kramer's birthday."

"He wasn't vice president yet. He was a senator like the rest of you, except he was running for the higher office. It made Lexie's confession to the Washington Post all the more serious."

"Those were silly allegations from an unhinged young woman." Senator Harrison shifted in the chair, now not able to get comfortable. He crossed his legs one way and then shifted to the other side. "I don't know why we are talking about this."

Kate had him now and she wasn't surprised how easy it had been given he seemed to be a man who was always bailed out by someone else. "Lexie was going to bring a lot of other women with her who had similar stories to tell. It was going to open a floodgate that would rock the Senate. Your name was on the list of accused offenders. Did you know that?"

Senator Harrison remained silent. His refusal to answer told Kate what she needed to know. He pointed his finger at Kate. "Why are you dragging all of this up again? That's not why you're here. You're trying to distract from the real issues at hand. Someone is trying to destroy my reputation and blackmail me."

"You destroyed your reputation, Senator," Kate said, trying to remind herself that Senator Harrison was technically a victim in her case. "What happened that night? Who decided that Lexie needed to be silenced?"

"She killed herself. I assume she knew what she was about to do was wrong and decided she had no other way out and took her own life."

Kate shook her head. "You and I both know Lexie was murdered. It might help your reputation if you finally come clean. You can come out the hero in this."

Senator Harrison fixed his icy cold stare on Kate. "It wasn't me, but I wasn't sorry that she was gone. She was going to destroy everything that we had all been working for. We did what we had to do. I didn't kill Lexie Bell, but I'm not sorry she's dead."

Kate assumed he didn't realize his admission in the middle of his statement.

He was protecting the killer.

Senator Harrison shoved himself up from the chair then. "I'm not saying another word without my lawyer present."

Kate stood too. "That's certainly your right, Senator."

"What are you going to do to stop this blackmailer?"

Kate shrugged. "I don't know that he can be stopped. Seems he is on a mission of his own."

Senator Harrison's jaw dropped and his stunned expression told Kate that what she said wasn't expected. "I'll have your job for this."

"I doubt it, but you can certainly try." Kate walked out the door without looking back.

# CHAPTER 36

Kate fumed as she walked from the library down the hall and then crossed the foyer and down another hall to the office where Declan was interviewing people. She was grateful when she reached the room, he was sitting at the desk alone. "Are you done?" she asked, dropping down in a chair and folding her arms across her chest.

Declan raised his eyes to her. "You look like you've had a rough morning."

Kate gave him the rundown of her interaction with Senator Harrison, including what he said to her before they even left the living room. "I didn't get much from him until the end. He all but admitted that he was involved with Lexie's murder. *We did what we had to do.* It's as close to an admission of guilt as we've had for anything."

"I should talk to him. He has no right to treat you like that," Declan said with anger in his voice, folding his hands on the desk. The blood had drained from his fingers from squeezing them together so hard. "I know you don't like me coming to your rescue but maybe he needs to have a man-to-man conversation to see the error of his ways. He shouldn't speak to you or any woman like that. You'd think with all of this going on he might have learned his lesson."

Kate appreciated that but she shook her head. "There's no point. He lawyered up so we can assume that he'll convince the others to do so soon. What's most important now is what Ditch told me."

"What's that?" Declan asked, annoyed that she'd brush it off so easily.

Kate explained about Allison's brother, Eric. "Ditch is sure he's responsible for the hack. If he was getting the information that was used in the blackmail then it's probably not a big leap to assume that Allison would be involved."

"What about Maven and Chase?"

"I don't know if they are connected." Kate stood from the chair and began pacing around the small office. "There are so many moving pieces that it's starting to get confusing. Chase and Maven were trying to stop the sexual harassment and had focused on Senator Cutcliffe. Maven indicated to me that now that he's dead there isn't much more for her to do with their lawsuit. She had hoped taking him down would be the first step in stopping the others. The first big tree to fall, so to speak. With him and Chase gone, there's not much she can do. She has no motive for killing Senator Cutcliffe or the others. But Maven did say someone was financing them and only Chase knew who."

Declan caught her eye. "You're thinking whoever might be financing Chase and Maven might have also been financing Eric?"

Kate turned and locked her gaze on him. "That's exactly what I was thinking. I'd assume they'd also have enough money to pay Nagy Barna."

"I'd agree with that," Declan said, leaning back in the chair. "What's the end game then? Do you think it's to stop the harassment or is it something else?"

Kate wasn't sure. There were still too many moving pieces of the puzzle but she was sure she was getting closer. There was something right there at the edge of her brain that she couldn't quite grasp yet, like forgetting a name she'd always known. The information was right there just out of reach. "If it's not about the harassment, then what could it be about?"

Declan didn't know. "We'd be back at square one."

Kate rested her hands on the top of the chair. "Someone wants to make all of them pay for all of it, Declan – Lexie, the ongoing harassment, their continued power, not taking responsibility for things they have done wrong. That's the core of all of it. People in power getting away with things. I don't think the blackmailer is going to expose any of them. Death was the only outcome. Otherwise, they wouldn't have connected with someone like Barna."

"But he only killed two of them and then Chase and Matt," Declan said and looked to Kate for her response.

Kate took a deep breath and then sighed it out. "Maven suggested something interesting to me. She suggested that Senator Cutcliffe was not like the other three murders. That the others were supportive of the victims that Senator Cutcliffe and the others were harassing. Senator Abbott was talking to Lexie before she died about possibly coming forward with allegations of abuse. She said that Matt Pike was a good guy. Chase was helping them. She's right that Senator Cutcliffe is the outlier in this."

"What does that mean, Kate? You think there are two killers?" Declan asked, confusion in his voice.

"It's possible, right?"

Declan looked at her with his eyes wide. "Wasn't Senator Cutcliffe killed at nearly the same time as Senator Abbott? Their cottages were right next to each other. Wouldn't it make sense they were killed by the same person?"

Kate couldn't argue with Declan's reasoning. It made far more sense than what she was proposing. She slumped back down in the chair. "I'm spinning in circles."

Declan looked over at her with a sympathetic smile. "We're making progress. Barna is dead and we know who the hacker is. I say let's confront Allison together and go from there. The other aides didn't have much to say when I interviewed them. I think we've narrowed down the core of who is involved."

Kate wasn't sure that was true. She agreed with Declan's plan and then added, "Maven said that she wouldn't be surprised if Nathan is involved. She said he is Kramer's right-hand man. He could direct Nathan to do whatever he needed without the Secret Service ever being the wiser. Did you get any kind of vibe from him when you interviewed him?"

"He's highly intelligent and arrogant." Declan paused for a moment and considered it. "I have to agree with Maven. I wouldn't be surprised if Nathan was involved somehow. He didn't seem to have any sympathy for the women who had been harassed. He suggested they might all be lying. I tried to keep my personal feelings to myself about that to connect with him, so I asked him why he thought they were lying. He said for attention. When I explained that this isn't the kind of attention any woman wants, he said that if it was happening they encouraged it."

"Sounds like you have concerns about him," Kate said, holding back what she wanted to say – that Nathan seemed like he was on his way to being just like Vice President Kramer, Senator Cutcliffe, and the others.

Declan stood from the chair and came around the front of the desk. "Let's go interview Allison. If someone is paying her brother, then she might know who is financing the whole thing." As Kate turned toward the door, thunder roared and lightning flashed brightening the whole room. She laughed nervously. "I wasn't ready for that," she said as the lights flickered.

"Before you came in, I checked the weather. The hurricane's outer bands are close and the eye will follow soon after that. We are in for it today. I'm sure by this afternoon we will lose power."

"They have a generator," Kate said, reminding him.

"It won't fully operate everything. I'm not sure how much wind damage this place can withstand."

"That's true." Kate didn't want to feel rushed to get through the day but she didn't want to get stuck here either. "Let me get Allison and I'll meet you in the library."

Kate found Maven and Allison sitting at the dining room table together in front of a laptop and their heads low in conversation. They were supposed to be in the living room with the others but they were alone. "Maven, you should go back to the living room with the others. Allison, I need you to come with me."

Allison's eyes shifted to Maven and then she stood up slowly. "I don't have anything else to say since we talked before. I'm not sure what more I can say."

Kate gestured for her to follow. "We have some specific questions for you that I'm sure you'll be able to answer."

"What if I don't want to speak to you?" Allison asked, remaining behind the table. She might have spoken with confidence, but it was clear to Kate she was testing the waters.

"You have every right not to speak to me, Allison, if that's what you choose. We have a killer on the loose who is not going to stop once this weekend is over. If you're not afraid of that, then I assume you know who the killer is and you feel safe."

"I don't know who the killer is."

"Then you shouldn't have a problem speaking to me."

Maven nudged Allison's side. "You need to let the FBI help us. Just tell them what you know and everything will work out fine."

Kate focused her attention on Maven and they shared a look. What Kate had initially taken as Maven telling Allison everything that they had discussed wasn't that at all. Maven was trying to help Kate gather information. She could see the look in Maven's eyes. She had learned something. "Allison, I want to help you. The only way I can do that is if you help me."

Allison nodded slowly and then came around the table and followed Kate to the library. She'd speak to Maven after she interviewed Allison and cross-reference the information each had gathered. They didn't speak until they got to the library and closed the door.

It was then that Allison saw Declan standing near the window. "I didn't know Agent James would be here too." Her eyes darted back and forth and she wrung her hands as she sat. She smoothed down her skirt and looked up at Kate. "Am I in trouble for something?"

"You tell us, Allison. We believe that you know more than what you told me before. It's time you came clean," Kate said and then Declan came over and joined her. He hung back and stood near the fireplace. Kate remained standing too. She wanted Allison to feel the pressure of them both bearing down on her. This wasn't a friendly chat.

"Do you mean about Lexie?" Allison asked and then said, "I wasn't around when Lexie was working as an aide. I never met her. I didn't think to tell you about her death because all I ever heard were rumors. I know that Maven was talking to you about that."

"No. That isn't why I wanted to speak to you. Did you know that Chase and Maven were working together to uncover information about Senator Cutcliffe?"

Allison raised her eyes to Kate's. "Not at first. Then they came to me to ask me if I'd be willing to go on the record about what Senator Cutcliffe was doing to me. They wanted me to talk about the harassment and I wasn't sure that I could do that. They assured me that I wouldn't be alone. Maven told me about her experiences and assured me that there were others. They didn't tell me at first about the lawsuit. Chase told me that later."

Declan asked, "Did you agree to tell them what happened to you?"

"Yes. I wanted the harassment to stop and I was afraid of losing my job. I didn't see any other way." Allison shrugged and shook her head. "I assumed that if I went along with it, I'd lose my job anyway, but at least, I'd help put a stop to the harassment."

"What about your brother, Eric?" Kate asked. "Was he aware of what was happening?"

At the mention of her brother's name, confusion fell over Allison's face. "What does Eric have to do with anything? I didn't tell him what was happening. I didn't tell anyone other than Maven and Chase."

Kate looked at her skeptically. "You never told your brother anything?"

Allison shook her head. "I was embarrassed and I didn't want my family to know. What does this have to do with Eric?" She seemed genuinely confused by the line of questioning.

Kate wasn't going to stop though. "What does Eric do for work?"

"He works for a software company in Arlington. He's been there a few years and has been involved in many government projects."

"Does he know people in government? Like any of the people who are here this weekend?"

Allison furrowed her brow. "Eric has come with me to events and parties for work when I can bring a guest. I'm not dating anyone and it's nice to have him along with me. Is there a problem with Eric?"

Kate didn't answer her question. "You worked directly with Senator Abbott. Has Eric ever met her?"

"Briefly," Allison said slowly, trying to put the pieces together. "He's met a lot of senators when he's been with me. I don't know who he's met through his work. He has security clearances and isn't allowed to talk about what he does. The same for me. That's part of the reason why I didn't tell Eric about the harassment. We don't talk about work at home."

Declan folded his arms across his chest and stared down at her. "What kind of computer setup does Eric have at home?"

With that question, Allison seemed to catch on to what they were insinuating. "Do you think my brother has something to do with the blackmail? Is that how you think he got all that money?"

"What money?" Kate asked, taking a step toward her.

Allison snapped her mouth closed, realizing what she had said. She looked between Kate and Declan, seeming unsure of what to say now. Finally, she sank back on the couch and looked defeated. "Several months ago, maybe a year ago now, Eric got new computer equipment – a lot of it and put it in his room. He said he was working on a project from home. He also added a lock on the door. After that, he had an influx of money. He was buying designer clothes and two expensive watches. When I asked him where the money was coming from, he told me not to ask questions." Allison looked up at them with her eyes wide. "You don't think he was involved in the blackmail, do you?"

Kate didn't pull any punches. "That's exactly what we believe. Now the only question is if you're involved."

# CHAPTER 37

llison's face contorted in fear. She held her hands up. "I'm not involved, I swear to you. Until you started asking questions about Eric, I hadn't even considered that he could be involved. Why would I? He has a government job and I thought he was having to work on a special project and be available at all kinds of hours, which is what he told me. That's how he explained having all the computer equipment in his bedroom and the lock."

Kate believed what she was saying. "When the blackmail started, did you tell Eric?"

"No, absolutely not," Allison said her voice rising an octave. "Senator Abbott would have been embarrassed and Eric and I rarely spoke about work."

"You said *rarely*. Does that mean you told Eric some things about work?" Declan asked.

Allison corrected herself. "Minor things about my day or stress I had. There was never anything that crossed the line to sensitive information. Senator Abbott was demanding and had high expectations. I loved working with her but sometimes it wasn't easy. We shared work stress, that's about it."

Declan kept on the same line of questions. "Did Eric ever share anything like that with you?"

"Sometimes. He had a demanding job and an even more demanding boss." Allison looked past Declan out the window at the rain coming down. "Now that we are talking about it, Eric seemed particularly stressed when the new project started. He also got a lot more secretive, coming and going at all hours of the night. I jokingly asked him once if his new project was for the CIA. He assured me it wasn't but said that it was a bit cloak and dagger and apologized if he woke me when he came home late or left in the middle of the night. He said it would be over soon enough."

"Is the project still going on?" Kate asked, drawing Allison's attention back to her.

Allison nodded. "But not with the intensity it was before. He doesn't seem as stressed and hasn't been going out at all hours of the night. That stopped a few weeks ago." Allison pinched the bridge of her nose and sucked in a deep breath. "What do you think Eric did?"

Kate still wasn't ready to answer that question yet. She looked to Declan to see if he had any other questions.

He took a few steps toward them. "Allison, was there any part of the project that seemed more stressful than the other for Eric?"

Allison sat there for several moments, long enough that the silence was making Kate uncomfortable. Finally, the young woman said, "Eric complained once that he had to get into a cellphone but that it was impossible. He had tried everything. The only reason he brought it up was that I had the same phone model and he wanted to know if I had ever gotten locked out of it. I hadn't so I wasn't very much help."

Kate tried not to look over at Declan and draw any attention to what Allison just said. She knew what they were both thinking. Lexie Bell's missing cellphone. "Do you remember what kind of phone that was?" Allison gave Kate the brand and model number of the phone. Then Kate asked, "Do you know if Eric was ever able to get into the phone?"

"I don't think so. He never said he did, but then again, he never told me much."

Kate asked a few more questions and Declan followed up with a few of his own. It was clear to Kate by the end that Eric Manning was someone that they needed to interview and should be picked up by law enforcement immediately. The only way Kate would have a chance to interview him herself was to get back to D.C. or over video chat. Neither would be likely right now. She'd have to hand it off to someone else.

Kate walked Allison back to the living room and then gestured for Michael to follow her back to speak to Declan. "Has there been a break?" he asked as they walked.

"I think so but there's not much I'm going to be able to do about it right now." Kate finally explained about Nagy Barna and the rest of the details she had been keeping from him. While she did, Kate's mind reeled with all the possibilities. It made sense that Eric was so well-connected in D.C. He was working for someone with a lot of money and made connections through Allison. It was also just as likely that he had met someone through his employment, particularly because he was on government contracts.

By the time Kate and Michael made it back to the library, they found Declan on the phone with Spade. He was giving him Eric's information and explaining what Allison had just told them. When he got done, Declan handed the phone to Kate. "You'll be able to explain better. You know more about Lexie Bell."

Kate took the phone. "Spade, all that's important to know right now is that Eric Manning is the hacker who broke into Fitz's server and stole information. Ditch confirmed it. Eric's sister is Allison Manning who was the most senior senatorial aide for Senator Abbott. I have no reason to believe that Allison knew what her brother was involved with. She did know he was trying to access a cellphone that we suspect might have belonged to Lexie Bell." Kate gave him the brand and model of the phone. "I don't know if it's in a police report, but we need to see if this is the same kind of phone that Lexie had. Eric needs to be brought in for questioning for the hacking and to see what, if any, direct involvement he had in the blackmail. I suspect he might have been helping with all of it. Allison said he was coming and going at all hours of the night. That might be indicative of him picking up the blackmail money."

Spade didn't say much as Kate explained. When she was done, he said, "Good work to the both of you. I was able to find that Nagy Barna was a hired hitman. He came into the country a few weeks ago. Whatever they were planning for this weekend has been in the works for that long."

Kate was surprised by that news. "Barna wasn't already in the country?"

"No, Kate. He came in from Hungary a few weeks ago." Spade asked her to hold and then gave her the specific date, which was nearly three weeks prior.

"What about other trips into the United States?"

Spade asked her to hold again and then gave her a full rundown of the previous dates going back six years, none of which matched up to when Lexie Bell had been murdered. "What is it you're looking for, Kate?" Spade asked with concern in his voice.

"I've been going on the assumption that Barna was hired to kill Lexie. I assumed they relied on him again for this weekend." As Kate explained, she was reminded of what Maven said about Kramer and the others not outsourcing. That hadn't made much of an impact when Maven said it, but now Kate believed the young woman might be right.

Spade mumbled to himself as he scanned the dates once again. "No, Kate. I don't see those dates here connected to his passport or the other names he had in his car. He could have used a fake passport, but he came into the United States legally so many other times, I don't see why he would have used a fake name that time. I assume after this weekend, he planned to go back home with no one being the wiser. This guy has no record. He was flying totally under the radar. I was only able to find out that he is a hitter for hire through some backchannels. Otherwise, the man's records are clean. His biggest mistake was underestimating the two of you. I don't think he would have been caught."

Kate was glad they had gone toe-to-toe with him and won. It just left a big gaping hole in her theory. "If Barna didn't kill Lexie then who did?"

"I hate to tell you, Kate, but that's not your case to worry about right now," Spade said, his tone bordering on scolding her. "You need to find this blackmailer and whoever you feel is connected to Barna. Someone is masterminding this whole thing."

Kate didn't say it to Spade but she knew in her gut that Lexie was connected to it all. "We have Barna and we have Eric. He may confess and give us his boss."

"I don't think you can rely on that. It's going to take a while to pick him up and bring him in. I'll interview him myself and let you know what he says. There's a bigger issue right now."

"What's that?" Kate asked, surprised to hear that Spade was going to do the interview. She didn't want to witness that. Spade had been involved in all kinds of interrogations for a long time. She only hoped that his style of interrogation was legal. He had been rumored to have done some work with the CIA in his younger years, and everyone knew that Spade had skills that went beyond the FBI.

"The White House press secretary has been fielding calls from reporters asking about the deaths of Senators Abbott and Cutcliffe. They don't seem to know about Chase or Matt Pike yet. We are going to need to tell them something soon. Your only saving grace is the hurricane barreling toward you. No one else can get on the island."

Kate hardly saw it as a saving grace. "We never even talked about notifying the families."

"That's been handled by Dr. Coburn's office and the FBI. I took care of that for you so you could focus on the investigation. All the families have been notified but cautioned about speaking to the media. You're in the clear, but it's only a matter of time before the media gets more details. Once the storm clears and the ferry is running again, you can be assured they will be there."

Kate couldn't worry about that now. She was running out of ideas for finding the truth in the situation at hand. Vice President Kramer wasn't going to speak to them again and Senator Harrison had already lawyered up. "Do you have any suggestions about where we go from here?"

"Follow the money. Whoever is in charge has access to a good deal of money that they don't mind spending. Why don't you give Ditch a call and see if he can explore some of the financial records of the senators there."

Kate questioned the legality of it and Spade reminded her that a lot of it was a matter of public record when they ran their campaigns. When Kate hung up, she explained to Declan and Michael the overview of the call with Spade. "Not only is the storm heading for us, but the media will be soon to follow. We need some answers now."

Michael looked between them both. "What's your best course of action? Is there anyone you can rule out?"

"That's probably the best way to go about it," Declan said, agreeing with him. He went to the dry-erase board. It had been flipped around to face the wall so those being interviewed couldn't see their notes. Not that there had been too many besides the photos of each person that Michael had tacked up there. Declan pointed. "If we want to follow the money as Spade said then we need to rule out Senator

Bailey because we, including his bookies, know he doesn't have any. What are your thoughts on Senator Taft?"

"His name hasn't come up related to sexual harassment claims. He and Senator Bailey seem to be out of the loop on that. Senator Bailey was also supportive of Lexie and cleared of any involvement. Senator Taft wanted her fired, so he was on board with the coverup." Kate saw Declan's face at the mention of Lexie's name. She rolled her eyes at him. "I know we aren't looking at that case, but it bears mentioning here."

Declan didn't address that. "Can we rule out Senator Yates and Senator Stone?" Declan asked, jotting some notes down on the board.

"No," Kate said, surprising them both. She wasn't sure why she didn't want to rule out either of them but she held firm to that decision. "Senator Stone didn't seem to care about the sexual harassment other than the young women needed to just get over it and deal with it. Senator Yates seemed to be neutral in the whole thing. Let's table them for now."

Declan turned back to Kate. "That leaves Senator Harrison and Vice President Kramer. I'll be the first to say what everyone is thinking. The pair of them are our best suspects. They were both named during the sexual harassment claims and the gun was found upstairs with Kramer. They are both the most non-compliant so far. They both have the most to lose if these sexual harassment claims become public."

Kate couldn't argue with anything Declan said. "Kramer is at the top of my suspect list, but I don't think he's doing this alone." She turned to Michael and asked a difficult question. "Is there any chance you think Barry could be involved in all of this? He works as closely with Kramer as you have. Do you trust him?"

"You've asked me that before, Kate. I trust everyone on my team. No one has given me a reason not to trust them. I know you said Barry lied to you, but he's a long-time agent who has a good track record I can't imagine him being involved in this."

"We rule him out?" Declan asked Kate.

She hated doing it but she said no as she watched Michael's face fall. "I don't have solid evidence, but I don't trust him. Let's keep him on the board but table him for now with Senators Yates and Stone. What about the aides?"

"Nathan is on the list," Declan said, writing down the man's name. "Also, like you don't trust Barry, I don't trust Allison."

Kate wasn't sure how he could have sat in the same interview and heard the same information as she had and say that. "Is there a reason?"

Declan looked past Kate to the couch where Allison had sat. "Call it a gut instinct. If she's not involved, then I suspect she might know more. I can't prove that, but the way she's trickled out information has me concerned."

"That's fair," Kate said and gestured toward the board. "I know you also said you don't trust Nathan." Kate turned to Michael. "Given how close Nathan is to Vice President Kramer, I'm sure you have an opinion about him. Maven also told me not to trust him. Do you have any thoughts or impressions to share?"

Michael opened his mouth to speak but was silenced quickly by the piercing scream that echoed through the house. All of them reached for their weapons and took off in a run toward the sound of the woman screaming.

# CHAPTER 38

Declan and Michael made it to the hallway just outside of the dining room and living room with Kate pulling up the rear. She could see between them that Barry was sprawled out on the floor with a gash on the back of his head oozing blood. A crowd of people stood around them as Allison continued to scream. Declan and Michael rushed to Barry's aid, pushing everyone back and demanding room.

Kate rushed to Allison to calm her down. "What happened?"

Senators Bailey and Yates shouted at Kate but she quieted them down. She wanted to hear from Allison who looked the most impacted of the bunch. Kate thought she might know something the others didn't.

Allison took several deep breaths to calm down. Her face was wet from the tears she had cried. She leaned into Kate. "Vice President Kramer wanted to go back to his room so Barry took him. While they were gone, we decided to take a break. A few people went back to their rooms and others went to the dining room. Stanton put out some pastries and hot coffee. I was in the dining room with Maven and the others. They heard something and reacted and then there was a thud. I heard the thud but not the first noise. We came rushing to the hall to see what had happened and found him here like this."

Kate leaned over Allison to Maven who stood on the other side. "Is that what happened?"

Maven looked equally shocked but she was more together than Allison. "I heard a grunt. It wasn't a word spoken or a yell. The best I can describe it is a grunt. That was quickly followed by a thud as Allison said. There was no one else in the hallway just Agent Noble face down on the floor."

"Who was in the dining room with you?" Kate asked, scanning the crowd.

Allison listed names and when she was done, three people were missing – Senators Stone, Taft, and Harrison. There was someone else noticeably absent.

"You said Agent Noble was bringing Vice President Kramer upstairs. Where is he?" Kate asked as fear came over her. With Michael in the library, Barry was the only one left to guard Kramer. Neither Maven nor Allison knew where he went. The last they had seen him they were headed upstairs together.

Kate put a hand on Declan's back as he bent over Barry. "Is he okay?"

Declan angled his head to look up at her. "Looks like a head wound, not a gunshot. He's got a strong pulse, but he's been knocked unconscious. Get me something to put under his head to stop the bleeding."

Maven disappeared into the living room and called for Stanton. She returned a few moments later with some towels and a bag of ice that Kate assumed wasn't needed yet. She set the towels down by Kate's feet.

"Who would do something like this?" Senator Bailey demanded.

Kate didn't have an answer for him. She advised them to get back in the dining room and remain there. "We need room to work here." No one argued with her and she was thankful for that.

Kate waited until they were gone and then said to Declan, "I need to find the vice president."

Michael, who was bent over on the far side of Barry speaking to him and assuring him he was going to be okay, snapped his head up and focused on Kate. He looked stricken. "He's not in the dining room with the others?"

"No. They said he went up to his room." Kate explained what Allison and Maven told her and before she could stop him, he took off in a sprint to the stairs.

Kate said to Declan. "Do you have this or do you want me to stay? I want to go upstairs and check on the rest of the senators. Allison said they went to their rooms when it was time to break but no one seemed to hear her scream." Kate didn't think that was possible and she wanted to know what they were doing. Outside of Taft, those missing were those she trusted the least.

Declan waved her off. "You go and check on them."

Kate left Declan there in the hallway applying pressure to the back of Barry's head. There was a good deal of blood. His gun was still holstered to his hip, so whoever did it took him by surprise. Kate made it to the stairs as Senator Taft was coming down them. She met him halfway.

"What's going on? I was on the phone with my wife and heard a scream. I was assuring her everything would be fine before I could get off the phone and come down here."

Kate briefly explained and told him to head to the dining room with the rest of them. "Don't leave that room either. Until we can figure out who attacked Barry, I need all of you to stay in the same room, which is what you had been instructed to do beforehand." There was anger in her voice or maybe it was frustration. Kate was feeling a mixture of both and she didn't care who she directed it at. All she wanted was answers.

Kate took the stairs two at a time and started knocking on doors at the start of the hallway and then continued down the row of them.

She had no idea what rooms Senators Harrison and Stone were in. As she knocked and then ran to the next door, the previous one creaked open. Senator Harrison popped his head out of the doorway. He had earbuds in and his cellphone in hand.

"Did you just knock?" he asked her with confusion on his face. "I was trying to get some work done during the break."

Kate went directly back to the door. "Barry has been attacked. How long have you been in your room?"

Senator Harrison pulled out his earbuds. "I've been up here since the break. I had calls to return." He showed her the screen of his cellphone and then pulled up his recent contacts and showed her the timing of his calls. "I don't know what's going on, but I'm not involved. I know I asked for the questioning to stop until I spoke to my lawyer. I did that because you seem to think I have some involvement in what's going on. I assure you I don't know who's doing this."

"But you do know who killed Lexie Bell," Kate said, a statement not a question. She knew it wasn't the time to do this and that he wouldn't disclose anything, but Kate needed him to know that she knew. When he said nothing, Kate urged, "You should go downstairs with everyone for your safety."

"I'll be safe in my room," Senator Harrison said, stepping back into his room and closing the door in Kate's face. She heard the lock click into place.

She turned back down the hall and called for Senator Stone. When no one responded and the woman didn't appear, Kate called for her a second time. Again, she was met with silence. Kate cursed and went back to the staircase, taking the stairs two at a time until she reached the top floor. The door to the vice president's room was slightly ajar. She pushed it open and called for Michael.

He appeared from the bedroom of the suite. "He's not here, Kate. There's no sign of him. What are we going to do?"

"Senator Stone seems to be missing as well." Kate holstered her gun and put her hands on her hips and looked around the room. "We need to search the rest of the house."

Michael ran a hand down his face. "Do you think they are together?"

"I don't know what's going on. Do you have a way to reach Kramer?"

Michael holstered his gun and pulled out his cellphone. He scrolled through the phone and then called a number. A phone rang from deep inside the suite. "His phone is here somewhere." The ringing stopped and Michael said he got voicemail. He tried the call again and they followed the sound of the ringing phone until they found it tossed on the far side of the bed. It was half under the bed and covered by the bed skirting. "He doesn't go anywhere without this."

Kate knew then that something was seriously amiss. "Do you have any other way to track him?"

"No. He's never alone unless we are in a safe location like his office or house and even then we are nearby. We can track his phone if we need to but we've never had the need." Michael started pacing the room. He cursed several times under his breath and then apologized to Kate. "This whole weekend was a bad idea. I told him from the start that we shouldn't be here but he insisted."

Kate had no words of comfort because this was bad and there was nothing they could do about it. "Let's go and start searching for him. It's all we can do. Do you have a master key to the inside rooms?"

"No. It was just the outside cottages."

Kate texted Declan to send Stanton up with the master key. She had their permission to search their rooms earlier in the weekend and with the vice president missing she wasn't going to seek that permission again.

They met Stanton on the second floor. He seemed hesitant to let them into the rooms without the guests' permission. "You don't have a search warrant or anything," he said as he paused at the first door.

"It doesn't matter," Michael said, his growing anger and frustration on his face. His shoulders tensed as if he were ready for a fight. "The vice president and a senator are missing. For all we know, they are both dead in one of those rooms. We need to find them now. You'll open the door for us or give me the key and I'll do it myself." Michael didn't wait for Stanton to respond. He snatched the key from the man's hand and went to the first door in the hallway.

Stanton stood back but didn't say a word. It was clear that he was only trying to do his job but was far out of his depth given the current circumstances. Kate looked at him with a touch of sympathy. "It's okay. You're not going to get in any trouble. Sometimes things have to overrule your protocol."

He nodded once and then turned to walk back down the stairs. Kate assumed he didn't want to be a witness to whatever they were doing. Stanton wouldn't stop them but he wasn't going to stick around for it either. Kate called to him. "Do you know what room Senator Stone is staying in?"

Stanton stopped on the stairs and turned back to her. "Last room at the end of the hall."

Kate thanked him and he continued down the stairs.

Michael opened the first door and they stepped through. The room wasn't as nice as the suite upstairs or the cottage outside but it was a step up from even the nicest hotel room. "Whose room is this?" Michael asked.

"I don't know. Just start looking around." She held out her hand for the key. "You start here and I'll go to Senator Stone's room." Michael gave her the key and she advised him, "If you see anything suspicious, snap a picture of it but let it remain. We don't have a search warrant so we aren't technically in here looking for evidence. We are looking for any signs of Vice President Kramer and Senator Stone. If we find anything in the process, we need to document it. I don't want to cut corners and have evidence thrown out of court."

Kate left the room and closed the door slightly. The last thing she wanted right now was to arouse the suspicion of anyone downstairs. The less the other senators knew right now the faster she could get the job done. She moved down the hall past Senator Harrison's room. She'd have Michael ask if he could search his room. Kate didn't want to deal with him anymore.

Kate knocked once on Senator Stone's door and called the woman's name. There was no response. Kate knocked one more time and then used the key to open the door. She stepped inside and closed the door behind her. The room was tidy and the bed made as it had been on her earlier search. A stack of three books sat on a table near a chair. There was one dirty coffee cup sitting on the desk and a stack of files next to that. Kate glanced through the papers quickly but didn't see anything other than research on pending legislation.

Kate moved on to the bathroom. She flipped on the overhead light but there was still no sign of Senator Stone. She was about to turn off the light and exit the room when a small object on the bathroom floor caught her attention. It was partially hidden under the bathroom rug. Kate bent down and pulled the rug back to reveal a 9mm bullet. It wasn't a shell casing but looked like a bullet that had been dropped. Kate snapped a photo of it but left it there.

A sense of dread came over her and she stood in the bathroom looking around the space. There was nothing else though that caught her attention. Kate left the room and searched the bedroom and small sitting area again but found nothing suspicious. Before she retreated from the room Kate slid open the closet door. There were clothes hung up neatly and three pairs of shoes in a row. A suitcase sat on one side of the closet on the floor. Kate dragged it out to reveal a black leather bag big enough to store a laptop. She hadn't seen that on her first search.

Kate reached for the bag and tugged it off the closet floor. She expected to feel the weight of a laptop but the bag folded in on itself as if there wasn't much inside. Kate lifted the bag and set it on the corner of the desk. She was sure she might be breaking a few laws but the senator was missing and nothing else mattered.

Kate unzipped the bag and the corners of file folders poked out. She reached in and pulled them free. Kate flipped them over and couldn't believe what she was seeing. Each folder was labeled with a different name for the six senators and the vice president. Senator Stone was keeping a folder on each one of them. Kate opened the first folder and found copies of the blackmail letters, the supporting documentation, and a record of payment.

Kate knew then that Senator Stone was behind it all. What she didn't know was where the woman had gone and if she had Vice President Kramer with her. Kate closed the last folder and placed it on top of the desk to take a photo of it. As soon as she pushed the button on her camera phone, a boom of thunder roared overhead and the whole house went dark.

# CHAPTER 39

Kate tore out of the upstairs bedroom and met Michael in the hallway. He appeared as frantic as she felt. She had waited for the generator to kick on but they remained in the dark. Kate took a few steps toward Michael as Senator Harrison yanked open his door and stuck his head into the hallway.

"What's the meaning of this? Why did the lights go out?" he barked the question to Kate.

"The storm, Senator Harrison," Kate said not hiding her annoyance. She didn't care anymore how powerful this man was. She wasn't going to afford him the respect he didn't deserve anyway. "Just go back in your room and deadbolt yourself in or go downstairs with the others. We are dealing with a situation right now."

"What situation?" he demanded.

"I'm not at liberty to discuss it. For your safety, I suggest you choose one of the options I gave you. I can't be responsible for what happens to you."

Before he could respond, Michael stepped behind him and nudged the man's door open wider. "I need to search your room."

"You most certainly will not." Senator Harrison tried to step back into the room but only ended up colliding with Michael's tall frame. "You cannot go in there without my permission."

Michael didn't listen. It seemed whatever had been holding him back before, the veil was lifted. He charged forward into the room and was out of Kate's sight for several moments while Senator Harrison threw what amounted to a temper tantrum. When Michael returned, he shook his head and then proceeded down the hall to the next room.

"What is going on?" Senator Harrison shouted and tried to stare down Kate. She waved him off and continued her search of the rest of the rooms with Michael. The only light they had was from their phones but it was good enough to do a cursory search to make sure that Senator Stone and Vice President Kramer weren't in any of the upstairs rooms.

When they determined they weren't, they descended the stairs to the first floor. Kate and Michael walked into the living room where they were all gathered. Stanton was lighting candles around the room and apologizing that the generator hadn't kicked in. They'd be warm enough with the fire going, but they'd be in the dark for now.

Kate was glad to see Barry sitting upright in a chair and Declan holding a compress to the back of his head. Barry's face was white and he was slumped down in the chair barely able to hold himself upright, but he was awake.

Michael headed toward the foyer and told Kate he needed to get outside and search as quickly as possible. There was no time to waste if Kramer's life was on the line. Kate still wasn't sure if Kramer was an accomplice. They needed a plan or it wouldn't be safe for any of them.

Kate nodded her head to the hallway and Declan asked Maven to hold the compress on Barry's head. He followed Kate out of the room. "Barry doesn't know who hit him. He was on his way upstairs with the vice president, but as soon as he walked into the hallway from the living room, someone hit him and he fell to the floor. He heard a scuffle but passed out before he could get help. He'll need stitches probably. I've tried to slow the bleeding as best as I can. He has a concussion, but there isn't any more we can do for him here."

Kate gestured down the hall toward the foyer so they were far away from the room. Michael was already in rain gear and ready to go. Kate asked him to wait one moment.

Once she was sure the three of them were alone, she explained to Declan what was happening. "I found evidence in Senator Stone's room that she's the blackmailer. I think either she's working with Vice President Kramer or she's kidnapped him. They couldn't have gotten far. We need to search the rest of the grounds. They are out there somewhere. Did you ask Stanton if this place has a basement or anything like that?"

"No, there's nothing like that. I did a walkthrough earlier with Stanton when I was interviewing him. Everything is on this floor and no basement. The only other spaces are those outside in the cottages."

"I assume that's where she must have him. I found a bullet on the bathroom floor, so it's a safe assumption that she's armed." Kate grabbed for their wet weather gear that Stanton had hung in the foyer to dry. "Without power, none of the cottages will have lights on. We have a little bit of daylight left but not much. Not that we could see much through the rain." Kate glanced out the front window. "It's coming down sideways out there. Do you want to search each cottage together or break up on our own?"

"On our own," Michael said not giving it more than a second thought. "We need to cover as much ground as possible."

Declan caught Kate's eye and she could tell by his expression that wasn't the way he wanted to do it. They potentially had two armed people who had a lot to lose. One or both of them had conspired to have several people killed already. Declan didn't want to take any chances.

Kate understood Declan's position but she agreed with Michael. "We'll do it your way. Can you shoot with that arm?"

Michael nodded and led them down the hall toward the back door that led to the small courtyard. He put his shoulder into the door and forced it open against the wind. Kate slipped through and tried to hold the door for Declan but the wind and rain whipped her face, stinging her eyes and cheeks. Michael took off in a run toward one cottage while Kate followed right behind. She needed the only key they had to unlock the others. He unlocked the door and she took off in a sprint toward another, unlocked it for Declan, and then sprinted toward another.

Kate crouched low outside after unlocking it. "Senator Stone, we know you're out here with Vice President Kramer. Drop any weapon you have and come out with your hands up."

Kate put her shoulder into the door and opened it with one push. She steadied the gun in front of her and stepped into the dark cottage. She realized then she was in the cottage where Matt Pike had been murdered. The blood stain on the floor was dried a dark red. She stepped around it and made her way to the back of the space, shouting commands as she went.

As she reached the back and found no one, she turned to face the front in enough time to see Senator Stone outside with her hand on Vice President Kramer's arm pulling him forward. Senator Stone saw the open door to the cottage and shot blindly once into the doorway. Kate threw herself to the side narrowly missing the incoming shot. With the cottages so dark, the senator couldn't see inside. She was shooting blindly but that didn't stop her from trying again.

Kate couldn't return fire without hitting the vice president. Senator Stone lowered her weapon and shoved Kramer forward. With the senator's focus otherwise engaged, Kate ran from the back of the cottage to the front and then stepped outside in the torrent. She shouted for Michael and Declan, but her voice didn't carry far in the storm, which made a loud symphony of sound drowning out nearly everything else.

Senator Stone continued to shove Kramer toward the back across the property. At first, Kate thought they were heading to the path that led to the beach below, the same way they believed Barna had entered. She didn't turn around once to see who was behind her. She just kept shoving Kramer forward, nudging the gun into his back.

Kate still didn't have a shot so she took off in a chase. "Senator Stone!" Kate shouted the woman's name for her to stop. Whether the woman didn't hear Kate or was just ignoring her, she made no motion to stop or even acknowledge the command.

Kate's feet slipped and skidded in the muddy grass as she sprinted toward them. Senator Stone stopped dead in the path as if unsure where to go. Kate thought she might have a chance to catch her and yelled again for her to stop. Senator Stone looked over her shoulder at Kate and then pulled the vice president in the opposite direction.

All at once, Kate realized where they were headed and panic set in. She had to get to them before they reached the area of the grounds that had no fence. It was open land right before a sharp drop to the ocean below. No one could survive the jump or fall. Kate didn't know what Senator Stone intended, but she had to stop her.

Kate fired off a warning shot but even that didn't seem to slow them down. The pelting rain and fierce wind prevented Kate from seeing if the vice president was struggling to be free or saying anything to her. Kate glanced over her shoulder and saw Declan and Michael closing in on her. The warning shot must have alerted them.

Kate kept running and refocused her attention on Senator Stone, who had dragged Vice President Kramer right up to the edge of the cliff. She had him by the arm and aimed the gun at Kate.

"Don't come any closer or we both go over!" she shouted.

Kate was worried they might go over the side no matter what Senator Stone did. They were right on the edge and the ground had to be unstable. Kate ran up to a point and then stopped. "Senator Stone, let Vice President Kramer go and we can talk about this."

"I'm done talking," she spat. "I've been done talking for over a year. We finally have our first woman president and this fool is going to try to take her down by primarying her! He asked that buffoon to be his running mate. What about me? Didn't I pay my dues long enough? I've let these men run all over me and I still have nothing to show for it. He promised me!"

Kate wasn't sure she understood any of it. "Who promised you?" she shouted.

The rain and wind whipped around them in a frenzy. Three lightning strikes hit not too far from them. Kate inched closer and Senator Stone aimed and fired a round in her direction, missing her by a few feet.

"I want to understand," Kate said, lowering her gun.

When Vice President Kramer tried to pull free of her, Senator Stone hit him on the side of the head, not enough to knock him out but to keep him still. She turned her attention to Kate. "I lost the vice-presidential nomination to this drunken idiot and then when he said he was going to primary next term, he promised me the nomination. If he had to do something so disrespectful at least he'd still have a woman in power with him. But he gave it to Cutcliffe, even knowing how toxic he was. Men and their power. They stick to their own."

All the reasons Kate thought the crimes had been committed came tumbling down. It wasn't about sexual harassment. It was power pure and simple. Kate shouted above the rain. "Were you there when they were killed?"

"There?" she scoffed. "Still thinking I need a man to get the job done. I shot them all! You should have seen Senator Cutcliffe's face when he realized what was about to happen."

Kate wondered then how Nagy Barna fit into the mix. There was something else more important to know. "Why did you kill Senator Abbott? She didn't have anything to do with Kramer and Cutcliffe."

"Same reason as Chase and Matt Pike," she shouted back. "They were going to expose Senator Cutcliffe and the rest of us for not taking action against the sexual harassment. It would have ended my political career had they gone forward with it. *Senator Stone is not a protector of women*," she said, her tone mimicking the news. "If I had to step on a few backs to get where I am, then so be it. Once I got to the top, no one would question me and I could expose them all. I'd be the hero. But they were going to deny me getting there so Cutcliffe and Kramer deserved to die. The rest just got in my way."

Kate was confused by that. "Didn't you help Chase and Maven pay for their investigation?"

Senator Stone didn't respond, but by the look on her face, it was a clear no.

"We need to neutralize her now!" Michael shouted from behind Kate. All he cared about was protecting the vice president. Kate knew if he shot her, they'd both go over the side.

Declan figured that out quickly too. "We can't, not yet. Let Kate do what she does best."

Michael and Declan argued behind her while Kate focused on Senator Stone. "Why did you cook up the whole blackmail scheme?"

"I wanted them to feel the way all of us women feel – exposed, raw, on edge. I needed all those who knew about the sexual harassment silenced. It started as a good distraction while I worked behind the scenes. Even with the blackmail, Chase and Maven and Senator Abbott were going to blow it for me."

Kate had no reason to hold back any information now. "Why use Nagy Barna?"

Senator Stone jerked forward as if she was surprised Kate knew the name. She wasn't going to walk out alive. Kate knew it and so did she. "You were getting too close. I had to finish what I started and you kept getting in the way. Barna was my backup in case I got in trouble. I don't understand how you survived both attacks."

"He's dead. Declan killed him when he broke into my house."

Senator Stone smirked and shook her head. "You've got luck on your side. It's a shame. I was told he was the best."

She had no regret for her actions, but the look on her face told Kate she wished she had killed more. "Who else were you targeting?"

"Maven but she didn't separate from the rest of them. I even tried to frame Kramer but none of you did anything with the gun. Did you even find it?"

"We found it," Kate said, understanding now that it had been Senator Stone who hid the weapon used to kill Chase. "Did you start the rumor that Kramer had a gun?"

"I did what I had to do! They all need to pay!" Senator Stone shouted and pointed the gun at Kramer.

"You're insane!" Vice President Kramer shouted as he decided enough was enough. He wrenched his arm free of her and tried to shove her back. Senator Stone grabbed onto him and they went back and forth, wrestling as they slipped closer to the edge. They screamed at each other as they swayed in the rain. Kate was still afraid to take a shot with the wind.

Kramer got his footing faster than Senator Stone did and took off running toward Michael. Senator Stone raised her gun to shoot but never got off the shot. Kate aimed and fired, hitting Senator Stone dead center of her chest.

Her body absorbed the impact and she dropped the gun on the ground. As her hands started to rise to her chest, her footing betrayed her and she tumbled back as if in slow motion. Kate scrambled forward trying to grab the senator's hand. Her fingers slipped through Senator Stone's as the woman tumbled back and over the side of the cliff. Kate landed hard on the edge of the mud as she called the senator's name one last time.

Kate wasn't sure how long she remained there right on the edge with the rain beating down on her. It was Declan's hand on her back and his words in her ear telling her she needed to get up and that nothing more could be done. She let him help her up as a mix of emotions washed over her.

# CHAPTER 40

Late that night, after they arrived back at Kate's house, she showered and put on pajamas. When she finally felt comfortable and settled, she sat on the edge of Declan's bed and waited for him to get out of the shower.

Earlier that night, after she shot Senator Stone and they brought Vice President Kramer back into the house, it was a blur of activity. The local cops couldn't send any help that night because the storm was making a mess of the island and they were needed elsewhere. With the threat neutralized, they should be fine.

Dr. Coburn stitched the back of Barry's head. It was good enough until he could seek medical treatment at the hospital the next day. By then, he might not need any, but she was sure he was dealing with a bad concussion and recommended it.

Vice President Kramer remained tight-lipped for most of the night. The only thing he said was that as they left the living room to go upstairs at the break, Senator Stone was in the hallway. Kramer and Barry passed her and it was then she struck Barry over the head and rendered him unconscious. From there, Senator Stone took Kramer by force to one of the cottages. When Kate pressed him about what happened at the cottage, Kramer shut down. He wouldn't say anything about it. It didn't matter what they asked him, he refused to answer. It made them all a little suspicious as to what the two had discussed.

With Senator Stone dead and Vice President Kramer not talking, there wasn't much more they could do.

When Kate and Declan explained to the senators and aides what had happened, they stared back too stunned to speak. They had all been looking for someone outside of the group who was blackmailing them. They hadn't stopped to consider that one of them could be faking their blackmail, which is what Senator Stone had done with her bad business dealings.

Senator Yates pulled Kate aside before they left and admitted that it was she who had been helping Chase and Maven with the lawsuit. She had done so much wrong with Lexie that she had guilt and wanted to help. Kate thought it was too little too late. She simply nodded as the senator spoke but didn't respond much in return.

Ditch had called hours after the incident to explain to Kate that he had found Senator Stone's offshore accounts with millions of dollars. She hadn't needed the blackmail money. Senator Stone had ambitions for the vice presidency and one day the presidency. She wasn't going to be overlooked again.

When it was all said and done, the rain had started to let up and the wind howled a little less. The power in the estate still wasn't back on, but the candles and fireplace had made it a cozy environment for them to ride out the rest of the storm, which was leaving faster than it had arrived.

By the time Kate and Declan made it back to her house, the rain had turned to a drizzle. Her house didn't have any power but Declan quickly made a fire and they lit several candles.

Spade called them and congratulated them on a job well done. They still hadn't located Eric but the local cops were searching. He promised to call back when he knew more. For the time being, Kate and Declan were free to wait out the storm, get her house in order, and then return to Boston.

Kate sank back onto the bed and propped pillows up behind her back. She pulled the covers up to her lap and breathed a sigh of relief. They had made it out of the case with their careers intact and had enough of an explanation to tell the media. The only regret Kate had was that Senator Stone hadn't admitted to killing Lexie. It was the one loose end on the case.

"What's on your mind, Katie?" Declan asked, coming out of the bathroom wearing flannel pajama bottoms and a worn FBI tee shirt. His hair was damp and sticking up the way it did when he didn't tame it in place.

Kate smiled up at him and patted the other side of the bed. "We are both sleeping here tonight unless you want the couch. I don't want to sleep in my parents' old bedroom downstairs and the guest bed isn't made up. I assumed you wouldn't mind. My room is still…" Kate trailed off not wanting to think about that room. They had closed the door and hadn't reopened it.

"A bloody crime scene," Declan said with a grimace. He went around to the other side of the bed, pulled back the covers, and slid in next to her. He got himself comfortable against the headboard and then glanced over at her. "Are you okay?"

Unlike the last case, this time it was Kate who had killed the suspect. It would weigh on her for a time. "About as well as can be expected. I just can't help but feel let down by Senators Stone and Yates. Both were aware of the sexual harassment and were in a position of power to help. Instead, Senator Yates kept quiet, traded her silence for the promise of a cabinet position, and only after Lexie's death decided to help Chase and Maven. It was far too late then."

Declan nodded in agreement. "There will be a reckoning in Congress over this for all parties involved."

Kate wasn't feeling positive that it would stop. She leaned her head on his shoulder and pulled the covers up higher around them. The room was colder than she would have expected. She snuggled into him and closed her eyes.

Declan laced his fingers through hers. "How tired are you?"

"Exhausted," she said, knowing what he was asking. They had started something earlier that she wasn't ready to continue now even if she was snuggled up with him in his bed. "Another time and place. Is that okay?" She knew it was okay but she still uttered the words.

"It's more than okay." Declan dropped a kiss on the top of her head. "We've had a rough case and a weekend of no sleep."

"Timing is everything," Kate said and opened her eyes and tilted her head so she was looking up at him. She felt safe for the first time in a long time. After a few minutes, Declan shut off the light and they got comfortable lying down in bed. Kate rested her head on his shoulder and he wrapped his arm around her. She kissed his cheek sweetly and then closed her eyes to sleep.

Three days later, they were back in Boston after spending a few days cleaning up Kate's property from the storm and addressing the onslaught of media that arrived on the island as soon as the ferry ran again.

Kate didn't hold back in her interviews about Senator Stone's crimes or the reason behind them. Kate stressed that it appeared there was a systemic sexual harassment issue in Congress that the FBI would be further exploring. While she didn't name names as Spade had requested of her, Kate was sure just highlighting the issue ruffled many feathers in D.C.

She also made a plea for Eric Manning to turn himself in. Fitz thanked Kate and Declan for help finding the hacker and promised to turn over any evidence he found about the sexual harassment to the FBI as soon as he got back to D.C.

A day after they arrived home, Kate was sitting at her office going through the mound of paperwork the case required when her cellphone rang. It was Spade.

"Kate, your plea to Eric worked. He turned himself in this morning and I just finished interviewing him," Spade explained with an edge of excitement in his voice. "He admitted working for Senator Stone but denied knowing that the information he hacked from Fitz was going to be used for blackmail. Senator Stone didn't tell him why she wanted him to hack Fitz but she paid handsomely for it. That's not all he said, Kate."

"What else did he tell you?" she asked impatiently.

"I want you and Declan wheels up within the hour. You're coming to D.C. to arrest Vice President Kramer. I got the warrant about ten minutes ago. Simultaneously, we will have agents arresting Senator Harrison and Nathan Channing."

Kate let out a breath she'd held as soon as she heard the words *arrest Vice President Kramer*. "What…" she started to ask but was too stunned to form the question.

Over the next few minutes, Spade detailed the evidence they had against them. "I want you and Declan to have the honors of the arrest."

Late that afternoon, Kate and Declan stood outside Number One Observatory Circle about to execute the search and arrest warrant of the Vice President of the United States. Kate felt the weight of history on her shoulders. She radioed in that they were a go – which was the signal to the other teams making similar arrests that day.

Declan knocked loudly and called out that it was the FBI. When the door opened, they flashed their badges and proceeded in. Kate found Vice President Kramer sitting at a dining room table with Michael not far from his side. Kate had not been able to give him warning that they were coming, but he nodded once and then stepped back and let them do their job.

"I need you to stand, Vice President Kramer," Kate said with an air of authority.

"What is the meaning of this?" he shouted, looking to Michael for help.

Kate pulled him up from his chair and then read him his Miranda Rights. She pulled his arms behind his back and cuffed him.

"Get me out of these cuffs right now." He cursed a tirade at them. "What is going on?"

Kate had never been more pleased to explain. "Conspiracy to commit murder, sir. The night of your party, Alexandria Bell recorded you and Senators Cutcliffe and Harrison admitting to the harassment and telling her there was nothing she could do about it. You threatened her right on the recording. You told her that you could easily kill her and make it look like a suicide. She may not have taken the threat seriously, but she had the evidence she needed for the Washington Post."

Vice President Kramer struggled against Kate's hold. "That's preposterous. I've never killed anyone in my life!"

Kate gripped him tighter, not letting him wriggle free. "That's right you didn't. You sent Nathan Channing to do the job for you."

Declan chuckled. "It's only a matter of time before he turns on you. That phone you gave to Eric was your downfall. Not only had Lexie recorded all of you, but she recorded Nathan in her bedroom and the fatal injection of fentanyl. By the time Nathan realized she had recorded it and pried her phone out of her hands, the screen had already locked. He wanted to smash the phone and get rid of all the evidence, but you said to keep it. You wanted to make sure she hadn't sent the evidence to anyone."

As Kate led him through the house to the front door where the media was waiting, she explained, "When Eric found all that evidence, he panicked. No one had told him anything about a murder. He wanted to go to the cops but worried they'd suspect him of being involved. He just kept telling all of you he hadn't cracked it yet while he held onto the phone deciding what to do. He's told us everything including that it was you who paid him." She gripped his wrists tighter. "You're not walking away from this."

"I want my lawyer," Vice President Kramer said with his posture rigid and his voice tinged with arrogance.

"You're going to need one," Kate said and smiled over at Declan.

This had gone better than expected. Eric Manning had already made a deal with a federal prosecutor. Kate assumed that either Nathan or Senator Harrison would turn on the vice president. Either way, there'd be significant jail time and accountability for all of them.

As Vice President Kramer stepped out of the house with Kate and Declan flanking each side, a wave of reporters shouted questions and pointed their cameras at him. His career was done no matter how it went in the courts.

Declan caught Kate's eye at that moment. "Looks like we live to serve another day."

Kate smiled over at him. She was still the luckiest person in the FBI to have Declan as her partner. Where it would go between them was still anyone's guess, but their partnership was more important than anything.

# About the Author

Stacy M. Jones was born and raised in Troy, New York, and currently lives in Little Rock, Arkansas. She is a full-time writer and holds masters' degrees in journalism and in forensic psychology. She currently has three series available for readers: paranormal cozy Harper & Hattie Magical Mystery Series, the hard-boiled PI Riley Sullivan Mystery Series and the FBI Agent Kate Walsh Thriller Series. To access Stacy's Mystery Readers Club with three free novellas, one for each series, visit StacyMJones.com.

**You can connect with me on:**

- http://www.stacymjones.com
- https://www.facebook.com/StacyMJonesWriter
- https://www.bookbub.com/profile/stacy-m-jones
- https://www.goodreads.com/StacyMJonesWriter

**Subscribe to my newsletter:**

✉ http://www.stacymjones.com

# Also by Stacy M. Jones

Watch for the next book in the FBI Kate Walsh Thriller Series in Fall 2023

**Access the Free Mystery Readers' Club Starter Library**
    PI Riley Sullivan Mystery Series novella "The 1922 Club Murder"
    FBI Agent Kate Walsh Thriller Series novella "The Curators"
    Harper & Hattie Mystery Series novella "Harper's Folly"

Sign up for the starter library along with launch-day pricing at
    http://www.stacymjones.com/

**Please leave a review for Dead Senate. Reviews help more readers find my books. Thank you!**

**Other books by Stacy M. Jones by series and order to date**

**FBI Agent Kate Walsh Thriller Series**
    The Curators
    The Founders
    Miami Ripper
    Mad Jack
    The Fuse

**PI Riley Sullivan Mystery Series**
    The 1922 Club Murder
    Deadly Sins
    The Bone Harvest
    Missing Time Murders

We Last Saw Jane
Boston Underground
The Night Game
Harbor Cove Murders
The Drowned Boys

**Harper & Hattie Magical Mystery Series**
Harper's Folly
Saints & Sinners Ball
Secrets to Tell
Rule of Three
The Forever Curse
The Witches Code
The Sinister Sisters
Scandal Knocks Twice